THE SIGNS OF NO

UNIVERSITY OF CALGARY
Press

the signs of no

JUDITH POND

Brave & Brilliant Series
ISSN 2371-7238 (Print) ISSN 2371-7246 (Online)

© 2024 Judith Pond

University of Calgary Press
2500 University Drive NW
Calgary, Alberta
Canada T2N 1N4
press.ucalgary.ca

LIBRARY AND ARCHIVES CANADA CATALOGUING IN PUBLICATION

Title: The signs of no / Judith Pond.
Names: Pond, Judith, author.
Series: Brave & brilliant series ; no. 35.
Description: Series statement: Brave & brilliant series 2371-7238 ; no. 35
Identifiers: Canadiana (print) 20230519040 | Canadiana (ebook) 20230519059 | ISBN 9781773854816 (hardcover) | ISBN 9781773854823 (softcover) | ISBN 9781773854830 (PDF) | ISBN 9781773854847 (EPUB)
Subjects: LCGFT: Novels.
Classification: LCC PS8581.O46 S54 2024 | DDC C813/.54—dc23

The University of Calgary Press acknowledges the support of the Government of Alberta through the Alberta Media Fund for our publications. We acknowledge the financial support of the Government of Canada. We acknowledge the financial support of the Canada Council for the Arts for our publishing program.

Editing by Naomi K. Lewis
Cover image: Alfred Stieglitz, *Lake George*, 1922, gelatin silver print, 19.7 × 24.4 cm, Art Institute of Chicago, https://www.artic.edu/artworks/66503/lake-george.
Cover design, page design, and typesetting by Melina Cusano

This world is all we have.
It is not too much for you.
You will not be rescued.

Margaret Atwood

For Esme, wherever I may find them

The Time Before

A gray day at the season's transition, the playground empty except for the child in her red hat, her red coat.

The child runs through the playground, pauses, runs some more. Her redhood helps her to run. She is such a fast runner, and she calls out to her mother. Look — she can run anywhere!

Just watch her.

She straddles the teeter-totter, leapfrogs the rocking horse, shoots down the slide under the cold sun; she is faster than anyone!

The mother sits on a bench beside the gingerbread house, reading. The mother is always reading. She reads a book about not going to the lighthouse. About how the weather might not be fine, and about how the little boy, James, longs to stab his father, who says mean things about the weather, how he wants to get him with a red-hot poker.

On the far side of the playground another mother and a father and two children pretend-drive a play car.

The family sees the red-coated child, and the children wave to her.

Do they know her? The mother wonders. Have they met her here before?

The mother looks up from her book as the child crosses the playground to join her fellow-travellers in their fantasy car. The genial strangers welcome her as though she were one of them, as though she could be theirs.

The child looks briefly back from under a gleaming wing of auburn hair, temporizing, testing the waters. "Bye bye, Mama, see you later."

The mother smiles dreamily, her mind on her book, on dinner, the cold wind, the dark sky not much bothering her. After all, how often does she get to sit and read for a whole hour?

This was in the time before, that endless time of playgrounds and Kraft Dinner, that the mother mistakenly imagined would never be over.

I

SIGNS

Rose

At the end of winter semester, Rose decided to drive (normally she'd walk) over to the showcase of the art students at the college. After all, she taught there; this way she could demonstrate approval and solidarity, while getting a break from marking, and from the echoing house. It was a dark March night, the piled-up sky hurling snow and rain, but she got herself bundled into the car and over to campus without incident. She even figured out the parkade, despite her dread of such terrifying subterranean spaces, and found a parking spot whose location and number she thought she could remember. *P1, L2. P1, L2. P1, L2,* she murmured like a mad woman as she ascended the steps into the atrium, where people, food, and art were on display.

Then she stood uncertainly in the entryway, dripping.

"Take your coat, ma'am?" The artist-students were acting as coat checks, baristas, and general traffic directors, in addition to their role as presenters.

"That would be lovely." Did that sound pathetic? Probably. Despite being on faculty here (English, critical thinking), Rose had imposter syndrome; she was alarmed by artsy places and the people who hung out in them. Such people, with their hacked-off hair and mismatched prints and beaded wrists, always seemed to know things about how to be cool in the world, that Rose was never going to get a grip on. But she was here now, at the cool people's art show; there was nothing to be done but to pretend she was cool, too. Handing over her coat, she walked into the space where the show was set up. Black candles flickered on Classical-looking plinths. Ominous music came jaggedly from concealed speakers. Edgy hipsters sipped wine out of plastic cups with short stems. Covertly, she hoped, Rose glanced around. Strange machines crouched like homunculi in corners. Abstract paintings dripped latex and dangled bits of rags and lost buttons. Dead hens' heads, larger-than-life vaginas, atomized words, and intelligent shards, seemed to expect her immanent attention.

So did a wiry man leaning near the appies. He was dressed in clothes an off-duty jogger might wear, Lycra splash pants, and an expensive-looking microfibre jacket, from whose zippered opening an athletically ropey neck craned. He was propped against a pillar, breezily texting.

Rose was impressed. Most people the man's age, which was give-or-take hers, stabbed haplessly at their phones with one finger. Morrison — it would turn out that that was his name — was adept. She wondered where he'd learned to text that way, and where he did his jogging. Did he prefer streets or hills, track or trails?

(Rose was a runner, too, when she had the time, usually on Saturday mornings, if the weather was good. She secretly thought of running as a kind of offering to the gods of aging and deterioration. Maybe if she continued to haul her descending behind over concrete for an hour or two a week, those gods would soften, and grant her the opportunity, at last, to find that special companion, the one who would love to plug in her phone at the end of the day, and cuddle her in bed, while outside, the storm raged on.

Should she say something to Lycra man?)

Now or never. She crossed the room. Mouth dry, heart fluttering, she remarked, "I just love all these — hearts in containers, don't you? I mean, right now, I can think of about half a dozen ways I could use a heart in a jar."

Immediately, she wished hers was in one, along with her big mouth.

The man replied, pointing. "That one's Lucy's. My middle girl. She did it after her mother died of a heart attack. She calls it Dis-heartened."

Oh, Jesus, of course. Why else would a middle-aged professional — for, despite the Lycra, he looked like one — be here, except to support a child artist, in this case a grieving one?

"Oh my God, I'm so —"

"Oh, hey," He waved his hand dismissively. "That's okay. To be honest, I couldn't agree more. And anyway, that's not true about their mother, I was joking —" He peered over a bony shoulder in case of daughters, revealing just the beginnings of a bald spot under his close-cropped salt-and-pepper hair. "She's actually still alive and giving me hell, even though I haven't been married to her since the Flood. The real problem is" — he looked around at the art — "all that tuition, and I don't even get a lawyer out of it. Who'll pay for my elderly foibles?"

(And when was the last time Rose had met a man who knew the word 'foibles'? *I will*, her inside voice cried, *I'll pay for your elderly foibles!*)

Her outside voice said, "You have unusual taste in jokes."

Morrison deftly lifted a bacon-wrapped scallop from a passing tray. "May as well laugh as cry." He popped the morsel into his mouth. "Eh?"

In addition to being a runner, Morrison soon told her, he was a twice-divorced master gardener. Also a social worker with a sideline as an anger counsellor and curiosity collector ("though Abbey — that's my ex — likes to call me a hoarder"), three times a father (two with the ex before Abbey, and a never-known 'accident' with the wife of a college mate, long ago), and finally: a cottager. He told Rose, while picking out a chicken wing, that he liked to deal with all those angry guys he worked with by going to his cottage on weekends. And if that didn't do the trick, his boat "gives me an excuse to wear my captain's cap." With a nautical wink, he doffed an imaginary one.

Rose listened and learned as the two of them moved to the foyer, where stolid students, shaved-headed, nose-ringed and Doc Martened, were churning out cappuccinos faster than flapjacks at a pancake breakfast.

"I work quite a bit with the guys in the emergency professions," Morrison drawled, sipping, and Rose could imagine him competently counselling in his captain's cap, "firefighters, first responders, police, guys like that. You'd be surprised how many messed-up people there are in the police." He chuckled, adding that so many of them came to his workshops, they'd given him the nickname of 'Dr. Whackjob.' "Because on the force, by the time you gotta come see me, that's pretty much what you are."

The angry guys liked Morrison, though; he was on permanent retainer.

Rose wanted to know how he'd gotten into anger management.

"I was pissed off," he joked, selecting a glass of wine from a passing tray. "That's how most people get into the professions they're in; not because they're pissed off, maybe — that's my kink — but because there's something in it they're drawn to. Think about it. Ministers become ministers because they wanna be God; shrinks shrink cause they're fucked up themselves, etc."

Rose wondered ruefully why she was teaching critical thinking. Then she imagined what Bean would have said to that one: "Because you're critical?"

Anger management was another thing Morrison had picked up along the way, back when he was still with ex number two. When not managing anger, he'd had taken up the gardening, then the collecting, then the running. But jogging wasn't enough. Morrison wasn't satisfied until he'd turned himself *and* the ex into a pair of lean, mean marathoners. "She got right into it, and for a while there, we raced all over. Still do — though not like before. Got one coming up in Santa Barbara in September. The Santa Barbara International. Good wine country, Santa Barbara." A server passed by, and Morrison chose a salmon canape, lifting it high before downing it whole. "We usually take a week or so off when we run a race, make a bit of a holiday of it."

Morrison and this excellent ex apparently demonstrated similar zeal when it came to gardening. An early attempt at growing their own lettuce had morphed into husbandry, then to horticulture. "Us two could grow garlic anywhere," he laughed. They even produced kiwis, quarter-sized cousins of the imported ones, in which Morrison, now separated from Abbey, still took pride. "They're just little wee ones, you can't grow anything else in this climate, but they taste the same as the big ones. You can eat em like strawberries, they're great on your cereal." Now he was sipping a cinnamon spice latte, into which, from his hip flask, he'd snuck an inch of Captain

Morgan. "You know, why don't we — it's getting kinda warm in here; how bout we step outside for a minute."

"You don't mind the rain?"

"April showers . . ." he stood aside for her as he opened the door, and they breathed in the moist air, "make my garden grow."

Rose smiled and stepped out into the night.

"Hey, you should come see my place sometime," he said holding the door, "it's a slam dunk to find."

A slam dunk for *who* to find, Rose wondered on a breezy April day a week or so later, as she toiled bleakly up and down the sweeping highways, sudden ramps, and stunning overpasses of the city's rapidly developing northwest, Siri's canned voice insisting with calm menace, that she "make a U-turn and proceed to the route."

"What route?!" Rose wailed, as she and her little black Toyota plunged and dived, "What *fucking route?*"

It was not by accident that Rose lived in the inner city, in an old house, on a street with large trees. She lived there because it came with zero highways. She was aware, of course, that such concrete mazes as the ones she was now at the mercy of existed somewhere — Detroit perhaps, or Singapore, but she sure didn't plan to ever go there.

Yet: *there*, thanks to Siri and a man she hadn't known a week ago, she might as well be.

"Shit, hell, fuck!"

Rose had a love-hate relationship with Siri. She knew she would never get anywhere without her — she thought of Siri as some sort of brisk, yet mostly trustworthy female enforcer — but she resented the fact that, depending on where you were in town, an address innocently entered could result in a sudden, unexpected, and inevitable commitment to a superhighway. It had happened before. Home Depot hubcaps, Costco mini-lights, even an after-work flu shot could without warning end you up on some terrorizing off-ramp, white knuckled and sun blinded, hungry, and hellbent for Lethbridge.

Not to mention experiencing a desperate urge to pee, which could happen to Rose anytime.

Famished, bloated hours could pass before she laid eyes on terra firma again. Hours? With Rose, it could be days.

Though to Siri's credit, she had to admit: you'd have the best deal on mini-lights when you staggered through your front door at midnight, inhaling a Clif Bar for your dinner; you'd be five steps from your end-of-the-day glass of Naked Grape, that you got a deal on at Willow Park Winery because profs got a discount; you'd have that fucking flu shot under your belt.

You'd go to bed feeling immune.

Morrison — thanks to Siri's blandly threatening ministrations, Rose eventually found him — lived on a cul-de-sac, in one of those brand new neighbourhoods whose streets all looked exactly the same, and whose 'drives' and 'closes' and 'crescents' and 'ways' bore maddening variations on each other's names.

Hunterbrook Way, Rose would soon discover, looked exactly like Hunterbrook Close, which was the spitting image of Hunterbrook Place, and a dead ringer for Hunterbrook Crescent. In impeccably manicured beds, waxy daffs bobbed. Along the tidy medians, young trees tilted like synchronized swimmers in the spring wind. The same wind seemed to fill with a satisfied secret all the people washing and polishing the gleaming SUVs, and trundling the rosy infants in stylish baby wraps along the perfectly even and crack-free sidewalks, and setting out glossy begonias in freshly painted window boxes.

What was their secret? Oh, what? If only Rose knew. Somehow, too, even the sky — orderly scrolls of cloud unfurling in the warming air, WestJets making their stately progress into and out of YYC against a background blue as a brochure — yes, here even the sky wore an aura of lives rightly lived, evenly proceeding, touched with a designer's flair. What was Plato's phrase for the cosmos?

Beauty and good order. A state mostly unfamiliar to Rose.

A small flutter of panic strove in her as she pulled up in front of a bald suburban behemoth bearing the numbers Morrison had texted her: who knew what went on in there? She'd only just met him; what if the house was a serial killer's lair? Was Hannibal Lecter going to meet her at the door? Was she soon going to find herself descending into a via a basket? More importantly: how was she going to get home from here?

Ah. Siri, of course. She patted madly for her phone. Siri would get her there. Dear, irritating, fairly reliable Siri.

The phone's screen told her she was early. She looked up the street, then down: no one. Now she realized she was exhausted, wrung out from the mayhem of getting there. Maybe — driving terrors aside, she'd been finding herself unusually tired this spring — she'd just ease her seat back, and take a little rest until it was time. Just a small rest, she so needed one.

Rose opened her eyes. Could she have fallen asleep? God, could she have? Slumped like a drunk in her car in the middle of the afternoon, in a respectable neighbourhood in front of the house of a perfect stranger? A stranger she had hopes of dating!

She couldn't have, but she had. Because the sun was lower, and Morrison, brown as a bran muffin and wearing nothing but running shorts and a Tilley hat — was grinning in her window. He was the picture — or rather: the billboard — of health and wellbeing. His trunk burst with worked pectorals; in the thick mat of chest hair, a gold chain glinted. A crown gleamed coldly somewhere toward the back of his well-tended smile.

"Catching up on your beauty sleep?"

Rose sat up, grabbed at her watch — 4:32! — and gave her hair a scandalized shove. Had her mouth been open? Was there drool? Dear God, had she been snoring? "Oh no, I'm so —"

"Hey, no worries, I like a woman who's relaxed! Come on in, I'll show you around."

A microfibre running shirt was knotted around his boyishly skinny hips, just below a winking navel. As he spoke, he dropped his hat onto her car roof, took the shirt off, and yanked it down over his head, veiling the outrageous view, thereby giving Rose a chance to grab her purse and check her lipstick in the rearview.

"All set?" And courtly as a Marriott concierge, Morrison the anger-management counsellor and marathon runner bent to open her door.

Too late. Rose, not quite awake yet, caught her foot in the seatbelt, and landed slap on her knees in front of her host, a more than mortified supplicant.

'Slap on her knees' aside, Rose is not entirely without aplomb. Compared with many of the people she grew up and started life with — so far away, so long ago! — she is practically daunting. All by herself, unlike all those people, she lives in a big city, owns a solid house, keeps a decent car. All by herself, she holds tenure.

She doesn't hold a husband or a child, though she used to. The husband, preferring to be held elsewhere, left a couple years after the birth of Bean, so nicknamed for her legume-shape on an early ultrasound screen. Once Bean was born, the nickname had stuck. After all, she continued to resemble one, shiny and smooth and packed with potential, all her secrets locked inside.

Back then, Rose's house, with its creaky floors and too-large yard and weedy flowerbeds, made better sense: the husband, not yet gone, would chase a squealing Bean down the hardwood halls at bath time; Bean would come running in from the garden with fistfuls of spring chives, crying, "Mama, they smell like the sun!"

Even now, it was sometimes hard to believe that both man and Bean were gone.

The first few years after the ex's exit had been bracing, optimistic even. "Now you can paint the walls any colour you want," her old friend Mab had urged her in their weekly phone call from Toronto. "You can have boyfriends, you can be bad, you can have sex on the kitchen floor. Rose, you can have a salon and invite smart people over!" She chortled sagely. "You'll never go back."

Rose agreed, nodding hard, the phone hot against her ear, and she readied herself for the single-gal adventure. She pumped new colours into her wardrobe, found buttery Larousse recipes, got out the special china and those wedding-gift placemats she'd hardly ever used; she bought Liz Claiborne pillows. Once a week, whether they needed it or not, she laid on a ladylike tea party for herself and Bean, who was too young, back then, to know what all the fuss was about. In bed at night with the lights off, she wondered, pleasurably, when *he* was going to happen: the man who would understand everything, and be good-tempered and organized, and sexy besides. Would he be someone at work, known for a long while and then suddenly aware of her, revealed to her, as they stood at the photocopier, shoulder to tweedy shoulder? Or maybe he'd be a new hire. Someone she'd have to mentor . . . Or how about a fellow C-train passenger, whose book she could notice and be insightful about. "Man's Search for Meaning! My all-time fave; I love where he talks about how suffering is the *task*!"

Or she could be introduced to him at a party.

The thing was, there weren't that many parties, not really, in a grown-up life, and after work on a Friday, the halls just got quieter, and eventually the offices shut down and the cleaning staff made their tidying rounds. "People have their lives," reflected her mother over the phone, not meaning to be mean.

At the end of her walk back from work every evening, there was her house, with its frowsy grass and peeling front steps and blank windows that had gone unwashed for another year. The front bushes were a little shaggier, and the fence — did she expect it to paint itself? — showed a bit more of a lean. Last season's birds' nests clung frailly to the eaves, and depending on the season, there was weeding to be done, or leaves that need raking. Again. When she slid her key into the lock, it made a precise click, like something finished. "Maybe you should lower your standards a little bit," said her mother, "well maybe not *lower* them, just — you know what I mean."

That was a long time ago. The house is still solid, and Rose is still in it, her car parked outside it the same as always, though these days nobody runs down the halls or brings the chives in. Instead, they advance further each year, a green battalion. She keeps meaning to sell the house, soon, depending on the economy. But for the time being it's her and it, and Jeoffry, the leftover cat.

It's always the women, Rose thinks, who end up with the leftover cats.

"Whoopsie daisy." Morrison caught her in her fumble from the car door. "Y'okay, there?"

Somewhere at the back of everything, a wormy little headache, a tag from her end-of-semester bug, gnawed. She laughed to cover her misery. "Never better." Even to herself, she sounded like a liar or an insurance adjuster. There must be something more friendly, more first-date-like, that a person could say. What was he interested in? His garden.

"So . . . where are the kiwis? Can I see the kiwis?" She felt pleased with herself for fishing that one out of the murk of her half-awake brain.

Morrison grinned indulgently. "We're about four months out from kiwis. But I got lemons growin in the living room, and a homemade blueberry pie in the fridge." Over his shoulder he eyeballed her. "And you look like you could use a cup of tea."

Rose had no use for pie and less for tea. She said, "I'd love a cup of tea."

Ex number two (Abbey-the-dancer, who was apparently a good deal younger than Morrison) left — "isn't that what they all do?" — because of a volcano. "The Volcano Marathon, that is," Morrison supplied as he showed Rose his velvet beds of yellow, coral and scarlet roses, the little herby outcrops, the trellises of wee, wee kiwis.

"World's highest desert run, a real bitch, ever heard of it?" He gave a proprietary snort. "She trained like the devil for it, lifted weights in the sauna, ran at high noon pullin a pair of tires all around the neighbourhood with the kids hollerin at her. Went without water. Girl was crazy." He paused to straighten a weathered trellis that still trailed a few curled leaves from an expired season, and Rose saw that his fingers were deft, intelligent. Why did men's hands and other parts hold up so much better, to time, than women's?

"Yeah," continued Morrison, "she was down in Santiago for it, I didn't run that one, I had a conference up in Vancouver I go to every year, it was on replacing aggression patterns with 'assertive anger,'" (he air-quoted), "funny how some things stick in your mind, and there were a bunch of key people speaking, some of the best people in the field." Another pause, this time to pick up a flier that had strayed onto his trim lawn. He straightened with a comfortable groan. "Figured there'd always be another marathon."

Now he reached a well-toned arm across Rose to open his front door. The door faltered back with an aluminum clatter. He shook his head. "That was one helluvan expensive conference, lemme tellya."

"Sounds like it." Rose stepped into the living room. Mirrors were everywhere, and plants, and the plants were doubled and echoed, as was Rose's own blurred and startled face, in the mirrors. Never had she seen so many plants. Ferny ones, feathery ones, some with needles, some with fronds, some with leathery dolphin fins. A thirsting branch strained toward the bow window's painted-on panes, holding out its burden of small, sun-hungry lemons.

"You really do grow lemons!" cried Rose, trying to avoid her reflection and clutching her purse, "how . . . citrus!" She winced at her own bad manners.

"Man of my word," grinned Morrison, who appeared not to have heard her lemon gaffe. "Now, tea . . ." He gazed toward the ceiling, counting off. "I got Raspberry, Lemon Ginger, Lapsang Souchong, Sleepy Time . . . but you don't need Sleepy Time . . ." The chuckle again. "Or we could skip the tea and move on to wine, I make my own, and I'm not bad, if I do say so myself, just opened a pretty good case of homemade Pinot Noir from 1999."

Rose set down her purse and herself, both of which had suddenly become too heavy. Ninety-nine was the year Bean was born. Back into her head came the long night of agony, the hours of pushing, the fevered begging and swearing, the last gush with a live baby in it. Then: her. There. Forever.

Not.

"Wine for the lady?" Morrison called from his pass-through.

Hell, why not? She couldn't leave for at least a couple hours, that was long enough for her liver to process a glass of something. Anything. "Wine would be great."

"You got it."

Rose looked around. Several large chairs were stationed with baronial coldness under a row of the mirrors, in front of an unlit fireplace. She sat down on one, a middle-aged Goldilocks on the father bear's throne, staring up at the four bear walls, and wondering what the real Three Bears had on their walls. Hives in trees, honeypots and bees . . . Morison's were covered in large winter scenes — sparkling hoarfrosts, loaded sleighs, watchful huskies with ice-blue eyes.

A small chill touched Rose's bare arms, as though somehow a breath of winter had escaped the picture.

"Here we go!" A reassuring clink of glasses sounded from the kitchen, along with the homey sounds of drawers opening and biscuits shaken, the good cheer of a cork loosened. "You like brie? I got some fantastic brie!" Around his questions and preparations, Morrison was humming the theme from *Chariots of Fire*. Ba-*ba*-ba-ba-*ba*-ba . . . Rose pictured him flowing slow-mo down some exotic beach, tunic blowing, gulls dispersing. Those long, hard legs.

She called, "I love brie!"

On a rough blue easel in the corner stood a large square of Bristol board to which was affixed a gallery of vigorous pictures: Morrison and a tanned and sinuous blonde — Abbey, it must be — standing drained but ecstatic in front of a crashing California surf; Morrison and the same female phenomenon virtuously spent against the backdrop of a hip Riviera; the two of them splendidly weary, surrounded by bountiful Honolulu palm trees; the same pair resting their blisters poolside with serious-looking mountains behind; fist pumping on the Great Wall of China; crossing a Finnish finish line: in every case both of them sweat-drenched and rapturous, holding aloft medals in one hand and champagne flutes in the other, the epitome of the fit power couple.

But: weren't Morrison and wife number two divorced?

"Never run a marathon unless it's in wine country," exhorted Morrison, who was suddenly back in the room, Pinot Noir in one paw, glasses and a well-stocked cheese tray teetering on the other.

A pang of shame shot through Rose, as though she'd been caught spying. And had she, by studying Morrison's wall of triumph? Though she quickly recovered; teachers get good at that. "So, is that Abbey? In all the pictures?"

And ... was that an even worse gaffe? It wasn't just in artsy places that Rose felt like an imposter.

After two glasses, the Pinot Noir was pretty good. After two-and-a-half glasses plus the biscuits and brie, even the nasty little headache was pretty well-behaved. Morrison was getting better, too; actually, the whole thing was getting better. Though a cautionary thought floated through, about those appalling highways, that, with Siri's help, had delivered Rose to Morrison and his vernal world, so long ago, in the waning afternoon — but the thought was pleasurably remote, thanks to the wine, and soon gone. She would deal. Of course she would deal. Rose always would deal.

Later.

Morrison, a man not just of his word, but also of industry and interests, wondered if she would like to 'take the tour.'

"I'll take a refill first."

"Ok*aaaay*!"

Rose never means to do this — actually she always means to *not* do it — but she occasionally finds herself in situations where she drinks more than she means to. Not too much more, just a little more. And not at home, and not alone, but —

She blames boredom. She does. Baby showers, faculty parties, work events with their catered chicken wings and radish roses and white macadamia nut cookies that always look better than they taste, and self-promoting conversations about travel and pedagogical innovations and technical revolutions and twins — all these perfectly fine and admirable things make her bored; the excellent families of people, and their pedigreed dogs and their Disney Land holiday plans make her deeply and dangerously bored.

Boredom makes her anxious.

Wine makes her friendly and edgy and earnestly interested, and finally panicky and headachy, because it also makes her tired. But by the time she's panicky and headachy, she's usually in the elevator heading down, worrying about check stops and cruel police men. Always, she means to do better. To drink less, to care more, to take more time.

But she is so bored by people, and so pleased by wine.

The first stop on the tour of Morrison's house was the basement. Rose, with her wiry host behind her, creaked down the shag-carpeted stairs, fresh drink in hand, moderate concern about the size, shape, and firmness of her butt, as possibly noted by Morrison, in mind.

A question: If you're moderately concerned about the man's opinion of the size and shape of your butt, is that okay? Does it mean you're not well-adjusted enough not to care, or that you don't care enough? Rose can never decide, and she couldn't decide now, but she was looking forward to getting Morrison out from behind her.

A framed print of the kind students buy for their apartments at the beginning of the semester caught her eye, high above the stairs as the two of them descended. It showed two marble people, winged and yearning through all of time, the poster implied, toward each other. Pfffft, Rose thought, at the same time feeling a betraying little burst of, *Oh*. Did she really — did some part of her really still believe in that kind of love? Another thing to deal with later.

Morrison reached past her, and switched on a light. "Show you the playroom first."

Playroom? Were there younger children he hadn't mentioned? A stash of grandkids? A padded floor and stuffy toys for bad days, bad boys? She got the *Oh* about the marble people under control, and strove for poise.

Proudly, Morrison indicated a left turn past an industrial-sized washer-and-drier, revealing a twilit room a-bristle with stationary bikes and rowing machines, Bowflexes and bar bells, all arranged theatre-style around an iMax-worthy TV screen, complete with stand-alone fans for cooling the sweating athlete-in-training.

That kind of playroom. Rose gulped with relief, and half her wine was gone. She wondered if she should make an excuse to run upstairs — a bathroom break? — in order to fill it up again. "Is this all just — for you?" That sounded stupid. "I mean" — striking a coy and sprightly CBC TV interviewer pose — "are you the only one who uses these scary-looking machines?" She indicated a set of weights; a stretch-strap coiled near a workout chair that looked as if it might have been designed for Old Melbourne Gaol; a treadmill; two stationary bicycles.

"My one daughter'll take a spin with me sometimes, when she's over," Morrison said while pausing to align a pair of twenty-pounders, "but she's pretty busy these days, Lucy is, and I tell her there's not much point in bothering unless you mean it, I'll tell anybody that, quick as look at em." He paused to toe a yoga mat into alignment. "Well, like I said, I've never met the first one." Ever so briefly, he looked down. "My youngest lives in Japan. Haven't heard from her too much in the last couple years, but I know she wouldn't spend a calorie if it meant eternal salvation. He shot her a stern look. "You got kids?"

Rose felt herself heat up. It always happened when she was stressed, the backs of her hands prickling, an uncomely flush advancing up her neck, sweat trickling between her breasts. "Yes." She clutched her wine close to her chest and moved to the back of the room, where the Bowflex hunkered, like a wounded bison. "You certainly have a lot of serious equipment here!"

Morrison nodded, studying her. "I like to challenge myself. Come see the puzzle room."

He opened a different door, this time onto walls of meticulously organized tools, disassembled motors, lawnmowers renewed, chairs getting glued. A lick of pleasure arced somewhere in Rose. She loved the way men could do things, undo things, make stuff happen, or gone.

But this was a first date. She needed to be mindful. "So tell me about your puzzle?"

"You're standin on it."

She looked down. Sure enough, she was parked precariously close to one of those gazillion-piece jobs that feature images of Venetian canals, old salts in rowboats, kittens in yarn baskets, leafy autumn trails.

This one was tropical fish. Submarine blues and greens, delectable bubbles, sea fans, bright fins. It looked a little bit like the toy aquarium that used to be attached to the side of the crib in the nursery, when Bean was around one. The aquarium had broadcast a reassuring deep-sea percolating, like a scuba diver adrift in his mask, and had helped the baby sleep, even through the loud — and as time went on, louder — conversations that would often be underway in the kitchen. The aquarium, that infant ocean, was still stashed in some forgotten box or closet, waiting to jump out at her, *Boo!*

An edge of carpet caught her shoe; she stepped back. "Oh, I'm so sorry! I thought you meant a different kind of puzzle, one of those giant Rubik's cubes, or maybe a climbing wall —"

Morrison smiled. "Nah. Just your everyday jigsaw. I worked on this puppy that whole first winter."

"First winter?"

"After the Volcano. Couldn't concentrate on much else."

Well, he'd brought it up. Rose figured it must be safe to ask. "So . . . what happened?"

By now they were heading back upstairs, Rose this time safely in the rear of her host.

"Just what usually happens." He reached to open the stairway door. "She met some guy."

"While you were at your —"

"Yep," he laughed. "Gave me a chance to try out all my new anger management tricks from that damn conference. To her credit, she told me about it as soon as she got home, and moved out three weeks later. Must have been restless for a day or two."

They had climbed back up to the wrought-iron railing that framed the opening of the stairs to the basement. Medals dangled all the way around it, serious-looking trophies from Tokyo, Boston, Chicago, Berlin, twinkling with solemn impudence between the balusters as Morrison affectionately rolodexed his fingers across them. "But hey, I believe everything happens for a reason."

Rose nodded and sipped, deeply disagreeing. There was no good reason those chives were taking over her back yard. The thought made her giggle, a small bubble of bleak merriment.

"Eh?" said Morrison, as though momentarily hard of hearing. Who knew, maybe he was; Rose had often noticed that men hear less acutely than women, that they miss things. Thank God he didn't wait for an explanation; Rose had none. "Most of these races right here I ran with her, some of them after we split. Bless my poor old heart. This one —" he held up the Tokyo medal "— we did just last fall. Harajuku, Ginza, Omotesand, all through that Sinjuku garden they got. Ever been out there?" As if he were referencing some nearby neighbourhood in their own city, some place with a good farmer's market or Italian deli. He looked up at her, hefting the weighty ornament. "I always say you haven't really been in a place 'til you've run a marathon in it." His face softened. "What is it about pain that binds you to a place? Or to a person, for that matter." He shook his head. "I liked that Tokyo medal so much I bought the jacket. Bought her one, too. "

"So you forgave her in the end," Rose said expansively, enjoying the wine's warmth, "that's good." And that sounded stupid. "I mean — impressive."

"I don't know how impressive it was. Sure, I forgave her, what choice did I have? After all, the race she dumped me for was her Boston qualifier. It's not every day a gal qualifies for Boston." An exasperated chuckle. "What can you do, eh?"

Rose had an idea of what you could do. By now she was getting curious about what was under all that microfibre, but she was a guest; she should behave like one. "What happened then? I mean, after."

"*Married* the guy!" He was canvassing his kitchen for something he could make dinner out of. "You hungry?"

"No way!"

"You're not hungry?"

Rose was always hungry. It was a point of mild mortification she had learned to live with. By now she was feeling cozy, comradely, dangerously pleased. She knew that this state could be one of those things Mab-in-Toronto used to call 'little bad signs.' But she'd been all through Morrison's house now. Despite the Guantanamo chair and the punishing coils of muscle-building equipment, it looked like a normal person's house. "No, I mean: sure, I could eat — I just meant about her marrying the guy."

"Yeah, married him and moved out to —" He was yanking on a drawer. "What the fuck's caught in there? Ontario." He straightened the drawer, laughed. "Lucy used to call it 'On to Tario.' When she was two." Rose wandered out to the kitchen. It was a bachelor's lair, albeit an intelligent one, and certainly a more capacious one than hers. Serious-looking cooking tools, many of them duplicated, gleamed along the counters. Baskets of lemons and onions and sundried tomatoes were arranged on the big kitchen table. A loaf of home-baked raisin bread stood under a heavy glass dome. In the window under a grow light, muscular house plants thrived. Morrison called Rose's attention to his asparagus ferns and aloes and Christmas cactus, and finally to his orchids. "They're a bugger to keep happy, you gotta put them in an east window and fertilize the hell out of them and give em just lukewarm water, never cold, but the blooms are worth it. I call them 'my girls' because —" he winked "— they're temperamental, and because they look like the best part of a gal."

Rose chose to ignore that. "So Abbey moved out to Ontario, then."

Morrison selected a second deep red bottle and held it up to the light. "Now, this is a good one. Brought her back from Madrid last time I was down there. God, they got some good wines down there, and cheap! That's where to live if you like wine. Yup, that's where he was from, the guy she married, nice little place, Kingston."

"Oh, I used to —"

"Marriage didn't last long, but she had a pretty good gig in a dance school by then, so she stayed out there. She broke up with a couple more dudes after that." He sucked a sip of wine through his teeth, appraising its profile. "Last I heard, she was about to go on a date with some guy with one of those different names. What was it? Dexter? Porter? Some 'er' name." He rolled what was left of his wine in its generous glass, set it down, drained pasta, squeezed more lemon into the frying pan. "Parker. That was it. Why do those alternative types always seem to have names like 'Parker'? Or Wilbur, or Gomer, or whatever. Apparently he's some kind of 'found' artist, too, Ab said, that's the type she'd go for. What she ever saw in me . . . Anyway, she's got a little fixer-upper up on the north side of town out there, what's the name of that street? Got some name of a province. Brunswick Street? Quebec Street?" He reflected. "Quebec Street. Been out there a few years now. You ever been to Kingston?" With comfortable ease, he set plates of pasta and shrimp and pine nuts on the table, tossed a salad, rolled more wine into their glasses.

Rose said, "You've got a good memory. For all things Abbey."

"I've got a good memory for all things, period."

There was no reason not to believe him, especially when he could recall such an obscure detail as Quebec Street, of all places.

Rose's face was warm. Quebec Street, back in Kingston, was where Bean had been conceived, or they'd figured that was where, in Mab's chilly upstairs spare. That was after Rose had moved to Alberta, and before Mab had gone to Toronto, as she euphemistically advised Rose, "for my career." Rose and the husband had visited Mab in Kingston, on a flying early spring visit on the way to somewhere else, and between the three of them, they'd polished off a bottle each of champagne. Sack-aerobics, as Mab was fond of calling sex, had occurred afterward, probably not quietly. Mab, who hadn't much liked Rose's husband and was far from sober herself, had yelled, "You go, girl!"

Even by that time, apart from such exceptions as this, Rose and the husband were hardly doing it anymore, and she figured she was too old to get pregnant anyway, so she didn't think about the three-bottle night until later, when she skipped a period, and then another. Mab and her damn champagne.

"Yes. I've been there."

In the ex department, Rose has not had the greatest success. Experience has shown her that when it's over, it's over. Lines are drawn, words are had, names are deleted from wills and insurance policies; you might as well be dead.

It seemed that Morrison and Abbey, on the other hand, were the civilized kind. They were the kind who make a point of seeing each other when in town, who keep in touch with the seasonal phone calls, who forward the family Christmas emails, who run marathons, "twice a year, whether we need it or not."

They were doing (Morrison called it 'doing') Santa Barbara in October. "As though the town were an activity," she would be carping to Mab a day or so later on their weekly phone call, "and Morrison and Abbey were some kind of jolly brother and sister, performing it."

Then she was sorry for being mean.

In the meantime, in the thick suburban dark, between Morrison's infrequently washed sheets, far away from her own quiet street (thanks to all that wine, going home was out of the question), she learned more about marathons, while her own house waited for her to lock the gate, give Cat Jeoffry his midnight snack, turn off the outdoor light.

But she wouldn't be getting there to do those things, not tonight. And tomorrow she would wake in a stranger's bed, headachy, parched, furiously contrite.

So old, and still so dumb. What was to be done?

It. *It* was to be done. She rolled toward Morrison; in return, a long, road-hardened flank clanked down over her hip, like some primitive engine being thrown into gear. Hands began travelling, parts were stroked, other parts nibbled and pressed and groped. More wine was sipped.

In Rose a warmth, faint but promising, began to stir. How long had it been?

Not long enough, apparently. Morrison's hand, eager at first, had now located her exploring one, and was gently but surely removing it from the part of him it had been working on.

"What?" Rose whispered, more than a little unsettled. "Is there something the matter?"

Morrison kissed her ear. "No, no, it's just. I just — not yet."

"Pardon? What?"

As her neck was insistently kissed, another expression of Mab's came into her mind: *It wouldn't happen to a dog, but it would happen to me.*

"Nothing's the matter. It's just that I can't . . . yet."

"Okay . . ." Where were her keys? Her underwear, dear God, what had she done with her glasses? She needed her glasses to find her glasses. And who was she kidding? She couldn't leave, even if she did somehow stumble on her specs. Rose didn't have many hard and fast policies, but she had one about drinking and driving: Never. "Be sure your sins will find you out," her mother always used to say. Behind her lay an evening's misbehavior. Before her, thick as a quilt, hung an endless night in the bed of a snoring stranger.

"It's not that I don't find you attractive," he murmured, " it certainly isn't that."

"What is it, then?" She hated how whiney she sounded.

"Remember I said I had a marathon? Coming up?"

Rose did remember. She also remembered that the marathon was months from now, but she managed to keep from saying so. Instead she lay flat as a carp at the bottom of a winter pond, while Morrison, his fingers companionably scribbling her arm, explained the peripatetically conjugal element of his races with the famed and golden Abbey. "We're not in *that* kind of a relationship anymore, not at all." He snorted at the preposterousness of such a thing. "And like I said, she does have this weird boyfriend out there, or at least she did have." He rolled onto his back. "This is just something we do."

"Sorry?" Wine-muddled head notwithstanding, Rose nevertheless believed this might be a good moment to pay attention, to hold on. "What's just something you do?"

"Well, you know we run races together."

"You and Abbey."

"Me and Abbey."

Rose pictured the lean woman in the photos and nodded, then realized she was invisible.

"Well, yeah, so we do a couple races a year, usually in a place we haven't been before . . ."

" . . . where there's a wine tour," Rose chimed in.

" . . . where there's a wine tour. Exactly. And like I said, we usually make a week or so of it, no point going to some new place it might be expensive to get to, and then not seeing the sights."

Good thinking, thought Rose, staring up into the foggy murk of Morrison's bedroom.

"And over the years, we've gotten into the habit of — well, you know — getting a double bed to save money, and at some point we just thought if we're staying in the same hotel room, we may as well . . ."

More bang for your buck, thought Rose. She said, "And that has what to with right now?"

Morrison yawned pleasurably. "Well, nothing, really, it's no big deal. It's just that Abbey and I have a bit of an understanding. About this one thing."

Rose wasn't interested in sex anymore; by now she was just interested. "And?"

"And we have this little thing where I don't have sex with anybody else for the six weeks or so before the race."

Really? Rose was intrigued. "What about her? Abbey, sorry. Does she do that too? I mean—not have sex with anyone before she races with you?"

"That's not quite how it works."

Rose was a sucker for stories. "What way does it work? If you don't mind me asking."

Morrison took a sip of wine. "How it works—least in my world, I don't know or care about other dudes—is that the woman is everything."

"Okay . . ."

26

"That means that she calls the shots, especially when it comes to sex."

Rose was half-smiling in the dark. "I think I could work with this."

"I hope you could." Morrison found her hand under the sheets, gave it a squeeze."

"So let me get this straight," Rose yawned; despite her curiosity, she was getting sleepy, "She—the woman—can do anything she wants and you—the man—have to—"

"You got er," Morrison confirmed. "In my books, the woman gets total freedom to fuck anybody she wants, and the man gets none, unless she lets him have certain moments of . . . allowance, shall we say. How that plays out with me and the Abster is that I don't get to even touch myself for those six or so weeks before the race, but she can . . ."

"Doesn't it make you jealous?" Rose asked, "I mean if you find out she's—you know—"

"Of course!" Morrison grinned. Even in the dark, Rose heard the grin, "the jealousy's all part of the excitement of it. As long as she tells me what she's doing, *especially* if she tells me, I'm one miserable happy fucking camper."

"Non-fucking camper, you mean." She reached for her wine. "You're also a bit weird."

"What I *am* is a lover of women. Of the woman. Of the female."

"What about Abbey, does she tell her boyfriends she has this arrangement with you?"

"Doesn't have to." He sipped again. "That's the whole point of our 'arrangement.' She's in control, so for that six weeks, it's up to her what she does, *and* what I do. Some people she tells about it, some she doesn't bother. I think once she decides if the guy's stayin in the picture, then she may tell him she runs marathons with an ex. She might even let him in on the arrangement. But it has to be a guy who can take it. Not all of em can. Did you know they sell cock cages on Amazon?"

"Uh, no. As a matter of fact." Was she really having this conversation? "The weirdest thing I've bought on Amazon is edible glitter." But she couldn't help it. Despite all she'd put herself through today, she was starting to feel a vague wave of pleasure. "So, if you and I got together, or whatever, and I felt like, you know, experiencing someone else at the same time as . . ."

"All you'd have to do is tell me what I could and could not do." Morrison sighed happily. "And all I'd ask is that you let me know."

He reached over, trickled a little more wine into his glass. "Bit more for you?" The wine smelled stale, vinegary. Rose craved water. She craved her own bed, her own bathroom. She missed Jeoffry, warm, indifferent, reliable Jeoffry. "That's okay."

"So I'm thinking if it's all right with you, I might just hold off with the — you know . . . with this part — until the run's done."

"You're a poet," Rose observed, "and don't know it."

"Man of many talents. I mean we can do all the fooling around and fun like this, but just kinda hold off on the — on the rest. Then, when it's over," he spread his arms and legs, "I'm all yours."

People have baggage, Rose thought blearily. By the time you get to this age everyone has baggage. And quirks. And unfinished business.

And narcolepsy. Sleep was bearing down on her now like a freight train, swift and sudden as Armageddon, a dark relieving wave; there was no getting out of the way. As the wave broke over her, she remembered her manners. "Okay, um, thank you for dinner," she managed to croak. "I enjoyed it."

Beside her, Morrison was already rooting and farting and blanket-yanking, nesting himself a comfortable spot for the night. "You're a good cock-tease," he sighed appreciatively as he snored off, leaving Rose staring up into the dark. Drifting uneasily toward sleep's dark pool, she thought of another saying of Mab's.

No fool like an old fool.

Rose was writing a book. So far her main output had been academic, but this time she was thinking 'outside the box.' A novel? Lots of other people wrote them, she reasoned, and she'd read plenty of them in her life, why shouldn't she have a crack at it? The book was going to be about the things that disappear, vanish, *poof.* Gloves, loves, lives. She was interested in the departures, the disappearances, the gaps that go unrecognized. "The chives among us," she laughed on the phone one day to Mab, "or not among us. Anymore." She laughed again. "Green today, gone tomorrow." Right now it was a long nothing, the thing she was writing, but who knew? It might turn into a novel or a memoir or a happy how-to someday if she could stick at it. How to use up leftovers with flair. How to restore your favourite boots from the salt of winter, without despair. How to make yourself get out of bed in the morning. Period. "A mere sixty-four-thousand words to go!"

Mab blew smoke into the phone, "Girl, you gotta get out more."

"But I do," Rose cried, describing the fresh pain-au-chocolate that she had just guiltily chosen for herself at the bakery not far away, and the pot of Saturday coffee that was ready to go with it. "I *do* get out more!" She poured herself a coffee, dribbled honey, added cream. "Plus I've got a reading coming up, in the fall, and it's not even here."

"Where is it?" asked Mab. "Where? You never tell me anything!"

"Oh, you're such a — Kelowna. It's just a professional thing, I've got a colleague out there, who asked me, I'm just reading a —"

"No, but woo hoo, you get to go a whole couple-a hundred miles from home, and read your own work to students not-your-own, how cool is that?"

"Pain in the —" Rose laughed as the doorbell started jangling. One, two, three loud times.

"Crikey," cried her friend, "what's that I hear, the friendly neighbourhood Gestapo? Do they have that in Calgary? Probably. You guys are so —"

"Mab, I gotta go."

"Okay, you go girl. Let's hope whatever it is, is something that's going to keep you good and busy. You've got too much pent-up energy from all that old —"

"What?"

"Well, that old stuff. You know, from before. What you need is to quit thinking so much and start getting out there with that cute little bod of yours. You hear?"

What it was, was Morrison. "Can I come in?" That marathon of a grin.

"You already *are* in." Sort of, Rose thought, dimly remembering how the evening at his place had concluded.

His shoes, at least, were in, all size nineteen of them planted squarely in Rose's tiled entryway, a family pack of well-marbled pork chops dangling from one hand, a portable stereo clutched in the other. An ominous clank sounded from the backpack he wore. "At your service!"

"You sure are!" Rose leaned forward to help with the unexpected provender, sweat filming her neck like cat breath. "Lord, Morrison, do you think that's enough pork chops?"

Morrison tossed the package of chops up in the air. "Person can never have too many pork chops, I figger." From where he stood in the front hall, he peered right through to the back window, beyond which Rose's untended beds sprawled forlornly in the warming air.

"I was just up at the nursery for my own stuff, so I picked you up some petunias —" dividing a sixpack with a practiced crack "— these little suckers'll grow anywhere, and I got you some marigolds, there's nothing hardier."

For the plant-killer, thought Rose.

"Radishes," Morrison warned now, and cucumbers and peppers, and two kinds of garlic."

Who needed two kinds of garlic? Who the hell needed radishes? "And —" wagging a glossy envelope in front of her "— ever grow nasturtiums? Not only are they gorgeous," he claimed, "they love tough conditions, they multiply like crazy, and they're not just for show. You can eat em on your salads with your very own garlic that you grew!"

Morrison maintained that "You can never have too much garlic, or too many nasturtiums, either."

Or too much salad, Rose guessed, remembering that she was getting fat. And she was, too. Look at her thighs and the tops of her arms. Look at the little ammo belt of lard snugged around her middle.

Bring on the nasturtiums.

Morrison dropped his backpack with a clank that sent Jeoffry scrambling and farting down the back stairs. "Jesus, what's that cat been eatin? And I thought you could try your luck with a few begonias in your shady areas, along by the shed there. We'll have to deal with the weeds first, and that damn twitch grass, don't you ever — ? But hey, don't worry," he shifted the weight on his back with a wink, "I brought my tools! "

Rose stood stunned, her coffee cooling, the pain-au-chocolate forgotten. But — so long ago she didn't remember — she had been raised to be a good girl, and this unfortunate schooling came home to roost at the worst times.

"Morrison, really, that's so —"

But Morrison's largesse was just beginning. "And I figured since we'll be workin up an appetite, we may as well cook up a nice little stew for later. You got a slow cooker?"

Didn't all ex-wives have slow cookers? Wasn't that where slow cookers went to die, in the basements of ex-wives? "Somewhere, I think I do. Maybe. I'll just —"

Then she remembered Mab. "You got your wish," she hissed, hanging up the phone on her way down to where the heavy-duty, never used stuff was still stashed against possible yard sales or unlikely family reunions. Sure enough, she found the slow cooker, which hadn't been in service since the chives era, and staggered back up the stairs, hurriedly rubbing the appliance's dusty lid on her backside.

But when she got back to the kitchen, Morrison, like the poor doggie's bone, was gone.

A weak rocket of hope flared inside her. Perhaps he had only meant to drop things off for a future day. After all, there had been no plan; and Saturday — hadn't she told him that? Hadn't she?

Saturday was writing day.

A stripe of green caught her eye, snaking vigorously through the dry backyard grass with all but a hiss: an extension cord with Morrison at the end of it, his white butt-crack winking above his boxers as he thrust the plug's prongs at an exterior outlet.

Soon the quiet Saturday air was rocking to "Taking Care of Business."

And Rose was taking orders.

"You can put a couple trays of the petunias and some of the marigolds over by the fence there, and then you can get me that bag of bonemeal and put that over there, too, for later. And where's your — do you have anything we can dig down and get at those damn roots with? When's the last time you got out here and got at that twitch?"

Never! Never had she gotten out here, and gotten at that twitch! She was a prof. She had students. She had papers to mark. And since when was 'twitch' a thing?

"Holy, look at the —" Morrison squinted down at his fancy runner's watch. "Eleven-thirty already; how'd that happen so fast? Can you just go in and throw those chops and a couple cans of tomatoes and some of the broth I brought in your cooker? That'll be just the ticket in a couple hours."

He patted his muddy T-shirt in anticipating circles.

"On it." She turned and sprinted up the steps. Thank God for a reason to go in, out of the noise and industry, the terrible sun. Except that the sun seemed to have moved right back into the kitchen with her, to have taken up residence somewhere in her brain, where it burned, weighting her eyelids like coins.

The house was cool, blessedly cool, her familiar, too-still house. Even if it was temporarily under siege, the siege at least wasn't in here, where Rose was, and Morrison — she looked gratefully around at table legs and counter corners — wasn't. She closed the back door, glanced at the slow cooker; she would deal with all that — later. Then she let herself down to the floor, her chin propped on her knees.

After a time, she began to dream.

Rose and Bean are in a Value Village, or someplace like that, on a drowsy summer afternoon.

Mother and daughter are browsing, milling, sleepily filling a shopping cart with things they might need, don't need, will never probably need, for the kitchen or for tomorrow, for school. The prices are incredible!

It doesn't matter what they put in the baskets, it doesn't matter at all. They are together, moving down the slightly stale-smelling aisles in the tired light of late afternoon, examining cuffs, caressing collars, considering possible heels.

Rose tries on a two-dollar apron that says I ♥ Timbits. She angles one knee against the other, brackets her hands at her ears, trying out an outdated version of cute. Bean is not impressed.

"Mom!"

Meanwhile, Bean herself parades the tired aisles in a 1940s hat decorated with a swirl of pink chicken feathers.

Rose smiles, laughs, hears her dreaming voice say, "It's so you!"

The two of them fall laughing against the wall, knees turned to water, who cares what anyone thinks, what anyone hears.

Until Bean, still smiling, disappears.

Morrison was standing in the kitchen doorway, the roil of chest hair pressing mossily against his soaked T-shirt, hands bristling with flower bulbs, a drop of sweat dangling from his nose. "When's the last time you divided these babies?"

Babies? What babies, Rose wondered. Scraps of dreams were still trailing through her mind, a secondhand store, an apron, an old-fashioned hat. She blinked. "Sorry, what was that?" Jeoffry crouched under the table, eying the intruder with yellow-eyed malevolence. Rose couldn't help smiling at his disapproving glare. "I mean, what babies?" She didn't know what 'dividing babies' could mean. It seemed she had long since divided hers.

"Your bearded irises. You should be dividing em every two to three years. Otherwise you can get soft rot and borers. You got a bit of it now, want to see, so you can recognize it next time?"

How was it men were so good at making you feel guilty? Who cared about soft rot? Who gave a shit about irises, bearded or otherwise? "That's okay."

Morrison was undaunted. "It's a bit of work, but it's worth it."

Rose, still plunked like a basket of laundry on the kitchen floor, looked up, she hoped with an expression of eager interest. She learned in this position that you can divide irises any time after they flower, "right up till the end of August."

"What you do's you get a pitchfork, you got one around here anywhere? And you dig around the plant, but you have to dig careful." Morrison, degrees and professions notwithstanding, enjoyed bad grammar, it seemed to make him feel like an honourary member of the working class. "So you don't puncture the rhizome." He paused, eyed Rose. "You with me so far?"

Doggedly, Rose nodded.

"Okay, so then you work the fork around the roots until you can lift the rhizomes, that's these things —" he held up a dirty knuckle of plant "— till you can lift them up with the fork. Then you just work at it until you can get the rhizomes out of the ground." He made digging movements, to demonstrate. "It's the digging's the hard part. These little gals —" he meant the irises "— grow with their bulbs practically right up on the ground. Once you get them loosened up, it's nothing to just collect them. Then you can divide them and clean out any weeds and stuff that's in around them. It's the only way, really, to get the damn twitch out of em."

"What a neat name," Rose mused, "bearded irises."

"I don't know why they're called that," Morrison said, "there's nothing on them that looks like a beard. Huh, I just remembered."

"What?"

"Iris."

"Iris?"

"That's the name of Abbey's dude's kid. Or ex-dude, or whatever, ex-kid?" He had set the muddy roots down on her counter, and was now rummaging in the cupboard for a glass to quench his thirst, just as if he lived there. Over his shoulder he added, "Abbey said she's like her name."

"Who is?"

"Iris."

"What," said Rose, "bearded?"

"Ha ha, apparently she's tall for her age, and real pretty." A pause. "Funny, the things a person remembers." He ran water into his glass, took a big gulp, sighed with manly satisfaction.

"Bean's tall for her age, too."

"Who?"

"My daughter."

"Since when do you have a daughter?"

Rose thought for a minute. "That is a very good question."

Rose was over forty when she became a mother. It wasn't anything like all the versions of birth she'd heard or imagined, the water obediently breaking on the due date, the last-minute canvassing of her tidily packed overnight bag's contents, the dramatic wee-hours-of-the-morning race to the hospital, it wasn't like that at all. For starters, she was two weeks overdue. "I'd promised myself I was going to have a Dairy Queen Blizzard the minute I dropped her," she told Mab on the phone as soon as she could hobble to one, "and then the little blighter refused to come out." She laughed. "Trust me to have a daughter who'd say no to her own birth."

Mab, usually quick to supply an answering wisecrack of her own, was quiet. Then, "She made it, though, Rose. She was born."

Rose laughed. "Actually, she was evicted."

The night before the birth, Rose had been given oxytocin, to start the contractions. All night long, the grind and twist of them, as though her organs were being drawn inside-out via some Elizabethan torture instrument.

After two days of hell and nothing but Popsicles, Bean was handed over to Rose, who was old enough to be her grandmother.

Sitting up in bed, holding the red-faced baby, she had made up a joking *National Enquirer* headline to tell Mab: "Woman Gives Birth to Own Grandchild."

"Rose, you take the cake," sighed Mab.

A crisp nurse in a pink-striped smock had sprinted soundlessly into Rose's hospital room the morning after, briskly slapping apart the plastic drapes on a dazzling fall day. "Time to rise and shine!" She pronounced it *razz*. Rose squinting, feeling for her glasses, wasn't ready to 'razz and shine.' She'd never be ready for anything again. Sleep, after the harrowing ordeal of the birth, had eluded her in the hospital's manic rush and clatter. Her stomach was empty. Her breasts felt like bullets. Her throat was dry as a London newspaper.

"Could I please get a glass of water?" The words were a cardboard croak.

"Bless up, you bet." The nurse complied with one competent hand, flinging the covers off what was left of Rose's rear end with the other. "Oh ma girl, do look like you was in some kick-up rumpus; what happen here?" Grimly surveying the carnage, she let out an exasperated puff of air, and more to herself than to Rose muttered, "Oof. For sure is a mash-up mess down there."

Rose managed a bleak grin. Maybe she really had been tortured, somewhere in the long hours of that natal struggle. Wasn't there one torture method where they hung you upside down and sawed you between the legs? Thank God she hadn't lived during the Middle Ages. Or maybe she had. Dimly, she remembered screaming for delivery from the pain as her heartrate soared and she broke a fever. Now, though, below her sadly exposed waist, she could feel next to nothing, and what she *could* feel was strange and terrifying. Her once quite tight abs resembled a collapsed pup tent. Her readjusting hips telegraphed a vague and ominous ache. Between her legs was lodged a soggy crust the size of a California steak. How was she ever again going to stand? How would she get to the bathroom, let alone find the strength to pee?

Dear God, how was she going to mother a baby?

Until she produced one, Rose had had few dealings with newborns. She had no clue how to handle one. She was alarmed by the desolate volume of the hungry voice, the whisper-thin but lethal claws, the colic, the infant wrinkles.

How could a person three hours old have wrinkles?

Because Rose's baby sure had them, a fan of transparent, but visible lines along both sides of the waxen button of a nose, giving her the appearance of a just-minted octogenarian.

Rose studied the baby's puzzling presentation. She herself was old; it stood to reason she'd given birth to an aged baby. This was the kind of thing Rose did, park in the handicap stall, forget to get her car registered, get pregnant too old, produce a senescent child.

She got up off the loo, and struggled back to bed.

"Here's somebody's beautiful daughter." A different nurse now — the Caribbean gal must have been the welcoming committee — placed the tiny Bean-shaped bundle in Rose's arms. Could anything be that small and still breathe on its own?

She felt like a fool but had to ask. "What do I do?"

The nurse chuckled. "Don't worry, she'll let you know." She winked. "They're pretty good at that." Then off she bustled on her rounds, leaving Rose alone with this terrifyingly vulnerable person whose entire existence was dependent upon incompetent, irritable, scared, imperfect her.

The two of them regarded each other, the baby's eyes grave inkwells, as Rose's fingertips touched and touched the downy forehead, so terribly new.

How had that brimming moment become twenty years ago?

It was the cruellest month. Marigolds, petunias, begonias, all loudly and lovingly planted and sorted by Morrison, were muscling forth in Rose's garden, and despite the interruption of writing day, she had to admit that she was enjoying the impromptu jungle.

The cruellest month, so named for exam time, plagiarism time, missed-deadline time, boo hoo, hey, nonny, nonny, take-a-tissue-they're-free time. So many shapely young rumps ensconced in the extra office chair, while Prof Rose for the millionth time went over 1) the course standards, that had been visibly posted since the beginning of semester, 2) the college policies, ditto, and 3) her tedious need-for-a-doctor's-note for those pesky missed deadlines.

There was rain.

And more rain.

And still more rain, dribbling down her office windows, dampening the birds, glistening on the hard green buds.

Rose hurried up her last consult, waving yet another sniffling girl out the door and down the hall. "You can always grieve it," she called reassuringly, "there's a process, there are forms, good luck!" The weather must be getting to her. She needed a break.

She got out her office mirror, and took stock: sunken eyes and porridgey skin, lank hair, energy level on a par with that of a Thirty-Years-War survivor.

And Morrison on his way to campus, to have lunch with her.

She did what girls do after war: she got out her comb and tidied up her hair as she bolted through crowds of students, to the campus diner.

"There she is!" roared Morrison over the noontime commotion. From the magnitude of his smile, you'd think he'd just caught sight of the Spanish Armada under sail, with his Amazon order on board.

Rose looked around to see who'd heard that. "Yeah," she laughed or tried to laugh, torquing her aching back into a plastic cafeteria chair, "It's me. Actually," she added, mindful of her role as campus grammar bitch, "it is 'I'." She could feel her nose starting to run, thanks, probably, to all those sniffling girls in her office lately, offering a side of germs, with their spreadsheet grief. She bet she was getting something; schools were germ factories.

She sat down opposite Morrison. "Doorknobs should be outlawed."

"Pardon?"

"Oh, it's just — this is a great place to catch stuff. So you should avoid doorknobs." She had to remember why she was sitting in the campus cafeteria with Morrison, the off-campus social worker. "What — how are you?"

Rain had caught her on the way, fat drops darkening her skirt, streaking her sweater; so much for the ambitious post-war combing of her hair.

Though she liked her short off-white Banana Republic skirt and fairly svelte black hand-me-down sweater. Didn't they make her look sort of kicky, sort of Gidget-like and frisky? For someone her age, didn't she look maybe a bit . . . young? Possibly just a bit rained-on and young?

She gave her hair what she hoped was a carefree L'Oreal fling.

Morrison — Rose saw this now — was sitting in front of a large book. "Girl, you're wet!" He half-grinned. "And late."

Rose shivered, felt the damn campus ague gripping her back as tight as a belt, and tighter — could it be? — than that aguey belt had gripped her yesterday.

Never mind. She indicated the book. "Looks serious."

Morrison shot her a look. "It's about the role of anger in the development of the animus." He took a slurp of black coffee. "That serious enough for you?"

"Sounds a little . . . angry!"

"Ha ha."

Students were rushing by, hollering and waving, giving Rose merry glances. She waved back, "Mind your business or I'll dock you marks for professionalism!"

Why did she suddenly miss them, those people who normally pissed her off? She wanted to follow them, tease them, surround herself with their ordinary mayhem.

Morrison didn't seem to notice the students. Instead, he let his book fall open at what appeared, by its underlining, its highlighting, its inked stars, to be a favourite passage. "Here." He stabbed. A muscular vein pulsed on the back of his hand. "Take a look at this."

Rose leaned forward, squinted, tried really hard, but the words scattered like so much salt over the page. All she could see was the vein. "Um, yeah . . . I didn't bring my glasses."

Morrison helpfully took off his own glasses and handed them to Rose. Rose wasn't good at not accepting stuff people wanted to give her, so she took the glasses, sweat filming her temples, as the weirdly magnified words swam woozily into view. *When the shadow appears as an archetype . . . it is quite possible for a man to recognize the relative evil of his nature, but it is a rare and shattering experience for him to gaze into the face of absolute evil.*

Rose gazed into the face of absolute Morrison. "I think I could probably absorb it better with something — you know — in my stomach. Should we maybe get a bite to eat?" Eating was the last thing she could imagine, but they were in an eating place, and it was kind of her place; she should make a gesture. "They have a pretty good salad bar."

Morrison saw no reason to spend money when he'd already paid to fill his fridge. He reached into the canvas bag at his side, and brought out a home-grilled turkey, brie, and apple butter sandwich ("my own invention") and a can of V-8 juice. "What d'ya think?"

Rose blinked.

"Of the book." He gestured impatiently. "The — thing. The — the Jung."

She looked down through the film of Morrison's boxy, unfamiliar glasses. *Through representation,* the solemn words swam, *the ego is able to integrate rather than repress unpleasant unconscious impulses. When merely repressed, the shadow finds a way through the cracks of the psyche and jumps out in disturbing ways.*

Morrison's brie-and-apple-filled smile jumped out at Rose in a disturbing way. "Well?"

She started back, took off the glasses. "I think I might have a jumpy psyche." She offered a lame grin. Definitely she had a jumpy something. Electric jolts were zapping her, pinging into her, making her teeth chatter and her knees thump against each other. Her hands in her lap felt like frozen laundry. Somewhere in her brain there was a power outage; her head, usually so reliably present, was as about as clear as a cabbage.

Morrison slid the book toward his backpack. "I shouldn't bug you with this boring clinical stuff. Tell me about your daughter. You said you had one. Or you 'might' have one." He raised a nautical eyebrow. "Something like that."

Rose felt her neck go hot. "It's kind of hard to put into . . ." She wasn't ready to talk about Bean, but when would she ever be ready for that conversation? She looked up at Morrison. "I have one. But I don't know . . . where she is." She clamped her freezing hands around her coffee. "Basically."

Morrison closed his book and shoved it into his backpack. "God, Rose, I'm so sorry. When? How long?"

"Two years and a bit, I guess it would be, now." A high-pitched sound began to repeat itself, an annoying bright-blue light was flashing. People were grabbing up their stuff. "Oh, shit."

Morrison sat up. "What's that?"

The sound squealed louder. Rose pointed at the annoying light. "It's the bloody emergency warning system. Stupid thing goes off once a semester. It's routine, but we're going to have to leave the building."

"The sound you heard," blared a recorded voice, "confirms that there *is* an emergency in the building."

Rose shrugged at Morrison. "As if we thought there might be an elephant instead."

But Morrison was busy stuffing the uneaten half of his brie-and-apple sandwich and his Jung into his bag, and eyeing the exits.

"And I should probably head home, get this cold or whatever it is, to bed."

Morrison looked around at the fleeing students "Lousy timing for it." He tightened a last buckle or two. "You were just about to tell me —"

"It always is. Lousy. I'll tell you. I'll tell you the rest another time."

Though, what *was* the rest? She wondered, as she reached the student union building's good old doors and uneven floors and sometimes-working elevators, all of it so manageable and familiar. That Bean's given name had been Stella, so that she'd always have the stars. That at fourteen, she'd developed an obsession with ancient wars, and that not long after this, she'd simply and as far as Rose had ever found out, willfully: disappeared.

She leaned against the doors, panting, watching Morrison dissolve down an avenue of soaked trees. Probably she'd never hear from him again.

Candied apples were on sale at a booth just inside the doors, Heaven only knew what for — weren't they more of a little kid thing? Though students, she reminded herself, weren't so far from childhood. In fact, they seemed less far from it all the time. For a moment Rose gazed at the apples' bright fraudulence, Then she bought one. For Bean.

Sometimes she still did things like that.

Rose doesn't talk to herself; it just looks like she does, or it would, if anybody was looking, which nobody is.

She talks to Bean. It's mostly an atavism, some fond nonsense left over from pregnancy, that ancient time of faith in the substance of things hoped for, in the evidence of things unseen, when you ate fish and mangoes for the baby's unborn eyes, and sang it lullabies, and played Mozart through your belly at it, read it reams of Elliot. When you actually believed that you could sing or read or *eat* hope and wellbeing and success into substance. When you thought that something you did, some bunch or set of things you did or didn't do, could cause whatever was quietly and determinedly assembling itself inside you to 'come out peacefully — with your hands up' — and turn into something you could know, relate to, hang on to.

After work most days, Rose comes home and crashes at the foot of Bean's bunk bed, the set of riveted Ikea slabs Bean used to call her 'bonk bed,' and stares up at the underside of the top bunk, studying the petroglyph stickers of princesses and poodles and smellable pickles, as if the peeling scratch-and-sniff decals might yet yield enlightenment, might even now give some hint of where she went, what was going on in her brain when things started to happen.

When *did* they start to happen? That's the fifty-dollar question. Was it that birthday party when she was seven, and while all the other kids were having fun, Bean spent the whole time hunkering glumly on top of the playhouse, not coming down? Was it when the teachers started telegraphing frustration, in Grade 8? The math-teaching principal who, when Bean asked for help before a test said, "I'm just gonna let the bus hitcha?" Could it have been Grade 9, when the other girls were trying out makeup and learning how to smoke, down behind the industrial arts building, and Bean spent all her noon hours in the school library, reading? As if that was such a terrible thing. Or was it earlier, was it maybe far before, when she was two? Could it have started in utero? Things can happen in there. And there'd been tensions in the house by then, those late-night arguments in the kitchen. Could the small clump of gathering cells that was going to be Bean, have heard the muffled arguments, made a self-preserving decision?

Maybe that wasn't such a joke after all, that old gag about Bean refusing to be born.

Rose is having a bit of a Bean conversation, now that the cold day is done and she's finally home and dried off and the lamps are lit, the doors locked but the deadbolt left open, in case, always in case. Unlike the gone one, the Bean in her brain is an avid listener, never interrupting, never challenging a thought or offering a 'yeah-but.' And unlike when she was actually there, she tilts her head, smiles when she's supposed to, her ink-blue eyes peacefully downcast, her face in shadow.

"Yeah," Rose sighs, getting comfortable, elbow under head, "so, like, remember I was telling you about this student who came up to talk to me after the exam and told me he missed it because his *dog* ate his *C-train* pass? I mean honestly, what are they going to come up with next, do they really think I'm . . ."

Bean listens and nods, calm as eggnog, hands so smooth they could be carved from soap, crossed in her lap like funeral statuary, a dreamed-up teen memento mori. Rose shifts for more comfort as drowsiness moves in, feels the irresistible pull of its dark train.

" . . . and then there was this other one whose son got sick at daycare and she asked if she could bring him to class, and you know what a softie I am when it comes to . . ."

Bean's shadowed smile turns inquisitive, and Rose knows that's about Morrison.

"Oh, well, you know. You know how it is with me and men." She yawns, gives a little laugh. She always knows what Bean will want to know. "Yeah, I might. If he lets me, I might see him again, if he calls sometime."

Morrison did call again sometime, just before the long weekend. Not only that, he said was sorry, on the phone. He shouldn't have been such a pushy bitch at lunch, he shouldn't have made her wear his glasses, shoved his damn Jung at her. "I don't even really care all that much about Jung!"

Rose laughed. "I've had worse things shoved at me."

"But I really am so sorry. It's my damn temper, Rose. I didn't tell you, but I got a ticket that morning, just running in to grab some grapes at Safeway. And getting tickets drives me to absolute — and I took it out on you." He chuckled unhappily. "I guess I need to make an appointment with myself."

"What, with 'Dr. Whackjob?'" Rose giggled, "Oh, spare me, it was —"

Maybe it was nothing to Rose, but Morrison was determined to make it up to her. Would she let him?

"Don't worry about it, it was nothing, I hardly remember —"

"Let me cook you dinner. I'm not bad in the kitchen."

"What, here?"

"Here, there, anywhere. When? Tomorrow?"

"Morrison, tomorrow's Thursday. I've got an eight o'clock class on Thursday, remember?"

"Not Thursday? How about Friday?"

Of course she should hold out, be attractively evasive, play it cool. But who had time for such nonsense anymore? Especially when food was involved and she didn't have to cook it. "I'm free Friday."

"Okaaaay!"

But when Rose hung up, she didn't feel so good. The next day she felt less good. She made it through her Wednesday classes, but by Thursday night, she'd come down with what the department admin assistant, who had seen it all, was fond of calling the old razor-blades-in-the-throat thing, the old killer-lower-back-ache thing.

Rose called up Morrison. "I don't think I can do dinner. I don't think you'd want me to, considering."

"Considering what?"

"How much snot I am producing."

"Hey, I don't mind snot."

"Handsome of you, but —"

"Anything I can do?"

"Well, since you ask, I'd love a Popsicle."

"What flave's your fave?"

By the time Morrison arrived on Friday night bearing a six-pack of 7-Up, several pounds of white grapes, two monster-jugs of Gatorade, Lemon Neocitran with rum "to put the hair back on your chest," and three different kinds of Popsicles, Rose could barely move.

"Girl, I think you got the Plague," he studied her, "complete with buboes; what's that on your nose? Just kidding."

Rose managed a dismissive croak.

"You want me to take you over to Outpatients?"

No, Rose didn't. "All I need is to lie there and drink water. Really."

"Well, you're not going to do it alone."

And Morrison moved in. Just like that. He peeled her a Popsicle, then hoofed it back to his place to set timers and find clothes, running shoes dental floss, his precious *Jung*. In an hour he was back, and setting up temporary digs between the closet and the computer in Rose's office.

The next week was a blur of sweat, snot, and grateful Popsicle consumption. By Friday Rose had decided lime was her favourite flavour. Also, that she was on the mend. She told Morrison so.

Morrison high-fived her, then announced he had to leave town.

"Really?" A desolate little wind stirred in her heart, which, unbeknownst to Rose, had started to like Morrison's noisy commotion.

"Just for the weekend." It was time to get the shutters off the cottage, and, he hoped, put the boat in. Could Rose manage on her own for a couple days? Did she think her cold had steadied out?

Well, for heaven's sakes. All she had to do was stay prone for two more days, and read her book (what better summer to be grinding through Moby Dick?); likely, even she could manage that. Plus — gaps were showing up between headaches — she thought maybe she was feeling well enough to start getting up. She smiled stoically.

Somewhere along the line, kisses had got to be a part of Morrison's expert medical treatment, and he gave her a friendly one, then made her promise: "You're to do absolutely nothing strenuous."

And Rose was true to her word. The only thing she did all weekend was sleep, hydrate, and hold her head.

Though she hadn't anticipated or remembered how very long and quiet, and weird, a sick weekend alone can be. Not since studying for exams in university had she been so aware of the hours of a day. Of the way the sun can rise and slowly climb the wall and slide over the covers of your bed, tracking minutely across your dresser and the clothes-covered chair, to take a reproving last look back, before finally disappearing. Of the long minutes in all those blank hours, the dust motes turning, shimmering columns of them there, then not there. Of the inane details of wallpaper. A crack that becomes a snake; a stain that morphs into a long, thin, sallow man, pursuing you in dreams.

Thanks to Morrison, she hadn't been alone much since things really got going. She had become used to the jolly splutter of the arriving Smart Car, and to the ubiquitous running gear, to Morrison's rummaging in her cupboards, even to his outrage over her untended fridge and duplicated spices. She actually missed his cheerful hectoring.

She missed his kisses.

On Monday evening the phone rang again, wakening her from fevered dreams about tiny ships battling white leviathans.

It was Morrison, back from his nautical weekend. Never had she felt so glad to hear a human voice. She wanted to kiss him, grab him, reach right down the phone and be inappropriate with him.

But Morrison sounded small and distant, like the stars, seen through the wrong end of the telescope. Or, in Morrison's case, was it the sextant? Rose wondered if there was a bad connection. "Can you hear me okay?"

He could.

Was he going to ask her how she was doing, after two days and nights alone with her own leviathan?

It wasn't looking like it.

Somebody had to do it. "Well, like, how was *your* weekend?" Her voice, after two day's silence, sounded like a bullhorn in her ears. "Did you get the shutters off? Were there mice? How about that boat, did you launch it?"

It was a tender evening. She was up and moving cautiously through the rooms. Now that she was vertical, she could see the ghostly spring light on the new leaves outside her windows, the kids next door playing hopscotch in the quiet street, the plants Morrison had put in before he left for the weekend beginning to lift their leaves and take stronger hold. She went out on the deck as she asked her greedy coming-back-to-life questions.

"Was it fun?"

"No."

"Oh."

"Yeah; something came up and — I'll call you later. Can I call you later?"

"Okay . . . sure."

Rose hung up. She sat down. She stood up again. She felt woozy, not in the flu way, but in a new way: in the realizing-you've-worn-out-your-welcome way. Of course! It must have been too much for Morrison, all this moving in to take care of her, all this suspending of his real life to run to the drugstore for ice packs instead of training for his race. No wonder he had to take off for the weekend, poor man, he probably didn't really have to put his boat in at all, he probably just went wherever he kept it, to lean against its keel, and breathe. Finally: invalid-free! Why hadn't she valued him more, when he was there? Why had his pork chops shocked her? Why had she had to go and ruin everything by getting sick?

She shuffled back to the bathroom and splashed water over her gray face. Didn't it always seem, with Rose, that by the time she realized what she valued in this life, it was too late?

The phone rang again; it was Morrison, again.

"I think I should come over."

When Morrison got there, Rose was on the deck watching Jeoffry show off his moth-catching-and-extreme-running skills. Heedless of the humans' glum presence, Jeoffry leapt into the air, zoomed as far as claws could take him up Rose's prize oak tree, fell back down the trunk sideways reproachfully rolling his eyes, and disguised his embarrassment by shooting between Morrison's long legs.

Morrison, usually up for the game, failed to be enchanted.

Rose sat on the deck drinking pomegranate juice and ogling Morrison's strong back; she hadn't eaten in so long the juice tasted like steak. The air was soft as lake water, a pink moon was rising in a smudge of silvered cloud, and for the first time since the bug had hit, she had managed to get cleaned up and be somewhere else besides bed. She was relieved to the point of pride.

But why was Morrison wandering around down there in the garden, and not coming up to tease her, cajole her, demand a beer? Why did he keep not turning around and seeing her? How come he didn't he get his cute ass up here? The wearing-out-your-welcome thing, that must be it. All that work she'd put him to. All that tea-brewing and ice-pack-toting, and Popsicling and encouraging.

Not to mention the missed marathon training.

She decided to try the tragicomic line she used with clasped hands in the classroom, when the students sat as far away as possible from her, which was pretty much always. "Was it something I said?"

Morrison turned, then, and came up onto the deck. "No. It wasn't anything you said, or anything you did." He looked like Humphrey Bogart in Casablanca, in that scene at the end, where Rick has to put Viktor Laslo and Ilse on the plane after all their triangulated Moroccan shenanigans: stricken, in a half-shameful, rained-on way.

"What's wrong, then? What's the matter?" She hadn't been up an hour, and already she was feeling tired again.

"There's something I need to tell you. About the weekend."

Rose put her juice on the table beside her and licked her lips, which suddenly felt dry. She hoped she didn't have Kool-Aidy pomegranate brackets on the sides of her mouth. "Okay."

"So I didn't end up getting up to my camp."

Rose let that sink in. "Did you go home to your house for the weekend? That's totally okay, I've been realizing you probably needed a —"

Morrison was studying the wood grain in the deck. "I didn't go home."

It was starting to feel more like *Casablanca* by the moment. Next, the World War II propellers would start to roar; actually, they were already roaring a little bit now, perking up like hunting dogs, flinging off the rain, preparing to take flight into the velvet North African night.

"I was on my way up there, to the cottage, and I was just at the turn-off to the lake when my phone rang, and, well . . ." He looked up from studying the deck, "it was Abbey."

Abbey? For a minute Rose had to think who that might be. Then she remembered all that stuff about the marathons. And volcanos.

And the sinewy gold creature in all those exotic photos.

But then Jeoffry did a particularly inept somersault, and she had to laugh at his waggery. "Look at him, the silly, he's been seven times around that tree!" She had to get hold of herself. "So, how *is* Abbey — marathon-ready, I hope?"

"Oh, yeah, she is. She sure is." Morrison kept on inspecting the woodgrain. "She's in pretty good shape, all right."

Wheels were turning in Rose' brain. *Got a phone call at the turn-off, didn't get to the boat.* "You went there. You went . . . there."

Ontario.

"Like I said, I was just about to turn off to the lake, and then the phone rang, and it was Abbey, and she was in . . . she had quite a situation." He batted away a stray cabbage moth. "To deal with."

"Let me guess," said Rose . . . her Lycra didn't like her? She misplaced her Espresso Love replenishing gel? She had a nasty-though-not-disqualifying fall?

Morrison chose to take the higher ground. "Well, you know all that rain they've been getting lately, out in Kingston."

The rain in Kingston stays mainly in the . . . thought Rose.

"So the thing was, her basement flooded."

"Oh my — my goodness," managed Rose. She herself lived in dread of fridge breakdowns, sink leaks, drywall, trolls. She couldn't help feeling actual almost-sympathy. For Abbey and her basement perils.

"Yeah, so . . ." Morrison glanced sidelong at Rose's oak tree, as if recalling that he'd flung his socks up there ". . . so, like, she called me."

Rose nodded. "Right. She called you in Alberta . . . because her basement flooded . . . in Ontario." She gave Jeoffry — "Oh, go." — an irritated little punt with her bare toe.

"She didn't know what to do, okay? She was panicking." Morrison looked with hard helplessness at Rose. "So anyway, I figured I can put the boat in any weekend . . ."

"Right." Rose gave a nautical nod.

"And I just — I couldn't very well leave her stranded, Rose."

Rose thought about that. "Didn't you say she has a boyfriend? Some Palmer or Potter, or whatever? Where is he?"

"Out of town. As it happened, his ex needed help with a door, and he went and helped her."

Jeofffry clutched a cork between his front paws, where had he got that? And was putting a pounding on it with his cruel back claws, pretending it was a hapless rodent, whirling it up into the air. Show it who's boss, thought Rose, then started counting in her head.

Ten years. Didn't Morrison once say that Abbey'd been in Kingston for ten years? And didn't that mean Abbey and Morrison had been separated for at least that many years? Her fluey brain stumbled over the unwelcome calculations. Didn't ten years mean you dealt with your own basement, when it flooded in another province? Ten years was about the same amount of time Rose had been separated from the husband, who would sooner see her drown in her flooded basement than miss his turn-off to a Denny's All Day Breakfast joint, let alone a weekend on a boat.

Your own boat, at that. She had to almost laugh. "Do you really mean to tell me you went *to Ontario* this weekend?"

"I'm a frequent flier," Morrison grinned, clutching for a bit of his customary self-deprecation. "And Abbey had a real situation out there. On her hands."

Rose thought, I bet you did, too. In yours.

"Yeah, and by that time," Morrison continued, "Jeez, the sewer system got involved, too." He shook his head. "Seriously not nice."

Rose nodded slowly, soaking it all in. "You went to Ontario. This weekend. While I was . . ."

"To help an old friend." He jammed his hands in his pockets. "And it *was* the long weekend."

"Long schlong. Abbey is an old — well, not so old, I guess — *lover*. A not-so-old lover you're training to run a marathon with, and that you —"

"And that's all. That's it. When the marathon's done —"

"There'll be another one; aren't they quite common, marathons?" In the back of her mind, Rose heard naughty Hamlet, whom she taught to the second years every semester, interviewing his uncle-fucking mother, who insists that the death of fathers is common. *Ay, madam, 'tis 'common.'* And she snorted an unfortunately snotty chuckle at her own, and Hamlet's, private joke.

"What?"

"Oh, nothing."

"Rose, it's just a race. Abbey and I've done this for —"

"Ten years, I think you said . . ."

"Yes. It's a tradition. And like I said, she's a good friend. And I was halfway to Edmonton by the time the call came. And there's an airport up there, if you remember. I don't work Mondays, I set my own schedule. Somebody I've known for over a decade needed help, and I was lucky enough to get a last-minute flight on points, so I went. So what. It's not as if you'd have been able to pitch in."

Rose toed Jeoffry's cork out of the corner where it had gotten stuck and shot it back to him. The moon brimmed in the newly leafed trees. "Cain't deny that," She drawled meanly, and then felt bad.

Morrison added, "It's not the kind of thing that happens every day."

"Well, no. There'd be the jetlag . . ."

"Okay. Okay, I know you're mad. You got a right to be mad. Especially when you're not feeling well. I'm sorry for my baggage. People our age have baggage. Didn't you tell me that one time?" He held out his hands.

For once — probably for once in his whole goddamned life — Morrison had nothing to say.

And Rose knew what that 'nothing' meant. And Morrison was damn right she wasn't feeling well. Her headache was coming back, dull water rising in the gray beaker of her. "Okay. It's okay." She gave a weak wave, as though at a bug. She didn't really want to fight; in fact, she was impressed she'd managed to convey any annoyance at all. All she really wanted was for Morrison to do what he did before, to scold her about her spice cupboard and deplore the state of her flowerbeds, to condemn her freezer, and bring her the occasional cup of chamomile tea. She wanted things to be back to normal.

She just wanted him to stay.

Morrison grabbed onto the small shred of hope Rose had let dangle. "Well, enough about me and my stupidity. What about you. What did you get up to while I was gone?"

Rose shot him a what-do-you-expect look. "I read a lot of *Moby Dick*."

Back bounced the irresistible Morrison grin. "That's a whale of a book."

"Ha ha, a regular beluga."

Abbey

Now she was in for it, And when was she not? Never, it felt like, was she not in some mess or other. Okay, so she was a late bloomer. Aren't most creative types? Which she sort of was, right? She was a lefty and everything. Though, trust her to finally land a decent job, only to have the place go tits up for the downturn. For that's what it was looking like. For months, attendance at the studio'd been falling off, and now there were rumours. So-called 'retiring' instructors, no more new-hires, certain mean-seeming economies, such as the brand-new requirement that instructors pay for their own parking, and no more free coffee in the staffroom. And didn't they just get told the cleaning staff had been let go, and they were going to have to take out their own frickin garbage?

It was starting to feel like back home, after the cod went sideways.

She wasn't getting any younger, either, that was sure. Thirty-six, and already she had a fine pair of bunions for her trouble. And the other day she'd found a new gray hair. Sometimes, too, she had to catch her breath for a minute when the kids weren't looking, and her ass was far from the pair of merry nectarines it used to be. More like a couple loaves of rye. Would she be scaled down, right-sized, categorized, God forbid: dismissed? She was already slowly but steadily going into the hole a little bit between paychecks. Where would she get the money to dry out the basement and fix all that damn drywall? (Which now predictably was starting to smell.) Also: Why, when she had the chance, hadn't she gotten more education, or a different one? She had a problem with Business? With Law? Doctors apparently weren't hurting.

Somewhere under that mop of bottled blondness, she had a brain, surely. Didn't she? Why, why, hadn't she stayed with Morrison? Did she really have to chuck a man who sundried his own tomatoes and had money, in order to take up with a skinny scamp with a temper and no real job, and whose name she now could hardly remember?

Of course, she knew she shouldn't have called Morrison and hauled him across the country, what with the new lady friend and all, but she wasn't sorry she'd fucked him. Life is short, and Abbey's one great gift was knowing it. On Abbey Baxter's tombstone no one would ever be able to write, "Here lies Abbey, who rarely got laid." No effing way. Plus, the marathon was getting closer. No sense starting a long trip without testing the equipment, right? Abbey always liked to test the equipment before a race; it was only reasonable.

And Morrison'd be fine; that by'e always landed on his feet.

Unlike Abbey, whose feet weren't satisfied till they walked her straight into the Parkers of the world.

Which they had, a few semesters ago, in front of a coffee place called Jerry's Diner.

By her usual bad luck, she'd been standing in front of the Diner after breaking up with Mr. No Name, trying to tell if she should go in and get a chai latte and a muffin. Teaching — she'd just done two hip-hop classes back-to-back — was done for the day, and she was hungry enough to eat a horse and chase the rider. Maybe she'd splurge and have two muffins, and spend some time perusing the good old *Whig Standard*.

And suddenly there was Parker, world-class delivery dude, deck fixer, and competitive swimmer, kneeling right beside her over his ailing bike tire, smelling like WD-40 and sunshine. Movie-star cheekbones and grand big hands, all tanned up the way she liked them. And that darlin little half-moon of bum, grinning between the bottom of his T-shirt and the waist of his pants.

His eyes, when he looked up at her, were bright brown, and pleased as a squirrel's.

Plus, he was no fool.

"It should be called Jerry's Boner," he'd reflected merrily, as he hand-pumped air into his tire, "don't you think it should be called Jerry's Boner?" Studying her with glinting intensity from his crouch beside the wheel. "That'd be more original." Then up he'd stood with a grunt on behalf of his popping forty-year-old knees, and, with mock entreaty, wondered if 'Mademoiselle' would "enter the

Boner, and enjoy a coffee avec moi?" Standing there in his hairy bare feet, which weren't one bit cleaner than they should be.

Abbey's warning bells were banging out a five-alarm warning, but Parker'd called her mademoiselle despite her own proximity to forty, and translated *Jerry's Diner into Jerry's Boner* She couldn't resist a man who could make up shit on the spot like that. It was the devil to pay, and no pitch hot.

She looked down, she hoped not unkindly. "But where's your shoes? Did you not wear your shoes?"

"Don't need shoes in the summer."

As if they were already an item, he was guiding her toward the counter. "Don't worry about the feet; I'm a regular. You'll see."

They found a table and moved toward the counter, Parker's hand near, but not touching, her lower back.

"Hey Park," yelled a tall tawny guy in an apron with a grinning croissant on it. "I thought you didn't go in for blondes!"

Parker grinned and waved. "There's exceptions to every rule. Hey, bring that java over here!" He turned back to Abbey. "That's Jerry. He runs the place. Lets me show my stuff in here."

"You are deep as the grave," she'd replied. "What do you mean, your stuff?"

Parker'd raised a sovereign hand to call attention to an assortment of odd objects placed along the ceiling-high moldings at the top of the café walls. There were featureless thumb-shapes that might be ossified sausages or grim hand puppets, plus an assortment of homemade candles fitted with alarmingly toothy smiles. On a table under the window — Parker pointed these out too — lay items of jewelry, made from what appeared to be human hair and bits of beads, and modelling clay, and braided string. He tilted his head. "What d'ya think? Think they'll make me my fortune?"

"Wait a fair wind, and you'll get one, I guess. Are you sayin it's for sale?"

"Yup. I'm one of the featured artists (he struck a dramatic pose and pronounced it 'arteests') of the best Boner in town." Jerry the proprietor passed by with the coffee. "Ain't that right, Jer."

"Absolutely." Jerry grinned at Abbey, then turned to the tables of other regulars. "Parker's famous at the Boner. Right guys?"

Up went a unanimous round of laughing applause for Parker, the featured arteeste, and his famous Boner.

"See?" said Parker, "even got me a fan club!"

"Well," Abbey managed. "It's not every day Morris kills a cow. Dare I ask where you get your inspiration from?"

"From Life." Parker said, with a capital L. "Hey, maybe you should come by my place sometime, and view the current project." With a bicycle-oiled finger he lifted a corkscrew of her hair. "You know? Yours is almost the same shade as my Tadpole's."

Abbey coloured. "Your which?"

"My kid's. Can you believe she'll be ten on her next birthday?"

Was he simple? Of course she could believe this. Since she knew nothing about either of them, she could believe the man's kid could be any age on her next birthday, or have yarn for hair, or be one quarter centaur. But she shook her head to show appropriate wonderment.

Parker felt for his phone and thumbed up a picture of a suntanned child in slight summer clothes. "There. See? Same colour as yours, practically. You're just about the same size as her, too, you're not much bigger than a tadpole yourself, are ya." He nodded appreciatively.

"More like my Uncle Tom's cow, but I'll take it; what's her name? I mean, her actual name."

"The tadpole's? Iris."

"She's a darlin, all right." Abbey studied the child's expression, a mixture of mischief and puzzlement, not unlike her father's. "Sure, she's like a faery's child."

Parker slipped the phone back into his shorts pocket. "Nah, she's mostly a little fart. A fairy's fart. You should drop over sometime, have a beer, and meet her. I bet you and her would get along."

Abbey was still recovering from the one after Morrison. She could see that Parker was an uncertain direction to be heading in. She said, "Fuck off out of it."

But she was cod-stupid, like Mum always said. And beaming like a Fuller Brush man.

Rose

She was sufficiently over the flu and Morrison's Kingston news
to make it to Kelowna, but was remembering now how much
she hated readings. Her own, and others'. At others' readings she
felt cripplingly shy and profoundly cross. She would go there,
determined to yap on about all the cool projects she was immersed
in like you're supposed to, and to pitch her latest project, and say
witty things, like you're also supposed to. Instead, she lurked,
monosyllabic and homesick, clutching a paper plate; predictably,
when she turned to be introduced, celery and cherry tomatoes
would drop from her unbalanced plate and roll at her feet. Shit like
this didn't happen to other people, she was sure. Only to her.

She was going to be reading from her own so-far unfinished
and unpublished manuscript, which of course made everything
worse.

For starters, she hated what she was wearing. She should have
worn black, you can't go wrong with black, when did she forget
that? Instead, she had on a tweed skirt and a tailored shirt that
made her look like nothing so much as the teacher she was. At the
same time, she despised all the fervent black-wearers, with their silk
neck cloths and their chic shoes from Gravity Pope, their high-end
leather and their saloned hair.

She couldn't stand her hair.

There must be parties afterward, avant-garde events in edgy
places with names like Proof or Frenzy, and smoke-throated
saxophones and black garlic aioli, but Rose could never find those
parties and places, and she'd be terrified if she did. Instead, she'd
hurry along the deserted post-reading streets, astonished to find her
unticketed car where she'd left it, and to manage all the things you
had to manage, in order to cause said car to take her to the rumpled
safety of her bed.

Even reading at her own school, which happened less often
these days, she felt like an imposter. What else would you feel like,

when you were past a certain age and not a little burnt, and all your books were out of print? It was so good of the people to come, so lovely of them! She had to quell an impulse to bring home-baked shortbreads, to pray, to offer coupons for Swiss Chalet.

And yet. Once more, thanks to arts grant funding and a connection, here she was on a plane, in a hotel, on an unfamiliar street in strange city.

Queen for a day.

That thought, about being queen for a day, made her remember a birthday, as she fumbled with the room key. Bean's seventh or eighth, a limpid day; a bunch of little girls in the back yard, roaring through the flower beds, climbing the trees, trying to yank doll clothes onto a wretched but equitable Jeoffry.

And where had Bean been? Crouched with pale balefulness on top of the doghouse they'd inherited from the previous family, looking like Anne Boleyn on her way to execution. *I have a little neck.* Rose had been exasperated. All those nice children to play with! All that pizza, the presents — the modelling clay and crayons, the hours of medieval fun with the longed-for game of Carcassonne! Not to mention the work of making the party happen.

Because if there was anything Rose despised, it was little girls' birthday parties.

Of the drum Bean was hearing, and was gearing up to march to, she'd had no clue, back then.

Why not, though? Why hadn't she? Remember the time in the playground, when Bean was two and all set leave her mother? And hadn't her favourite kids' show been Dora the Explorer? What about the time when Bean was ten and mad at Rose for a moment's reasonable discipline? Do most kids go to their room, wrap a spare pair of shorts in a tea towel, tie it to a stick, and ask for the bus schedule? And then had come the rejection of all things high school — "but Mom, these people have no values!" — and her permanent retreat to the library, where she spent her noon hours reading about bog people and black holes, and Jenny the ghost ship that ended up full of dead bodies somewhere off the coast of Cape Horn. What was the common thread, the police asked, later, much later, when Bean had really been proven gone.

Had they meant to suggest it was Rose?

And had it been?

She slid the hotel room's plastic key card stripe-up, then stripe-out, without success. "Fuck!" She huffed and fumbled, a warning wetness dribbling from her bladder, her purse slipping off her shoulder. What if someone was watching? Of course someone wasn't watching, it was early afternoon, the place was a total tomb, and nobody watched a woman Rose's age do anything.

Finally a green light winked on, and with an unfamiliar exhalation, the heavy door whooshed open. She'd done it; she was in.

Silence. Tidiness. Unstirred air. That delicious feeling of being delivered, untethered, of not a soul knowing who you are. She could be a movie star, a bus driver, a lover; who knew what she might be, by the time the reading was over! All possibility — she still was vulnerable to such nonsense — lay in a band of afternoon light falling on foreign sheets. She dropped her bags on the anonymous bed and crossed the soft carpet to the view of shops and restaurants and streets, and beyond these, a sculpture of wings or sails, flying like white muscle, in front of a shining lake.

Home, sweet not-home. No students. No long-not-so-lost lovers, with their basement-floods and helpless exes. No disappeared daughters. In a hotel room, even history was powerless.

One of not a few arguments she could come up with, for no fixed address.

An oversized brown leatherette chair reclined behind her and she turned to it, plunking herself down with a sigh and kicking off her little black suede boots, bought on sale at The Bay, just for this trip. The boots rubbed the small toe of her left foot.

And that was only one of the many things, like her fear of the dark and the mole on her back, that no one was ever going to know about her.

She pulled out her weird new manuscript and placed it on the generous arm of the chair. She hadn't worked on it in ages.

A narrative must be figured out, an order, some way to present the damn thing as though it hadn't gone stale and practically unfamiliar to her.

Mom, there's four hours till the reading, come on. You got this.

You got this? Really? Did ghosts keep up with the nonsense on social media?

Several times on the plane she'd read over the passage she was going to deliver. She could always count on adrenalin. Though maybe she should give it one more go. For good luck. She eyed the mini bar.

Mom, and how long has it been since you've gotten out of town? Plus, don't get into that shit before your reading. You know how stupid wine makes you.

"Okay, kid, you win."

She hauled her little black boots back on, applied a hopeful streak of lipstick, and went out with a view to finding something for Bean. Always when she went places, she'd pick up something. Sometimes for the younger Bean, sometimes for Bean the age she would be now. A candy apple, a book, any little unusual object, however much the practice made her wince. She thought of it as a form of defiance. Though there was an illogical sort of logic to it, which was another thing no one was ever going to find out about Rose.

And the thing was that if she still bought things for Bean, her daughter must still be out there somewhere.

And someday, Rose might find her.

At the last minute, she slipped into her folder a stab at some poetry she'd been working on, just in her spare time. May as well.

Soon the little suede boots were trudging through unknown streets in the winter sun, and Rose was passing stationery-cum-china stores, organic food bars, funky boutiques full of unique clocks and scented candles, locally made jewelry, designer smells. The almost-winter afternoon gnawed her fingers in their light gloves, and for a moment's relief, she stepped into a shop called Green Ideas.

What idea wasn't 'green' these days?

A fake-nurturing smell of beeswax and cloves flowed out the tinkling door, and immediately Rose was greeted by a smart-looking woman with excellent hair. Her lapel pin said, *Hi, I'm Evelyn.* "Looking for anything special?" In her spare time Evelyn probably fundraised for the symphony, while being married to a doctor.

Rose should have worn her other coat, she knew it, not her comfy old walking-to-work one; Evelyn of the perfect hair regarded her with brisk authority, as if she might be a thief, or possibly a tract hander-outer. An imposter, essentially. And that's what she was, of course. Imposter writer, imposter teacher, imposter mother most of all; a fool could tell. Rose assembled what she hoped was a confident smile. "Do you have . . ." As always in such situations, she was covered with confusion, certain the impeccable Evelyn would find her craven, if not outright criminal. "Would you have, maybe —" looking brightly around; surely a place like this must have them "— um, T-shirts?"

Why did the Evelyns of the world make Rose want to commit hari-kari?

It turned out that The Green Idea actually did have self-consciously excellent, artsy T-shirts, hanging on a circular rack near the earthily expensive pottery. With Evelyn hovering, Rose thumbed through the overpriced glad rags until she found a black one with a green design of spiky leaves marching across the front. She thought of Bean at four, her little fist full of chives, running in from the garden, calling her.

"I'll take this one."

It was late afternoon when she got back to the hotel, not just one toe burning from the new shoes, but several, a traveller's weariness filling her head and limbs. The reading wasn't until seven; there was time. She kicked off the shoes, toward which she no longer felt friendly, tossed the oversized decorative pillows into the corner, and crawled under the comforter of the huge double bed. The last thing she saw as her eyes closed was the fancy boutique bag containing the T-shirt, resting on the chair in the corner.

Rose and Bean used to watch Teletubbies on TV. Bean couldn't get enough of the fat pastel creatures with their saccharine voices and freedom from gravity, and the way the sun dawned at the start of every program, its face that of a vast, happy baby. The sun in Rose's dream reclined at an odd Teletubby angle in the sky, and she was back out on the streets she'd just come in from, walking, walking, though now her footsteps made no sound, and she wasn't the least bit tired. This time it wasn't winter. A warm breeze flowed in from the sea, tossing gulls and sails, the infant sun lighting the trees, the buildings, the faces of shoppers and runners and drinkers of designer coffee. Turning the corner, she suddenly spotted — right there! Almost in front of her! — Bean again, just a little ahead, floating along, as though her feet made no contact with the pavement. She could tell it was Bean, despite the eccentric clothes and the ragged hair, the antique-looking spear.

But when she tried to call her daughter, no sound came, and Bean flowed on, serene and unaware.

Undaunted, Rose hurried behind her, following the downy neck, the familiar shoulders, her eyes tracing the longed-for shape, throat straining to sound the lost name. And behold: Bean slowed and turned, a radiant smile softening her face, and Rose rejoiced, relief flooding her brain, her empty hands. Bean was so close now! So nearly reachable! Just a few more steps. But each advance of Rose's seemed, by some strange polarity, to repel the girl further ahead, behind a door, around a corner and then another, Rose gamely following after.

She could see her! She had been there!

The scene changed. Gone the coffee drinkers and runners, the Teletubby sun, all replaced by gaunt, haunted buildings, a bullying wind. Unwittingly, Rose had followed Bean into a darker part of town, or a darker town. A crosswalk appeared, and Bean entered it, indifferent as a saint. Rose had no choice but to huff along after her, into the river of cars. But there were so many of them, going in so many directions and at such terrible speed that it was all Rose could do not to get hit. She had to keep her head down. The next time she looked up, Bean was gone. Instead, her disembodied voice remarked, calmly and reasonably, "This dream is a cliché." Rose woke to find herself drooling into the pillow.

As a wannabe writer, she had to agree.

The reading was in a college classroom. Security had to come open it, but they weren't there yet, so Rose found herself standing in the hall with the audience, most of whom were unisex creative writing students, on notice that their marks depended on attendance. Proud-boned Eritrean cleaning staff zoomed past on their hallway Zambonis, with the hollow swishing sound that means: everybody else in the world has gone home, what's wrong with *your* life? The students stood shy and silent, woven together in a protective little pod like a nest of baby snakes. So Rose, since she was the entertainment and the grown-up, automatically launched into professor mode, interested and persistent, middle-aged and ridiculous. Thank God Bean wasn't here; she'd die at the sight of it.

"So" — some of the students were going to be reading their work, too — "are you all writers?

. . .

"I love your campus, it's so . . ."

. . .

"You know, I'm from Calgary; do you realize what it's like there at this time of year? I'd give my cat for your weather!"

Nobody laughed, and Rose repented. Also, she secretly apologized to Jeoffry, and made a mental note to bring him salmon treats. Not the ones from the grocery store, either. No sir, Jeoffry was going to get the low-ash, organic, expensive kind you buy at the vet's. She made a mental note to have the cab stop there on the way home from the airport.

The baby snakes exchanged furtive, fluttering sideways glances, gliding closer to each other and minimally wincing, as though suddenly exposed to too much light. Bean would approve of them, thought Rose, the milk-skinned girls in their long flowered Value Village dresses and combat boots and delicately militant tats, the softly bearded boys in vintage skirts and skull-patterned tights.

Not to be unkind, Rose found herself wondering, but how did such gentle souls cope with life? How did they manage its tedium and inconvenience? What did they do about schedules, and bills, and deadlines, and dirt? How did they survive things like bus stops and plumbing, landlords, and grocery shopping? How the hell did they get though anything?

Their beauty was staggering.

Also, it was boring. Rose had seen beauty before, she'd even had some once upon a time, she now realized, and she knew what was under it: the hard and touching gleam of the will to survive, which had brought them out here tonight to see if fame awaited them, and which eventually resulted in marriages and daycares, and mortgages and lives not so very different from hers, they'd find out, skulls and all. Eventually everything came down to luck and DNA, and whatever you could flash before you were thirty.

"Okay," she said, to no one in particular, as the security person clanked toward them, "last one in's a rotten . . . Elliot??"

This time she got a groan out of them.

She read, doing her best to invest her stuff with something fresh; she answered the questions, and in return, dutifully listened to the efforts of the next generation.

A burly spoken-word dude chanted the entire Halifax explosion in rhyming couplets.

A graduate-level sonneteer cleverly delivered a great many elegant facts about the coastal weather.

A soft-bearded boy in a thrifted kilt recited his contemporary verses of queer-courtly love, while strumming on an actual lute. To judge by the young man's song — Rose had to conceal a smile — queer love was just as fraught and wondrous and ultimately doomed as the other kind.

Now the student with the boots and the delicately militant tats stood to read, her shyness so painfully mannered, they amounted to a form of inverse arrogance. Keloid scars shone on her inner arms as she raised her papers, to tell all about how love is murder, then, seemingly shocked to find herself in public, quickly sat down.

The shy girl's lines Rose segued with some conveniently arterial strokes of her own, inspired by those gleaming friends of Bean.

> You sit or rather
> tilt, for the undead do tend to tilt,
> on a sheet or maybe a doormat, it's hard to tell which,
> your eyes holes, a further hole drilled into
> your gut and soaking darkly through
> your wet bedsheet. The way you lean against
> that tree, at night, in nothing but
> snow. How either that's a big red smile
> you're wearing, or your mouth
> has been widened
> somehow.

There were further verses, all variations on a theme of blood, and redolent of walking dead, stakes through hearts, and Halloween, but all that spookiness was metaphors, merely, for the inscrutable need to cut, to pull the skin taught and see the spurt, feel the wound's warm rain, private ecstasy of incision.

A collective stretch rippled through the room when she finished, ardently hoping she hadn't sounded too lame. Questions were invited from the audience, and they kindly came up with some.

"Who, or what would you say are your influences?"

"Bean," she wanted to scream. "Atwood," she tossed off instead, "and I suppose Louise Gluck, and of *courth* Plath," hazarding a semi-lewd wink, to show that her lisp had been intentional.

"How many drafts do you typically write before you're finished a poem?"

"I haven't finished any."

"Do you ever feel frustrated by the limits of language?"

Let me count the ways, she was about to say.

And then, "Is there anywhere I can buy that?"

"Pardon?" said Rose, "Excuse me?"

"How can I get that, what you just read out? About that girl?"

A woman in the back, not anything like any of the other audience members, in their boutiquey get-up. Small, dark, a swollen face shadowed in a hoodie, possibly attending the reading as a way to keep out of the cold. Again, the question, "Is there anyplace I can get them words of yours?"

She could feel herself colouring. "It isn't . . . I haven't actually published —" the audience holding its breath, "— Um, you know what? Here." She dug into her folder, found the poem attempt, and handed it back to the woman with the swollen face. "You can have it. Here. It's yours." She smiled. "You can keep it. Please have it."

The woman took the poem. People exhaled, smiled, then laughed uncertainly and with relief the way you laugh when you're watching somebody do something you can't imagine being able to do, like changing a tire, or making a meringue.

Almost immediately, the reading was over, and it was a weeknight and still winter and damn cold, and nobody, least of all Rose, cared much to linger. A cab delivered her to her hotel. She was glad to be back in the neutral quiet of her room, to kick off her tight shoes and pour a drink, lift the soft T-shirt from Green Idea out of its stylish bag.

Studying the shirt's faux-arcane design, feeling its impossibly soft folds falling through her hands, inhaling a scent that didn't yet, and might never, inhabit it, Rose thought that Bean had loved the things that weren't supposed to happen or be given, and the ones who needed them, like the homeless man she had offered her coffee to on winter streets, and the dogs — so many! — that she used to want to bring home, and the swollen-faced woman who'd asked for the poem. She'd have fit in seamlessly with the pod of baby snakes, with their manskirts and sad madrigals. Somewhere, Rose believed, Bean must be one of these. She held the shirt to her tenderly.

Somewhere, Bean must be.

Morrison

Morrison stood at the bottom of the airport escalator in clean jeans and a navy blazer, a dozen Safeway roses clutched in his arms.

"Morrison, you old —"

He stuck out the roses, grinning. "Got you a baker's dozen!"

"You're impossible."

"When a ma-an loves a wo-man . . ."

"Oh, spare me . . ." She looked around in case anybody'd heard that.

"Madame, the night is cold, and your chariot awaits."

"You've got the car here?"

"Well, I didn't drive a horse and buggy. You hungry?"

"Sorry. Dumb question." She studied the reluctant shuffle of bags on the luggage conveyor belt. "Yeah, I haven't had much except pretzels, and those mean little Oreos the size of your thumbnail. Why do they even make Oreos that size?"

"I can't comment on the size of airplane Oreos, but we do have reservations at the River Café."

There was a reason Rose had intended to be mad. What was it? What had been going on before she'd left for Kelowna? Ha. Abbey. Abbey and her oh-so-convenient basement flood. She felt her face start to heat up. "I teach at eight tomorrow, and I'm getting over a cold, Morrison, if you remember."

"In my experience, there's nothin better for the common cold than a plate of uncommon —"

"Is this to make up for Ontario?"

" — paired with a crisp Sauvignon . . ."

"Because if it is . . ."

Olive oil and rosemary artisan crackers with red pepper jelly and mignonette oysters; shitake mushroom broth with caramelized onion, pickled asparagus, and charred cabbage; fermented fife-glazed sturgeon with parmesan and basil orzo. Oh.

And buckets of Sauvignon Blanc with dinner, followed by berries and Grand Marnier.

And a slow-burning hickory fire doubled against a turbulent pre-spring sky.

And a crème brulé to make you cry.

When they left the restaurant it was midnight, and almost spring and raining, and Rose's head was spinning.

Morrison

Mixers, blenders, coffee makers, planters, composters, garburators, toasters, coasters, dressers, bench presses, clothes presses, flower presses, garlic presses, letterpresses, anything that pressed: Morrison loved stuff.

He surveyed his kitchen, which contained two — or multiples of two, he was an even-numbers kind of guy — of pretty much everything. He could never be an astronaut, his ass floating in outer space; he liked to be restricted, held tight, spared the terrifying sense of: *alone*, a problem for a man who these days mostly shared his bed with no one. Though he was a problem-solver. And a reader. Jung, Freud, the romantic poets. These days he was even into Godart, with his radical ideas and his waif-like actresses, he loved that Jean Seberg with her little skinny pants and her wispy hair and her big awake eyes; she reminded him a little bit of Rose. Too bad Seberg died the way did, rotting in her car somewhere, like he was gonna be if he wasn't careful.

How he hated the word 'single.'

At least he had peeps. Jung, Freud, Seberg, the poets, they and their books and the journals that wrote about them were his family, and he kept them where a person of another era might have kept his actual family: in bed with him. The books and mags were everywhere, but there was an order. A spine of magazines down the left side, a light bedspread of paperbacks over the middle, hardcovers to anchor down the night. And Morrison in the middle, where it was safe and sound, and barely enough room to crawl between the covers at beddy-bye time.

And that was the way he liked it. For Morrison, the unpeopled wasteland of a blank bed was a nightmare.

He turned to his second-best coffeemaker to top up his java, and caught his reflection in one of his careful arrangements of mirrors. Not too glam these days, with his graying hair and his hungry eyes, but Morrison loved his mirrors anyway. He coveted their serene rendering of the world in all its eerily reversed detail, the way they forever held viewer and viewed, tranquil and doubled. Mirrors — often unique ones — could be found at auctions and antique shops, yard sales, even Home Depots, and Morrison had one or two of them in every room. Lying in bed in the dim early morning, he never tired of gazing at the silver oval above his dresser, offering its view of an identical world, luminous and cool, always-unreachable. In the dim light of early morning he imagined being Alice in Wonderland, floating up to the mirror's beveled edge and pausing in mid-air, then passing through to a place where nothing changed, where mantel, candles, plants, and the patient chairs, were held in a spell of stilled silver, as though suspended in a world of water.

But Morrison wasn't just a collector; he was a voting citizen, and if you didn't mind his saying so, a darn decent neighbour. When the folks to left and right headed down to the Dominican after Christmas, he made sure their lights turned on and off as programmed, brought in the mail, kept an eye out for anything unusual. In return, he enjoyed the same neighbourly regard when he was away, plus the inevitable gift bottles of Duty Free.

Though Morrison would drink anything.

He'd eat just about anything, too; he was always hungry, always had been. As soon as the neighbours were airborne, he'd be over showin the snow who was boss, emptying the mailbox, feeding the cat, checking out the contents of the crisper and the cupboards, whether they needed it or not.

His job of vigilance accomplished, home he'd trot triumphantly, bearing a flag of wilted kale, four spongy carrots, a Sherriff's piecrust, a net bag of lemons. With the veggies he'd Magic Bullet up a penitent health drink for morning, in order to justify the lemon-pie-to-end-all-lemon-pies he'd make for his dinner, and when that perfect pie came fragrant and golden-meringued from the oven, he'd pour himself a hit of something that seriously burned, scoff down the hooch, and inhale the whole goddamn pie while he worked it off on his treadmill.

Call him old fashioned, but there was nothing like washing down home-baked lemon pudding with a snifter of Appleton Estates at a three per cent incline while rewatching *Rocky* on a winter night. He had it down to an art.

As for art, he didn't know much about it, but he knew what he liked, which was anything that showed strong emotion: crucifixions, pietas, battle scenes, it didn't matter if it was Superman and Lois Lane or Greece on the Ruins of Missolonghi, as long as it had emotion.

At a yard sale on a cold November day among the Tupperware sandwich sealers and five-finger-rings and knobby packets of never-opened modelling clay, he once found To Go Beyond, a sepia print of two classical Greek lovers, faces rapt, marble arms raised, sightless eyes gazing upon each other, their stone lips hungering eternally for the those of the other.

The image had seized him, made him tremble. Somehow — he knew it as sure as he was born — he'd been there before, locked together with another in a place beyond time. But time had got in, heaven had ended, the beautiful room had been locked, and he'd never been able to find his way back.

Until the yard sale, and that astonishing, terrifying picture.

He'd had to steady himself against a table, nearly knocking over a stack of hangers. The piece had been priced at five dollars, marked down from fifteen. Unbelievable. He'd handed over the money and run, thanking the vendor absurdly, and half expecting someone to sprint after him, arrest him, demand the thing back. But no one had pursued him. He'd walked freely away, clutching the lovers to his chest. Now they hung in the stairwell above his race medals, their longing gaze casting an ecstatic hush over the space below. For hours sometimes, in the evening, Morrison could sit on the couch with his glass of wine, quietly studying the sculpted faces of the ecstatic pair, his eyes lingering over their reaching hands and great wings, their blank eyes and adoring gaze, which sought nothing but each other's. And nothing would ever interrupt that gaze. The lovers would forever be the same, their mutual worship exempting them from time. It was like that poem by Keats. *Forever wilt thou love, and she be fair*. Even better: not even death could ever separate the pair.

Out of all his strange collection of pots and pans and plants and mirrors, the framed world of Cupid and Psyche was his most prized find. The only improvement would have been to have two of them.

Somebody'd asked him once, "Is there *anything* don't you have two of?"

And Morrison had joked back that he even had two of him. Or did have. Because once, he'd been a twin. Before the start of time, with its losses and farces and bad bargains, Morison had been whole and peaceful.

Morrison had once been identical.

Did he remember the one who'd begun and floated beside, and then at nine weeks, quietly died, pressed into, impressed upon him? The one who'd been born, thanks to his own triumphing life, as a cyst with teeth somewhere in the deep folds and dark caverns of his own body, and who'd been delivered, not on their common birthday, but when Morrison was twelve, during a routine adolescent appendix operation. The doctor's pale blue mask mumbling to his mother in the recovery room, "There's something you probably should know," the news fit for a *National Enquirer* headline: "Man Born Pregnant with Mummified Sibling." Morrison's luck. Morrison's unbelievable fucking dork luck.

Why didn't you tell me?

His mother, looking down, looking away in her sad green felt hat, "We didn't want you to be sad. We thought —"

At least the doctors would talk. Now, Morrison learned why his left side had always been weaker; why he'd forever felt the absence of something inside him, but couldn't say why "— it's common; with time it'll go away"; why he'd always felt guilty for taking up space; why, as a kid, he'd for years had an imaginary friend, and why anything doubled delighted and unsettled him. "You absorbed your twin."

Ostensibly — he'd done his research — the cyst with teeth was the reason he'd never stopped longing for the *one*. For the You.

There was no memory of being with the twin, not in his brain. But his body remembered. In dreams, or with a bit of weed (it wasn't just petunias he started in his greenhouse) or in that liminal half sleep in the gray time before dawn, his limbs resumed the peaceful sway of being's beginning, his heart recalled the pulse of: not alone. Not alone. And he would relax, then, into the remembered rhythm of that other heartbeat so like his own. There were even times when his fingers, old now, and clumsy, could almost feel the answering touch of her tiny ones, other, and yet beyond near: There you are. There.

There.

That smallest of times together: an inviolable world with no beginning, no end. A time of being in, and of, each other, as though each were the one true and clear answer to the other, like water flowing into water, like the yearning lovers in his timeless picture.

But it had ended. The One had gone. The pulsing darkness sheltered himself only after she had slipped away. No way to stop. No way to help. No way, in that time before time, to understand or to find. No words yet, with which to shape anything into story, to create a reason; instead, there was only himself, condemned. Why? He'd taken too much inner space, and now must float eternally in an outer space forever unfillable.

Sometimes in the dusk, sitting under the picture of the stone lovers, he imagined how it would have been if she'd lived.

By week nine they'd have begun practising. Flexing. Reaching and touching, exploring their small room, taking its measure. By ten weeks, the first, ghostly smiles would be there, for none but each other. A year or so on, they'd be toddling together, plundering cupboards, scaling the furniture.

At five, they'd be stumbling over their first printed words, their green eyes widening when the funny lines on the page became *cat*, became *sun*, bloomed into *flower*. Even now, he could remember the bright green caterpillar on the opening page of his fifth-birthday board book, and how some part of him had felt the fascinated presence of his sister.

Because she would have been a sister, not a brother. Or so he had always believed. He knew she would have been his small, exquisite female double. The dark, hard, dire-smelling knob teased out of his body and bottled, in his twelfth year, would instead have been the little sister who now was absent every Christmas Eve, and who was missing on Easter morning, who haunted every Halloween, wavering behind each birthday's candle flames.

And who never had a name. At least not an official one, they didn't do that kind of thing back then, bestow names upon the unborn dead, or give them a burial's recognition. But Morrison recognized her, all right . And he damn well did name her, later, after he knew. Danica, he had pronounced her. For the morning star, to whose care he had finally consigned her, his dear double, the other one of him, his fellow tenant of the red chamber.

II

MEETINGS

Morrison

A year or so after the Volcano Marathon, Morrison and a discreetly concealed flask of Pusser's Rum (Original Admiralty Blend) attended the preview of the annual spring showcase at the art college. His daughter Lucy had some of her weird stuff in it, and he'd promised to go to the opening with her, but he wanted to go by himself first. He needed to see it before Lucy was at his elbow, demanding to know.

It was a bitch of a March night, and he took his time, figuring parking wouldn't be hard to find. Was he ever wrong. Instead of enjoying a half-empty parkade, he found himself maneuvering his car backward into a too-small stall beside a smugly tidy Toyota, in which sat a woman with greying hair and an intelligent face that looked as if it habitually converted worry to wry. He liked the look of her, but she was out of her vehicle and up the concrete stairs before he could think, let alone imagine a way to get her attention.

He caught a reasonable view of her ass, though. Not bad for a woman . . . he regarded her disappearing shape . . . of a certain age. Of his age.

In the foyer he caught sight of her again after the show's preliminaries, and by the time she and her drink wandered past, he managed to be casually texting against a column.

As if.

Morrison couldn't text for shit, and his digital acrobatics were all for show; he had bought the phone and the plan that very afternoon, because Lucy with her big blue eyes had hauled him to the Apple store when they were in the mall looking for running shoes, and made him sign up for it — "Look at it this way, Dad, if you can text you'll hear from me more" — but he'd seen the young ones with their thumbs flying over those infuriating little screens, and he hoped a good imitation might impress.

It did. The woman spoke first. Something clever about the possible uses of hearts in containers. The exhibits, she'd meant.

Morrison made up some story about his daughter and her bottled grief over her poor dead mother, wife number one, who was in fact perfectly fine, and living in Edmonton; Morrison did stuff like that under pressure, especially woman-pressure, he could never figure out why.

"Oh my God, I'm so —" The woman's pale face had coloured.

She was wearing a slender gray trench coat, and strange little green shoes with upturned toes, that riffed off the colours in her scarf, and that looked just right for a sixteenth-century Flemish butcher or a naughty teacher, he hoped to God the latter. She was so near, Morrison could almost smell where she'd been in her day, feel the energy in her, the grave, puzzled, breathing life of her. In his gut he felt the predictable awakening of the nameless gap, the familiar stir of the terrible hope: would this be the time? Might this be one who brought him back home?

"That was actually . . . kind of a joke. About my ex. She's unkillable."

"Oh," the woman said, looking mildly shocked; had he put her off? "Good trick, that."

"I mean . . . I totally agree that these whatever-they are's" — he waved in the direction of the art pieces "— beg to be messed with." A sip of his rummy London Fog, "You wouldn't be an academic, by any chance . . ."

"Oh no, does it show?" A regretful smile.

"Hey, I meant it as a compliment!" A minimal wink. "I enjoyed your observations. Back there. About the hearts."

He sipped and indicated the gallery's high walls of dark glass, streaked with spring rain. "Wouldja look at er come down out there."

Rose laughed. "It's about time; we've sure had enough snow."

"Amen to that. So what do you —"

"Oh, look, they've got those smoked —"

"Would you like to —?" He hooked his thumb towards outside. "You know what, it's so noisy in here; we could —"

She looked out at the bare trees, bending in the wind. Her neck felt cold.

"Unless you're chicken."

"I'm not chicken." Appetizers were going by. "Just a sec." She grabbed three smoked-trout-with-garlic-cream-on-rye.

"That oughta hold ya."

Rose grinned. "I'm not known for my delicate appetite."

"That's refreshing."

Morrison held open the door. They stepped out into the rain.

Abbey

Parker held open the door. Abbey stepped through into it. Because, sweet Jesus, if anything was ever an 'it,' it was Parker's place.

"What do ya think?" He appraised her with an intensity that seemed part merriment, part mockery, his eyes boundlessly amused, shaggy head tipped to one side, bare feet brown and amphibian-wide. One of his large hands rested lightly on the small of her back where her sketchy summer top left it bare, and an annoying commotion was starting up in her. Jaysus, she had about as much control as two squirrels in a coffee can.

She eased aside a little, to dodge the hand and stop the feeling, which soon, if left unguarded, would take a turn for shagging. "Gimme a minute."

After the brightness outside, her eyes struggled to penetrate the vague shapes and humps that hunkered in the dim twilight.

Parker asked again. "So, yeah, what d'ya think?"

What she thought was the look of the place gave her the bivers. But she couldn't say that, right? "Oh, it's great, where should I sit?"

Parker took that as a compliment. "There's lots of furniture! See all the furniture?"

As though furniture were someone he hadn't clapped eyes on in a while. Good old Furniture.

"I do see . . . shapes. Is that what — ?"

"Shapes? These aren't just shapes, they're my dear old granny's chairs! And that's an ottoman. Ever see one of those puppies before?"

"Yeah. I had a grandmother. Ottomans are big on the Rock. Or is that Ottomen, ha ha?"

"Huh?"

"Oh, just me being a chucklehead."

Gradually through the murk she discerned what could be either the inventory of a used furniture store or a serial killer's lair.

Parker was magnanimous. "Have a seat!" A cheerful smirk, head to one side. Abbey sat, the thick fabric of the Ottoman tickling her bare legs. For distraction, she looked up. Industrial-strength drapes were shoved aside or looped up over their dowels to let in the light, dust and dried moth husks shimmering in their sun-blasted pleats. Below the drapes, struggling rubber plants stood forgotten in ceramic pots, their gray trunks like elephants' legs, vast and lost in the strange twilight. Melancholy monoliths of dining-room chairs stood along walls and crowded against a defunct fireplace, whose mantel sprouted cereal-box action figures, static in their plastic postures. GI Joes reigned silently there, and Ninja Turtles, stiff Star Wars characters. A jar of — dear God, was it toenail clippings? — glowed like yellowing eggshells high on the windowsill.

Abbey swallowed. "What would, uh, that be?"

"That's some of my work."

"Your work?"

"My art."

"Did anybody ever tell you it's weird?"

"I'm a loner, Abbey," he said with mock drama. "A Rebel."

"I thought you were a market gardener."

"That is my day job. One of them."

Parker fixed decks, too, and operated a one-man delivery service, and sometimes worked on people's boats. "But my real thing's my art."

"So your art is putting toenails in bottles."

"Toenails are important! You'd be pretty sorry if you didn't have any."

"Can't deny that."

"Anyway, it's not just art, it's 'guerilla art.' It's a form of commentary."

"Commentary on what?"

"On everything and anything. On Life. It flies in the face of convention."

Try putting that in your artist's statement, Abbey thought. "Where'd you study to be an artist? What do you mean by 'flies in the face of convention?'"

"Didn't have to study." Parker smoothly redirected a fart. "I told you I'm a rebel. My art is the art of subversion. It doesn't need books and courses. Books and courses are part of the establishment. An artist needs to remain outside the establishment, so he can see things for what they are."

Abbey gazed around the dim room's strange collection of lost objects. "And that's what you do." She took a sip of the Double Double she'd brought. "See things for what they are."

"Rather see em for what they are than for what they were. Hey, that's pretty good. Don't you think?" Parker smiled magnanimously as the large hand once again found its way to the bare part of her back, and began moving ever-so-lightly up and down, making the hairs turn. "I see, and I comment. I call it Kamikaze commentary. It's got a nice ring to it, don't you think?'"

Abbey moved away from the hand again. "Some would say your commentary was a tad ghoulish."

"It's not goulash, it's stew! No, seriously, it's preservation. I, Parker Darlington, am preserving the otherwise lost toenails of mankind — and womankind — for posterity. He grinned. "I also make cat-hair finger mice, and earrings out of molars. Any time anybody I know gets their teeth out, I make these really cool earrings to give them." He squinted at her mouth. "You got any teeth you need out? And I paint. Right now I'm doing a series on fire hydrants. There's more challenge to getting those puppies right than you'd think. Like, at different times of the day, depending on where the sun is, and that. And wait'll you see my peanut-butter art."

"God, you're takin a rise out of me," Abbey murmured. Should she leave? Should she be getting out of here right now? Anyone smart would say she should.

Instead, she imagined getting fucked in the gloom of Parker's bizarre home, getting thrown down over the Ottoman in the half dark, her legs kneed roughly apart, face pressed with no mercy into the crusty upholstery, Parker finding her and thumbing her wet with his own spit while pulling off his shorts with the other hand, Parker thrusting into her —

"Hey, and what d'ya think of my Luke Skywalker?" Tenderly, Parker regarded the rubber homunculus. "Just got this baby. Took Tadpole to an estate sale in Elgin last weekend. Got her some great little flippers, too, for when we go to the lake, a dollar fifty and hardly used!"

Abbey knit her brow. "The tadpole. . . That's your daughter . . ."

"Yup. The one I showed you the picture of the other day at the Boner."

"You mean the Diner. The café."

"Hey, you're catchin on!" He grinned like a pleased teacher. "I got this Luke and Yoda for five bucks a piece. Unbelievable deal. There . . ." He reached the Luke Skywalker down from the mantel and gently handed it to Abbey. "These bad boys are going to be valuable." He called into an unseen room, "Aren't they, tadpole!"

A child's uncharmed voice from somewhere in the back of the house: "Sure, Dad."

Rose

An August afternoon, aspen leaves dropping like coins, the first signs of the season's waning. It was the day after her surprise dinner with Morrison, and she was stealing time for a cup of coffee and a read of the new *New Yorker* on her deck before heading in to work. A feature article on postpartum depression, its sweats and fears, its boredom and isolation, lay open on her knees, perfectly and shockingly describing the brand new, old mother she'd been back then, making her remember how, in the middle of an autumn afternoon just like this one she had hugged her denim knees on the front steps of a rented house with a wobbly deck, warped siding, and wary marital energy. How, sitting on that deck she would sweat, then freeze, then sweat again in the almost invisible sun, her baby crying for attention, her body a wounded alien. She'd been past forty, she'd just delivered, and she was caught in the crosshairs of rampaging hormones and impending divorce.

The afternoon street of memory was still as a witch's spell. Parked cars tilted downhill like desert boulders, clutching their tight black shadows. The grass on the parched lawn was crisp as Easter basket straw. An insect sawed its saw. Behind her in the little house, the newborn paused between howls. Rose the old, new mother counted, the way people count after lightening. One thousand, two thousand, three thou —

— sand. And here it came again, the terrible sound, primitive and wet and riveting as the horn that took down the walls of Jerico. And like those walls, the walls of Rose, the new-old mother were being shaken down. For she was exhausted, and there was no one but her, to go in.

Rose went in. And she sat on the bed in front of the mirror, buffeted by the baby's cries, staring at the ruin of herself: unloved skin, dribbling breasts, sad thighs — and thinking about resumes. She didn't have one. How, at such an age and with an infant, could a person have no resume? How, at such an age could a person have an infant? And no resume, and no references, and not a soul to recommend her, not one.

How, at such an age, could a person be alone? Which, even though the husband hadn't left yet, Rose was.

And this was the moment in her life when Rose met fear, which was real, and which looked nothing like Hitchcock, with his well-trained birds and obedient vertigo, his safely framed rear window. Real fear was so much more ordinary and scary than the scariest movie. It was a credit-bought car seat, big as life on the kitchen floor, the cats stalking it in circles, sniffing at the wailing new family member. It was the kitchen floor itself, worn and spotted, and the clank of the rented aluminum door, and the over-and-over, wind-up recording of Inky Pinky Spider, who never ceased to go up the waterspout.

Down came the rain and —

It was the dreams of the new-old mother, when sleep came, in its snatched fragments —

— That the baby had somehow been left outside on the punky deck, at night, in the weather, in nothing but a diaper.

— washed the spider out. —

That the cats in the night had leaped onto the counter, pulled down the carcass of a raw turkey, and gnawed it bloody, while the roof let in in the rain.

She hadn't known, at the time, that such thoughts were normal, that she wasn't about to become a baby killer, that there could be life after birth.

The child cried on, and Rose, the new-old mother, woke, listened, fell back down into dreams . . .

— and the itsy bitsy spider climbed up the spout again.

But Rose couldn't dream, didn't dare to dream. What if there were more bloodied carcasses? More circling cats, further forgotten babies freezing their poor little newborn butts? What if she finally fell asleep, and something really did happen to Bean?

Night after night she lay awake, eyes watering from the effort to sleep, the house silent, the husband for the time being, snoring in the basement, the cats' yellow eyes regarding her with cold appetite, as she shuffled about the kitchen, pumping breast milk and looking for NeoCitran, hoping the NeoCitran would help her to relax, so she could get a grip on the damn nursing.

What a laugh all that coy granola parenting stuff was, what a myth, the notion that breastfeeding was so easy, so natural, so portable! Oh, please. On the phone she described to Mab the humungous hydraulic breast pump "— like a bloody outboard motor" they'd had to rent at considerable cost. "Don't you talk 'natural' to me. Don't anybody mention 'portable' to me, that thing's about as portable as a Steinway!"

'Blame' being the factory setting for mothers, Rose blamed herself. The birth had been interminable and gruelling, a famished march through the desert, a war, her organs seized and squeezed for hours, the terrifying torque of induced contractions, her heart working so hard she went from a sweat to a fever, "and thence to a fast," she quoted Hamlet to Mab. Afterward, amazed to be alive, she'd joked that if they'd invented the breast pump in Hamlet's era, childbirth could have been used as a form of torture. "They had the Catherine wheel back then, didn't they? They had St. Andrew's cross. They could've called this one the Wrack of Rose — or how about the Rose Wrack! That kind of has a ring to it, don't you think?"

"I think you should just say yes to drugs," said Mab.

By the time the ordeal of birth was finally over, Rose might as well have spent the weekend on the original Catherine wheel. It was one o'clock in the morning. She hadn't eaten anything solid for two days. Removed, at last, to her room, she stared at the glass of orange juice some humane person had left on the bedside table; she couldn't imagine lifting it. Oil filmed her hair. When was the last time she'd seen a shower? Her sex throbbed numbly, an expiring animal in a leghold trap. A cathedral of emptiness reigned where Bean had for so long been curled.

She felt like a bombed field.

Instead of engaging in the fight of teaching a reluctant newborn to feed, she allowed Bean to be taken to the nursery for a few hours, just a few, figuring a bottle or two that first night wouldn't hurt anything. But Bean was too smart for that, Rose reported to Mab. "Our little legume wanted the nice bottles back."

Mab, who was trying to break a daily wine habit, sighed, "Don't we all."

But Rose had been determined to nurse, no matter what it took.

It took plenty. The hydraulic pump became her constant companion, its rubber suckers cupped over her aching breasts hour after hour, its engine grinding out its mean whine. In front of her as she pumped, a music stand, poignant reminder of things urbane and sane, stood bravely holding up a copy of the *New Yorker*, Rose hungrily devouring details of Danish architecture, innovations in music, political skullduggery, excellence in dance. She even read the letters to the editor, those signs that somewhere there was a world in which people held opinions, built stuff, went to movies, strolled along caféd streets, finding quirky new places to eat.

When it became clear that the pump was getting her nowhere, in came the lactation consultants, the milk stimulants, La Leche League, with their meetings and advice and arcane devices. For months she wore around her neck a small plastic box from which two tubes of stingy milk extended, one tube taped to each breast. This she would have to try to trick Bean into mouthing, in the hope that eventually the child's work would stimulate more, and that one day, presto, she and her daughter would turn into a contented Madonna and child, complete with dreamy smiles and pre-Renaissance halos.

One breast worked slightly better than the other. "The things I did," she groaned to Mab, "to keep her at it. I'd have her lying on her back on the bed — I had to, with that ridiculous box thing around my neck — and I'd turn myself into a human pretzel, trying to keep her on the good boob, and spare her the other one so her work would be easier, and she wouldn't quit."

But the tubes would tickle the roof of Bean's mouth, and she'd turn into a wailing, spluttering prune, tiny red heels kicking, wafer-thin nails raking Rose's sweat-soaked breasts. Eventually Bean put her foot down. "Metaphorically, I mean," Rose laughed. "There came a day around four months in, when she turned her head in a way that I knew meant business, and — I was worn out, Mab; I had to concede defeat." Had that been one of the signs? Bean's final refusal of Rose's meagre offerings in the nourishment department? Rose sighed. "After that it was bottles. Period." Another sigh. "Kind of like last night."

"You mean dinner with Morrison?"

"The same."

"Well, you know what they say," reflected Mab, "I'd rather have a bottle in front of me than a frontal lobotomy."

Rose sighed, "Mab, that is so old."

"Kind of like me," quipped her friend.

Mab

Mab never meant to live in Toronto. "Put that one down to youthful folly," she once laughed on the phone to Rose. This was a few years after their tearful, teasing parting, Rose to the West, Mab to the self-proclaimed hub of the East, when the good rates were on, late one night. "Put it down to, like, *extreme* youthful folly."

Rose laughed. "You're such a harridan."

"Mom always said I was a vixen."

What she was, was a librarian. And don't believe that old cliché about librarians. Mab was no bespectacled, cat-mothering, Dewey Decimal handmaid. And unlike the librarian cliché, she had no cat. "Can't stand the fleabags, with all due respect for the venerable Jeoffry!"

Mab, who despised cats and gave zero shit about the Dewey Decimal System, did her post-university librarian internship in Kingston. For a while, needing friends, she also sang in a pile of choirs. "You should have seen my schedule. One day I was Anglican, the next Catholic. Never Baptist, though. I have my standards." She sighed comfortably. "I used to call myself a choir whore."

After signing up for the librarian program, she'd needed a place to live. Through the student grapevine, plus somebody's well-connected mother, she inherited an artsy and universally coveted apartment not far from the waterfront, which caused her — "there were people who would have *killed* for that place!" — to end up staying on after her program was finished, and working at the main branch of the Kingston public library.

"That was a great old place, and so nice and close to the Pilot House; their french fries with a cold one were the best!"

That was where she met Heathcliff, whose actual name was Heath, but (Mab confessed to Rose on the phone) Heathcliff suited him so much better. "As in, '*God* won't have the satisfaction that I shall.'" Mab snorted. "Yeah, right, Mr. Wuthering Heights."

Rose had interrupted. "You know, you've referred to Mr. W.H. plenty, but you've never really told me the whole story. You've never even said how you actually met him."

"Oh, didn't I? So this one day it was the kids' story hour, and I was prepping "The Wheels on the Bus" when I caught sight of him, swanning along, tanned as a Kardashian, you should've seen him, with the little handknit socks and his Oxfords (he got those made for him too) and his cravat — who in their right mind wears a cravat! — and his Armani shades, looking for books about sail repair." She snorted. "Yeah."

"Must've been quite the sight," Rose chuckled.

"I'll say. He caught sight of me, too. Did he sniff my secret weakness for early Christian motets? La, la, la."

"Must've sniffed something," said Rose, egging her on.

"You're terrible. Anyway, up he trots to the front desk wanting help finding his books. The man didn't have a clue how to look anything up. How did he get through school?"

"That's men for you, they see a woman and forget how to —"

"Ain't that the truth."

Mab was busy, she had to set up the chairs and the props, and put out the juice boxes and the snacks, so she thumbed the direction of the card catalogue — "We still used card catalogues back then, imagine!" — but directions weren't enough, oh no, Mr. Handknit Socks couldn't be happy until he had her all to himself in the stacks, digging up obscure manuals on everything from celestial navigation to Tasmanian sailmakers. "For his boat, don't you know. Well —" Mab struck a pose Rose could hear "— for his yacht."

"Oh, Mab," laughed Rose. "*You* on a yacht?"

"Hang on, I'm getting there. Yes, on his yacht, which he kept down at the King Street marina. You know, for his Kingston getaways." She huffed. "Maybe the question isn't so much how he got through school as, 'What woman in her right mind dates someone who wears handknit socks and a frickin cravat?'"

Because two nights later, Mab dated a person like that.

Rose hastened to subdue Mab's embarrassment. "Well, what single gal's not charmed by a dashing doctor?"

Which Heathcliffe was, and not just any old doctor, either. He was a heart surgeon, no less.

Though Rose couldn't see it, she could sense that Mab was placing her hand over her chest, to demonstrate sincerity. "Oh, he was all heart, that one." She chortled shamelessly at her own pun. "He was spending the summer in Kingston, to take a break from it all. He claimed it was sort of a mini-sabbatical."

The date had taken place in the marina, on Heathcliffe's boat, Mab, in her full dirndl — "Oh, the good old eighties!" — and sluttily lacy blouse (purchased that very afternoon, at punishing expense, for the occasion), perched with voluptuous alarm on the polished bench in front of the gently rocking cabin. "All that brass, Rose," she squeaked. "All those winches and charts and sextants, and what all. I was practically having a coronary myself, I nearly needed his surgical services!"

"You must've swooned."

"I wish that's all I did."

Mab described an early August night in Kingston. Horses and carriages for the tourists; a jostle of street vendors and buskers; St. George's carillon hourly serenading the couples who strolled the King Street cobbles in the sauna-soft air; the summer smells of bus exhaust and fast food and lake water, while a darn-good local band on the patio of the Holiday Inn played *If I Had a Million Dollars*.

"And here's me on deck in all my cheapo finery, pretending I dated doctors on yachts every night; Crikey, I was scared out of my gourd!"

But it had been a delicious evening, there'd been a steady supply of excellent rum, and — after the Holiday Inn shut down there was the Allegri Miserere (Heathcliff, a former cathedral chorister himself, it turned out, had his own hots for early music) pouring ecstatically from the Bose speakers in the cozy little cabin, the swallows darting on the lemony air, the marina wavelets lapping.

Redde mihi laetitiam salutaris tui: et spiritu principali confirma me, soared the clear voice of the soprano soloist, O give me the comfort of thy help again: and stablish me with thy free Spirit . . .

"Free spirit, all right, the canny bugger. He had the instincts of an accomplished criminal, *he* knew the Allegri would get to me."

"Well," reminded Rose, "speaking of spirits, there was also the rum . . ."

Mab was unused to doctors, much less to rum. The next thing she knew, it was very early the next morning, she was stickily pinned under a snoring, post-coital stranger who looked like the grandfather of the man from the night before, her head hurt ("OMG, there are no words"), and "I had a new understanding of thirst." She described for Rose how she'd held onto her head while fumbling for her watch, and seen the bitter hour of 5:30 a.m.

"Rose, I bet you've never been that dumb."

"Oh," Rose had replied, "I have. I have been."

Rose

After the boozy back-from-Kelowna dinner at the River Café, Rose and Morrison lurched their way to Rose's place. Luckily, Morrison had left his car there, and they'd walked to the restaurant, which wasn't far, for dinner. It was raining harder. Rose didn't care anymore, that she had an eight o'clock class in a matter of hours. The semester was nearly over, and at least it would be a Friday morning; half the students wouldn't show up. She could give the ones who did surface a work period, she would be too hungover to think of anything else. Maybe she could find a way to give bonus points for having a pulse.

"Did you want to come in?" Far away in some wiser part of her brain, she could discern the faint throb of warning.

Morrison perked up. "Can I?"

"Well, you can't drive home that way." Rose fumbled up her keys and opened the door, smelled the warm, reassuring cabiny smell of sun on pine that always for some reason lurked in her front porch. As usual, the smell, so suggestive of summer holidays, lake-splashed docks and Nancy Drew mysteries, made her feel unaccountably homesick for the cottages and cabins and canoes that had not been a part of her childhood.

Then she remembered, with a sudden little jab of annoyance, that she still had to unpack from the flight. One thing Rose could not tolerate was unpacked bags. "Shit."

Morrison stood on the top step behind her, surveying her lawn, which, as usual, needed cutting. "What's up?"

"Oh, just —" She gestured toward the luggage pile in the entryway.

Morrison grabbed the bags. "Where do you want 'em, Ma'am?"

Rose flicked on lights, kicked up the furnace, dropped her wet coat, which showered the hardwood floor, irritating her more. "Doesn't matter. Anywhere, just off the floor." It occurred to her, with the thought of getting wet things off the floor, that a smarter person would have turned off the water to the house before heading into the blue for two days. She might have come home to a flood for her trouble.

And that was when she thought of Abbey.

Morrison, on his way down the hall called merrily, "Gotta pee."

Rose snatched their dripping coats and gave them to him to toss into the spare room on his way. "Feel free."

A woman, she reflected as the bathroom door clanked shut, will do anything to relieve herself quietly. She'll crawl down the inside of the toilet bowl, hide behind a door and do it in a yogurt container, anoint the back yard with her stricken piss, anything for privacy. Why did men always have to make such an event of their business? With their slamming of doors, and their flinging back of toilet seats, and their cheerful announcements about their bodily functions. You'd think no one else had ever relieved themselves before.

In the kitchen, she turned on the tap and slammed the dishwasher on Rinse to drown the halting squirt-and-pause of a well-watered man of mature years. But she couldn't drown his voice. "Hey girl, your tap in here's leakin, I think you got a wrench in your toolbox, can you go look?"

Rose didn't even know she had a toolbox, never mind a wrench. As she tried to think where it might be, a movement caught the corner of her eye. A child's drawing, that had been tacked above the sink for so long she mostly only sensed it there, and rarely took note of. Grade 3, it must have been. A happy cat with a tiger tail, and a polka-dot grin. Caption simply: 'Mom.' As she watched, the drawing fluttered brittle and frail into the sink, resting for a moment on the sudsy water, before swaying the rest of the way down.

She must have jarred it off the splash tile when she slammed the dishwasher.

The toolbox was downstairs, now she remembered, on the same shelf as the slow cooker and other tools and gadgets no longer much used. "Just a sec," she called, as carefully, so carefully she lifted the drawing of the polka-dot cat out of the sink and set it on the drip tray. She leaned hard into the counter, remembering Grade 3. The dire Miss Macumber and her learning centres: Computer, Store, Library, Family: aka organization, provenance, civility, regularity. All those elusive things Rose in her hard-working, self-indulgent singleness had failed to provide.

At Centres, the children had acted out going-to-the-store and paying for things, visiting the library and taking out a book, getting along in a family. The Centres family featured a slim blonde Mother, a strong handsome Father, a sturdy Big Brother, a frilly Little Sister.

By then, Family for Rose and Bean was neither sturdy nor frilled. It was always tired Rose, and ever needy Bean.

And Jeoffry made three.

One day at roleplay time, Bean, whose only idea of a sibling was Jeoffry, had a different plan than Big Brother or frilly Sister, and chose, instead, to be affable Family Cat. She'd purred. She'd pawed her kitty ears. She'd dressed up in her last year's Halloween costume, and meowed with conviction. But after roleplay was over for the day, Bean had decided she really was a cat. She took to navigating the classroom on all fours, purring, rubbing up against table legs, sniffing ankles. The other kids had loved having a pretend cat at school, but Miss Macumber on parent-teacher's night was less enthusiastic. "Of course, it's certainly too early for concern, but there are signs which may merit . . . our attention."

Rose stumped down the stairs to find the toolbox, and see if its jumbled contents included a wrench. She'd have liked to have given Miss Macumber some attention, all right. As she descended, she noted that the stairs were covered in cat hair, and needed vacuuming. She should have paid more attention, back then. She should have been watching. Maybe then she would have caught on to Miss Macumber's signs.

Signs of what, she asked herself, flicking on lights, flinging open the storage-room door, banging her knee. "Fucking ow." The signs of: *I can't, I won't, and you can't make me.*

The signs of No.

How far back does No go?

(Speaking of 'far back,' here was the toolbox, shoved in behind a bunch of preserve jars Rose had never in her life made use of, and behold: the wrench. At least Morrison was going to be pleased.)

Back then Rose had enrolled the two-year-old Bean in a toddler's movement class. A church basement, white cinder blocks, seven preschoolers, and a teacher with a portable stereo on one of those primary-coloured interlocking rubber mats. The kids were to march in a circle, and shake their sillies out. Then they were to wiggle their waggles away.

The movement class was on Saturdays.

The first Saturday, Bean stood to the side in her tiny pink T-shirt and yellow jumper, dark eyes reserved under the wing of auburn hair.

No.

"Sometimes it takes a time or two," smiled the teacher, an excellent young woman in designer jeans and well-used jazz shoes.

But it happened the next time, too, and the one after that. Each time, Bean parked herself farther from the center of activity, canny hands stuffed behind her back, chin tilted in elfin opposition, head slow-shaking. *No.*

No to wiggling. No to waggling.

No to pretty much everything.

Rose joked that Bean was like her, ever the observer. "Maybe one day she'll turn out to be a philosopher!"

But after the fourth time, the teacher took Rose aside. Something was wrong, she felt. There was a reluctance, a remoteness, possibly even a learning disability, just a slight one, nothing important, but if were caught early "— and I'd be happy to recommend —"

Rose smiled. "All this because she chooses not to shake her sillies out?" She thought, Screw you and the jazz shoes you danced in in.

But there were further No's.

No to ballet.

To Soccer: No way.

Nothing to do with Frisbees or bicycles, or the colour blue. No to making Christmas angels in the snow.

Eventually the No's of Bean reached Dr. Seuss proportions. Rose, to manage her frustration, took to making wretched rhymes out of them. Forget Brownies and Girl Guides and C.G.I.T., forget calling Grandma to say Happy Birthday, screw prom night and its tacky corsages, screw graduation and its future mirages, never mind the whole nonsense of getting engaged, to hell with getting married, getting pregnant, or laid.

Bean kept saying: NO, that little Sam-I-Am (Not).

What was a mother to do? What, oh what?

Work . . . yesiree, there was always work to be done. Rose girded up her loins and set her face toward town.

"You find that wrench?"

"Coming!"

Even when Bean was a baby, Rose had a job. She had to have one, the husband was gone by then, and those darn bills kept rolling in. She was still on contract, and she had to teach all the time, plus tutor and volunteer and be on committees, in order to prove she wasn't a criminal, and could be hired safely, Which left only the weekends to catch up on the marking and admin. She used to joke that she barely had time to take a bath; it was not that far from the truth.

They used to have a huge ugly couch left over from the previous owners, in this very basement — found wrench in hand, she looked around — in the big messy space they'd gamely called the family room.

Once on a workday, Rose was in a hurry, buttoning, tightening, checking her purse. It was seven o'clock, and she had photocopying to do before her eight o'clock class. What if there was a line-up at the photocopier? What if the damn thing broke down again? Bean and her babysitter sat on the awful couch, regarding Rose's frazzled departure, Bean naked but for a diaper and a pair of bright green froggy boots, eating cinnamon toast, and, by her own admission, getting bigger and braver every day. For a brief moment she studied

Rose from under her thatch of auburn hair; and then she remarked, "And I'm not even going to cry."

The words were still down here, suspended in the basement's nacreous air.

Rose took a quick last look at the furnace room and the water heater before switching off the ceiling light. Luckily, nothing had flooded while she was gone, or even leaked. A thought that returned bloody Abbey to her mind.

(A thought almost too unbearable to entertain: had Rose herself been one of the signs)?

Morrison, his pee completed, was leaning in Rose's kitchen door, looking like he needed to sneeze or had misplaced his keys. "You find it?"

"Find what?" Rose knew 'what,' and she knew she was being a bitch. She despised being a bitch. But there were times. Like right now.

"Ooh, here be landmines," Morrison warned himself aloud.

"Anything I can get you? Glass of water, glass of wine?" She fished in the cupboard for glasses. *How about a glass of turpentine?*

Morrison stepped to the counter and slid a filled glass toward himself. "I was just thinking . . ."

"About staying over?"

"After I fix that tap. You read my mind."

She winked, not especially friendly. "Not hard to do."

"Ooch."

"Fuck. Sorry." She put her glass down and stood looking out the window. "I mean it, actually, Morrison. You didn't deserve that."

"You could make it up to me by letting me share your bed . . ."

"I'd love to, but where'll we put Abbey?"

A fork of lightening licked the sky.

"That was a bit below the —"

"Wow. Hear that?" Rose, despising herself, cocked her ear, listening for the thunder. "Gosh, that was pretty close." She studied the ceiling with Pythagorean calm, counting the seconds. "One thousand, two thousand, three thou —"

"Rose."

"— sand.

"You seem pretty pissed off."

"I so love a good storm, don't you? Why don't we open the back door."

And why didn't she shut up? She knew she was being bad, but she couldn't help it. Badness was a dark part of her, had been since Bean's departure, and God knew, probably before. Like a hangnailed thumb or a phantom limb, it ached when she was tired and late at night and in the wee hours, and there was and would be no cure.

She found her keys and unlocked the back door.

A dark rush of rainy air, the curled cat picture stirring slightly on the counter. Her hand darted out and batted the drawing away. Why was it even there?

"Rose, I told you it was just until —"

"The marathon. Yup." She contemplated her hand, which actually did have a hangnail. She should shove it in her eye, a better woman would.

"It's just a couple months."

"And a hotel room." She pushed a stray wisp of hair off her forehead. "And how about a continental breakfast the next morning, would you like a latte with that?"

"You said it was okay." Morrison set his glass down. "I thought we agreed."

"Maybe I was talking in my sleep."

"Maybe you were; I do recall hearing someone snore."

Rose pressed horridly on. "So, do you do it with your medals on? I mean, after the marathon."

Morrison picked his glass up again.

"And when it's over, do you have, like, 'medal fatigue?'" She stifled a mean chuckle. "Oh, dear —"

"That was so not-quite funny."

"I'm sure you're so quite right. And I'm so going to bed." She grabbed her wine, wheeled and booted the door shut with her foot, to hell with the spring night, which was getting louder and wetter, big drops spattering the floor through the open screen door. "And you should probably . . . I think for tonight, we should probably call it . . ."

"I should go home, you mean. I agree. But I can't drive yet."

"Well, you know where everything is." She left the room, bypassing the bathroom and recklessly ignoring her bedtime chores. "Including the guest room." All she wanted in the world was to be in the dark, alone, while somewhere above the sad goddamn world, the thunder growled on. She turned out the hall light and stumbled, unwashed and unflossed, into to her bed.

And found — how on earth had he managed it so fast? — Morrison.

"Jesus, Morrison, you've got some nerve."

"And you've got some curves."

"Whoops, gotta wait till the marathon!" She took his hand, which had found her waist, and planted it firmly on the bed between them.

"Girl, that's enough."

"What's enough? You're the one who won't fuck!"

Morrison flung a pillow at the wall. "Honestly, Rose, fuck you."

"Fuck you, too! I bet it's not about the marathon after all, I bet the marathon's just a big front to hide that you *can't* fuck, I bet that's it!"

Rain raked the window as Morrison lay silent.

"Oh shit, I'm sorry! I'm really sorry, Mor — ."

Suddenly Rose was crying, hard, sitting up in the dark, still in her travelling clothes, hands shoved in her hair, snot mixed with the tears. "I miss her, Morrison, I just miss her."

"I miss her, too."

Morrison

Never rained in Calgary, but it poured. And tonight it was pouring outside and in. "Rose. Rosie, Rose. Come." He moved toward her and covered her with himself, then pulled the blankets up over her heaving shoulders. "You're okay. It's all gonna be okay." He patted her wet hair. "And we are, too."

Rose covered his hand with hers. "What do you mean, you miss her, too?" She rubbed her nose with the heel of her hand. "I mean — you never met her."

Gazing up into the dark room, he told her about the other dark room. The one where there was only himself and her. His sister. Where they were rocked and held, side by side, the universe of her his only need.

"Morrison, you never told me."

"No. It's just life, I guess. Or death. Not much to tell."

Stroking her back, listening to the rain, he described how the life in that room had been nearness, completeness, peace, a hand touching a face. How they'd floated together shoulder to shoulder, slow-dancing in the room's gentle sway. How sometimes they'd held hands. "They do, you know, womb twins, it's documented. And we — I just know this — sometimes we even kissed ."

"How did she die? I've been so selfish. Morrison, I'm sorry. Please tell me."

It had always been night there, in the room before time, the same long, good night, so sweet and private. That is, until he began to know she'd changed, become heavier, stiller, duller, her slack limbs flattening, flesh shrinking, no more *her* in her. Always before, she'd pressed toward him. Now she pressed him down, her heavy head lolling on his comfortless shoulder, her lifeless weight a disaster, a thing ill-starred. He couldn't move her, couldn't help her, there was nothing he could do for her, his sister, for Danica, his small dead star.

And it went on and on, until he wanted her gone.

And then she was gone.

Where are you? Why can't I find you? When I reach for you, why can't I touch you? There were supposed to be two, and now there's just me, all one in the dark with a dead thing. I can't go where you're going, and I can't go on this way. How could you do this to me? Without you I'm nothing. Without you I can't keep being.

He had had to make a decision, there, in the room before time, to let go of her hand. To let go.

"And that's what I did. I let go to save my life, and I made my sister gone."

Rose was finally asleep, he could tell, her breath coming in regular, weary puffs. Grateful to be allowed to stay, Morrison turned over, and listened to the rain.

Abbey

"Well, that's a damn fine Luke Skywalker." She handed the action figure back to Parker, sensed the wiry heat of him, inhaled his smell of bicycle tires and sun.

In her mind, she saw those blunt fingers and work-dirty nails undoing her bra, snatching off her panties, raking her ass . . .

"Dad," came again the child's voice from somewhere, "I don't *care* if your dumb-bum action figures are going to be valuable, I'm going out to the treehouse, so I can get back to my *reading . . .*"

Abbey looked at Parker. "Oh, no, are we disturbing her?"

But Parker was grinning. "Whoops, almost forgot the tadpole was here. Why don't you come meet her."

"What, now?"

"Tadpole doesn't bite. Hey, Miss Reading Machine, come on out here first, for a minute."

"I don't . . . I'm . . . No. . . ." Abbey squirmed.

"Take it easy, you're gonna like her; I mean it. She's cool."

"How about next time," suggested Abbey, "It sounds like she's —"

"No time like the present."

"No, Parker, I'm not —"

But Parker had her by the hand — "This won't hurt a bit." — and was pulling her out of the strange living room, then through a more or less normal kitchen, out the back door, and into a leafy summer courtyard.

Flagstones and grape vines and Japanese lanterns, a bright riot of nasturtiums, two red canoes. A shed at the back full of boat bits and boxes of tools. A tiny house in the middle of it all, complete with curved walls, flower boxes sprouting more nasturtiums, Middle Earth windows, gauzily curtained. There was even a working chimney, Abbey noted, and Parker, seeing her notice it, piped up, "That's for the cold nights. Great little place out here on cold nights." He winked, his hand once again straying to her back, and with the same troubling effect as before. "Tadpole isn't the only one who gets to use it. And she ain't always here." His hip brushed roguishly against hers.

Abbey made a face. "Dude, you got more brass than an orchestra."

Parker grinned. "It's never failed me yet."

The hobbit house was set up on stilts, like Noah's ark pre-flood, and you had to climb a shaky ladder to get to its shire door.

Abbey looked at Parker. "In there?"

"Tadpole likes it in there. You will, too." He coughed to hide a fart.

"I heard that."

It was June, everything waxy and green, a blue day showing through a network of trembling leaves.

Parker looked up with the sun on his eyelashes and yelled, "Hey, Tadpole!"

"Yeah, Daaaaaad . . ."

"Somebody here to see ya."

"Who?"

"Abbey."

"I don't know any Abbies."

"Friend of mine. She's a reader, too. Wants to meet you."

The curtains stirred, and Abbey glimpsed a blur of bright hair.

Parker turned to her. "You can go on up."

"What? Parker, I don't even —"

"Just go on up." He gave her rump a little shove. "She's waiting for you. Don't worry, I'm not going nowhere. I gotta hose off these canoes back here. Guy's picking them up this afternoon."

Abbey headed up the ladder, awkward as a bear on a bicycle. What if 'the tadpole' didn't like her? What if Iris despised her?

And what the devil was she supposed to do when she was in there? Levitate? Abbey didn't know any kids. But she remembered what she'd thought of adults before she was one of them, and the recollection did nothing for her confidence.

She called softly, "Knock, knock." Wasn't that what you said to kids, didn't they like knock-knock jokes? Knock knock, there's an idiot at your door.

An imperial ten-year-old voice sighed and then replied, "You may enter."

Abbey took a deep breath and ducked under the low door, into a walnut-sized cabin that smelled like canvas in the sun. The tented light showed sleeping bags tossed on built-in bunks, a yard-sale table with a bowl of granola bars and fruit, magazines with holes and shapes cut out.

Above the tiny room, the green afternoon filtered down through the warm plastic bubble of a homemade skylight. Even in the state she was in, Abbey could imagine lying below that skylight on wet and windy spring nights with the dark wash of the city sky billowing above, the rain pattering on secret leaves.

She could almost smell the sound of it, inhale the sweet safety of it.

"Hello." A small girl looked up from a large book.

Abbey ducked in, looked around, imagined she was back home on the Rock, with the nieces and nephews. And out of her before she knew it came a Newf expression. "Who owns *you*?"

The girl was not amused. "I am Iris." She laid a felt bookmark between her pages and gravelly closed the book. "But you may call me Mary. That's because I'm actually Mary Lennox. In this book." She held up a hard-used copy of *The Secret Garden*, whose cover bore the same illustration Abbey remembered from her own childhood. "Mary Lennox is an aristocrat," Iris studied Abbey. "And an orphan."

Abbey continued politely to wait at the door. "And how does she get on? Can you tell me more about her?"

"Certainly. Everybody in Mary's family and the *whole place*, that's *India*, gets cholera, that's a horrible, disgusting disease, where you throw up and get dehydrated and have an electric light imbalance."

Abbey fought a smile. "That would make you skinny. My mum used to say I was so skinny she could see the sin on my soul."

"And then," Iris continued, ignoring the comment, "They *all die*." She pronounced 'all' *ole*.

Iris waited for Abbey to be shocked and when she wasn't, she stuck out her small chin. "Absolutely *ole* of them."

Iris/Mary, the aristocrat-orphan, was orphan-thin, with fine tanned skin, like her father. Huge pale-blue, thick-lashed eyes, pink-brown cheeks, a rosebud mouth with slightly protruding upper teeth, restrained by braces.

In her Mary voice, and with regally raised eyebrows, Iris added, "You may enter."

Abbey stepped in and sat down on a paint-spattered stool, from which she could regard the girl. A long rope of bright blonde hair almost the colour of Abbey's own lay over her small shoulder, which, in Iris's sleeveless tank top, shone brown and bare. Books were everywhere. *Charlotte's Web. Anne of Green Gables. Where the Wild Things Are.*

Abbey said, "I like your place." Then she saw *Little Women*. "I had that! Back home on the Rock when I was a kid, I read that!"

"You lived on a rock?"

Abbey smiled. "It's where I'm from, the Rock. It's what they call Newfoundland. You know about that, right? Out on the other side of the country?"

"We did Newfoundland at school. It was all about cod." Through the window, Iris watched her father move back and forth, whistling and showering the canoes. "It was boring."

"Yeah. Hard to get excited about a cod if you're a kid in Kingston. Sometimes even if you're one in Newfoundland, if you want to know. Anyway, it's this . . . crazy wonderful place, the Rock. Nothing but mist and seaweed, and a porpoise or two."

"What's a porpisertoo?"

This time Abbey laughed. "They're similar to seals, but they look like dead guys. Big old whiskery heads and purple noses. If you're on the shore early enough in the morning, you might see one bobbing in the water."

Iris considered. "Yuck."

"I saw one once. I was down to the beach picking gooseberries for my mum to make a pie, you haven't lived until you've had Mum's gooseberry pie."

They heard the slap of water, the swish of the hose. Iris called, "Don't forget to wash my bike, Dad, you said you would!"

"Cost you five dollars!"

"You owe *me* five dollars."

"For what?"

"Hello? I paid for breakfast yesterday, remember. With my *allow wince*."

Parker called, "I pay your rent, and I don't even get an allowance!"

Iris rolled her eyes and turned back to Abbey. "He always says that. So what happened then?"

"Sorry? When?"

"When you were picking those goose bumps. For the pie."

"I thought it was some dead old soldier with his face all dark and swollen, come floating in."

Iris put her book down. "Did you scream?"

"Well, in Newfoundland, darlin, you don't scream, you screech. Sure, I screeched, all right. And I was up the bluff faster than a dog'll lick a dish, never mind the berries."

Iris reflected. "Did you have any brothers or sisters, on the Rock?"

"So many my mum darned near run out of alphabet." A rueful smile. "Had to name the youngest one Zane. Have you got any?"

"I've got a sister. I'm tons older than her, she's only, like, five. Plus I've got a new brother. My mom had them with dumb-bum Bob, after the split. From my dad. My brother and sister don't live here." She narrowed her eyes. "I don't either. Just on weekends."

Iris wasn't stopping her, so Abbey dared ask. "And where do you live when it's not the weekend?"

"With my mom and Dave."

"Is that your mum's husband?"

Iris frowned. "How come you say 'mum,' when everybody else says 'mom?'"

"Cause where I come from, darlin, your mum's your mum."

"Whatever." Iris made a face. "Anyway, Dave's my *mom's* partner. He's a dumb old workout guy, and he's going to be moving in with us pretty soon."

Abbey put her book down. "Is Dave a nice man, then, I mean, do you like him?"

"All he ever does is work out his muscles and drink his dumb *protein powder*, and yak on about grammar."

"Does he have big muscles?"

"That's all Dave *is*, is a *muscle*, just one big bald muscle. Like your porpoises or whatever, except he's not purple."

A chuckle bubbled up, and Abbey quelled it. God forbid Iris should think she was laughing at her. "I'm sure he's very nice."

"He's okay, for a grammar muscle."

Abbey smiled. "Once upon a time, you know, grammar was thought of as 'glamour.'"

Iris looked up, curious despite herself. "Like, okay . . . why."

"Well," Abbey reasoned, "that was because back then, folks who could speak correctly were thought to be more sophisticated, so people really wanted to have good grammar. It was sort of like the way nowadays, people want all the brand newest fashions."

"Well, I don't care about fashions or about grammar. And it's all I hear day in day out, at my mom's. Dave teaches it at the college, and he's always going around being 'correct.' Except when he's not."

Abbey was the curious one now. "And when he's not?"

"When he drops his g's, which I despise. He's always this'n and that'n. Mary Lennox would never drop her g's." She lifted her straw-coarse braid and began to twirl the end, which was nearly as wide as her hand. "I'm going to continue reading now." With that, she tossed the braid behind like a finished chip bag, and settled herself more comfortably. "Since you are familiar with it, you may borrow *Little Women* if you wish."

So Abbey sat down and opened *Little Women*, and began to read.

Iris

Over her own book, Iris secretly studied this Abbey of Dad's. For a grown-up, she was hardly even ugly. If she had to exist at all, it was at least good that she was so small. Normally adults were huge, smelly, and disgusting, for example: Dave. But back to Abbey. She had little hands like a kid, but grown-up feet with bumps on them by the big toe, like her mom's, and pink nail polish. Long skinny legs in her shorts. Her hair on her head was nice — yellow and all wavy and stuff, the way Iris wished hers was. And she had a fairly yummy face, with bluey-blue eyes and a kissy mouth. Probably Parker was planning to smooch her.

But until then, what did he do instead? Stick her in with Iris, for *her* to babysit. That was *so* Dad.

Abbey looked up, saw Iris staring, and smiled with her kissy mouth. Iris dove back down into her book.

Babysitting sucked, and one way or another, Iris was always getting stuck with it. At home her mom was always like, "Iris, you have to turn down your music, because Pippa's got a test tomorrow. Iris, you have to watch Odessa while I do the laundry." And like, "Iris, Hugo needs his *beans*, feed Hugo his beans *now*, please." That sing-songy doing-the-laundry voice she always used to mean, and *you can't get out of it, so don't even try*. Why should Iris feed Hugo his dumbass beans? He wasn't even her actual brother, he belonged to her mom and Bob the blob, who wasn't even around anymore. How about getting dumbass Bob to feed his own ugly baby. Except Bob moved out, and now it was Grammar Dave.

There were far too many Daves in this world.

Plus also, he looked like Humpty Dumpty, Hugo did, and he had humungous see-through ears like a baby elephant, and he never stopped pooping. Phew!

It seemed like all her mom did was get new babies. Hugo was as bad as a batch of them.

Iris didn't know which was worse, her mom's baby or her dad's girlfriends, which were pretty much the same as babies. They were always different and always the same, skinny, with long hair and girlie voices and necklaces on their ankles, and they always asked the same dumb questions.

Do you have any brothers and sisters?

How is school? What grade are you in?

What do you like for breakfast?

What does your dad like for breakfast?

And always, the girlfriends' annoying questions ended up being about her dad. Abbey's would, too, by the end of the afternoon.

She peeked over her book again. Blech! Look at her, reading away as if she meant it on the other bunk, and getting *Little Women* all covered in her germs (note to self: put *Little Women* in freezer later). Iris stifled a gag. Look at the pukey way she turned the pages *way* too fast, and how she was smiling already on page one, when the March family had just found out they weren't going to even have any Christmas presents this year (how insensitive!), and look how she twirled her hair around her finger to try to be like Iris, and how she dangled her bare foot down like a big fat question mark, like the foot was a person, like it was going, "Hello, there, can I please get some attention?" Some more attention; Iris had already given her more than she could spare. She turned back to her own book.

Mary Lennox was so lucky. She didn't live in two messy houses, with a stupid Hugo and a dumb Odessa, and grammar-glamour Dave, and a bunch of dumb girlfriends and dumber deck buyers and half the time nothing but beer and leftover takeout in the fridge, and a dad who took actual *pride in his farts*. Mary's parents weren't separated, they were just dead, which was so much better. Unlike Iris, she only had to move once, not every weekend. And did Mary arrive at her gloomy and romantic manor on the windswept moors in a rust bucket that smelled like Cheez Whiz and diapers? No, Mary was *escorted there by soldiers.*

And actual servants, not her dad's gross recycling box, greeted her at the door. And the servants said, "Good evening, Miss Lennox, not 'Hey Tadpole!,' like she just crawled out of a swamp.

Plus, cholera ended Mary's family — simple, sudden, incurable cholera, not fights and dragged-out times of nobody talking, and the grass not getting mowed and the house not being taken care of or the lights turned on.

And the dinner getting colder.

Best of all: thanks to cholera and soldiers, Mary never had to wonder if her family had died because of *her*.

Because, did it? If Iris had been a better kid, if she hadn't turned up her music at Pippa, if she'd humoured her dad and helped her mom, and not been a crabby pants, if she'd fed Hugo his beans, would those guys still love each other? She longed for answers, but she didn't know how to ask, and no one except possibly Mary Lennox could tell her.

The brown foot of Abbey bobbed up and down, up and down, boring as the afternoon. It would not be getting any of Iris's attention. She eyed it with disdain, then went back to her reading.

"Hey, Tadpole," called her dad from outside, "what did you do to Abbey, did you make a snack out of her?"

"Ha ha, no, loser," said Iris out the window. She had no desire to do anything to Abbey bum-babbey tee-Abbey go-fabbey. Who had a name as dumb as Abbey? Or hair as wiggly. Or toes as ugly or eyes as crossedly or a nose as bugly.

Though she had one thing going for her, Abbey did. Well, maybe two. She talked funny, and she didn't ask stupid questions after all.

The Time Between

A yellow June day, lawnmowers humming and lilacs blooming, coffee cups and finished Rice Krispy bowls scattered over the sun-splashed breakfast table.

The mother and the five-year-old daughter share a paper and pencil. The mother writes C-A-T.

"Cat," says the daughter, tasting for the first time the strange pleasure of letters tumbling into words, curling into creatures. "Cat. Like Jeoffry!"

"Yes," The mother laughs, throwing up her hands, hugging the daughter, "Exactly, like Jeoffry. You're reading, you can read!"

The mother writes B-A-T.

"Bat."

S-A-T.

"Sat. Sat, sat, sat, the silly cat sat on the bat!"

The mother and the daughter high five, hug, and hug some more, sharing their new secret of reading.

The bright new words taste like chives and sunshine.

Rose

After the husband was gone, Rose and Bean stayed on in the house with the overgrown chives and the creaky floors. It was more than she could afford, but Rose wanted to keep it so there'd be something familiar. The house was in a nice neighbourhood with a nice school, and all the people in the school were super nice people. The nice mothers drove Jeep Wranglers and wore Lululemon leggings, and stood about in small companionable pods after the school bell rang, clutching designer coffee cans while making the morning's Starbucks plans.

Rose couldn't imagine having Starbucks plans, much less Lululemon leggings. Even if she could afford them, which she couldn't, she wouldn't have a clue where to buy them. Thanks to these challenges, Rose believed, she was not much of a follower of fashion.

Also (the husband got the good car), she drove a beater — was that why she seemed invisible to the Lululemon mothers? No husband, nondescript jeans, and a shit car?

She had no leisure to need Lycra for.

All before eight-thirty in the morning, she had to shower and feed the cat and find something to wear, and make the lunches and fix the breakfasts, and shovel if it was winter, and pull the weeds if it was summer, and haul a resistant Bean out of bed whatever the weather, and wash and dry the gym gear she should have washed and dried the night before, and try to appear cheerful for the Lululemon mothers, while dropping Bean off and reminding her to go with the afterschool caregiver, "and nobody else," until she got there at four. Then she had to find on-street parking (who could afford a parking pass?), try to stop panting, and arrive at her classroom by the time the bell rang, looking like she knew something, like she'd actually prepped — another luxury largely foreign to her.

She hated leaving Bean at the school and walking away, but she did it every day, and every day she underwent the ritual of meaningless, jokey small talk with the coffee-can mothers.

Hey did you see that Kiss is coming to the Saddledome? How about that Flames game! Trial by playground over, she would hurry to work, grab a cardboard coffee at the nearest vending machine, and lean with relief against her office door. But as soon as she got there, her mind bloomed with questions. What was Bean doing now? Where was she? Was she okay?

Was anybody being mean to her?

At school, according to the teacher, Bean connected best with Newton, the classroom's fire-bellied newt, whose preferred lifestyle was lolling under his heat lamp, regarding the world malevolently and stirring only to knock back the occasional fly. Rose figured Bean approved of Newton because, incarceration apart, the creature was free to be his true lizard-self, which Bean could not figure out how to be, in a world of rules and halls. From day one, she had not fit in. Why, she wanted to know, must she sit at a desk when the perfectly good floor was there, put a pretend apple with her name on it in a basket, sing songs about numbers?

Rose's answers did not satisfy her daughter.

On day one, Bean wrapped her tiny plaid jacket around her teddy bear and laid them both on the windowsill, so that she could come back and rescue them later. "Don't worry, sweetie. We're going to get out of here." She did not want to paint or play hopscotch, or sing alphabet songs, and she had no use for numbers, a position — or a plight, to judge by her cheque book — Rose secretly shared.

Though she had to steel herself for report-card day. The comments never seemed to vary.

While Bean is a unique student with many potential gifts, a habit of distraction compromises her participation in class.

What was a habit of distraction, Rose longed to ask the teacher, something disruptive nuns wore? Who could be accused of such habits in Grade 4?

116

Bean is a bright and curious student. She appears to enjoy learning, but has trouble completing tasks. More concentration on finishing assigned projects would result in better grades and higher self-esteem.

Did Bean's forgetfulness about lids and deadlines — "Mom, how can lines be dead?" — conceal some significant lack of self-esteem? And what even *was* self-esteem, for that matter, Rose wondered. Whatever contented and incurious state it was, it had always eluded her.

Bean seems preoccupied in class, and has a tendency to daydream. Because of this she often misses important information.

A habit of daydreaming. What a terrible thing. How many unnecessary meetings, and uninspired conference sessions, and deadly, time-wasting hallway conversations had Rose spared herself the brunt of, owing to the same wayward tendency?

Bean seems to prefer solitary activities to interactions with other students. Reading is her go-to activity. Books about animals and war, or anything historical are preferred.

Reading about war — a delight, or a disaster? As sure as Rose thought she knew, she'd be wrong.

Two other comments also seemed unvarying, and Rose always saved these for last. She allowed herself another cup of coffee if it was morning, or glass of wine at night, just to savour them.

Bean clearly enjoys anything to do with art making. Her use of classroom materials is imaginative and unusual, even, one might say, defamiliarized. Suggest encouraging this interest, perhaps with an after-school program for gifted students. Additionally, Bean is reading well above grade level, and shows interest in a wide variety of topics.

Though tales about industrious beaver families and dragon-slaying princesses in sparkles and tulle, and talking pigs and pie-eating contests were not on Bean's preferred reading list. The ancient Mayans and their ingenious burial rituals, the punishing quarrying and creation of the pyramids, the lives of the viruses, the bog people's unholy preservations and undead vigour, absorbed and beguiled her.

The illustrated life of Joan of Arc ignited her.

Joan of Arc said *No.* She did not care about centres or pretty families, and she did not fit in. She had a mission. When all the other young village girls were busy brewing and baking and deferring and waiting, Ms. Arc was up and out early in the morning, surveying the horizon, and conferring with the saints who were wont to hang out in her father's garden.

Luminous and beautiful beyond bearing, these shimmering beings, Michael and Margaret and Catherine, told Joan to blow that popsicle stand. They advised her to lose the humbling hood and the confining kirtle; they wanted her to put on pants and take charge of the army, to muster the artillery; to lead the country to victory.

The saints told Joan to man up, and start herself a revolution. Wondrously unbehaving, they urged her to resist.

The saints left out the part about getting burned at the stake, which Bean learned about when she got to the end of the book. But she didn't mind. "Mom," she said, radiant, laying the book down, "can I be in a revolution?"

Rose smiled tiredly. "Honey, you are a revolution."

Revolution or no, Bean couldn't be happy until she had a jerkin and matching leggings, a crocheted snood for her head, a bow-and-arrow-to-go. She couldn't rest until she'd chopped off all her hair. One morning in the kitchen Rose held her breath and dutifully removed the silky auburn tresses, and then had to try to figure out how to improvise the martial gear, and finally to justify Bean turning up at school looking like a cross between a ragamuffin and a junior warrior. As a teacher herself, she managed somehow to tie her child's unlikely presentation into a passion for self-expression. When the real teachers showed concern, Rose claimed that Bean's new being was educational.

Bean and Rose had a little end-of-the-day ritual, back then. Rose would finish teaching her afternoon classes, pack up her stuff like the last life raft was about to hit water without her, and sprint with minimal dignity to the chain-link playground where Bean would be playing on the slides and the swing tires with the afterschool kids and Liz, the neighbourhood caregiver, whose hands were kind, and whose peanut--butter sandwiches were to die for.

Panic, unnecessary, mortifying, barely managed, daily accompanied Rose as she hurried along the outside of the enclosure, the desperate fear of not being able to see Bean yet, she was so small, Rose chanting: *yellow sweater, blue shoes, pumpkin orange overalls. Yellow sweater, blue shoes, pumpkin orange overalls*, as though her incantation could cause Bean to be there, as though the words could save her.

Then the small storm of yellow and orange and blue, the flash of auburn hair, hands like pale stars, hurtling toward her.

In Rose's chest, the everyday storm of relieved joy.

"Fence kiss!" Rose would cry, her heart rising, eyes filling, and Bean would pucker up as she ran, and Rose would get her lips ready too, and they'd both run like shaggy monsters until they found a kiss-sized opening in the links of the fence, to smooch through. *Mwah!*

Mwah to you, too!

And then the slow redemption of going home.

And day after day, they did this, for such a long, brief time.

Oh, Mom, chuckles Bean, *you're such a sentimental old thing.*

Rose rubs her eyes, yawns, stretches, wakening from a stolen afterwork nap at the bottom of Bean's 'bonk' bed, which she knows she should replace with office furniture. It's dark, or almost, and Bean reclines against one of the big pillows at the other end, her hands crossed in that perfectly marble way, her auburn hair still shining softly in what is left of the day.

"I am not sentimental, and I'm not a thing. What do you mean?"

All that old fence-kiss stuff. Maybe it's time you let that go. I'm all right, you know.

Rose wants to shout, Prove it. Show up or shut up. She wants to fall upon the thing she thinks is Bean, weep, shake her, beg her to come back. But she knows that if she shakes the thing that seems to be Bean, there will be only a pillow in her arms, a house without any lights on.

Of course Rose knows why she dreamed of her. This afternoon, after getting home from work, she realized she'd forgotten the thumb drive that contained all her marking. What could she do, but go back? She decided to walk, it was a mild afternoon and it was four-thirty, exactly the hour when the kids from Bean's old school were heading home in their green-plaid jackets and gray pleated skirts, their backpacks heavy on their shoulders just the way it used to be with Bean, their faces open with plans of parties and study and walkathons and graduation, knees and noses rosy from the startling June sun. Rose wasn't wearing her glasses, so they all looked more or less the same. Which meant that every one of them had been Bean.

That old thing, again.

Rose hauls her bones up and out of the bedroom door, not looking back — above all, one must never look back — and gets out the kibble for Jeoffry.

"I'm telling you," Rose tells Mab later that night on the phone, "parenting's not for the fainthearted. You know?"

Mab, adeptly turning a pained catch of breath into a laugh, allows that she is sure that must be true.

Mab

Another thing she never meant to do was get pregnant. That's what she did though, back then, back in Kingston. For all she knew, it might even have been that very first time with the heart doctor — such things had been known to happen — the night they listened to the Allegri Miserere, with its ecstatic chant and exquisite intervals. "It wouldn't happen to a dog, but it would happen to me," she'd laughed to Rose when she finally owned up. Though there were quite a few reckless evenings after that first one, and something that Mab, in her elegantly roundabout way, referred to as 'considerable mischief.'

Considerable mischief, as well, in Mab's apartment, and lots on the doctor's boat. Not a few late nights, and plenty of superior rum to go with them.

Plenty of hurrying back to Toronto, too, by the doctor, for his emergencies. Mab soon had to understand that important men like Heath were called upon and interfered with all the time, even on their boats and sabbaticals.

Even in their exquisite intervals.

Once, frustrated and gratified by such an interference, Heath had hissed as though to the great unwashed, "*This* is the life of a surgeon!"

Now they had less occasion for rum, the pair of them. And more for the Miserere. "Though if it was mercy we were after, you'd think we might've been a bit more proactive!" Mab carped on the phone. "Or would that be less? Maybe we were *too* proactive." She sighed. "Or maybe make that, too active?"

It was June when they found out the results of their boozy frolicking. Everybody else was strolling past the shops, picking up flimsy bargains at the sidewalk kiosks, raising rosy glasses under café awnings, soaking up the tender ephemera of the Kingston summer. Everybody else's life was still their life.

Mab soon got to see what some of the emergencies were about. Or, she joked, "what was rocking the boat." It turned out Heath was married.

"Can you believe it? Here he was, pretending he was the sexy single doctor dude on his yacht in the sunset, with his cravats and all the rest of it — and all along the guy had a bunch of kids and a brace of beagles. Back in Toronto. Those emergencies he was scramming back there for? That was his wife! She needed help getting the kids off to summer camp. Plus the beagles needed their teeth done, and there was the Mastercard bill, and what have you. "

"Oh, Mab," sighed Rose.

Mab meant to have the baby. Heath meant not to stop her, he could manage that much. "I guess he was honouring that oath they have, of doing no harm. Plus, there was God to deal with. The last thing he wanted on his conscience was an abortion, even if it was just mine."

Though now they had to figure out what to do about the surprising results of their equally surprising summer fling.

"This was back in the eighties, when it wasn't as cool as it is now, to be a woman raising a kid alone."

It seemed best for Mab to move to Toronto, where Heath could at least be occasionally useful, and for her to have the baby there. Mab had connections at the Bloor and St. Clair branches of the Toronto Public Library. She'd been half-thinking of a move to Toronto even before she met Heath. "Figured I'd submit a resume before the ship went down, in case I could land a job for later, when I resurfaced."

Meanwhile, Heath set about finding decent single mother digs on Queen. Mab found her apartment a good tenant, bid adieu to Kingston, "and I took a good hard look at the Great bloody Unknown."

Before that, though — "I was still an occasional jogger back then, and Heath was too full of himself not to join in" — the two of them decided one day to go for a sunset run.

They agreed to run from Mab's apartment — it was still going to be her apartment until the first of September — down to the

Confederation Basin Marina, where Heath, with the shock of extramarital fatherhood looming, had recently moved his yacht, marina fees being cheaper there. Their plan was to spend the night on the boat, talking about why Heath hadn't told Mab he was still married, and what the fuck, besides Mab relocating to Toronto, they were going to do now.

But a storm blew in while they were getting ready to run, and torqued-up funnels of gritty dust scattered the tourists and made the trees lean, and the clouds turned a sullen, inhospitable purple-green. It was the kind of bustling bad-tempered midsummer weather that Mab especially enjoyed, or had enjoyed, until the storm moved from outside, to inside her. Now suddenly, she felt vulnerable, small, weirdly assailable, even by her old friend, the wind.

Unconcerned anymore about appearance, she dug down in her running basket and found a nylon jacket and a pair of pale blue sweats, and hauled them on.

It was getting dark when they started, or maybe it was the storm that had made the dark. Car lights raked cruelly across them, lighting big cold no-nonsense raindrops; above them the trees thrashed and roared. Wet yellow leaves, the first too-soon sign of fall, slapped the pavement, stuck to their faces.

There was a smell. Mab noticed the smell before she found the wetness, hot and acrid, seeping between her legs.

Sucked pennies. Band-Aids. Expensive Scotch.

Iron.

She looked down. The pale-blue sweats were definitely done.

"The things we do," she jokes with Rose on the phone, even now not exactly telling what happened, "when we're young."

Rose said, "Don't leave me hanging here. Tell me what happened. Back then."

"Well, what you'd expect, I guess. Heath was busy showing off what a fine runner he was, even though he hardly ever did it anymore and was so much older, and suddenly I felt something going on between my legs."

"Oh my God. What did you do?"

"I kept going, what else was I going to do?"

And she kept thinking, *Baby, be there.*

Until that moment, she hadn't had a clue she'd wanted a son, a daughter.

All the way to the less-expensive marina, through the watery car lights and the driving leaves, she'd kept thinking, "Baby, be there."

Her lower back was aching by the time they got to the marina, which at that hour on a weekday was deserted. She went straight for the can, slammed into a cubicle, all soaked sweatpants and rust smell, shoved down her soiled clothes, and sat shivering until something plopped out into the toilet.

She opened her stained legs, then closed them fast, not wanting to see . . . an unformed forehead, an inky eye . . .

. . . so she flushed the toilet. And as best she could, rinsed out her sweats, and joined Heath back on deck.

"Believe me, I wasn't a pretty sight!"

"Oh, Mab, why didn't you —"

One thing she knew, "and that was that I was done with Heath — and his 'meth.'"

"His what?" Rose asked.

"His 'meth.' As in: mess. Haha."

"Mab, do you ever stop with the jokes?" Rose sighed.

A week or two later, she gave Heath the old heave-ho — or, as she joked to Rose, the old 'Heath-ho,' and headed out on her own, for Toronto. "That was the end of running, for me. But . . . life's a marathon, wouldn't you say? If you want to survive, you gotta put in the training."

Morrison

Santa Barbara was breathing down his neck. He was up on Nose Hill Park, doing sprints. Jesus Murphy, he better be. The race was coming closer, and he'd heard horror stories about that Corkscrew Hill on the course, six miles straight up before the drop into Ballard Canyon, a descent that'd be hell on heart and soul, not to mention the bunions. Of which he had his share. And there'd be Abbey to keep up with, beautiful damn long-legged Abbey, who, like your big — or small — sister, could never be kept up with.

Just like none of them ever could be kept up with, or figured out, or met. Women. He thought of Rose, so anxious and smart and vulnerable and inept. Her terrible cupboards and her rat's-ass lawn and those damn, stupid chives she wouldn't let him get rid of for her, didn't she care that chives will take over? And the closed-up bedroom door of that daughter, the lack of mementos, the pictures of earlier, hidden behind safer pictures.

The unfathomable gap she didn't know he saw, in the shape of a daughter. Sweet, desolate, wry Rose, with her sorriness for being mean and her touching attempts at redemption. She'd be here to pick him up in two hours.

It was barely nine o'clock. Already, hot light hovered above the clumps of sketchy trees, drawing out the scent of clover and wild roses, glancing off poplar leaves. People walking dogs were dots on the distant white ribbons of path, beyond which he could see the shimmer of the city, and after that, the foothills, fading into the pale blue swim of mountainous horizon.

It was going to be a wicked one.

His phone buzzed a reminder of Abbey's training instructions for the day, a 1.5-mile tempo run followed by a seven-minute recovery walk, before a whore of a long hill at his 10K pace, and a short one at a 5K trot. Then, if he was still breathing, a double repeat of the hill sequence, gearing down to an easy jog back to his starting place near that cute little clump of sage that the sun was already making fragrant, at his feet. Two hours, give or take. Two hours to solve the world's problems, or at least have a crack at his own. He loved that about running, the way your mind relaxed as the world flowed by, and stuff you couldn't figure out gradually began to look less gnarly. The way your head started to feel like one of those snow globes the kids used to get for Christmas, the impacted thoughts and preoccupations gradually stirred and then atomized, rising like lazy confetti, to fall in new and surprising patterns.

He took a good deep breath of the clover air. Maybe someday one of those new patterns would be 'the one.' The answer he was searching for. The answer to her. And to her, and her, to all those 'hers' he'd loved and found so mysterious and dear, so damnably not there. Didn't he always say, There's no problem a run can't solve?

One day, maybe, one of them would stay.

A quick yank on his water belt, a last look at his laces, one more slap of sunscreen.

Now or never.

Sun's brighting me.

A voice. Whose? Jesus Johnny, who else in this world knew those words? Slowly, very slowly, he adjusted his sunglasses and looked around, every sense on hunting dog high alert. Nothing there but grasshoppers in gravel, a light breeze whispering in vetch and timothy, the occasional nectar-drunk bumblebee.

But he knew that voice. It was hers. *She* would have said, *Brighting me,* he knew in his every bone she would've.

Was he nuts? How nuts would it be to answer?

He should put one foot in front of another. Sanity lay in putting one foot in front of the other.

A lifetime ago, on a high-school track on the other side of the country, he'd learned that the hard clean solitude of running could temporarily save you from the terror of *the room.* That you could send endorphins and blood and oxygen after it, build muscle and strengthen tendons and develop endurance against the red chamber.

That, even if you could never outrun the damn thing, you could at least fortify yourself, mount some semi-reliable defense against it.

Running was everything.

So he'd run for the track team, he'd run with friends, more and more as life went on, he'd run on his own. After a while the endorphins and endurance had become their own reward. Running cost nothing and could be had every day with minimal bother, didn't matter where you were, or the time, or the weather. No matter what, you could hit the path along a river or grab a piece of track, or roll off the red-eye at six o'clock in the morning, and you could run.

Brighting me, eh. The sun was bright; so what? It was nothing. Just his mind. Phew. He checked his watch, took a swig of his water, and put the good old engine in gear the way he always had, the earth of the path responding with its familiar sweet resistance. Giddy up. He began to relax into the long rhythm of his breath, the grab of his hamstrings, the easy swing of his arms.

He'd lost her in the first trimester, his outrageous life expanding cell by cruel cell while hers paused, then became smaller and quieter and flatter, stiffening eventually into a cyst that turned into fodder for his own appalling increase, his eager organs, the brazen demand of his bones, his brain using hers to build itself, even as his own gain deprived his heart and soul of her.

And his terrible secret: he took it all, he stole the works. How can you live with a secret like that? He, Morrison, had hogged the room before time, sucked up its nutrients, inhaled its oxygen, entirely at her expense. Not satisfied with that, he'd devoured his own sister and made himself empty forever.

Was some residual energy of her still here? Could a thing like that be? They said that, didn't they? That you can't destroy energy.

The breeze sent a faint sibilance through the poplars beside the path. *Danica*. A name like the murmur of the wind in those trees.

The path began its drop into the coulee he always got tripped up in — for its Biblical terrors he called it 'Holy Coulee' — all thorns and muck and loose stones and barked shins, with a cedar-snarl like the home of the undead at the bottom. The sky went cold above it as he descended, just the way it always did. A red winged blackbird swung on a reed high above, and cried.

Morrison had cried. In utero and out of it, he'd cried.

After birth he'd wailed for so many days they'd thought he was trying to cry himself back into nonbeing, but it turned out, on the contrary, that he was just too greedy for that decent fate. Somewhere in the storm of his newborn tears he'd caught his breath, sucked the life of his bereaved mother, and lived.

But he'd lived to grieve. From infancy right through to his Grade 4 report card, he'd been inconsolable.

And then, late one winter afternoon, he'd walked into his room and found her sitting on the end of his bed just as if she'd always been there, or as she would have been if she'd reached two, her smocked dress, her bright baby pigtails, her matching bows.

He'd called his mother to come see, but only he could see Danica in the slanting winter sun that was 'brighting.' And when he'd tried to touch her, to comfort her, there'd been nothing there but: *No*.

Rose

A gang of geese arrowed its way through the midsummer air. Didn't they know it was too early to head south? Maybe they were lost, had lost some fledgling member. Far below in the usual afterwork hurry, Rose hoofed it to her neighbourhood drugstore. She needed face wipes, batteries, cat food, onion powder. She needed nylons and dish detergent and bread, and nail polish remover. It was astonishing these days, what you could find in a drugstore.

A small wave of guilt, for once not mother guilt, passed through her. She knew she should be driving up to the Safeway, but figured what she lost in discounts, she'd gain in time. There were three sets of tests to mark, and she needed to get at it. House rule number one: No wine until the marking was done.

She passed a neighbourhood church. Lights were on in its concrete basement rooms, and people were singing, potlucking, AA-ing, such reasonable, good, and trusting things. Things Rose had somehow never got the hang of, and worse: never much respected.

Why? For most of her life until now, she'd imagined she'd known. Now she wondered if there was something she'd missed, some key ingredient about being human in all this after-supper congratulation and community serenity, that she'd failed to take in.

Her head was down, fists in her pockets, thoughts, as usual, a thousand miles away, a film of sweat gathering under her eyes.

Something pale sat on the sidewalk ahead, unmoving. A glove? Wrong season. A strayed baby rabbit? She had seen them around here before, even rescued them once or twice, from dive-bombing magpies.

But it was neither. She bent and retrieved a small ballet shoe, held it in her hand. Six years old, the dancer? Seven, maybe. From the orphaned slipper, her mind fashioned the slender leg, the tights, the satin ribbons, the living bones.

Would anyone have missed it yet? Would the small dancer, home now in front of the cartoons and waiting for her noodles and cheese, be holding up a shoeless foot? Would her mother, exasperated and tired and hurrying to prepare dinner, be wondering how she was going to pay for another pair?

Would the mother be scolding her?

Rose should return the slipper. She knew she should. She should do like other people did with errant hats and dropped mitts, and place the orphaned slipper on a branch, deposit it on a window ledge. She should take it into the church, and hand it to some genial facilitator or rosy potluck lady. "I was just walking by . . ."

She might do that. She might, one day. Soon. But she was due to pick Morrison up in two hours, she had to keep moving.

Tenderly, she lifted the slipper from the sidewalk, and tucked it away.

Was it because she'd never got the hang of things like potlucks and AA?

Was that why?

Abbey

Parker called up and said, "Hey Ab, headin up to Mud Lake to swim and spend the night at a friend of mine's cottage. Last weekend before they close it for the winter. You don't have any Thanksgiving plans, I know you don't, 'cause you told me. Wanna come? We could pick up a turkey and some of that cranberry shit and look like we meant it."

Abbey was just home from buying an antique mirror she couldn't afford, at the farmer's market. She'd bought yellow peppers and artisan bread, too. Organic, seven grain, handmade. She didn't feel like spending the night in some lean-to full of spiders in the middle of nowhere.

"I don't know how to swim."

"Dude, how can you be from Newfoundland and not know how to swim?"

"Nobody from Newfoundland knows how to swim. It's a thing."

"You'll be fine. Tadpole'll watch out for you."

Abbey's heart beat a little faster. "You never said you had Iris this weekend."

"Last minute change of plans, happens all the time. The ex ain't real good with tools." He chuckled. "Ali, yeah, she cracked her knee with a hammer trying to open a jar this morning, and had to go to Emerg. The little ones are at their grandmother's, and Dave, he's a pretty good guy, the kids like him, he drove Iris here. Bonus: he'll pick her up on the other end, and we can have a couple days up there just the two of us, after she's gone." He paused. "To be honest, Tadpole ain't in the best mood today. Might cheer her up if you came."

"Don't give me your ballyrag. What should I bring?"

"Just your bathing suit and your book, I've got the rest. You're gonna like it up there."

"I don't know anything about 'up there'; why will I like it?"

"It's pretty cool. Maybe like the Rock. People even think it's some kind of spiritual place. There apparently used to be a native burial site around there somewhere a long time ago, but nobody I know's ever found it. It's got an *energy*, though," he said spookily, "People I know've felt it. You got a bathing suit, right?"

"Why, sure. And a book. I've actually got two of them." Maybe she could sit beside Iris and read again. Maybe there'd be a hammock. A fireplace. Maybe they could roast marshmallows, tell ghost stories, make S'mores. She'd stop at the corner store on the way to Parker's, and pick up a bag, along with Graham Wafers and some trail mix or granola bars. She didn't like being hungry in the middle of the night at other people's places.

But where was her idiot bathing suit?

The last time she'd seen the article, it'd been in the back porch, down behind the drier; having no immediate use for it, she'd left it there. Now she peered down the snarl of lint and single socks and lost Bounce sheets, and there it still was, big as life and twice as ugly, as Mum used to say when somebody she didn't like was comin down the road. Would it fit? Too late to find another one. She grabbed the suit and shook the dust bunnies off it, then went upstairs, found an overnight bag, and threw in the suit and the peppers and a bottle of wine and the homemade bread, a book, and a wedge of maple fudge she'd been saving for a midnight snack.

Maybe Iris would like the fudge.

Iris was curled up on the couch reading Asterix comics and eating Xtra Cheddar Goldfish out of the bag when Abbey and her overnight bag clattered through Parker's aluminum front door. The kid's skinny brown bug-bitten arms and legs were sprouting from a green pop-top and matching shorts, her heavy hair dumped over her back. A pink plastic sandal dangled from one big toe.

"How's ya gettin on, me cocky?" said Abbey, being a Newf for Iris's pleasure. What else did she have to offer?

Iris looked up at her like a drowsy guard dog considering the potential danger of a dubious passerby, then returned, unamused, to her comic. "My dad's out back."

Abbey said, "I brought my book."

"Very well." Iris returned to reading hers.

Friggin Parker, thought Abbey, I could be home right now, hanging up my new mirror and making myself a lemonade, and instead off to a shack in the bushes, with Miss Crabbypants and her chucklehead of a dad.

Too late now, to fuck off out of it.

The drive was long. Iris sulked. Abbey regretted. Parker farted. The car was a rattling box of hot, evil-smelling wind.

Jaysus, the pickles she was forever getting herself in.

After two wrong turns on a rutty road they found the place, and it wasn't a shack in the bushes at all, but a gracious cottage, more like a house, appointed with warm hardwood redolent of past fireplace nights and colourful dishes and cozy furniture. Skinny, crammed, old-fashioned, bookshelves lined the walls. Joyce Carey and Eudora Welty and Malcolm Lowry looked out of them. Earnest Hemingway.

Readers, they must be.

All across the big front windows, the lake shimmered serenely.

Parker dropped the cooler, then his trousers, revealing shamelessly Hawaiian swimming trunks. "Last one in's a rotten egg!"

Abbey murmured, "Seems we're already blessed with a winner in that category."

Iris stifled a giggle, then strove to regain her bad temper.

Abbey regarded her with solemn merriment. "Should we find somewhere change, then?"

Iris's small golden face crinkled into disappointment. "Except, I'm *hungry.*"

Thank God she'd brought the cheese and that good bread from the market. Oh, and the fudge! "Tell you what. I'll fix you up a little bite and a glass of milk. Then we'll go join your dad down on the dock. Kay?"

Abbey watched Parker kick off his trunks and drop, brazenly naked, from the end of the dock, then butterfly away, his lake-slicked head rising and vanishing, powerful arms carving the water like burnished blades. She thought of later, in the dark, in the wood-smelling cabin — whose cabin? Who even knew? — with Iris asleep somewhere near, and the gold braid of Parker's arms around her.

What a sucker she was, for 'later.' 'Now' could be farts and peanut butter art and jarsful of toenails, but there was also — she knew in her loins and in her life that there was going to be also: the shuddering, silent striving of later; the lost, sweet, dark of:

later.

A breeze stirred the reeds.

Iris, unperturbed by her father's departure, was up to her ankles in the clear water. Minnows the colour of rain schooled and paused above her feet, arrowing them with fleet shadows. In the distance, Parker churned away. "There he goes," she said stoically, "and he'll be gone for the rest of the day."

It was only two o'clock. What was Abbey supposed to do with Iris until Parker showed up again? "What for? Why?"

"He always has to swim to the other side and back." Iris raised a glob of mud on her big toe, scattering minnows. "It takes forever-ever, and then he falls asleep. He snores, too, after he gets back," she added Mary Lennox-like, "That's something you might want to know."

Parker! Abbey wanted to yell, *ya stupid article!* but he was already a wedge of darkness far out; it was too late.

She studied the receding ripple and shimmer of his wake, looked down at Iris. "Well, then, what do you think us two should get up to?"

Iris bent forward and drew her hand through the water to startle the minnows, which had boldly regrouped above her feet. Her heavy hair slipped over a brown shoulder, and she batted it away as if it were a fly, as she squinted up at Abbey. "We come here like, lots. *I* know where there's noseypokers."

Parker

Out in the middle there was no longer any need for his showy butterfly. He lapsed into a quiet breaststroke, legs barely stirring anymore. The sun warmed his back. Now he wasn't anybody's father or lover or ex or fix, he was simply part of the lake. It was just him and the deep, pollen-dusted green of it, far out, just him and the long cool muscle of the water.

He rolled onto his back, felt the soft topple of his cock under the sun, thought about later, when the tadpole'd be in bed. How he'd come upon Abbey in her boxers and that stupid-cute tank with the lace on it, in the pretty ensuite, brushing her teeth. God, he loved watching her spit, with that frisky little tilt of her hips! He was going to come up behind her, and . . .

He stretched pleasurably. One of these days, he was going to get her pregnant, that's what he was going to do. One of these days he was going to knock that girl up. Even if she didn't rejoice in his peanut-butter creations.

The little head stirred at the big head's thought of knocking Abbey up, and Parker, floating dreamily, let his hand stray down to rouse it.

Abbey and Iris

"There's a path around here I'm looking for," Iris muttered over her shoulder.

Abbey waved away a persistent blackfly. "A noseypoker path?" She remembered how, growing up on the Rock, blackflies had been called 'noseeums.' A deft Indigenous name for something infernal and invisible. She felt a little wave of missing home. Not the Kingston one, the Rock one.

But that wasn't where she was.

"Just a path," Iris muttered. "As you can see, I am not feeling jokey."

"Sorry about that, love." Abbey sighed.

Iris glared.

Fine, thought Abbey, hoofing it behind her along the shore, where, here and there, herons stood like penitents over the water, and cattails leaned against each other, and horse flies zinged with elegant menace through the warm air.

Abbey surveyed the beach, the banks, the buttercupped fields shining above them. If she was going to get a run in — and she should, September and the marathon were around the corner and Morrison was hard at it out there — it would have to be first thing in the morning. By now they were already supposed to be into sprints. Morrison was into sprints. Of course. Every day came the friggin Sprint Report.

But where around here could a person sprint? She needed long and straight, not marsh and muck. In the morning she'd get up before the other two, and head out the road. She would.

"It was here before." Frustration nettled Iris's voice. "It was *right* here, the path. How can a path just disappear?"

How can it not, Abbey thought. A path can disappear easier than you can gain weight after forty. One minute you're fine, and the next — "Don't worry, my trout, we'll find it."

She swiped away a satchel-sized horsefly. What else was Morrison doing out there in Cowboyland, besides sprints and anger management? Was he having a good time with his brainy new woman friend? His texts since the flood had been all business. 'All business' could mean success at last, or bust. Which was it? And why did she care?

She did, though. Much as she meant not to, she did.

Iris stopped to scratch. "What do you mean, 'trout'?"

Abbey didn't know herself what she'd meant. She had to reel her mind back. The path, finding the path. "Now, you don't mean to tell me you haven't heard of a trout!"

Iris whacked a cattail, sending brown fluff flying. "I know it's some kind of a fish." She looked out toward the water, then peered back into the snarl of green. "Sometimes my mom makes it. Well, Dave does. He's the one who cooks. He puts stupid lemons all over it." Iris made a fish mouth.

"Sure, it's a rawny little fish, and it's the devil to catch. But, oh, when you get that b'y on the coals in foil with a bit of garlic and butter . . ." Abbey winked, though she knew Iris with her head down couldn't see, that Iris didn't have any intention of seeing.

Iris trudged on. "The devil can't catch me."

Abbey laughed. "No sir, no siree!" But could the devil catch her? Had he? Sometimes she exaggerated. She knew she did. About things like headaches and cheesecakes and snowstorms and pension contributions.

Floods, too.

It was true her situation hadn't been what a person might call certifiable, as in . . . insurable (supposing a person . . . had insurance). It'd been more — she held an irritating branch away from Iris's shoulder — a case of falling asleep in the bathtub with the tap running, after maybe just a wee bit too much of an edible. Depending where you got them, those things could be wicked unpredictable. When she'd come to, there'd been water from stem to gudgeon, her bathroom about the same as that lake there. She hadn't meant to be a mischief. She'd simply remembered, through the edible fog, how Morrison had always been there. How he'd taken care of her, how he'd forgiven and shored up, and cautioned and spared her. How, without batting an eye, he could sand a floor or change a tire, or dispel a nightmare, shimmy a warped shed door.

What about that, exactly, hadn't she found sexy?

It wasn't so much — her foot sank down into swamp muck and came out black — that she hadn't found Morrison sexy, though, sure, he could've been younger. Who couldn't be younger? It was that she could find pretty much anybody sexy if she looked long enough. It was just a thing with her — she watched as Iris ducked ahead of her — that thing of talking to somebody, maybe at a coffee shop or at a folk concert, even on a street corner, and all of a sudden: that lightbulb moment of really seeing them. Of seeing the glint of light in a person's hair. Or the sudden line of a collarbone. Or the glow of a summer shoulder.

That awful moment of seeing another. That's what Abbey could never stop getting in trouble for.

"This looks familiar," Iris called with the stern interest of a military general, "plus, I smell something. It might be up ahead here."

"Right behind ya!" She might have been awake that night, but she sure wasn't anywhere near sober yet, and her phone was in its customary taking-a-bath spot, the spot where Abbey-on-edibles should never have a phone.

Why was it called a smart phone, when it was so good at helping you be stupid? How could she have been so dumb as to dial him?

Though to be fair, how could she have known he'd up and come, right? If Abbey was bad, Morrison was worse.

Never look a gift horse.

Parker

He floats, half in a dream, his favourite dream. The dream of women. Tall ones, small ones, white ones and brown ones, silly ones, sober ones, slow ones and fast ones, right now: Abbey, Abbey, Abbey ones. The sun warms his face from above; the water cools his buns from below, while his hand, with nothing else, for once, to do, gently strokes himself. Through his half-closed eyes he sees a dark fringe of spruces on the far shore, and he imagines taking Abbey there. A picnic, maybe, sandwiches and strawberries, chocolate and wine loaded into the canoe, the silk of the water, a blanket for later. He imagines eating the sandwiches and drinking the wine, the strap of Abbey's halter slowly — oh, so very slowly — slipping down.

But oh-oh, now they discover a problem. Out on the water in the punishing sun, the chocolate has softened. What to do? With the reliable convenience of dreams, a shady copse comes into view, and Parker deftly turns the canoe. Out of the deep water, up the cool beach and into the trees, where instantly he spies a mossy glade, protected by tall ferns, grasses, a heaven-made bed.

He helps Abbey out of the boat, her long legs brown and shining, finds the basket, opens the wine, tenderly lays the blanket down.

Now he spreads her legs, and she lets him, and the leafy air is cool and warm at the same time on her naked body, and he can see that she is ready. He unwraps the melted chocolate, his fingers becoming slick with in it, and begins to work.

First he whorls and spirals her face, then he streaks the length of her neck and puddles chocolate in the sweet hollow between her collarbones. Her nipples become chocolate-smudged buds before he daubs her ribs, thumbs her navel, marks the dark line she'll wear when her belly one day starts to ripen.

Now he goes for the cunt with the sweet paint, touching it with chocolate until it is covered, and Abbey in her dark finery is spread on the blanket, her costumed sex a primitive God.

And Parker kneels in the dappled light, and worships.

Iris

Abbey wiped the sweat from under her breasts. They felt bloated as a pair of water balloons. Had she gained weight? All she'd intended out of this unplanned caper with Parker was to get laid. And now look at her, lost and sweating in some bunch of bushes, with an orphan of life like herself, looking for noseypokers, whatever the devil those were.

To make matters worse, her fellow orphan was losing her temper, whacking at grass and making worrisome squeaks and barks of frustration. Abbey'd looked after enough little brothers and sisters to know there'd soon be tears.

"We'll find it, trout." She lifted, then let go of, Iris's braid. "It's too hot, is that it? You want — should we maybe quit, Tadpole? Let's go back to the cottage and see what we can find for —"

"Don't call me Tadpole." Iris kicked the cat tails again.

Abbey felt a wave of something. A sick little watery wave. She swallowed, her mouth tasting her mouth. "Okay." (Where was the mother? Where was the father? Where was stupid fucking Parker?) "Promise."

And what had she eaten today, that hadn't agreed with her?

"I hate my mom and I hate yappy, take-your-stuff Odessa, and I hate Hugo and his poopy pants, and I hate *Dave*." She flung the name like a boomerang.

"I thought he was a good cook, and you told me he cares about grammar. Nobody who cares about grammar can be all —"

"He's my mom's *boy*friend, and he's a dumb-bum."

"Right, the one after . . . what was his name?"

"Bob." Iris whacked aside another offending stand of cattails. "Bob the knob, that made Hugo, who I hate also." The cattails swayed drunkenly, then toppled, the sun silvering them as they went down. Fiercely, Iris studied them, her eyebrows gold stitches above her furious eyes. She smiled at the cattails' demise. "It's almost like slow motion." She straightened. "Yeah, well anyway, now we've got Dave. And we've still got Hugo, even though Bob the knob's gone."

"Oh, trout. Do you miss him? Do you miss Bob?"

"No! Bob-the-dumbo-knob. He couldn't even. He didn't even. Bob was *retarded.*"

Abbey wasn't about to take on Iris's choice of adjectives, not out here in the middle of a swamp in the heat, with her own stomach upset. "Okay, so is Dave . . . is he okay?"

"Whaddaya mean 'okay,'" barked Iris, altogether forgetting Mary Lenox's vocabulary. "I just said he puts lemons all over the fish and works out all day, why?"

"I don't know. I just hope he's okay. That it's — okay." Why was she asking this? She shouldn't be asking this. It was none of her business to be asking a thing like this. But there they were, the two of them, a big Ruth and a small one, lost together in the alien corn.

She had to make sure the small Ruth was safe, in all parts of her life.

"Well, he's not." Iris gave another whack with her stick. "It's — not."

Another flutter in the gut. "Can you tell me? You can tell me." Should she be saying that? She couldn't help it. Always, always, Abbey couldn't help it.

Iris turned slowly, her heavy hair falling over one thin shoulder.

"Because all that guy *ever* does is drink his dumb protein shakes and call me *Charlie.* My name doesn't even sound anything *like* Charlie!"

Abbey couldn't help smiling.

But now Iris, too, was smiling strangely, looking down. "Here it is. *Here's* the noseypoker place, ha ha." Something half grizzled, part silver, lay in the stems and water in front of her. Flies buzzed bluely in it. A bone shone. A dog. The remains of a family pet, likely, skedaddled away on a cottage weekend just like this one, and never found. Except by Detective Crabby Pants. Must have a nose for it. In the high trees above the stinking heap, turkey vultures hunched, their ashen wings shining like undertakers' suits in the tired late-afternoon sun. Iris took a careful step forward. "This is how everything on the whole planet ends up, see. Protein powder *Dave* even says so." She looked up slyly. "Even my mom and my dad and Odessa and Hugo and Bob the knob, and even *you* are going to end up this way." She gazed softly at the unsightly display. "Even me."

Abbey looked down at the way all things are going to end up.

And gagged.

Parker

Deliciously spent, he stroked the water's silk, felt the sun's sweet gaze, closed his eyes. Could you sleep on water? And if you did, would you drown or dream?

Asleep or awake, Parker dreamed of being an artist, that was the real him.

Though nobody understood his stuff. Everybody thought it was a joke. How come? What about all those dudes in New York who made crazy shit and sold it for fortunes in the big galleries? What about that Kurt Schwitters guy? What about that Robert Rauschenberg, or however the hell you said it. What about all those Dada dudes with their weird collages, and their bike wheels mounted on ironing boards? Wasn't there even some crazy-ass guy who stuck a urinal on a stump and made money?

Duchamps.

Yeah. So that Duchamps dude made piss art, and Parker made peanut-butter art. So the fuck-all what? Tell him what the difference was between himself and the urinal guy, and the rest of them? All those dudes did was tie boots to goats and fling paint, and — he paused to watch a carp the size of a toaster ghost colourless below him — hey, presto: fame and fortune!

He bet his boots things would be different if he moved to New York. *There* he'd be taken seriously!

A dragonfly glanced off his shoulder, wings thundering, helicopter-body like mica. He took a little swipe, to see if he could touch it. Instead as if to tease him, it momentarily alighted on his hand, then vanished.

Art was like a dragonfly, in a way. No matter how well you could see the thing in your mind, you could never get that *particular* thing, you couldn't get the colour of it, you could never touch, never freakin reach that *exact* colour or shine before it was gone. Same with shape. Take your everyday old fire hydrant. Just a hump with knobs on it, right? Nope. People'd be surprised how hard a hydrant was to get right. Didn't matter how perfect the picture of it was in your head, the minute you picked up your brush to put that puppy on the canvas, all hell broke loose.

Because the trip from the mind's hydrant to the one on the canvas was no joyride. As soon as you looked at it, really looked at it, the fucker started to do shit. A false move here, a wrong line there, and next thing you knew, your hydrant looked like Snoopy.

Sometimes he had to fart, just to cope with the stupidness of it.

A cloud moved over the sun, sending down cool rays of violet and grey. Over his shoulder passed a trace of September, even though fall was still only a rumour.

Through half-meshed lashes, he gazed. The cloud was changing shape, growing an arm here, a leg there, developing a voluptuous swell like a hip there. Like Abbey's hip. Damn, she was a looker! His cock gave a happy little stir at the thought of her, and he stroked it, imagined it inside her later, thrusting, pausing, thrusting again with just the right pressure, his lips on her neck, fingers in her hair.

A second cloud crossed over, sending a less delicious shiver across him, and he eyeballed the sun's angle. How long had he been gone? Shit, fuck, and damn, he needed to get back to Abbey and Iris, and all that woman commotion. The two of them — he knew it — were going to hammer the arse off him for leaving them alone together so long.

How did ol' Dave do it, he wondered. He had four tadpoles, if you counted Iris, plus Ali, and no childcare breaks like Park had; the poor man must be half batshit. He guessed that was where the gym came in. A guy's gotta have an outlet somewhere.

He rolled over and started to butterfly again, arms clawing, butt clenching, his body a shining brown missile, heading woman-ward.

Well, that was one thing he and Dave had in common: too many goddamn beautiful women.

Dave

He slammed himself into the Hammer Strength machine, grabbed the handles and whaled on them. There was nothing for claustrophobia like discipline. Another forty minutes and he might start to feel human.

Note to self: before losing your temper with the kids or God forbid, the dame, hit the gym.

Which was where he was, in the weight room doing reps, that's one, and two, and three, and four, and listening hard to the Bird. Charlie Parker. The man. The one. There was nothing like the snap of the traps and the dizzy fidget of the horns, the player's improvisations, the piano's smoky black subversions. *We wanted music they couldn't play.* Imagine back then, what it must have been like! The dives and the diners and the midnight speakeasies, and the *women* — that's four, that's three, and two, and — fuck, man, what must it have been like to be *part* of that scene!

The tobacco he kept tucked between his bottom lip and his teeth burned satisfyingly. Upper body today. Dumbbell. Bench press. Superset with dips. Reps and more reps and sweat and more sweat, beats clamped down over his hoodie so he could generate more sweat.

What was *wrong* with this picture?

Him. That was what was wrong. Dumb-bum Dave, to quote an overheard Iris. But he didn't blame her. Poor kid, dealing with those noisy little sibs, shuttling back and forth between Ali and the Park and from bed to unmade bed, never knowing who was going to be her next substitute dad.

Why did people even *have* kids?

A riff of horn in the beats on his ears. He *should've* been part of that scene. Or some scene like it. He should've been on second sax, or at least in the back with a topped-up White Russian and a well-read copy of Kerouac, hell, or Hemingway.

Instead, where was he? Teaching compound subjects to accountants — accountants! — at Fleming Fucking College, a slave to a mortgage, and raising some other guy's kids. How the *fuck* did a thing like that happen?

Like, how the *fuck* do you get to be almost fifty, with no kids of your own, a pile of credit card debt, and a tattooed, forty-year-old girlfriend with a *brood*?

Reps, that's how. Reps are what get a man into *stupid* fuckin situations. Nothing like elder-abs to fool a forty-year-old.

Though it's the dude, in the end, that's the fool. Look at *him*, every day of his life. Up at five, walk the dog, book it back in time to make the breakfasts and lunches, hey, honey, don't forget to make the beds before you leave for work, and make sure you find time in the middle of the day, to run home and walk Fido again, and put another load in, and cut the goddamn lawn.

Kind of Blue. 1959. Those seedy, greedy midnight tones that can make a man swoon. The sweet, dark lean of the horn, till you want to 'cease upon the midnight with no pain.'

Imagine if Keats'd been born in New Orleans. Imagine if he'd been born in fuckin *Ontario*!

He got up to move from the hammer to the high row, grabbed the handles, and felt the bite of a worn joint in his elbow. Man, was he achin in the places where he used to play. Still, when he showed up with Ali at the park or the parent-teachers' meeting, the other parents eyed him good. Just the other day, some wife'd whispered to her husband, "Look at his back!" He gave another push. Yeah, that was still worth something.

Pecs against the press pad, deep breath . . . and fuckin give er. Oh, yeah.

He moved his chew, adjusted his beats. He'd always thought he'd have his own kids someday, back when he was riding the California coast, or down in Mexico, drinking tequila on the beach with his partying friends. So many years of parties and friends. But then the tequila got too strong, and the ride got too long, and the next thing he knows, he's got a borrowed family and white chest hair.

He completed his two sets of power cleans and moved on to squats. Was that self-pity? Maybe. A thing to always — he chomped hard against his mouth guard, took a swig of his vitamin drink — avoid.

Yeah, but imagine. Imagine if these kids — Hugo, Odessa, Iris — Christ, imagine if Iris were *his*! And some other guy was raising her. Fuck! He'd fuckin shoot himself, sooner than let some other dude raise his kid. He'd be gone, man. He'd go back to driftin around Playa Zipolite, lookin for ways to get killed.

He snorted in disgust, grunted up his eighty-pounders. If he'd had a kid of his own, he would have called her Ophelia. He'd have had a kid just to name somebody that. But he wasn't going to have a kid of his own. Why? Because there was a life. A *kind* of life you had to live, for your own kid to happen. And he hadn't lived that life, where you get married after college and saddle up in the entry-level job in your dad's company and buy the house with your father-in-law's help, and paint the pickets on the weekends. He couldn't face all that shit back then — the routines and the payments, the parent teacher meetings. And he'd paid hard for letting himself off all that, for not living that.

No Ophelia.

The Bird had a saying. *If you don't live it, it don't come out your horn.*

Rose

Saturday. The one semi-free day, recovery day, mop-up-from-the-week day. Rose was cleaning out the hall closet. She did such jobs sometimes on Saturday mornings to avoid other things, and since she was already being bad on those mornings, she also allowed herself an extra pot of coffee, which she drank very slowly. She had a theory that if you drank coffee slowly, it was less unhealthy.

She had that theory about wine, too.

Of course it was going to catch up to her. Someday, it was all going to catch up to her.

She was sitting on the low blue IKEA toothbrushing stool from when Bean was two. In front of her gaped the largest, lowest shelf, the one they used to call the 'terminal catchall.' What a mess! She found a defunct alarm clock, a pair of startlingly odoriferous jazz shoes from her brief Irish dance phase, a snake for unplugging sinks (very sharp, should not be in there), an augur, a pickle jar, a bunch of toy fishing gear.

Where (and when) had she acquired a samovar?

Jeoffry paraded past and regarded her squatting indignity, then padded away as she lifted out a pair of tiny red corduroy trousers and a matching plaid coat and beret. Two years ago, she'd gone through the house and put all of Bean's clothes and toys and books and journals, from every age and stage, away. Hadn't she? How had the junk closet harboured these small remains? The clothes themselves were the size of toys; maybe that was how. She held the soft plaid jacket in her hands, lifted it to her cheek, remembered the first time she'd seen the tiny getup, at a toddlers' consignment store, and the last time Bean had worn it, in their neighbourhood park, around the corner.

The way she'd sailed down the slide under the fall sky, her cheeks as red as her coat, yelling, "Mama! Mama, look, I'm a flier, I'll fly away!"

At the time, Rose had not realized that this was a promise.

Nobody else had been in the park that day, except a young couple with two preschoolers, shaking their sillies out on the opposite end of the playground. The happy family had been piled into a play-car that had a real steering wheel and tires from a truck, car doors that opened and shut, sturdy boards for a seat. Bean had spied the group from the top of the slide, and the minute her heels hit rubber mulch, she was off across the playground, climbing in with them, claiming the kids as her siblings and the parents as her own, taking over the driving as though she'd just been hired.

Rose had her book. She never went anywhere without a book, not even outdoors, not even in playgrounds. Not even in rain. She waved so Bean would know where she was, pulled her coat tighter, and curled up on the hard park bench to savour a few familiar lines.

That was all it took, back then, to make her happy. You think, back then, that you're overwhelmed: working, managing a house, chasing after a kid, spending time in the cold and wind, in half-deserted playgrounds. You think you're tired, overworked, overweight, that you have no social life, that you never get to be creative.

It never dawns on you, in the midst of all that, that you're happy.

"There'll be no going to the lighthouse today," warned Mr. Ramsay as Rose half-watched and half-read that day in the distant park, and James in Part I despised the red-hot pokers of his father's words like he always had — and longed to make a hole in Mr. Ramsay's breast, as he always would. And the odious Mr. Tansley in Part 2 echoed Mr. Ramsay's terrible words, "No going to the lighthouse, James," and in Part 3 Mrs. Ramsay, as she always did, tried to comfort and assuage: "But it may be fine — I expect it will be fine." The terrible hope of her words. And Rose, despite the cold, had eased down into the vivid and continuous dream, lulled and appalled, as she always was, when "someone had blundered," at the end of Part 1.

Time passed, just as it did in *To The Lighthouse*. The sun slid lower; a small wind worried the grass and blew a wrapper past her feet.

She looked up, and the trees were tossing, and it was getting on for dinner and Part 4, where Mr. Ramsay, bearing down upon Lily Briscoe, that poor little weekend guest who lives somewhere off the Tottenham Court Road, shouting, "Boldly we rode and well," nearly knocks over Lily's easel. And still Bean rode the play-car with the happy mother and the friendly father and the invented sister and the charming brother.

"Time to go," Rose waved, rising up and down lightly on her toes like someone waiting for the bus. "Time for dinner, how about we have chicken nuggets tonight?"

Boldly Bean rode, and well. She was not interested in what time it was, or in chicken nuggets, which she pronounced 'kicken nuckets,' or in going home.

What was she interested in? Rose, her book jammed under her arm, had by now trudged over to the play-car. "Say bye-bye, now, Bean. It's time to go."

"No."

"No?" A wry smile to the other mother. "So is this lady going to be your mommy now? And will he —" Rose extended her cheerful smile to the woman's partner "— be your new daddy?"

A firm turn of the steering-wheel, a flash of auburn hair. *No.*

"But chicken nuggets are your fave!"

"Don't want kicken nuckets."

"Are you sure?"

But Bean was already sailing down imaginary highways with her new, unknown companions, at home in their stranger-car, the last dazzle of cold sun brightening her hair.

Rose smiled again, not so easily as before, and walked backward in the direction of the slide and the swing and the bench she'd started the afternoon on. "Bye, then," she called, "see you another time, see you some other . . ."

A Toys-R-Us playhouse blocked her retreat, and she crouched behind it out of the wind, to see if Bean would reconsider. And Bean did unwillingly come, when it was finally time for her adopted family to go home for their own dinner.

Though not a minute before. Would she have gone with them, if she'd been invited? Would she have toddled happily away, supposing she'd been lured?

A cartoon Rose read in a magazine back then showed a desperately bored kid gazing up at a flying saucer. The caption read, "I will literally pay you to abduct me." Was that what Bean had wanted? Sweet capture by a real family, the kind with actual siblings and a nice, 'together,' mother and father?

Someone had blundered.

She quietly closed the closet door.

Had the blunderer been her?

The Joan of Arc phase lasted so long Rose wondered if she had a reincarnation on her hands. Grade 4 became Grade 6, which soon enough was Grade 9. As the other girls in Bean's classes moved from flowerpot crafts and sleepovers to tie-dying and lip gloss, Bean-Joan kept on being the intractable Maid of Orleans.

"I was in my thirteenth year when I heard a voice from God," she claimed one day when Rose innocently asked what was up, "to help me govern my conduct."

Apparently Bean was not inspired by the idea of gymnastics for improving the conduct of the young, or by Girl Guides, or by simply applying oneself to one's science homework.

The only discipline Bean was interested in was the life and times of Joan of Arc.

First came the costume, then the home reenactment. Rose and Bean had to go to the library, dig up books, study maps, consider logistics. Not just that. Furniture had to be moved, and rooms repurposed. The living room became Orleans, where Joan was born, the kitchen wasn't just the kitchen anymore, now it was Chinon, the seat of some bloody fourteenth century French royal court. "Pardon me if I turn on the dishwasher!" And God help Rose if she turned it on during a military exercise, or failed to comport herself with sufficient dignity between sink and fridge, mid-campaign.

Now, too, most of the time, Bean had to be called Joan, and Rose got in royal trouble one day, for calling her "Bean of Arc."

"That's not even funny, Mom."

They had entered the era where Rose got in trouble for everything.

But there was work to be done. Characters were needed, to play the parts of the pivotal people in the young warrior's life.

Bean sent Rose out to the shed one rainy fall night on the eve of Grade 10, to find the stuffies, banished there since the Grade 2 lice infestation and then forgotten, and never again brought back in. Until now.

"Oh my God," cried Bean, forgetting Joan for the moment, in finding her damp old friends. "Here's Polka-dot Puppy, aw . . . here's Pink Elephant. Here's all my Webkinz — how could I have forgotten my Webkinz?"

Try turning into an ecstatic saint from the Middle Ages, Rose thought as she grunted her way in with yet another box of potential princes, hoplites, knights, and prisoners. Try that on for size.

Now Bean set about deploying the long-discarded stuffies all over the house. Her big blue frog became the dreaded garrison commander Robert de Beaudricourt. Miss Piggy and My Li'l Pony found jobs as soldiers, Jean de Metz and Betrand de Poulengy. The Easter Bunny became the Dauphin Charles VII, who munificently granted Joan's urgent request to be equipped for war, and to be placed at the head of his army. One day, tired of all the military intensity, Rose said, "Girl, your bedroom's out of control — actually, this whole place is pretty much out of control. Time to clean it up and spend some time in the current century. Do you want help with that?"

Bean said, levelly, "I am not a girl." She looked at Rose with those quiet gray eyes, and she said that.

Rose wasn't fazed. At that time — Bean would soon be going into Grade 10 — she could still imagine that life made sense, and that she could have some effect on what went down in her own house, if nowhere else. She smiled. "And what does that mean, that you're not a girl?"

Bean conferred upon Rose a look of calm reproach. "It means that I am God's handmaid. Period."

"Oh, okay," sighed Rose, who had a lot of marking to do, "I guess there's worse things . . ."

"And I must be at the King's side." Bean paused to reposition a green velour bear. "The kingdom will perish if not for me."

"Darlin," countered Rose, silly Rose, still not getting it, "you might be God's handmaid, but your room's a mess, and you need to hop to it."

Bean merely looked up with a mild and distant gaze from the medieval map she was studying. "Although I would rather have remained spinning at my mother's side, yet must I go and do this thing, for my Lord wills that I so do."

Rose poured herself another cup of coffee and added a splash of Bailey's. "Well, it's your mother's will that you get your laundry down to the machine, and as far as I can see, it's your mother, and not the Lord, who's paying the bills." She sipped, leaning wearily against the kitchen counter. "And by the way, have you checked out — you know, with all your research and all — where Joan ended up for doing the Lord's will?"

Rose and her big fat mouth.

Though things weren't always so fraught with smoke and sainthood. There were Joan-of-Arc breaks. For an occasional joke, Rose and Bean still played hide-and-seek. The hiding times would arrive with no warning, usually after dinner or an argument one of them was sorry for, or before homework, somebody calling out the stern verse Rose learned when she was a little girl, that meant the game was starting . . .

Ready or not, you shall be caught . . .

. . . and then the other answering, from where ever she happened to be in the house, *for I am coming!*

You had to really stress the *I am* part of the verse, sometimes even stomping your feet, to let the other person know you meant business, that you really were coming. Then it had to be decided who was going to hide first, and the one who was seeking had to stand in the farthest part of the dining room, in that cold corner where it was always winter, and count all the way up to twenty before starting to search.

Long ago they'd used up all the easy and logical hiding places, the dark wedges behind doors, the teensy-tight corner beside the piano, the hall closet, even the lean of the ironing board. Now that they were getting older — soon Bean would be sixteen! — and too smart for each other, they were becoming cagier in their choices, and more outrageous in their responses, playing with the game.

Unfindable hiding became a thing they took pride in:

Rose, laminated behind the French doors, face pasted sideways in a jester's frozen grin.

Bean, balled under the piano bench, silently giggling.

Rose flattened under her duvet, ingeniously suffocating.

Bean, impaled between the bookshelf and the wall, unrelenting.

Rose, flattened under the toys on the 'bonk' bed, almost indistinguishable.

Bean, pasted behind the curtains in the front hall, delightfully stifled.

Rose not breathing behind the winter coats in the stairwell.

Rose not breathing.

Rose not breathing the day she found black electrician's tape pasted across the sensor for the security system in Bean's medieval room, the window ajar.

Bean nowhere.

Two hours, three hours later: Bean still nowhere. Not under the piano bench. Not under the toys on the bonk bed. Not behind the French doors.

It was hide-and-seek in reverse, and it wasn't a game anymore.

A text, finally, after two terrible days and a first police search: *I'm hitching to the coast with some friends. You don't know them. I'm okay. Don't come looking for me.*

Not God's handmaid any more, apparently.

Weeks, then months of nowhere, occasionally interrupted by a text with a hint of where. Where to wire money, forward transcripts, send the guitar. Bean long gone by the time Rose got there.

Rose going to work and teaching people things, then coming home and feeding Jeoffry the special new food she now indulged him in, herself living on gummy bears (the 'real' fruit juice kind) and wine, sitting up in bed in the wee hours, reading *New Yorkers* backwards, hunched over the pain.

Rose discovering the hard way that it takes forty-seven *New Yorkers* to make a year.

A whole, real year. A year of calling up people around the neighbourhood and making a fool of herself — *just wondering if you've heard from her lately* — making police reports, lurking ineptly on Facebook and Twitter.

Dabbling in prayer.

Until the letter, written and delivered on paper: *I'm living with my new friends, in a kind of community, I guess you'd call it. They're really cool people, who want to make a difference, and who actually believe in something. I've got a job in a bookstore, which you should like, since you're such a big reader, and I've got a different name. I'll tell you that later.*

I never was, and never will be, your 'daughter.'

Rose folded up the letter, and placed her hands across it, in her lap. For a long time, she sat without moving. She sat so long the house became a dark, cool, negative of its daytime self, the counter a blur, the cupboards ethereal above her.

The fridge a wedge of darkness.

And . . . *with the lamps all put out, the moon sunk, and a thin rain drumming on the roof a down-pouring of immense darkness began . . .*

And in that darkness, things could be put away. The black-and-white studio photo of the two of them, Bean standing behind Rose with her hands lovingly arranged by the photographer on Rose's shoulders, was tucked behind a safer picture; the fridge word-magnets, with all their messages and reminders and jokes and doggerel, were swept into a box that used to hold dominos, and the

156

box clicked shut, and put away; Bean's bedroom was tidied up and then closed up, her clothes bagged and stored, the stuffies carted back to the shed, her bathroom returned to hotel-neutrality.

More months went by, and Rose discovered that it was true, about those stages you go through when someone dies: the denial and the bargaining, and so on, though she never seemed to get to acceptance. Even now she'd sometimes hit *Send* too soon, or wing a shoe across a room. And she still had dreams that Bean was the little Bean, just that small apricot-skinned leprechaun in the dark blue jumper Rose found at a kids' secondhand store, and that Bean was falling and calling out to Rose, but that Rose couldn't quite reach her, that just at the moment when their fingers almost met, the leprechaun would smile, "Not yet," and glide away, fade away, calm and ghostly. And she still had times, Rose did, not as often as she used to, of thinking — of being certain — that she saw her daughter walking toward her, under a streetlight, late at night. But then, when she got closer, it'd be just some young person with a similar figure (or possibly similar, for how would Rose know anymore?) from whose hoodie escaped a flash of amber.

On the phone she'd tell Mab that, even though she'd been through all the stages four or five times, she was still vulnerable, when she'd had a bad night or too much wine, to bargaining. Though these days she was running out of energy, even for that.

(Was it because she didn't believe in something? That she didn't believe in something enough? Was that it?)

She still had the little red coat and the matching hat.

Seeing Red

A November afternoon in Grade 9, and she's for a moment alone.

She opens the door after the day's work, drops keys, flicks on lights, sees the winter afternoon leaning on the kitchen window, its old, cold thoughts, its dull motes.

Dinner. That tired everyday gesture of the mother.

Grilled cheese, Mac and cheese, Noodles and cheese. Too much cheese.

She turns on the tinny, ungrammatical clatter of the CBC, pauses at the adolescent warrior's bedroom door, surveys the strewn school paraphernalia, the leggings and the goofy Joan of Arc snood, the unmade bed.

She sees red.

Just a little bit of red, just flecks and streaks here and there, like the ones she's seen before, on a towel, a sleeve, a roll of toilet paper.

The furnace has come on for the season, that must be the matter. She makes a mental note to get a humidifier, against the cutting air.

Rose hugged herself at the end of a cold day, sometime before the Joan of Arc phase. Wind was grabbing at the house and tossing the lawn chairs, rain driving the Idaho Buckeye's long yellow leaves against the window. The furnace had come on, with its familiar clicks and complaints, its burnt dust air.

Rose and Bean were having the usual after-school dinner.

Or rather: Rose was having dinner, hungrily, greedily, in a hurry to move on to the dishes, so she could get a start on her marking. Bean was doing what she did nowadays, when it was dinner. Picking up bits of food, turning them over, putting them back down, quite near where they had been before.

Rose passed the Mac & Cheese.

"I'm not —"

"Wait — what?" Rose mopped her mouth. It was the special Mac & Cheese with the three cheeses and the bacon bits and the green beans and breaded chicken, that Bean particularly liked. That she'd always liked. That anybody in their right effing mind would like. "Bean, what —"

"I'll just have it later. I'm not hungry right now."

"You didn't eat breakfast. I sat here and watched you not eat it. And by the way, I found your lunch. But it wasn't what I put in there. What's —"

"All I did was trade with somebody, we do that all the time. It's a thing."

That was what she always said.

"You gave your lunch away. Or you threw it away. You did, didn't you."

Jeoffry swanned through, black bottlebrush tail held in high reproach above his smug pink bumhole. *Deal, people.*

"Bean, you tell me. What's going on?"

Bean held up a reddened wrist, placing it against her forehead, a swooning Victorian heroine.

"What's that?" Forget the fucking Mac & Cheese. "What's that on your arm?"

"May I please be excused?"

"Bean. Stella."

"Don't. Don't call me that."

"Okay, I won't." Rose put her fork down. "And . . . your arm?"

"I've just got these little . . . bites, or something." Bean turned her face down in that infuriating adolescent way, where the mother's not capable of knowing anything, but she's supposed to know everything, and it's hell to pay if she names what she thinks she knows, ever. "I'm not sure how I got them."

"Okay," said Rose, wanting to believe.

Rose had a bad secret. It was that she hadn't wanted to be pregnant by the time it finally happened, not anymore, her house was too small, and she was too old, and the husband didn't like her; at that time, she didn't even have a job. By the time the unlikely feat was a fait accompli, a bug would have known the marriage was over.

Even Rose knew it was over.

And she wanted it to be over, she was so ready for it to be over. She'd take only what she absolutely needed, hit the road, go back to school, live in an attic, wear red, get laid. She'd take law, art history, martial fucking arts, fuck, she'd take chicken wings, she'd take anything.

She was longing to kick things.

Though now the thing that was kicked was choice. There wasn't enough money, and certainly not enough time, for a proper divorce. It seemed the only viable option was to stay put, and for the two of them to try to make a go of it.

And Rose was bad. She took chances. She ignored the traffic, walking to the store. She signed up for hardcore aerobics, dug out flowerbeds, hauled furniture. If that baby was going to be there, it was going to have to be damn determined to be there.

But then a bunch of chemicals flooded her system, and made love arrive. In Rose's head and belly and bones, even in the world itself, strange, luminous things began to happen. The days became slower, the pale spring leaves opened into summer, her skin glowed. Her hair, which had always before been wispy, grew fuller. She waited for, and gasped at, the first tiny flutter, somewhere deep inside her; every morning she checked her reflection in the mirror, to see if she was any rounder. Before she knew it, she was reading the books, taking the vitamins, and wolfing down fish like a herring choker.

Soon art history, martial arts, wearing red, and getting laid were out the window. Even chicken wings were out the window. Instead, she found herself wandering around in high-end baby stores in the middle of the afternoon, holding teensy, outrageously expensive outfits with archly intelligent-looking bunnies on them, and sniffling at the thought that one day she would be putting such things on a real infant. Her own!

Cautiously, in secret, she began talking to it. *We'll go to the playground. I'll push you on the swing.*

I'll teach you the words for everything.

The third ultrasound appointment was on a Friday morning. It was raining. Beethoven's *Ode to Joy* came on the car radio as Rose drove to the appointment, and it seemed that the triumphant chorus and symphony were soaring just for her, as she drove through the rain, imagining pearly toes, a rosebud mouth, the curves of ears, the silken skin.

Then the ultrasound technician, who looked thirteen, spoiled it all by saying, "I know what you're having."

Rose sat up. "What? I mean, pardon?"

She didn't want to know what she was having. She wanted a daughter, that was all, her goal was a girl. She didn't want to jinx it by knowing. Though somebody else had told her that if the technician says she knows what you're having, it's going to be a boy.

"Don't tell me."

The technician managed not to tell, but the damage was done; Rose put away her dreams of a girl, and set about loving a boy.

Liam, Brian, Finn, Jack. At least there were excellent names for boys. And boys adored their mothers, which was less likely with girls.

Rose decided she could love a boy.

It was August. The world dried and yellowed, the infernal cicadas clicked and sawed, the caragana seeds came singing out of their pods. Sitting, sweating at the kitchen table in the mornings, Rose set her coffee cup on her ballooning belly and watched it jump to the beat of two hearts, while magpies screamed on the rickety deck and the days got hotter, and the due date came and went.

Two weeks past the longed-for day, Rose's doctor laughed, "Looks like this baby doesn't want to come."

Her heart clutched. "And that means . . . ?"

What it meant was that very early a couple of mornings later, an intern young enough to be somebody's kid brother broke her water, and the next day: there was Bean, red and rough with the work of her coming, eyes full of glycerin, tiny fists hurling left hooks at the air.

"It's a girl," somebody in the busy delivery room managed to call out, "you have a beautiful little girl!"

Rose, weeping with exhaustion and relief, while the doctor whaled on her nether parts like a sailmaker: "Can I see her?"

The doctor ignored her. "You've got a great placenta. Look at the veins running through it; looks like a New York steak. Kid's going to be a holy terror."

And the doctor, in his way, was right, considering Bean's later choice to live life as a mail-wearing warrior. Was it because she knew in utero that, for a month or a moment, her mother hadn't wanted her?

Rose couldn't bear to think of that, the blade of that, to an undefended heart.

When the husband left, he took the things people usually take. Benefits, pensions, policies, gloves. He laid claim to the gourmet knives, arguing that he was a better cook than Rose (which was true), and that, after all, he'd brought the knives into the marriage. That was what people learned to say about things like policies and knives and couches, once divorce got underway. As if they'd hauled them down the street and through the front door on their very own shoulders, which subsequently imploded under the load, and must now be duly compensated for.

Washer and drier: $2,500

Water heater: $900 plus tax

Lawn maintenance x 10 yrs.: $2,000

Those knives that had sat beside the toaster forever and cut birthday cakes, Thanksgiving turkeys, Christmas hams: priceless.

After the spouse cut loose with the knives, Rose, the not-so-good-cook, replaced them gradually with stoicism and no-name ones from Safeway. She would pick them up from time to time when she felt the need to buy something besides groceries, some little diversion or comforting kitchen bauble, usually on a Friday night or a family holiday, in the deserted Bake Time aisle.

The Safeway knives came in brittle plastic envelopes like the ones for dried mushrooms and organic thyme, they weighed about as much as organic thyme, and they worked until they didn't, which as far as Rose was concerned, was fine. Their shafts were thin, and their plastic handles sported fraudulently bountiful shades of prickly pear yellow, key lime green, dragon fruit red.

They couldn't hold a candle to the ones that were starting to show up in Bean's bed.

A Tuesday afternoon tilting toward late and Bean not home yet, the house quiet, rooms awash in pale October light.

Rose turned up the furnace, fed Jeoffry, emptied the dishwasher's load. A glance in the fridge revealed last Friday night's Hawaiian pizza leftovers, three half-used bags of wilted kale and cabbage salad makings, a punky English cucumber — why did they always go off like that? And so fast! — a couple of whole wheat bread heels in the bottom of the bag. Rose was not one of those people who could take a look at a bunch of sad-assed fridge items, add a bit of garlic and ginger, et voila. Plus, Tuesday was her six-hour teaching day, and she was Tuesday-beat. When Bean got home they'd order in Chinese and watch the Discovery Channel. It was Bean's favourite, and Rose could stand it.

But right now, for a few minutes, for once, there was nothing to do.

A habit she had was to stand in Bean's room before she got home from school, to inhale its adolescent scent of vanilla lip gloss and dog-eared textbooks, and sleep, and gym socks, to tidy the room, make it warm, her half-irritable bustle an attempted-amulet against harm. As usual, she straightened the bed, lined up the textbooks and tossed the stale grilled cheeses, fluffed up the comforter, and resettled it over Bean's small — so small! — smudge of a sleep hollow.

But what was that under the top sheet? Something sleek and alien and elegant, too elegant for this room, this house, reclined, cool as an eel, under the pillow.

A knife.

Not some half-baked Safeway job, either. Nothing key lime green or dragon fruit red about this baby. This was a serious brand from a real kitchen, its silken burden almost satisfying in her stunned hand.

Blood on it. A thin rust seam, barely discernible, but real. Which suddenly somehow, nothing else in the room was. The books about dinosaurs and bog people, the closet mirror with its familiar cracked corner and decals of Walt Disney princesses, their entire make shift hide-and-seek life together.

Not a molecule of it real.

She had to marvel at her stupidity. All those fears of terror out there in the world, and the svelte killer instead comfortably chilling in her child's bed.

What could it mean?

Nothing much; just murder and mayhem.

She moved to return to the kitchen and staggered, dropping to the small stool by the fridge. Her legs were aching, heart pounding, eyes moving from table to sill, to sink, to phone. Should she call someone? Was this a thing for 911? Should she wait until Bean got home? Cry wolf? Use the slim weapon on herself?

Rose was chicken. She dreaded needles, caved to authority, shrank from the first sign of rain.

Though she was capable of shameful things, if they helped her avoid confrontation.

So she let herself believe that the knife was an aberration, and that because that was all it was, she could put it away. That's what mothers do, isn't it? She reasoned with herself. Put stuff away?

Back she went to Bean's room, picked the thing up with two fingers, carried it to the kitchen, and put it somewhere up high.

Maybe it could just stay there, she cravenly thought, and it did, complete with its edge of dried blood.

But then came another one, and after that a third, each one a little larger and sleeker than the one before, as if the bed itself were deftly birthing them, one killer after another.

Came a day when Rose couldn't stand it anymore. She grabbed Bean by the shoulders and shook her. "Now, tell me. You tell me where those things are coming from, and what they're doing in there!" Though she knew. Somewhere, behind a door she hadn't let herself open yet, she knew.

Back came Bean's usual cool, impenetrable gaze. "They're my blades." Her face arranged in a private half-smile. "They're my friends."

What kind of friends land you in the hospital Emergency until three o'clock in the morning, face blanched, arms scored like flank steak? That was where Bean's slim new pals eventually sent her.

They landed Rose there, too, naturally, her face in the same white state, heart stopped, guts in a knot. Though by now she'd done some reading, called a helpline, scrolled through the horrors on various sites. You were supposed to stay calm. Err on the side of understatement. Maintain your composure.

And that was what Rose did. She sat there all night beside a contritely bandaged Bean, waiting for doctors, and marking papers. That bitter January night she marked an entire class set of first year essays on Hamlet's antic disposition, that doomed caper that let him spy on and survive — for a while — his uncle's evil. *The treacherous weapon is in thy hand, unbated and unvenomed*. Right on, Laertes. *Now* you tell me.

Grimly, she supposed that in certain contexts, marking could be considered an antic disposition, and this was the night, if ever there was one, to don one. Like Hamlet himself, she didn't break. She didn't even crack.

Not so anyone could see.

Though, should she have? Should she have wept, pounded her breast, staged a tantrum, made ultimatums? Would that have been better? Would that have been right? Was that what Bean had wanted, needed from her, that bloody night?

Abbey

Some corker of a night this one was turning out to be, with the sobs echoing down the hall of the cottage, and Parker snoring like a backhoe. Abbey didn't know what to do. One thing she wasn't going to do, she could tell that right now, was sleep. She got up and eased herself into Iris's room, touched the little girl's shoulder. (Because under the boldness and the lion's mane, Iris was so small, when you actually looked at her, all bones and questions under the shimmer of attitude and tanned skin. And the parents all over everywhere, not least in the bed of Abbey herself.) It was midnight, and Parker was as hard and gold as only Parker could be, and he smelled like lake, and this was what Abbey had come here for.

But down the hall, Iris was crying again. It sounded like winter rain, that weary and desolate drop, drop, drop of the end of a cold season, too tired even to demand attention. Abbey rose up on her elbow, listening.

Parker reached for her. "Hey, you."

"Shh . . ."

"Wha — ?"

"She's crying."

"*I* know. So?"

Abbey made her eyes big, though of course Parker couldn't see them, in the dark. "She's upset, Park."

"I'm aware." He tousled her hair. "Come 'ere."

"Shouldn't we, I mean, shouldn't somebody —"

"She'll be fine, the tadpole's always fine."

"She surely doesn't sound fine."

"She does that sometimes, when she has to switch. She doesn't like moving back and forth between houses, that's all; bothers her at night."

Parker reached again. "Mmmmm, you smell good . . ."

"Parker, for Lord's sake, I can't, not with — I'm just going to go see her for a minute. I'll be right back."

166

Parker rolled over, yawned, farted contemplatively.

"Oh, for — Jesus, Parker, on second thoughts, maybe I won't be back."

"Suit yourself." Another, this time much bigger, yawn. "But you know where the good stuff is."

"You've got more nerve than a plough horse, you know that?"

Abbey put on Parker's long Boat-Builders-Make-Better-Lovers T-shirt and padded down the pine-panelled hall.

From behind one of the dark doors came the sound of a child who was working on keeping crying.

"Iris?"

The crying paused.

Abbey took that as permission. She pushed open the door, felt for the bed, found its small prisoner.

"Can I sit down? Can I sit here?"

"I *wish* I could cut off my hair!" Iris found her tears again, and started crying harder. "I wish I could just — burn it up!"

Abbey felt for the edge of the bed, and gingerly lowered herself down. The Iris-shape began to resolve out of the dark, a small girl's lean and lonely back.

"Whyever don't you like your hair? You've got hair like a fairy's child."

"I hate it! It weighs more than Hugo, and it's so hot, and I've had it forever 'cause Mom likes it, and it's ugly, plus there's mosquitoes in here!" she cried, as though Abbey'd put them there.

Abbey listened. But she heard no tell-tale insect whine. "What's the worst thing, the hair or the mosquitoes?"

"The worst thing is *being* here." Iris spit out the last two words like pits. "I *hate* this place."

"Okay."

"And I can't sleep. And it's too hot. And I want my mom. I just want to go *home. Why can't I ever be home?*"

Iris wasn't the only one who wanted to be home. Abbey thought of her calm white bed back in town in the moonlight, the streetlight, its beauty and good order. She'd never had to deal with an upset kid in the middle of the night before, and she knew dick-all what to do. But Iris's lament made her remember something.

"When I was your age I couldn't sleep sometimes."

The Iris-shape held still.

"You remember I grew up in Newfoundland?"

"No."

"I told you. Doesn't matter. It's the Rock I told you about, out in the Maritimes, with the ocean all around."

"With the whales and stuff?"

"Oh, whales by the bucketful. And dolphins, and porpoises, like we talked about. Anyway, out there on the Rock we had this goofy little house in the bushes, up between my gramma's and cousins' places, not far from a pond. We kept a turtle in it, on a chain."

Iris considered. "I wish I had a turtle on a chain."

"Well, it's not right to keep a turtle on a chain, trout. But people didn't know any better back then. Some places they still don't."

"What was his name?"

"Tom. Isn't that a silly name for a turtle?"

"I think it's a nice name." Iris shifted a bit toward Abbey. "When I can't sleep, my mom lifts up my hair. Off my back." Abbey could hear Iris scratching at a bite. "And she blows on my skin."

"Would you like me to do that?"

"I don't care."

Abbey fumbled and found the heavy hair, what else could she do? And lifted it, and saw that Iris was right, the hair did weigh a lot, and it was dense as a Home Depot doormat, and damp with sweat. She leaned in and blew, cautiously at first, then with more gusto.

Iris breathed out in weary relief. "What about the pond."

Abbey canvassed her memory. "Well, there were other things in it, besides the turtle."

"Like what."

"Snapdragons, and water spiders."

"What are snapdragons?"

"You don't know what snapdragons are?"

"Are they scary? Do they bite?"

"Snapdragons are flowers, trout. They're a beautiful orange colour, and they have a . . . almost like a face with a big wide-open mouth, and in the middle there's something that looks like a tongue sticking out."

Abbey could feel the child listening. She took courage. "And their seeds are these long little sock-looking things. And when they're getting ripe, if you squeeze them just a wee little bit, out comes the seed. Pop!" She snapped her fingers.

"What are water spiders, then?"

Abbey smiled, remembering. "Oh, they're the coolest little things. They look a bit like the other kind except more friendly, and they're so light they can flitter across the top of the water, without falling in. Imagine." Abbey ran her fingers lightly across Iris's back, and the child smiled in the dark; Abbey could always tell when someone was smiling in the dark. "Some people call them water skippers. Their little spider feet make round shadows on the top of the water, like when a raindrop lands on it."

Iris yawned. "That's nice. What else."

"Frogs. Do you mind frogs?"

"I never saw one."

"You never saw a frog?"

"Not a real one, just in books."

"You poor darlin, I'd never have made it through childhood without frogs." Abbey laughed. "That's all we had, was frogs. In the morning Mum would say, 'Out you go, and don't you let me set eyes on you till dinner.' We spent all our time down there, messin in the water. That pond was wall-to-wall peepers."

An actual giggle.

"And at night, after the sun went down, they sang like sixty."

"What's sixty?"

"That's just an expression. It means loads. A lot."

"I never knew frogs could sing."

"Oh, it's a lonesome sound. Used to make me sad when I was a kid and it was bedtime, and I heard them down there. I'd always be worrying they were shivering."

"That's so sad. Were they? Shivering?"

"Nah, little beggars are cold-blooded, they don't mind a bit. No place they'd rather be at night, than a nice chilly pond with the moon shinin down to get them going. But when I worried, my mum used to sing a little song, to help me get to sleep. It went, *Peep, peep, the water's deep, my belly's cold, I cannot sleep.*

"That's a nice song." Iris yawned. "When I can't sleep, my mom draws on my back."

"That's a good idea; what does she draw?"

"She draws," Iris yawned again, "about Alexander."

"Who's Alexander?"

"A mouse. He lives in the . . . in the garden, and the garden is my back, and he walks all around on my back, and he has . . . . . . mmmm . . . . ventures."

"Tell me more about Alexander. Tell me one of his adventures."

"When there's more than one tadpole, what's that called?"

But before Abbey could promise to look up the word for 'more than one tadpole,' Iris was quiet, her breath coming in regular small snores. Abbey smiled as she covered the child. She never knew that anyone below forty could snore.

Morrison

God's teeth, it was hot. He booked it up the last small rise of the park, before the washrooms and the parking lot. His singlet and hat and shorts were soaked. His arse, as Abbey would call it, was going to need major Tylenol tonight, that much was clear already, but it'd been a good run, all things considered. He thought again of the voice, or whatever it was, that he'd heard up there. *Sun's brighting me*. Weird, the shit your mind can do when you've had too little water and too much sun. Ghostly interference aside, though, he should be ready for Santa Barbara with a few more runs like this one in the can. He fanned himself with his hat; thank God he was almost to the parking lot. Sweat was burning his eyes, but he could make out Rose in her car, texting like a pro.

Rose and her texting, a trick he was never going to learn. The sight of her after all that lonesome work made him grin.

III

THE EYE OF GONE

Rose

It must be getting close to time for Morrison to come in. Waiting in the Nose Hill parking lot, Rose was watching a YouTube video on her phone. It was one of those goofy, dark-side-of-the-internet things that Mab, who these days wrote for an inflight magazine, was always sending, and that Rose was too self-respecting to watch unless she was stranded, which, until Morrison turned up — she peered into the shimmering distance — she was. Her car's A/C had tanked again. Hot noon light sizzled on her neck, her arm. Greasy sweat swam under her glasses as she squinted at the smudged screen.

The YouTube video — where did Mab get this stuff? — was about synchronicity rituals, and how they had evolved as a way to get people to leave their individuality behind and work together, to make personal sacrifices for the benefit of 'the group.' It showed the finale of the North Korean Mass Games (who even knew there was such a thing?), a stupendous exercise in choral bombast, vast-scale choreography, and small, brightly decorated people leaping with whirling scarves and sashes in front of fin-de-siecle fireworks, all deployed in an arena the size of Saskatoon, while Kim Jong-il serenely flicked through a magazine with one hand, occasionally waving at his subjects with the other.

Rose thumbed up the sound. All those happy, hopping people. All that unison joy, striving away under an alien sky. How did it happen? How did entire acres of people just glaze over and give it up to one small, rumpled man who looked like he'd recently rolled out of bed?

Mab claimed that the North Korean people's frantic joy wasn't so different, really, from what happens when we get together with other people to raise funds, or recite the Apostles' Creed or sing the national anthem at a hockey game. "It gives people a sense of purpose. Of motivation. You know, they feel like they belong to something. People want that. Well, most people."

Apparently Rose wasn't most people. Her motivation, however solipsistic and imperfect, was her own. It belonged to her. Apart from her compulsory participation in the teachers' union, she had never belonged to anything.

She had no intention of reciting the Apostles', or any, creed.

"Research has shown," Mab soldiered on, "that when people perform synchronized activities like singing songs or reciting chants or even walking in step, they feel more connected to the people they're doing it with. They experience more . . . buy-in. It causes people to bond." Rose didn't answer, so Mab double-texted, "I just thought you might be interested."

The North Koreans danced ecstatically on, draining Rose's battery. While she still had a few G's, she finally answered Mab, "It sounds like an interesting piece you're doing."

One day, a week or so before driving up to collect Morrison on Nose Hill, Rose had opened the mailbox and found the usual stuff: bills, fliers, politicians' promo, a real estate agent's appeal to sell her house for her, should she ever be interested. These came fairly regularly, thanks to her location and the size of her property, which was bigger than most inner-city lots, conveniently close to all the things people want, and graciously quiet. Uninterested as usual, she was about to toss the pile when she discovered, caught between the folds of a bargain sheet, a postcard. It had been sent from someplace martially named Fort Nelson, B.C, and showed dark mountain peaks rising out of a remote sunset lake.

An image of heartless beauty.

A message in Bean's handwriting.

Rose gripped the banister, heart pounding, mouth dry, and got herself sitting down on the front step, to read its few terse words.

I'm not where I was before.

Tell me something I don't know.

We've moved into the interior.

We. So she was still with the others. The ones who 'actually believed' in something. Or maybe she wasn't with those ones anymore. Maybe — Rose was starting, too late as usual, to wise up — maybe by now it was a whole new bunch of 'others.' Were they studious types, bookstore types wearing Harry Potter glasses and homespun cable-knit sweaters, the way she'd naively imagined the West Coast ones had done? Not bloody likely. And neither were the first batch, probably. All of them were surely the type that 'move into the interior.' Rose pictured a teetering trailer, rusting car batteries hunkering in wet grass, a pile of kindling covered with a rained-on tarp, mangy dogs yapping on fraying ropes.

We're in community.

Roll call. Five a.m. prayers, evening taps. Confessions, *Community.*

Rose hadn't heard that one since her own misguided youth, when somehow in a moment of first-year university homesickness she'd fallen in with the Evangelicals. A church outreach program, in the student ghetto. A prayer-line. A tearful, jerry-rigged conversion.

The 'fundies in their undies,' as the sane people called them back then. They were in community, too, that lot, babbling in tongues and having penitential potluck suppers, taking things up in prayer, energetically shunning each other. A married pair of them once lured twenty-three-year-old Rose into a dire scenario that had posed as a dinner invitation (she was always hungry back then), but that was actually an introduction to a pyramid scheme. The menu was meatloaf and tinned peas, and the event was hosted by a person who pushed the pyramid scheme while drawing zealous Sharpie diagrams in his crisp white sleeves. He kept asking Rose what her hot button was.

"What's your hot button, Miss? You want a trip? You want a yacht? How 'bout that brand new fridge you've been thinking about."

We have a whole system. It's pretty cool. Everybody works together, and we share absolutely everything. And we haven't sold out. We've got real ideals. We believe it's possible to reach the truth in our bodies, here on earth. We know that we can be whatever we believe we are, whether it's male, female, vegetable, or animal. I've been told I have potential.

Right, Rose thought. First the Chinese food and the flattery. Then the indoctrination and forced worship of the leader, a fat forty-two-year-old with six child wives and a Rasputin beard, followed by — wasn't this how it went in those groups? — gradually intensifying sexual abuse and eventual waterboarding: *you had potential. You blew it.*

But what did Bean mean, about 'reaching the ideal in our bodies?' Was that in some weird way what the knives had been about? And the forsaking of food until she was practically transparent, and that whole absurd Joan-of-Arc nonsense? With which an equally absurd Rose had played along. And what was she going to be now, 'here on earth,' as she called it? An oak tree? A bunny? A very excellent round of havarti? Sweet Jesus.

Though none of these questions was the important one, the real one. The real question was: what was it deep inside herself, that Bean, through all these bizarre manifestations and bewildering rejections, had had to say no to?

I know this must be hard for you, and I know you won't understand. Because you actually never have understood me.

Rose had understood high fives. Hadn't she?

Nobody could fault her for her fence kisses, could they?

She hadn't been unusually terrible at hide-and-seek, as far as she knew.

On the basis of such flimsy evidence as this, she'd had the naiveté — no: the arrogance, the complete and touching foolhardiness — to believe she'd been a good-enough mother.

Though clearly there was something she'd missed, and what she'd missed was the only thing that mattered, and that was Bean. She'd missed Bean. Somehow she'd got through all those slow and fleeting years of school and work and backpacks and report cards and decent dinners and itchy winters, without having a clue who she was living with. To who her own child was.

I am not, and never will be . . .

Her daughter was never. That was it. Her daughter was not.

Mom, can I be in a revolution?

What kid asks such a question? And what, in that question, hadn't Rose heard? What darkness had she harboured, what cruel indifference or denial, covert or casual, had made her deaf, and caused Bean to run?

And . . . she could no longer avoid the question: What kind of mother makes her daughter run?

You can rent my room or use it for storage, or do anything you want. Feel free to get rid of my stuff (and my stuffies, LOL!).

All the best,

Arc.

Arc. That must be the different name the last letter had alluded to. Which actually was an old name. Did Bean think Rose had forgotten? After the house renovations and the wardrobe innovations, and the stuffy-installations for the Maid of Orleans? After Bean had gotten so mad that time when Rose, stupid Rose, called her 'Bean of Arc'? Had she forgotten that? Time passes. Bean must have. Forgotten. Because now Bean was 'Arc.' Nothing else, just that. Rose supposed that was her fault, too, like the economy and the weather, her kid needing to change her name to something celestial and electrical, something blatantly neither-nor.

All the best. A phrase as chaste and hateful as a terminal diagnosis. You've got stage three cancer. Too bad about the Alzheimer's. Best of luck.

Probably Rose had sucked at hide-and-seek.

A cold little wind had come up while she had sat with the postcard, but she didn't get up and go in. Instead she sat dumbly rereading the mercifully ordinary words of the brochure from the real-estate promoter, the one who was always wanting to sell her house for her.

This time she hadn't tossed it.

Rose switched off her nearly depleted phone. So that was what Mab had been getting at, with all the Kim Jong-il, people-belonging-to-something hoo-ha. *Community*. 'Real ideals.' She looked up. A dripping Morrison was leaning in her window.

"I gotta tell," he started to say, then stopped.

"Morrison?" Rose put down her phone. "Are you okay? Morrison, what's wrong?"

Morrison looked at Rose, not seeing her. "Danica."

"Morrison, what, what's —?"

"I felt her. She — she was right here, Rose." His hand batted the air beside his jaw as though what-or-whoever it was, were still there, a tiny breeze, moth's wings.

"What on earth are you talking about?"

"I saw her."

"Morrison, I think you need —"

Morrison leaned into Rose's window, sweat squirming down his singlet and dribbling from wrist to elbow, one stumpy finger raised as if to tell of the Gethsemane terrors of Holy Coulee. "I'm tellin ya, that place down there's enough to give you the —" He slid down the car door. Rose could hear him grunting somewhere down there.

"Morrison!"

A pair of runners about Rose and Morrison's own age were coming in off a training run of their own, and Rose called them over, to where Morrison was now gamely struggling to stand. The man handed his water bottle to the woman. "Sask, take this and pour it over him, while I get him up and in the car." He turned to Rose. "Nothing to worry about, just a little heat exhaustion." He shook her hand. "Actually I think I've seen this guy in a few races. He's tough, he'll make it." He grinned. "I'm John."

The sky was closing in after the hot day. There might be hail; it was only four o'clock, and it was dark as hell. Under the couch, Jeoffry growled; he was nobody's fool. Above him on the couch, Morrison was resting in Rose's living room, his bony shanks planked across the space between couch and coffee table, a freshly filled glass of water and one of wine on either side of him, an ice pack to his head.

He wasn't worried; "It ain't the first time I've been dehydrated."

But Rose was fretting, and she wasn't impressed. She was listening to Emmy Lou Harris's "Prayer in Open D," and making her special pasta with parsley, toasted pine nuts, and pecorino cheese, the one that Bean, the rare time she would eat, used to tolerate, and that Morrison, who never stopped eating, was always asking for.

Morrison called out to the kitchen, "You're lookin pretty cute in those jeans. Man, I'd love to . . ."

"I forget," Rose answered, "do you like pepper? On your —"

"You know there's other ways to get it on. Besides A into B, I mean . . . until after the marathon . . ."

"Rest your ass, Morrison, and shut your face."

She loved the guitar in Harris's Prayer, its midnight chords laid orderly down under the words of brokenness, as though brokenness were as unremarkable and necessary as laundry. *There's a valley of sorrow in my soul.* Whites first, then colours. Then the fucking end of it all.

Where every night I hear the thunder roll.

Big drops of rain had started to fall; while she thought of it, she should get out and take the cushions off the lawn chairs. She was always forgetting to do that.

Morrison hollered, "I love pepper, and I love you!"

Rose muttered, Screw you. She got out the pepper grinder and set the pesto, in its metal bowl, to warm over the pasta, a part of the recipe that always for some reason pleased her. She turned then, and propped herself in the living room door, one ankle crossed over the other. "Morrison, what was that about?"

"What was what about?"

She wiped her hands on her hips. "And don't play dumb. Up there. In the park. You come staggering up to the car window, going on about some 'Danica,' or whoever, and then you drop like a shot gull, and I have to ask random people to help me haul you home, not knowing if you're Jim-dandy or packing an aneurism. I mean" — she licked a drop of lemony olive oil off her thumb; the pasta was going to be reasonable — "is there something I should know?" She poured them both more wine. Morrison might be annoying sometimes, but he always brought good wine.

Morrison turned over his ice pack, and clamped it to the other ear. "It's nothing. It's really . . . Jeez, Rose, how should I know?"

"How should you know? Okay. Let me remind you." She could tell that her voice was getting that edge. That shitty, whiny, so unsexy edge. "One of the last things you said before you hit the ground up there, was something about 'Danica.' That sure doesn't sound like nothing."

Why was she such a negative bitch? Was that why Bean ran? Because she had a bitch for a mother?

"Danica kind of was." Morrison had tossed the ice pack, and was now fiddling with the remote, trying to make the stereo show the time of day and the date.

"Kind of what? Morrison, I've got a clock, I don't need the stereo one. Could you just —"

"She was kind of nothing." He frowned at the TV. "Don't you want to be able to see the time on your stereo? Your stereo can —"

"I don't give a rat's ass what my stereo can do."

Morrison laid the remote on the coffee table. "Okay. She was . . ." He wiped a hand hard across his mouth.

Rose sat down. Heat pricked her cheeks. "Morrison, is this something to do with her? With whatser — Abbey?"

"Rose, for. No. No, Rose!"

"Well, who is she? You tell me. *Who* is this Danica?"

Morrison jumped as though a bird had hit the window. "She died. Danica — died. That's all." Something happened to his face. An ashen sinking. Under the start of his five o'clock shadow, you could discern every one of his ancestors. "Danica was lost."

"Who? *Who* was lost, Morrison? Why have you never said anything about this person?"

"Because it doesn't make sense, that's why. I don't go around telling people. It's hard to tell anybody about her. Because she sort of never was here to begin with."

"You're right, you're not making any. Sense."

Morrison gave a sharp nod. "And anyway, I did tell you. About her. That night in your bed when you were crying about Bean. That night when we had the storm."

Rose felt herself blushing. "Okay, I'm sorry. I remember now, you telling me. But *now* you're telling me you passed out up there because you lost and then saw someone who's not real?"

Morrison chuckled, but it was more like a snarl. "Unlike some."

"What's that supposed to mean?"

"Well, we all know who's got the corner on losing people."

"You are — wow." Trembling, Rose went back to the kitchen, turned off the pasta, and set the pesto on the counter, one of those careful gestures left over from being a mother. Then she started for the door.

"Where you going?"

"Out."

"You're gonna get wet."

"I'm willing to risk it." She snatched her keys off the hall table, grabbed her sunglasses despite the rain, and was gone.

Morrison

Morrison listened to Rose's front door clunk shut, then shudder back open the way it always did, thanks to its eighty summers and winters, the latch and the strike plate long-since frosted and blasted out of true. Rose knew dick about latches and strike plates, much less about true, but she was the only one who knew how to give that extra, exasperated, proprietary little press that coaxed the old mechanisms to catch. And she was clearly too pissed off — and too not there — to care.

He listened harder. Sometimes, even at moments like this, times when they had that extra half-glass and said that one more thing, the thing they shouldn't've said, she wasn't really gone, not really.

But this time she was. This time she really was.

He looked up at the window above him, its panes old and cold, the kind of warped and wavering antique glass people went online nowadays to find, and that they paid through the nose, and upped their energy bills for. He was always trying to get Rose to replace the damn things with those new super-efficient double-thermals — Christ, he'd put em in himself! — because he thought of her. Because Morrison thought of Rose more than he thought of anyone.

And just like 'anyone,' Rose was gone.

Gone had a sound. It was the minute settlings, never usually heard, of a house recently or long abandoned, and it was the wind nosing at eaves troughs, the refrigerator cycling on and off, the forlorn sift and swish of one's own head blood.

Gone sounded bad.

Nose Hill had been harder on him than he'd realized; now, five hours later, he didn't have the energy to move. Instead, he studied the room's books and objects, the unplayed piano, the mullioned ceiling's delicate cobwebs and pockets of lost light. Finally he considered his hands, which lay white and useless, curled around each other in his lap, a pair of dead twins.

The wind, stronger now, sent slants of rain down the windows. Leaves drove themselves against the panes. No lights were on.

This was it then, the eye of Gone.

He pictured himself standing up, hauling on his coat, shoving his feet into his shoes, finding his keys, watched himself getting in his car and driving away. How hard could that be? To get in the goddamn car like a grownup, and drive the fuck away.

Not so hard, maybe, if you felt like a grownup. But Morrison had never felt, could never altogether feel like one. He couldn't get the hang of it. That whole thing of being able to fall asleep at night and hop up refreshed in the morning as though your room weren't a shrinking cell and yourself its leftover criminal, as though you weren't something stopped, trapped, frozen. As though the dark weren't the dark of a dying sun. Such innocence — of sleep, of rest — was too good for the likes of him. A person like him had to watch his back; if he let his guard down, the walls could close in.

So he ran. And ran. Twenty years ago he'd started, huffing around the block dizzy as a whacked cat in the sun, after wife number one scrammed. First one block, then two, then a Running Room training group, and finally, at fifty, the marathon. He would never forget the feeling of crashing through that first finish line alone, hat soaked, back screaming, legs on fire, heart pounding, for her.

Toronto, Halifax, Tokyo, Tofino, he'd run them all, some several times over, always for her, always with her. Nowadays the only place he really felt at home was sitting in his living room with his fellow angry guys, or on a marathon course any time after 32K, that place of brute strength and sheer extremity, of near-ecstasy. Of Danica.

To date, he'd run twenty, and he had the knees to show for it.

Sure, he could run marathons and healing workshops on substance abuse and anger, and how anger affects relationships, and managing anger in creative ways. He could fool women for a while into thinking he wasn't a lost child. He could raise kiwis in a cold climate all day till the end of the world. And he lived in a serious house with a sauna and a security system, its own gym.

But he couldn't escape the room with no security and no end, ever, in sight. Thanks to it, the only thing he knew how to do was wait. All the gardening and the counselling and the running and the spinning, not to mention all those good vintages he and Rose put away — all of it was just a form of waiting.

Waiting was what he did best.

And so he waited, hearing the dead sound of a door pulled tight, seeing the cat hairs on the couch, the crumbs on the carpet, the afternoon dust, calm and terrible, its fibres rocking microscopically on the coffee table.

A person could get lost in dust.

Once, as a kid, he'd been sent out after a big snowstorm, to play. The world white, the leafless trees dark against the winter air. As always in his mind, he'd taken her by the hand. Or had she taken him? Holding hands, they'd found an edge, an end, a sheer drop from backyard to swamp, its peril disguised by leagues of lovely, powdery snow. One of them — which one? — had called to the other, and Morrison had found himself falling through white silence, his lungs gently filling with snow.

A lifetime had unrolled since then. Wives, children, marathons, friends. And yet his lungs, knowing nothing of time, were filling with the same cold and mortal softness, now.

Rose

Rocking forward in her crouch under the shed's overhang, she tried to spare her neck the steady drip of rain, as she watched the dirt turn to rainbowed mud in the lane. Morrison was right, goddamn him and the horse he rode in on. Why could she not kept her cool, at least long enough to find herself a jacket?

Pride.

Worse than pride. Stupidness. Was it John Wayne who was supposed to have said something about stupidness? *Life is hard; harder when you're stupid.*

Well, life was plenty stupid right now. For here was the true and actual state of Rose: she was full of shit. What business did she have, scolding Morrison for his weird grief, when she hadn't dealt with her own?

Though, how did you deal with a grief that had no end, no conclusion? Whoever Morrison's Danica was-or-wasn't, she was dead. Death at least had a shape, a definition. A door closed, and decently locked. Maybe it was cruel, but at least it was clean. The one left behind could eventually stand up again and open another door, start over.

But how did you start over when a person just . . . passed through a wall and faded away? She thought of the postcard, its impeccable refusal. How did you say goodbye when all you could see was trees? *Couldn't say goodbye for the trees*, her soggy head joked bitterly.

The rain had finally ceased. In front of Rose shone a puddle still as a fairy's pool, stirred only by the occasional breath of wind. Watching the wind stitch and release its cloudy surface, she thought of the Bible story about the pool of Bethesda in Jerusalem, where the invalids sat, waiting for healing. How they'd wait, sometimes for days, on the steps that descended into the pool, in the hope that an angel would come and trouble the waters. According to the story, or parable, or whatever it was, the first person to enter the pool after the angel had stirred it would be healed. A miracle. Was that what Rose was doing, crouching here like a fool in soaking clothes? Waiting for a miracle?

A leaf of wild rhubarb stirred beside her, and a tiny orange kitten, this season's, it must be, stepped with wretched delicacy out from under it, shivering and wet. A tiny sound came out of it, a needle-thin cry of supplication.

Rose cupped her hands, and the kitten stepped in.

Morrison

The furnace hadn't come on since before Rose left, and the house was cold. The couches, the table, the walls were old-house cold.

He craved the reassuring clatter and whir of warmed air, but he couldn't make himself get up and go to the thermostat, it was too far. Anything was too far. Morrison was a prisoner, chained to an IKEA coffee table, in a house that wasn't his, in a storm. That was the kind of thing that could happen to people like him, to orphans of the time before. They could be chained, owned, left behind, because they didn't know any better.

Because they were only half there.

A blanket was draped over the couch, that Rose kept there for the rare time she watched TV, and Morrison sheltered under it, not moving, the storm's darkness wedging him, gradually, into a shape, a hump indistinguishable from other shapes, in the fading room.

The light went yellow, then gray, then down. Morrison's eyes drooped, fluttered closed. His breathing slowed.

He is walking somewhere dark, and the path, if there ever was one, has been lost.

This is in the woods, that snowy inferno, lightless and timeless as always, with that airless wind, Morrison holding his sister's hand. The two of them walking farther, then farther in, Danica forever slightly ahead of him, her tiny feet bare, her smile merry and eerie as a Christmas elf, and not there.

Morrison as always, wanting to protect her from the cold, to wrap her and hold her.

And knowing he must not follow her.

Come back, Danica, this way, come this way.

But Danica's in a hurry, she has something to show him.

Okay.

They float together above the snow until they come to the mystery his sister wants to show, and then, as always, just as they get to the moment of revelation, she's gone.

A branch was banging against the window when Morrison woke up, and his chest was exploding. A freight train, the usual one, was bearing down with the knowledge it always delivered: That Danica had never been.

Which meant that his waiting and searching, in dreams and in waking, in running and in spinning, could have no end.

And that sucked major butt. When in his life had he not been waiting on some vanishing female? Since before he was born he'd been hunched over a pain of waiting, for her to come back, for her to forgive, for her to say yes, for her, whichever 'her' she was, to grant release, good riddance, good luck.

Well, fuck that. The car needed attention, he had seedlings to tend to, and a laundry to do. Maybe he should go buy himself those grow lamps he'd been coveting.

Maybe it was time he stopped waiting.

Rose

Screw her pride. Rose was done with sitting in the rain. "Let's go, Scottie's little wet one." She pocketed the kitten and lurched out from under the semi-sheltering shed roof, then scrambled back to the house, dripping, hoping.

That none of the neighbours had seen her sitting out there.

That she could salvage dinner.

That Morrison might still be there.

She dropped her wet stuff in the porch and pushed open the door.

Morrison drawled magnanimously, "Looks like you could use a towel."

Of course he was still there, the blighter. He was even half-assedly texting somebody, one eye on the phone, the other on the towel he had ready for her. She was annoyed at the relief that swept through her. "And I guess you've never — wait, are you leaving?"

"Car's leakin' oil. Gotta take er in." He clicked the phone off. "But she'll keep till tomorrow."

"Since when do you have an oil leak?"

"Since when have you turned into a jerk?"

"Fuck you, and I mean it."

"Okay." Morrison stood and moved toward her. "I will."

"Excuse me? What about the marathon? And —" She let the rest dangle.

"I've done Santa Barbara before. Twice. Decided to just run er any old way this time, and come home. Got friends out there I haven't seen in a while, I can stay with. I already ran it by Abbey. She'll find her own digs. She'll be fine. It'll be fine."

Rose looked up at Morrison. "You don't say."

"I do —" Morrison started tugging off Rose's wet clothes. "— say."

"Morrison, the floor's going to get wet. Look, it's going to —"

"Girl, can you think of a better way for a floor to get wet?"

IV

DEPARTURES

Rose

Spring was unfurling with its end-of-semester chaos, meetings and marking and Morrison bringing porkchops to slow cook and plants to plant. He'd taken his car in, but also himself, scared enough of his episode on the hill, to get a check-up. "Turned out I got high blood pressure; who knew a runner could get that shit?"

But he had the pills for it now, he'd survive.

Meanwhile, Rose had finally taken Mab's advice, and decided to get busy. She'd been sitting on her butt feeling sorry for herself for going on eight hundred days, and now it was time to do smarten up, get out, do stuff with other people, maybe even make some friends. She joined a book group full of people smarter than she was, and tried to fool them into thinking they weren't. She bought tap shoes and took Celtic dancing, and went at it so hard she broke a toe. For a while she sang in a community choir. There were rehearsals and practices and submissions to prepare, there were coffee dates and potlucks and parties at the end of the year. She made up a pretty good short story about porkchops, improved her pitch, got promoted to the first soprano section when somebody had to go have a baby, and lost the ammo-belt of fat around her middle. She decided that maybe, after all, she could let herself have a life.

But one morning she woke up and knew a new thing about grief. What she knew was that you can have gaps — terrorizing, unforgiveable gaps — in your concentration. That you can stop concentrating. On a person. Or say, on the place where that person used to be.

You can catch yourself not wondering. And that's when you have to make a plan.

That very night she spoke with Mab on the phone. She told her "I'm going to go up to that Fort Nelson."

"Oh, Rose, really?"

Rose was in bitch mode. "Your point?"

"Well, it's been, like, a while, right?"

"A year. It's been a year or so."

"It's been over two years, Rose. Don't you —"

"So?"

"I mean —"

"What, Mab. You mean what?"

"Rose, what glass are you on?"

"What cigarette are *you* on?"

"Okay, you got me." To prove it, Mab exhaled noisily.

"I said, what do you mean?"

"I *mean* that at this point, it's mostly just a gesture, isn't it? Rose, isn't it?"

"I know it's mostly 'a gesture,'" Rose snapped, sipped, "and I also know there are gestures you can't not make."

"You and your double negatives." Mab exhaled again. "Though you're right, I know you are."

"I have to go there. Mab, I have to — be there."

"I know, doll. I know you do."

"I have to walk on the streets she walked on."

"Are you —"

"That she could have walked on. I have to see those fucking mountains."

"I wish I —"

"I have to stand on the shore of that goddamn lake. Do you not get that?"

"I get it, Rosie. Of course I get it."

"For a couple of days, a weekend, I have to live. Up there."

"Well. When?"

"I'm thinking Thanksgiving. I don't teach Fridays, and Monday's a holiday. That gives me five days off."

"Really, Rose? At Thanksgiving?"

"Never been a fan."

"But —"

"It's supposed to be beautiful. Lakes, mountains, untouched wilderness, and all the rest of it. I'll take the laptop. Maybe I can even get some work done."

"You better take your long underwear."

"Ever the optimist, you."

"Rose . . . do you want me to — ?"

"No."

On her lunch break the next day, she went to a travel bureau, a thing that would have scandalized Bean, who, medieval rigours aside, had been part of the Expedia generation. A perky girl who was probably about the age Bean would be now, expertly eyeballed a screen, and clicked her up a 'flexible fare' ticket. "So, you can pretty much go any time that suits you."

"Perfect."

"Do you mind small planes?"

"I'll deal."

"Window or aisle?"

"How long is it, the flight?"

"From Vancouver . . . about three and a half hours."

"Window, then. And can you find me a hotel?"

After the travel bureau, she went to the post office, picked up her mail, and dispatched to Annie's Northern Suites in Fort Nelson B.C., a small and heavy, pricey parcel.

"Thirty dollars?" Rose squeaked.

"It's the shape, Ma'am, as much as the weight."

"I bet you tell that to all the girls."

A Second Cup was next door to the post office, and Rose went in, to see if they had their maple lattes in yet, for fall. They didn't. But they had Bean-aged people, a rumpled clump of them, in thrifted clothes and nose rings and rainbowed hair. She stifled the impulse to ask the usual have-you-seen question, and instead ordered a coffee, pulled out the plane ticket and sat staring at it, in its crisp paper folder. Calgary to Vancouver. Vancouver to Fort Nelson.

Central Mountain Air.

Two years plus. Hundreds of days of waiting, of wondering. Of not wanting to leave the house in case. Of memorizing every line and grain of that postcard's elusive and tantalizing message and picture. And now it seemed that it was a real place, existing in the world, and not even all that far from here, as destinations went. And that a person could simply pay money, and get on a plane, and go there. She packed warm clothes and long johns to please Mab, added earplugs and a bottle of hooch for insomnia in a strange bed, found her copy of *To The Lighthouse*.

Locked the door.

Dusk was falling, unrolling its long wing over the slumbering tundra as the little plane bucked and shuddered through the thermals, Rose's reflection pressed like a tired ghost against its plastic window-bubble, seeing the pale spectacle of itself.

Was her daughter down there? Was Bean or Arc, who or whatever Stella was now, somewhere in all that darkening nothing? Trees were. Lakes, blank mirrors of the day's last silver, were. And animals were, in their holes and lairs.

Somehow, it gave her comfort, thinking of all those little bodies snuggled in their burrows, invisible and safe.

The seatbelt sign flashed on, and she cinched herself tighter, as if that would make her safer. Descents were hell on her; she had no faith that a plane — for all its optimistic hardware and confident procedures — wasn't it really just a souped-up tin can? — could actually go up in the sky and take people across great distances, and decently deliver them to their chosen destinations.

And if it did land intact, and by some miracle she walked out alive and into a northern town called Fort Nelson, what would happen?

Suppose the impossible happened, and she actually found Bean. What then?

A long time ago, when Bean was two, Rose and the husband enrolled her in a daycare, just a little morning program in the same church basement that Bean had refused to dance in. The program had been called 'Tiny Tots,' but Rose and the husband, who at that time were still trying to believe they liked each other, had renamed it 'Tiny Twats.'

Rose couldn't remember, anymore, which one of them came up with that.

How it worked was that you could drop your child off after breakfast and go do your errands, then pick her up before lunch, and it cost next to nothing because it was charitable. Agnostic Rose guiltily took advantage of it a couple days a week. They didn't have any money; it was a godsend.

Rose was young then, relatively. She thought pain was your period or a headache. She thought running after a little kid was exhaustion. She didn't know anything about what can happen.

She left Bean at the Tiny Twats on a bright fall day and did her errands, buzzing about in her third-hand car, dropping things off, picking other things up, the autumn wind tossing her long, freshly darkened hair.

At noon she arrived to collect Bean. But instead of finding her playing amiably with the other toddlers, Rose found the child seated like a marble figurine on the lap of a caregiver, her small face frozen. It was like a Pieta, the young woman ample, simple, and enthroned, the infant solemnly ensconced upon her wide knee. It was almost biblical.

Until Bean realized she hadn't been abandoned, after all.

The moment of silence before the squall, so breathtaking even the other tiny twats paused in their games of Lego and ball. The little face reddening, shattering in a primal howl, mouth an inverse Jack-o-lantern smile. Bean in her red jacket and matching overalls so devastated to see Rose, she didn't even think to reach for her.

Did Bean think she was a goner? That she going to have to stay at Tiny Twats forever, that her mother was never coming back?

The seatbelt sign came on, to indicate turbulence. *Never coming back.* What must happen in a child's heart and brain and body, believing a thing like that?

Now Rose, in her own heart and soul, might be going to find out.

The Budget place was closing by the time she found her luggage, but the people were decent about it. They let Rose be the last one in, and she apologized and cracked wise and made fun of herself all through the credit card and the insurance arrangements and the keys, and the forms for the rental car.

Not for the first time, she felt like a nutcase and a bother.

Though by the time it was all done, she looked and behaved like anyone getting off a domestic flight and heading for the interior. Sliding doors whooshed open in front of her as she exited the little airport, letting in air that felt less like Thanksgiving than November.

A bright November morning long ago, Rose found herself remembering as she found and unlocked her car.

The two of them together in the sunny kitchen. Outside: a dazzle of hoarfrost on thin trees. Inside: reheated coffee, a tableful of crayons, Britten's Hymn to Saint Cecilia on the CBC.

I cannot grow;
I have no shadow
To run away from,
I only play.
I only play.

The strange words, nimble and dangerous, enchanting the child, who dances and spins. "Look at me, Mommy!" But Bean can't quite say 'Mommy' yet, she's only two. "Woe-ie, she says, "See Bean, Woe-ie."

Rose, standing at the counter, doing mother-things: stirring up healthful muffins, keeping track of immunizations, stacking the dishwasher, worrying: *What if I don't/what if I can't/what about —*

"Woe-ie see," Bean calls again, and Rose smiles, to show she sees, thinking, *what if I don't, what if I can't, what about . . .*

. . . as Bean dances like a leaf on the strange words . . .

I cannot err;

There is no creature
Whom I belong to,
Whom I could wrong . . .

"Woe-ie!" once more calls the little girl.

"I see you, Beanie, I sure do." Rose sees also what the child can only sense: the world's immanent destruction, the kitchen gone, the family torn. What if she won't be able to make enough money? Suppose she doesn't have enough education. What if she can't make it on her own? Suppose it all comes tumbling down.

Such things happen.

The pigtailed child twirled and twirled in the vanishing kitchen, her dance a dazzling question.

Rose settled herself in the unfamiliar car, and turned the key in the ignition.

Annie's Northern Suites was eight minutes north of the Fort Nelson airport. The billboard beside the *Welcome to Resourceful Fort Nelson* sign said so, and Rose hoped to God it was true. At the best of times she was terrible at the wheel, daunted by other drivers, bewildered by gears, mistrustful of mirrors — and now look. Budget Rent-A-Car had put her, of all people, in charge of a frighteningly new-smelling vehicle and its righteous papers, and let her loose on a night road, in a strange land.

Rolling off the lot, she caught sight of her forehead, fretted and pitted, in the rearview. Crazy, she felt. Dizzy. She who could barely deal with a downspout, was hellbent, all by herself, at night, for Mile Three Hundred of the Alaska Highway. Woe was she, who once was someone's 'woe-ie.'

Fumbling for the CBC — did wavelengths, or whatever they were, even reach this far north? — she grimly set forth.

Except for her own timid headlights, the road was intergalactic dark and weed fringed, and as far as Rose could tell, without end. What if there was a critter? Fuck, what if a moose lumbered out in front of her? Things like that happened up here, didn't they? She couldn't imagine much else of note happening in a world so forsaken. There was nothing to see but her own dashboard. Cold, now real winter cold, was seeping in all around her. Where was the heater, the damn defroster? This was practically the North Pole, and well on into the fall. Suppose it snowed?

Boots, despite Mab's mothering, had not occurred to her.

She gripped the steering wheel with one hand, shoved her glasses higher along the bridge of her nose with the other, as if that would affect the polar weather. What in God's name was she doing here, where the foxes said goodnight to one another, a day and two thousand hard-earned dollars later?

Since the one she sought could be anywhere. Or — not.

But she couldn't think of that. She could not let in the image of that final door and Bean alone, quietly passing through it, into that undiscovered country from whose bourn no traveller returns. Almost worse: the thought of never knowing, of never finding out. Of that silence going on and on, unanswered. Though surely Rose would know? Wouldn't she feel that passage somehow? Wouldn't a mother, the one who gave birth to her, know if her daughter had passed on, passed through?

Rose had to believe she would know, and that this meant Bean was still here. Somewhere. That stubborn belief was all she had.

Lights blazed in her mirror, a transport roaring up behind her like some northern monster, its outrageous grill grinning cruel uproar.

Not your daughter.

The truck geared down and passed her in a swirl of dust and gravel, as the CBC told about Canadian Thanksgiving traditions, from Samuel de Champlain to Stuart McLean. The turkey. The Vinyl Café. The perfect pumpkin family.

What were the names of McLean's so-normal protags, she tried to recall for sanity, as the dark grass blasted by.

Dave-and-Morley. The exasperated, ordinary, long-suffering couple Rose and the husband had never been, could never have been. What had undermined them? Lack of money? Lack of trust? Or had it been something less obvious, more devious? Some cruel piety, or willful laziness, that showed itself as the unlove it was, and finally brought the house down. Someone she once knew used to say that not to love another person is a failure of imagination.

Drive, she told herself. Just fucking drive. So she did.

And before long, just as the sign had promised, a red-and-blue welcome light flashed in the dark ahead.

Slowing to pull off the highway, still, amazingly in one piece, she heard a small, almost forgotten voice: *Woe-ie.*

A bell tinkled at the push of the motel door. Rose stood in the foyer of a place that had nothing to do with her.

Except that it did. She so desperately hoped it did.

An alphabet soup smell greeted her at the counter, a whiff of towel and bath water, a bedtime interrupted.

Whose?

She paused, ill at ease, part orphan, part criminal. Was this even a motel?

Though it must be. Behold the MasterCard sign, the routine and prudent shoe shine, the ATM machine.

A sign behind the counter stated, *Imaginary friends stay free.* How about invisible ones? Rose carped inwardly, as she waited for someone to greet her. How about friends who were spectral?

Maybe she'd come to the right place after all.

Brochures in a rack on the counter glossily offered local activities. You could spend time on forest trails that were home to an impressive array of northern wildlife. At certain times of year you could bask in the unearthly glow of the northern lights. She touched her car remote, to be sure she'd locked it, stared out at the enormous night.

Fort Nelson boasted camping in pristine provincial parks in summer, ice fishing or snowshoeing to one's heart's content in winter, she read as she waited for someone to attend her. Great. She scanned her watch, studied the counter. Was she too late? Was that why no one came out to serve her? She read further.

Despite its remoteness, Fort Nelson offered the traveller a visitors' centre, a curling rink, three churches, thank God several Tims. Not far from the motel, you could visit a heritage museum, a health store, a gourmet coffee emporium. You could take nature walks, observe rare birds, go on hikes, rent bikes. A charter service on the edge of town sold reasonably priced day trips to untouched mountain lakes. In season, you could ski.

A small yellow dog spied Rose, scrambled up from a cushion on the floor, ran in circles, barking. From somewhere in the back, a muffled voice snapped, "Jesus, Harley, I'm not deaf!"

Rose was so tired, startled, and alarmed, she felt weirdly warm. She loosened her scarf and let it fall across her arm as a commotion of aggrieved thumps and shuffles sounded from a neighbouring room.

The proprietress of Annie's was shaped like a Maytag, wore a unisex sweater in a pattern of green-and-black stags, and bore a good start on a Charlie Chaplain mustache. Her bright, appraising eyes considered Rose from under a sturdy fringe of salt-and-pepper hair.

"You the lady from Calgary?"

The badge clipped to her sweater read, *Doris*.

Rose pulled her London Fog bag closer to the counter. "I'm so sorry to arrive so late, the plane —"

"Hey, no problemo, we been waitin for ya. Ain't we there, Harley!"

Doris gave a comfortably outraged sigh as she hauled herself onto a high stool behind the counter, and simultaneously, with one short, surprisingly deft leg, skittered the little dog out of the way. "Go lay down. Gwan, now, and quit makin them goddamned *smells*." She waved a hand in front of her nose. "Dogs, eh. God knows what this one's been into." Briskly then, getting down to business, she fired up her computer. "Don't mind him, his bark's louder than his bite." She shot a merry look over her shoulder. "Harley, ain't that right!"

Rose smiled. "He's got quite the pipes." She was dying to get her teeth clean and lie down, she hardly cared anymore on what.

"Okay, now," Doris hummed, squinting shrewdly at her computer monitor, "Where's that damn spread sheet? And I'll need some photo ID." She turned to look fondly at the mutt. "He's never lost for words, that one." A half hitch of her formidable shoulder, "*Are* ya, ya little —"

A young tortoise shell was curled on a small hand-braided oval mat beside the computer, enthusiastically grooming its nether parts. Doris paused, pressed a key with a thick, yellow fingernail. "Now, if us girls could do *that* for ourselves," she sighed, "we wouldn't need men, would we." She gave a melancholy chuckle and stuck her pen behind her ear as a bright schedule bloomed on her screen. "Okie dokie, here we go. Yup, here's you. Room 22." She massaged the cat's frostbitten-looking ear, and it elicited a throaty purr. Then she looked at the wall behind her shoulder. "Oh yeah, now, and I see there's a parcel's come in for you. Come up from Calgary a fair little while ago."

Rose woke in the middle of the night in a strange room, with a dry throat. Generic drapes let in a sodium seam of parking-lot light.

The room was too warm. She kicked off the covers like she did every night anywhere, reaching for water, gulping for air. That much was familiar.

That, and the parcel on the chair, a little the worse for wear and not seen since she sent it from Calgary, back in September. She shook it, felt its familiar weight.

A car swished by on the highway, its lights bouncing off the shiny tape of the package, and bending away up the wall to nowhere.

The wind was up, woe-woe-ing around the building. Apart from her own airline-tagged bags and rumpled clothes and tossed shoes, the shadowed room looked like any room: Acceptable.

Intolerable.

But Rose had a cure for intolerable, a partial one, anyway. She dug into her carry-on and found her last-minute airport purchase of Appleton Estates and the Stephen King she'd picked up at the kiosk beside the liquor place. *Joyland*, the cover sporting an alarmed young redhead in a scant emerald dress, the byline: *Who dares enter the Funhouse of Fear?*

Rose dared, that was who. Just bring on the fucking funhouse of fear, she fucking lived there.

She burrowed deep into the cheap covers, novel held aloft, grateful for her handknitted bed socks, an ancient Christmas present from Mab, who'd be glad. The next time she woke, she recognized the book but couldn't remember what she'd read, there was the usual dull ball of ache in her head, and it was a long time till morning.

Daylight was brightening the drapes when she woke again. How had she slept so long? She couldn't face Harley the dog and Doris in her stag sweater, or the tiny dinette of Annie's Northern Suites. Not yet. There was a Tim Horton's down the road, she remembered. There might be a clue there. A decent coffee, at least, would be there.

Nobody at the Tims had heard of a group of idealistic young people living in the bushes anywhere around.

"Not 'less you count the Baptist youth group," one old guy chuckled, "they may's well be a community, can't get em apart on a Friday night for love nor money."

Rose grinned — "Kids, eh?" — and bought him a Red Velvet muffin, then sat in her car afterward sipping a Double-Double, feeling like a fool.

What had possessed her to come up to this godforsaken place? She wasn't going to find anything after this long. There wasn't enough to go on, and probably there never had been; plus, it was the nature of such groups to move on, and to turn into something else and then something else again before they were done. Their final morph would be a predictably unapologetic transformation into earnest young parents with starter homes and entry-level jobs in law firms, the former rigour of lentil stew and dreadlocks channelled into mortgages and daycares, with just enough time left over for Pilates classes and therapy to cure them of their discarded and terrible parents.

Rose didn't care. No, sir. But there'd be no moving on with her own life without a stopover here. Somebody she taught with once used to say, "Jest git er done."

And there were worse ways to spend Thanksgiving than being somewhere where its ghosts couldn't get you.

As well as anywhere, Fort Nelson would do.

The visitors' centre was an environmentally friendly green-roofed building covered in tan siding and bird houses. It was open. Rose walked through the pine tree-framed doors and into the hushed museum dusk of lighted cabinets, instructive displays, glossy brochures.

Two bright-and-shiny young people ran the information desk, eager to draw circles on crisp maps, dispense northern knowledge, twinkle local welcome. In return, Rose would offer urbanity and cheerful self-deprecation, the usual lead-up her bleak question.

But not yet.

Her Tims was still warm, and there seemed no prohibition on bringing it inside. The sweetened caffeine was slowly delivering its quotidian mercies; after the parched and headachy night she'd just spent, she craved every one of them.

Coffee in hand, she smiled *I-come-in-peace* to the shining ones, and entered the display area, demonstrating touristy interest, paying attention, genuinely reading about how the First Peoples hunted and fished, how the fur trade attracted European explorers who introduced new customs and built trading posts, and how the Alaska Highway *opened up this splendid land for commerce and travel*.

Also, apparently — Rose gazed now along a hushed walkway of tasteful display cases — to roadkill. Beside her, perfectly preserved chipmunks nibbled accurate nuts on lifelike branches. Nearby towered a bison, its arrested mass still tremendous, its spent energy caught in egg-sized eyes of furious glass. From a clump of preserved indigenous grasses arose "A Startled Stoat." Next door, a tawny cougar in mint condition leapt to take down a long-dead mountain goat.

There was a view. You could turn from the educational cabinets to see Jack pines and rustic fences and forest meadows, framed by a Walmart-sized window.

Or you could cut to the chase, and ask the goddamn question.

The young man and woman shook their heads, and were so sorry.

Rose said, oh, not to worry, that was okay, she was just passing through and thought perhaps . . .

She thanked them, got back in the car, and drove up one straight, strange street and down another, gazing between the blank-eyed houses and behind skimpy trees, as though one of those houses or trees could possibly be harbouring a temporary Bean, as she herself once had. In the business district she made some actual stops, just random drive-bys. Had Bean gone local, perhaps, and taken up curling? She walked into the rink, and for a while watched laconic young men and women leaning on brooms, breathing on rocks. None of their faces looked like Joan of Arc's. Could she be working in some store? Rose canvassed the post office, the hobby-&-craft place, the Overwaitea, the IGA. She asked the people there, just casually.

Ever hear anything about a group of young people who might have lived together somewhere around here?

Ever notice an unfamiliar girl, about eighteen, delicate features and intense eyes, short boyish hair?

Please, please, please, have you seen my daughter?

St. Mary Magdalene's Anglican, Fort Nelson, was tiny and old and cold, and, surprisingly, open. Altar guild ladies breezed in and out with Brasso and buckets and clean linens, chortling cheerful gossip. They did not mind that a lost soul from who-cared-where had slipped into a back pew.

A choir was rehearsing in the chancel, the early words falling like rain. *For man walketh in a vain shadow, and disquieteth himself in vain.*

Rose inhaled spent incense and slid to the padded prayer bench. There, on her knees, she took out of her purse the dog-eared postcard of sunset mountains over a remote lake. The lake was called Maxhamish. It was a forty-minute flight, she'd found out, from here into the interior. The day trips by small plane were insanely expensive, but they went to that lake.

And it was only money.

In nomine Domine.

A text lit up her screen as she headed back to the rental. *Hey girl, been thinkin about you up there. Any signs or wonders?*

Not unless you count Harley the farting dog, she texted Morrison back, leaning against the car, and remembering, with a little spurt of annoyance, the whole thing about Abbey, and Morrison's emergency visit back east. She supposed Morrison was on the phone with her, too, consoling her for her domestic ineptitude and behaving like some kind of long-distance hubby.

Damned Abbey.

Abbey

High in Iris's window, a cold coin of moon hung amongst tiny clouds, tissue-thin, eerily bright. Abbey woke to find herself still sitting beside the child's bed, all her limbs tight and the cottage deeply quiet.

Iris in her bed was as remote as that moon, her shoulder a serene line. A small and satisfied sigh escaped her lips; what was she dreaming? About ships and sails and sealing wax, and Alexander the mouse's elfin voyages across her back?

Abbey was always the one left out of sleep. Car trips, sleepovers, Girl Guide camp, everybody else snoring, and muttering about frogs and toads and Tater Tots, herself staring up into the dark, forever the one still awake, watching out.

That was what you had to do if your old man was the town drunk.

You had to be on it, had to be watching, to *know*. Somehow by your own willpower, you had force his car back to safety. With your strongest thoughts, you had to guide your father home through rain and snow and the haze of booze. You had to get him home safe, and you could do it, you'd managed it every time so far, by staying awake, by staring awake.

A small sound caused Abbey to look down. Iris had stirred and opened her eyes, but she wasn't behind them. She was dreaming, eyes open, gazing back inside herself, an uncanny sight. Then she was gone again, the thick lashes a dark seam. Abbey envied her.

Somewhere in the childhood commotion, she had forgotten got how to close her eyes. Now, no matter where she was, sleep was fleeting. She had a few tricks. Reading, keeping her glasses on, keeping the light on. Anything to beguile herself out of the eye-watering torture of trying.

She reached down and sorted Iris's surprisingly heavy feet from her damp sheets, then drew the covers up over the cool cliff of her shoulder, which shone like still water in the moon.

Parker snored hard as she stumbled back to the bedroom. The stars were almost gone.

Abbey woke up. She had no memory of finding the bed or falling asleep. Bacon was cooking when she appeared in the pretty kitchen. It smelled disgusting. Parker grooved up to her, extending a steaming mug of coffee, his PJs dangerously low on his skinny hips. He looked pointedly at the coffee. "Say, 'Good morning, Mr. Breakfast.'"

"Parker, for — Look at yourself. What if Iris —"

"What?" He looked down at that hairy frond of his on his lower belly, as if it was a friend of his. "Tadpole doesn't care. Half the time I don't wear anything when I get up in the morning. He winked, then executed a fairly convincing runway move. "Put these babies on just for you."

"Parker Darlington, sometimes you can be stunner'n Tom Tucker's goat."

"Ah, but you can't resist me." A second swirl and wiggle, to show off his scantily clad buns.

"Listen, Park, she's not a baby any more. She's —" Abbey sniffed in the direction of the crackling bacon. "Oh. God. Phew. Did that get put in the fridge last night?"

"Everything did. Why?"

She waved a hand past her nose. "It doesn't smell right."

"What doesn't smell right about maple syrup and hickory smoke and —" He did that dangerous thing with his hips once more "— just you and me in the woods, in a funky li'l ol' cabin?"

Abbey had forgotten the part about 'just you and me in a li'l ol' cabin.' She felt a pang. "What about Iris? I forgot. When does she go?"

"Dave'll be here tomorrow afternoon, sometime before dinner."

Abbey remembered. "Okay." She tried to sip her coffee. "What's he like? Iris seems vexed with him."

"What's 'vexed'?"

"Don't be a dick. 'Vexed' is she doesn't seem sure she likes him."

"Tadpole's tired of boyfriends, is all. She'll get used to him. If he sticks around." He snorted. "Ali doesn't make it easy."

"What does he do? Dave."

"Teacher. Up at the college. That's where him and Ali met. She teaches in the business department up there, and she's smart, like him. She met him at the college gym, they're both crazy fitness geeks. For them a good time's a Friday night in the weight room, followed by a bowl of kale." Parker rolled his eyes. "But he's a pretty good ol' guy, Dave. He's good to Ali and the kids, and he doesn't bullshit."

"Good. I'm glad." She looked around. "Speaking of kids, where's ours — I mean, yours?"

"Still sawing logs." Parker went over to turn the bacon. "You want some of this?"

Abbey felt her mouth water, not in a good way. "I'm not hungry, yet, Park. I think I'll do a quick run. Maybe that'll sort me out."

"Watch out for the bears."

"Ha ha, fuck yourself."

"That's *your* job."

"In your dreams."

"Sure was last night."

Abbey grinned. "Ooh, burn."

"Different story tonight, better be."

"Depends how you behave yourself today." She yawned, scratching under her arms. "Back in an hour."

"K." Parker drifted toward the door. "Gonna go wake up the tadpole."

Abbey headed to the bedroom to deal with her gear. What a mess, everything mops and brooms. The bed unmade, bags and backpacks yawning open, dental floss and socks and Parker's boxers in strange places.

Somebody had to clean it up.

But her back was aching; it must be her period coming. She sat down on the bed to start smoothing and sorting, then — she was so tired — she lay down for a few minutes.

Abbey opened her eyes. No one there. No sound, not a thing familiar. Where the devil was she? Was it morning or evening? The late afternoon light gave nothing away.

Her hand found its way to her ribs. Somewhere under them, a high hollow feeling. Like there was no connection, no digestion. No stomach to anything.

The clock beside the bed read 7:13. Parker's watch lay beside it.

The cottage. Iris. Alexander the mouse. All that. Phew, now she knew.

She rolled off the laundry-littered bed and trailed back to the kitchen. Thank God, no sign of bacon. A note on the table said, *Gone to the store for briquettes. Tadpole with me. Back soon. XO.*

Briquettes. He'd actually spelled it right. Amazing.

Early evening, then. She must have caught that bug that was going around at the dance school last week.

She'd slept the whole damn day.

The light was colder by the time she was trotting down the cottage steps, and taking to the spruce-fresh path toward the road. Between trembling trees, she could sense the first, sobering hints of fall.

And of marathon. Jeez, and of Morrison. As far as Abbey could tell, he'd been faithfully following her training instructions, all that cut-and-paste bull-crap of tempo run and recovery walk she'd been finding online and feeding him all summer, and figuring that she, being so much younger, could pull it off at the last moment.

She didn't feel younger any more. What was wrong with her? Sure, she was running. One foot wearily following the other. The legs and elbows and shoulders all doing what they were supposed to be doing, the ligaments and bones bravely cooperating.

Though she might as well have been running under water. There was no power in her, no hint of a second wind, no hope of resurrection.

But she kept on, eyes down, ignoring. That's what runners did. *Come on, girl, dig deep, giddy up.* Runners — and she was one of them — believed that running could cure anything.

By now the day had divided the way it does at lakes in late summer, the afternoon shrunk to a cold glitter in the tops of the trees, the night's tide rising like ink in the hollows of the road.

Suddenly she didn't like the feel of the road. A chill descended over her shoulders — didn't Parker say this place had once been some kind of holy site or something? — and she wanted to get out of there; she didn't know why, just that she wanted to get out of the trees and back to the cottage, and faster than hell.

A slogan from one of her race T-shirts came to her, and she obeyed it: *Run like you stole.*

Mab

During the time she called her 'plaid period,' Mab lived for a while in a basement apartment in a Victorian house in Cabbagetown. "I chose that place because it was right across from the St. James Cemetery, and the Necropolis."

"Wow," said Rose on the phone, "dead neighbours, what fun."

"Yeah, I know," laughed Mab. "Instead of my plaid period, I should have called it my dead period. Speaking of cemeteries, I saw something, you know, when I was living there."

Rose heard Mab blow away a breath of smoke.

"And not just once, either."

She called it her plaid period because of the eighty-seven-year-old Scotts landlady, who dressed in Kinloch Anderson tartan, wore her hair in a dense brown beehive — "She looked like a Beefeater!" with a rakish bow to match her skirt, and who was forever bringing Mab samples of her famous macaroni and cheese pie. "She was always saying, 'pasta in a pie equals perfection,' while she stared over my shoulder at my deplorable housekeeping."

Rose wanted to know what it was Mab saw, back then.

Mab didn't know. "I'm sure I was just all stirred up from — you know, all that business in Kingston — and scared of my shadow, and thinking I was seeing things."

Living in the permanent semi-twilight of a basement full of shrouded furniture hadn't helped, either. "Or maybe it was that the ghosts in the necropolis liked going out at night, and wandering into peoples' basements for something to do." She giggled. "Guess they didn't get out much."

What did it look like? Rose wondered.

"A lot of legs. Like, and I mean hairy ones."

"Oh fuck, Mab, you're creeping me out; what was it?"

"What you're thinking." Mab exhaled. "What you're probably thinking."

"Centipedes."

"Yup, and not just a few. You had to be careful at night, opening the door."

Rose sipped her Bengal Spice tea, a new kind she was learning to like. "Oh, God, Mab, why?"

Because centipedes, startled by the sudden light, would fall off the heating ducts that ran across the ceiling, and skitter, that was why. "It was horrible. There are no words. There was this one time when one of them fell onto my bed. It was the size of a flipping bottle brush!"

Rose shuddered. "What did you do, did you complain?"

What she did was, she grabbed the can of Raid she'd bought soon after moving in. "And I sprayed it and sprayed it and crikey, I sprayed it" — until the creature was hobbling, shuffling, not knowing where it was going, and Mab was sobbing, down there, in some damp basement in Toronto where she'd never meant to be.

"I dug under the counter and found a plastic yogurt container and a brick that were under there, and I clapped the container over the thing" — by this time, still slowly moving, still trying to move, white as a weed in a hoarfrost — "and I put the brick on the container, and fell into bed."

"Sounds straight out of Hitchcock," sympathized Rose.

For another two days she'd left the weighted container with its now freeze-dried prisoner, in the middle of the floor. "I couldn't make myself go near it."

"Oh, Mab."

When she finally took the container off and saw what was left of the centipede, "I howled!"

"It was yourself you were howling for, you know that, right?" Rose said. "It's always ourselves we wail for."

It rained all the time when Mab lived in that apartment. Mildew grew like dark flowers in the damp corners. The landlord's sad black lab lived chained like a homunculus outside Mab's bedroom window, through which the smell of his pee drifted reliably.

Heath was history.

"Thank God I had a job." Though she hadn't gotten on at the Bloor and St. Clair branch, she'd ended up, postpartum "or whatever it was," and mortally disoriented, at the University of Toronto's Art History library, just in time for the fall semester.

This was just after the D&C and before digitization, when everything was still real. Ortrud, Mab's supervisor, who above all things prized order, showed her how she was to type up strict little cards and stick-on labels for the two hundred thousand slides of paintings and sculptures and buildings and textiles and ceramics that the library housed, and then how to paste the labels on the slides, and finally to file the slides behind the cards.

"But you couldn't file them just anywhere," she told Rose on one of those late-night calls. "They had to be under Century, then Artist, then Medium, then date range, and God knows what else, besides." She laughed. "Oh, there were a thousand things!"

Mab hadn't stopped bleeding. Sometimes there were still contractions; she was prone to crying jags.

In the wooden drawers that held the slides were even more cards in sober colours, pale orange, light gray, hospital green, painstakingly typed out and installed there over the years by Ortrud, to denote art's centuries and categories, its endless and orderly subcategories.

The little cards in the drawers — so many of them! — were often a teary blur. Ortrud, thanks to Mab's somewhat freer interpretation of her centuries and categories, soon was politely pissed off with her.

But Mab hung in there. She managed to keep the crying to her bathroom breaks, and to contribute appropriate trivia during the long, somnolent afternoon coffee times with the art historians and the other librarians. Soon she was familiar with their stories.

Lilian (circulation desk) had just hit menopause. Her partner was less sympathetic than you might think. "All she ever says anymore, is 'deal with it'!"

Lilian spent the coffee breaks slowly rolling a chilled can of Pepsi up and down her long golden neck, and puffing out little spurts of unhappy air, which flipped her straight blonde bangs up, then down in an approximation of refreshment. Her skin shone constantly with exasperated sweat.

Anne (early modern) was renovating her house. A criminal was doing the renovations. "How could I have known he's a criminal? I found him through a friend, and she thought he was all that and a bag of chips!" He was only supposed to create a little bathroom in the basement. "But the next thing I know he's telling me the house needs new wiring, then that the plumbing's not to code, and the sewer lines aren't going to last another year — why not, they've been there for eighty reliable ones so far. But that's more cash for him, right?" She'd fling herself back in her chair, thinking about him. "Every time he turns around, he says, 'That's a problem.' But what it is, is more money out of my pocket."

Every afternoon while the women, it was mostly women, sauntered in, and the percolating coffee clucked and chuckled, and the fall air stirred the reddening vines at the window, there was a new chapter of the renovation. Frost had been found between the walls in Anne's root cellar. "That's a problem." There was no insulation on the outside walls. "That's a problem." The basement bedroom had no egress window. That was a two-thousand-dollar problem.

Bruce (Byzantine textiles) was looking for a long-term care facility for his wife. She had third-stage Alzheimer's, and should have been in care eighteen months ago. Bruce hadn't had the heart to consider it up until now. Timetabling made sure every semester to give him a schedule that allowed him to scram home by four, so he could feed his wife and shower her and read her a story, tuck her into bed at six with her stuffy toy.

But he had to do something. He knew he did. Every day, Ortrud and Lilian and Anne, and before long Mab, who was slowly getting the hang of things in the art history world, agreed.

Liz (Italian Renaissance) and her husband, Paul (ditto), were in the process of adopting a baby from China. This was complicated in a number of ways, not least by the fact that now they were expecting already. They'd applied to adopt after losing their first baby during his birth; then when they knew they were going to be successful in adopting, they'd conceived again, and it was twins. Liz threw up her hands. "Twins! Please! Might as well make it triplets!"

But the Chinese adoption was almost complete, the papers signed, the tickets bought. They had to go through with it. Now, here they were, getting themselves ready to welcome not one baby, but three.

"This kind of thing happens so often," mused Ortrud, sorting through a new set of Matisse slides in the wooden tray on her lap. Lilian, puffing and Pepsi-ing her neck, mused that adoption, thanks to its certainty of a baby, allowed the grieving mother to relax. The next thing you knew: Bingo! She dabbed at her face with the sleeve of her cotton sweater and gazed out the window, as though on the lookout for a breeze or Houdini.

Liz was fond of telling about the funeral for the first, lost baby, who had slipped so quietly away. The ceremony had been held at a lake, on a fall day. She described the autumn colours, the leaves dropping into the water, the family and friends who'd attended, the scattering of ashes on the still air. She told about how, back in the cottage at the other end of the dock, a splendid feast had later been shared.

Now, on a bluff above town, a young oak with a plaque grew as a memento. "We wanted him to have a really good view of the city."

At this point in the story, Mab, who would rather not hear any more about the well-mourned baby, would set about cleaning up from the coffee, it had gotten to be her job anyway.

There would be no memorial, no plaque or sturdy tree, for the unformed forehead, the inky eye.

What if — one day she set down the coffee pot and stumbled to her office, closed and locked the door. What if someday she didn't remember anymore? Back then she'd been far from thirty. What if someday all this was in the past, and eventually she had a husband and a normal life and a for-real baby or maybe even a couple of them.

What if life made her let go of the memory? What then?

V

LIFE

Rose

Lines for a possible poem, Scribbled in a Roadside Motel.

It is the last hour of winter. Bare and gleaming, the child races through the darkening rooms, her clear laughter echoing.

Outside, the spring light descends.

The mother and the child are playing the game of me catching you, though the child is moving far too fast for the mother ever to win. One by one the stars wink on.

Here are the child's small clothes, discarded on the floor of the kitchen. The mother raises them to her face and breathes them in, as though the game were just a dream, as though already it were an echo, the child gone.

One good thing about getting away, Rose thought. You can be a poet for a day.

She shoved her papers into her backpack, and took the cab she'd called to the airport.

A pink stain of sun climbed the sky above the tarmac as Rose and her package and her neuroses, and her stab at a poem, buckled themselves in beside somebody vaguely her own age and suffering from the same spinal issues, it wasn't hard to tell. The way he climbed into the little plane in stiff stages, the joke of a grunt, the apologetic grin, the wince that could be pain or sun, Rose recognized it all, and was tempted to mention Tylenol. *Extended Relief's best; do you use Extended Relief?* The kind of old-person conversation starter Bean had always despised. Instead of starting it, Rose checked her phone. Even here, where Bean could actually be, she went through her daily 'in case' phone routine, and found the usual smugly blank screen.

Sun on the instrument panel shimmered, a sight both eerie and ordinary. She was marvelously far from Calgary.

The pilot checked his controls, fished for headsets, eyed Rose's seatbelt to make sure it was secure. "You good?" he yelled, his aviators like two huge fly eyes, in which she saw nothing but her own dishevelled self. He was wearing a plaid shirt and leather jacket, jeans, and cowboy boots, gray-flecked black hair in a neat braid. Like everybody else here it seemed, he could be a misplaced rodeo guy, except maybe more skinny.

She yelled above the engines, "All good!"

They were headed for Maxhamish Lake, wherever that was. Where the hell was anything these days? When you're spending Thanksgiving weekend hurtling over the horizon in a tin can. When a foreign sun is throwing its darts in your eyes.

When the only kid you ever had turns into a scorched saint from 1200 AD and vanishes into the mapless trees.

"Takeoff's a bit on the loud side. Some people don't love it; you want something for the noise?"

The pilot had in-service earplugs to put on under the headsets, a ham-and-avocado sandwich, and a Double-Double.

Rose craved the Double-Double. "That's okay."

"Name's Byrd by the way." He reached to toss his jacket into the back. "Bill Byrd. But people just call me Byrd."

"Any relation to the composer?" Rose yelled into the wall of noise.

"What?" yelled the pilot, "to what?"

"The composer," she hollered back, thinking of Mab, who'd been partial to that one because apparently he had the best Miserere. "William Byrd."

The pilot looked blank.

Rose shrugged. "He's from a long time ago. Way before airplanes. That's okay."

Byrd canted his head out of mock respect for the long-dead. He must think her demented.

Two other people, two hunters, were supposed to be on the flight, but their connection had got messed up. Byrd laughed his satisfaction. "They're parked at the Jugo Juice in Edmonton Airport right now," he yelled over the roar of the propellers, "waiting for updates. No big game for them good ol' boys."

So Rose, all by herself and for a handsomely reduced fee, was destined for some desolate lake for which the ratty picture she carried in her purse was apparently a not-bad match.

She reached the postcard sideways as the engines revved. "You ever see this spot?"

"Eh?" Byrd shoved his glasses up, cranked his head in the direction of her hand.

Rose yelled, "Does this place look familiar?"

Byrd took a mouthful of coffee, gave a shrugging chuckle. "Yup!"

Rose quickened, leaned. The familiar painful stir of hope. Its desperate flutter.

"They got a stack of em up at Bickerton's drugstore!"

Very funny, you fuck, Rose thought, then repented. Not only was she getting fat; she was turning into a bitch. Why should some decent-enough guy doing his underpaid job out back of beyond care about her, or guess that she harboured a cold cavity where there used to be a daughter?

Rose settled back in her seat, determined not to be terrified as the tiny plane rushed to the end of the tarmac then shot straight up, a calamitous dragonfly, parallel to a dark wall of ominous evergreens.

Her stomach lurched.

"Take a look," the pilot said, slurping and pointing the index finger of the hand holding his cup.

"What?" Rose didn't see anything. "Where?"

"There, see. Over there in that underbrush."

"All I see is trees!"

"Use your eyes."

Rose did. The tree trunks started moving. "Oh. Oh my —"

"Moose," he said, still pointing, "See? Mother and a calf." He set the coffee down in the cupholder. "Sure you don't want any?"

Rose took a sip, nodded thanks, peered. They were higher now, though still not far above the trees, which churned and stormed against the propellers' commotion. "Isn't that a bit unusual? I mean, for them still to be together in the fall?"

She wanted it to be unusual. She wanted it to be normal for all mothers, after a reasonable season, to be exiled from their children.

"Nah," the pilot yelled, "not really. They can stay together sometimes till the calves are around two years old. Mother punts em then, especially if they're bulls."

"How come?"

"To keep from breeding with em."

The afternoon sun was glinting on Byrd's smooth, tanned arm. Finally, they were in the air. Rose watched the moose family until it disappeared. A colleague used to say, When you're ready for your kids to move out, stop cooking with cheese.

"Aw," crooned Byrd, pointing, "look at that little sucker runnin after his mama."

Rose smiled. "You got kids?"

Byrd glanced at the radar screen, then took another sip of his coffee. "I'm all done with that scene."

Abbey

Why was it cottages were always so damn dark? Abbey closed Iris's door and fumbled back to the room she was sharing with Parker.

But Parker was face down and deep asleep, one long leg half off the bed, one muscled arm flung up over. The moon lay bright as arrows across the gold of his shoulder.

Abbey craved those arrows. She craved to scoop them into a silver quiver, to claim them, to aim them deep inside her.

Part of a hymn quoted in movie about runners came back to her. *Bring me my arrows of desire.*

She slipped off her clothes and arranged herself beside him, the curves and the hollows of her. She studied him like an observer.

If her lips touched the shoulder . . .

If the tips of her fingers passed across his jaw . . .

If her hand traced the dark stem travelling down his belly . . .

Her hand found her own belly, sliding between the twin hooks of her hips and descending through to the place of desire.

And desire was there, waiting for her.

Her hand caressing the familiar topography, she began thinking about locker rooms. Abbey always got going by thinking about those cold metal cubby holes, with their mysterious contents, their smelly shoes and floral deodorants, the creams and powders, the scents and unguents.

Aveeno, Oil of Olay, Dove.

Somewhere above, the drip-drip of institutional water, its strict and aimless clatter.

And then: her. The swimmer. Right there. Just a locker or two away from Abbey.

She might be about to set sail, or fresh out of the pool, limbs gleaming, wet eyelashes clumped together, hair a tawny coil on her neck, that long neck.

The swimmer stands before her locker, unaware and offering full view of an ass that could only be illegal: a long and lazy inverted heart cupped in black Lycra, its curves like raindrops, teardrops.

Add to this the soft swell of the collarbones, the sweet scribble of the ribs, the darkly perfect nipples, breasts forbidden as Eden's apples.

Abbey loitering on her own bench meanwhile, in the opposite bank of lockers, doing up her shoes or toweling off, nobody but the two of them in the room, with that gentle drip-drip of water.

Abbey crossing the room then, pressing the swimmer into the cold door of a locker, peeling away the wet bathing suit, kissing the slick hair from her shoulder, that shoulder all muscle and water, both salt and fresh together, the nipples hardening under the tongue's hunger. The lines of her, arcane and silken as scripture, the divine commandment of her.

Stay me with flagons. Comfort me with apples. For I am sick with love.

Beside a dreaming Parker, Abbey came as quietly as air.

Parker

Buttery autumn light splashed the blue wainscoting of the kitchen walls as Parker, still horny from listening to Abbey come in the night, made the cruel discovery there was no coffee. This day — no day — could begin without coffee. "Hey, Tadpole," he called to Iris, who was firing off caps with a rock on the back step, "want to take a run up to the store?"

"What about *her*?" She indicated the still-dark hallway where the bedrooms were.

"Hey, now," Parker warned gently, "Are you a tadpole or a 'tupid'? *Abbey* didn't sleep so good last night, we have to try to be nice to her. We'll surprise er when we get back with a nice fresh can of Folger's . . ." He paused, less than pleased. ". . . cause that's all they got up there." Then he brightened. "They got cinnamon buns, though, and it's early so they won't be sold out yet; we'll get a whack of those, too."

"Can I buy myself something?"

"Don't buy anything bigger than your head."

Iris groaned. "Dad, you say that every single time."

A Chinese family owned the store, which was called 'The Store Famous,' and which was really just the sunporch of their small house, fitted up with a cash register and essentials for the cottagers — cigarettes, ice cream, butter tarts, Band-Aids. Parker had found his buns and coffee, as well as a pack of filters, and was ready to hit the road, but Iris wanted to linger.

"I'll see you outside then, when you're done."

He stepped out into the trees, sniffed the lake air, and it made him hungrier. For Abbey. For every little part of her, and for one part especially.

He was one horny dude. He knew it, and he didn't give a fuck. Except that right now, a fuck was what he did give.

He looked back to make sure Iris was still busy in the store. From where he stood, he could see her, earnestly considering the comics and the goofy sunglasses, the Dubble Bubble gum. A stand of young spruces grew near the car, and he concealed himself behind them. Then, cock in hand and Abbey in mind, he leaned behind the car, under the stunning sun.

Holding his breath, he barely had to touch himself, to come.

And then he came again, and it was harder this time, and more intense, his body one long shudder. It was all he could do not to yell.

He had a minute, Iris hadn't emerged from the store yet, and he made use of it to sort himself out, reflecting as he did, that not many guys could come twice in a row, but he still could, at almost forty, given the right circumstances, and he was pretty proud of that wee fact. In a way, it was an art form. Another one. His peanut-butter critters and his swimming and his tooth jewelry and his market gardening — who grew better peppers than he did? — were art forms too, in their way. But there was nothing like the sweet, hard art of coming.

He shoved himself back into his damp swim trunks and sighed with satisfaction, then looked up from the sheltering bushes, his gaze travelling along the road, which was already crossed with cool lengths of morning shade.

An uncanny feeling raised the hairs on his arms, he had no idea why, and he broke into a run. Around the back of the car and up the path to the store, his own breath loud in his ear, suddenly afraid he wouldn't see her. But there she was, pouring over an Archie comic, golden and serene, his beautiful, smart, demanding daughter.

"Tad, let's get out of here!"

"Why?"

"Because I love you, that's why!"

And he grabbed her and scrammed like he didn't know a just-come dude could scram.

Rose

If anyone was the queen of weird situations, it was Rose. Here she was on Thanksgiving weekend, not in her office, marking, which would have been a very good thing to do, considering the one hundred and twelve essays on confirmation bias stacked on her desk. Instead, she was soon to be marooned for two nights with a stranger in some remote northern cabin. At least, she reminded herself, it would be half-price, thanks to the no-show hunters from Edmonton.

Byrd-the-pilot had gallantly offered to overnight in his cockpit, but Rose was apologetic. "Hey, I do it all the time. It's kind of part of the job." He winked. "Plus, I got crackers."

Was he joking? "Well, aren't you, I mean —"

They were starting their descent; Rose's ears were popping.

Byrd indicated a foil package on the console. "You want some gum? Gum helps on the way down."

Rose nodded, took some.

"And this coat makes a dandy pillow." He grinned.

"Oh, for —" said Rose, "Didn't you say there's two bunks in the place? And you're going to need some way to keep warm, besides —"

"Got whiskey for that."

"You have actual whiskey?"

"No good pilot leaves home without it." The lake was zooming toward them, a canopy of cattails and foam, and rolling water.

Now the skis were down and they were skimming the surface, the little plane tipping and shuddering, caught in the lake's weather. Byrd glanced over. "You okay?"

"Okay." Rose swallowed, yelled. "Yeah. I'm okay."

"We'll land and haul the gear up to the cabin, it's just up in there." He gestured toward a wall of impenetrable forest. "Then how about a sunset campfire? Otherwise it's a long night up here. There's chips and stuff in the place." He grinned. "And I'll share my whiskey."

"I won't say no."

She watched his hand grip and thrust the throttle forward, aviators glinting, the fringe of his leather jacket swinging. Had she really said that?

And did she really feel the stir of that foolish old familiar danger? She laughed to think what would Mab say about that.

One night the summer Bean turned four, Rose and Mab were on the phone. They were remembering Mab's bad old days, back in Kingston. Rose said, "Why didn't you ever tell me?"

"Why didn't I ever tell you what?"

"About the miscarriage. Jeeze, Mab."

"I did tell you."

Through the phone, Rose could hear Mab fussing with something. "Yeah," she had carped to her friend, "five years later, you told me, after blithely pretending you'd moved to Toronto for your career!" She listened harder. "Are you smoking? Was that a cigarette I heard you light? Since when have you been smoking again?"

"Since I felt like it," Mab exhaled. "Anyway, I did move here for my career. Behold, I have a career. Well, practically two, if you count the travel mags. And yes, I do smoke occasionally. Only the light ones. I suppose you have no vices."

"You know what my vices are." Teaching was over for the summer. So was daycare. Bean was bored. So was Rose. It was a good time to travel. "I'm coming out there."

"What for? That's so old hat, Rose. I'm over it now. God, I better be!" Mab gave that girlish laugh of hers, the way she did when she talked about early music and little bad signs, and exhaled again. "And anyway, we're having a heatwave. Bean wouldn't be able to sleep."

Good point, Rose thought. She said, "Screw that." Then she got to work and found a deal on a ten-day stay. She needed to see Mab with her own eyes. It was time. Plus, it'd been a while since she'd hung out in Toronto; she could do with a shot of Upper Canadian urbanity. The Beaches. The Planetarium. The St. Lawrence Market. All that. Already she was thinking about spending time in those obnoxiously precious Cabbagetown boutiques, with their overpriced produce and specialty coffee.

Rose and Bean arrived a week later on the red-eye.

"Yoo hoo!" There was Mab, over by the carousels, looking thinner and less young and more handsome than Rose remembered. "Look at your dear wee babe!"

Bean frowned and turned to clasp Rose's knees.

Rose grinned, waving over Bean's head. "Look at *you*, so sharp and trim!"

"Don't let that fool you. Deep down I'm the same fat girl as ever. Speaking of which, did they feed you on the plane? Have you had any breakfast? Let's go get something to eat, I know this great little place!"

Mab's apartment was the middle floor of an Edwardian house that had seen better days. It was one of a row of such houses, genteel and slightly down at heel, that bordered the Riverdale Zoo. Bean, homesick and stern at first, was nevertheless pleased with its deep window wells and its deeper bathtub with claw feet and a curved back that you could slide down, into the water. She loved Mab's Jasmine-&-Lavender bubble bath in the evening, and her 'famous French toast' in the morning. She carted around Okie, Mab's rescue cat, and kissed its partly missing ear. Mab showed Bean how to get Okie to stand on her hind legs for treats, and how to keep her litterbox clear.

One day Bean said, "We stay here?"

A routine of sorts developed during their visit. In the morning, long talks over coffee and Bailey's, followed by walks to the park and through the Zoo, to see the animals. Later they might do the rides on Centre Island, or stare up at the stars in the Planetarium. One day they bought sausages and hot-cross buns at the St. Lawrence Market; another time they went up the CN Tower, and had lunch there. Later, Mab showed Rose and Bean her job at the Toronto Public Library. She had them come to story hour, to hear her read *Where the Wild Things Are*.

It seemed that it was true, about Mab's miscarriage, that it was 'old hat.' Mab kept on being her same old recklessly cheerful self, cracking jokes, reminding Rose of bawdy old times, being irreverent about new times. "Oh my God, wait till you meet Mrs. Gory. That's my landlady. She looks like a talking haggis."

Rose said wryly, "We all will someday."

Bean's favourite part of Toronto that summer was the dogs. Everywhere they went, she had to stop everything, so she could pet them. And every dog she saw made her ask Rose when they were going to get their own.

Who had time to walk a dog? Rose hardly had time to pee; she couldn't get a dog. She kept putting it off.

That summer and other summers, she put it off.

Already, it was Thursday. Rose and Bean were set to return to Calgary on Sunday. The promised heat wave reigned in Toronto, and Mab and Rose, after Bean was finally asleep in just her undershirt and panties, were sitting on Mab's little balcony, drinking plonk and watching the summer night thicken in the trees.

Mab said, "You're so lucky." She'd had a glass or two by now, and the 'so' sounded like *zo*.

Rose was in the same shape. "How zo?"

"Isn't it obvious?"

"Um . . . not exactly. Can you give me a hint?"

"Well, you have *her*, for one." Mab tipped her chin in the direction of the room Bean was bedded in.

So it wasn't so old-hat after all. "I'm so sorry, Mab. I mean —"

"Nothing for you to be sorry about."

"You never did tell me what actually happened."

"I had a bath!"

"You're being a little cryptic tonight."

"You've heard the term 'bloodbath?'" Mab sipped. "Well, I had one. Literally."

"Couldn't Heath have done something? The guy was a friggin doctor!"

Mab poured them each another. "He did something, all right."

Rose put down her glass. "Oh my God, Mab —"

"Oh, it wasn't anything nefarious, he just covered his elegant ass, more or less."

"How? What did he do?"

"Took me to my place — we'd been down at the marina, remember — and ran a bath of warm water, and stuck me in it. That's where I sat all the rest of the night, bleeding until I was practically cross-eyed. Well, actually: until I was close to passing out. I remember everything going sort of sepia at around three a.m." Mab sipped. "It started at around midnight. By four or so it was over, so that was that. More or less."

"What did you do? I mean, after?"

"Nothing. I just wanted it to be over. I just wanted things to be back to normal. If you can call the life I was living at that time 'normal.' So I went to bed after the bleeding mostly stopped, and the next day I pretended it never happened. So did he, believe me."

"Sweet Jesus."

"Here's the thing, though." She paused to wave at a neighbour, and agree about the terrible heat. "It did happen. And it keeps happening. What made me think I could just flush something like that — a *life*, Rose, well the start of one — down the toilet? I see it even now sometimes. In my mind. The hard little lump of it with that eye-thing in the middle of the — I guess it would've been the head. If it'd lived."

"Mab." Rose remembered the night Bean was born. Her daughter. The pink-skinned nurse the next morning, placing the tiny Stella-bundle in her arms. Could anything be that small and still be viable? She'd wondered. "What do I do?" she'd asked the nurse.

"Don't worry, love, she'll tell you."

The two of them seeing each other for the first time in that hospital room. Rose beholding the tiny body that had come from her body and realizing suddenly, that, "I haven't even touched you yet."

The vague new face turning to the sound of her known voice.

Rose's fingertips grazing the downy skin, eyebrow, under eye, nose, chin. The baby's face easing, eyes closing.

"I'm so sorry, Mab."

Mab picked up the hem of her summer skirt and wiped her eyes. "It would've been old enough to play with Bean by now. Imagine. Our kids could've — that was my chance and I fucked it up." She bit her bottom lip. "And I could never even tell it goodbye. I'll never be able to say goodbye properly. Because I *flushed* it down the toilet. I flushed my *own child* down the toilet." She was sobbing now, her whole skirt stuffed against her face.

"Oh, honey."

"God," Mab laughed, remembering herself, "I'm going to ruin my dress. It's a homemade tie-dye. It'll be every colour of the rainbow, or I will!"

By the time they'd finished the bottle, the two of them were singing all the Gilbert and Sullivan songs from *Chariots of Fire* and boo-hooing like banshees. "Will you come back next year?" Mab sobbed, hiccoughing, laughing at herself. "Can we do this again?"

So after that, Rose and Bean went to Toronto for a few days every summer. It got to be a tradition. When Mab still had the apartment, they'd go to the specialty shops for treats, and to More than Cabbages, with its outrageous prices, for more treats. Some days they'd hang out on the Beaches; on others they'd walk over to the zoo together, stopping, like they always had to, to pet all the dogs, and for Bean to beg for one of her own. When Mab eventually bought her fixer-upper, Rose and Bean came out to Toronto, and Rose helped Mab set up the new house, which had a room for Rose and Bean, and then one just for Bean. If Rose had to go to an academic conference, Bean would get on a plane to see Auntie Mab. The time Mab broke her ankle, it was Bean she called for. When Bean hated Grade 7, it was Mab she had to see. By Grade 9 she was splitting her summers between Calgary and Toronto, between Rose and Mab, and that became another tradition.

That is, until the summer Bean disappeared.

Was it because there'd never been a dog?

Rose

The stove had long-since gone out, and the cabin was cold. Rose had one of those headaches that feel like a worm behind the eye, drilling, drilling. No pill could kill it. And she deserved it.

She crawled out of bed in the dim chill and laid eyes on the pilot. Byrd or Brad, or whoever he was, lay quietly snoring on something that looked like a cross between a couch and a sled, and no coffee was made. A small high window, flecked with fly bodies and cobwebs, showed a steely horizon under a quilt of low cloud. It was going to rain.

A hungry squirm in her stomach reminded Rose that she hadn't eaten anything since last night's shared supper of Ripples, tinned beans, and more than enough wine. What had she said, done, told this man last night? She knew there'd been tears. Hers. Lots of them, before she'd finally crawled into her damp and lumpy sleeping bag. She'd never learn. Blushing and fuming, she fished in her purse for a granola bar, shoved at her hair, struggled into her damp jacket. Behind her, the pilot gave a short snore and dug himself deeper. A snarl of greying hair showed above the covers.

Rose heaved her backpack onto her shoulder, tip-toed to the cabin door, and slipped outside, clutching her jacket tight.

Silence. A fall wind, small and steady as her headache, and cold as charity, out of the north. Cormorants rising like torpedoes on the winter air above reeds leaning in bright water. Her mind's dull freight was struck by a spill of sullen light. It was 5:40 in the morning, and Rose was hungover and cosmically tired, and shivering under an inscrutable fall sky.

She remembered that today was Thanksgiving.

Thanksgiving had been the end. The husband's lease on his new place would begin on the first of November, and he'd packed and hauled all the long weekend, never mind dinner; a moving van had waited outside on the curb; in the emptying dining room had stood

Bean — she'd been only eight then — asking if there was going to be any pumpkin pie.

Rose studied the empty sky. Was she here? Did Bean lurk somewhere in all this reddening green? And if she did, what rig or configuration would she manifest in, this time? Would Rose even recognize her daughter, anymore, supposing she actually found her? And how *was* she supposed to find her? Should she just go and stand in the bushes like when Bean was little, and holler?

And if she did, would there ever be an answer?

The postcard was where she always kept it, in her jacket pocket. She drew it out, gazed at its shapes and lines, long-since memorized, compared it with the wall of trees and water stretching in front of her, the same as trees and water anywhere. What had she been thinking, coming up here with nothing more to go on than a tattered postcard?

And that was where she finally knew it. There wasn't going to be an answer.

A whitened log lay half buried in the fine, damp sand, where ants and beetles, their day innocent of calamity, worked and scurried. Rose lowered herself down to the log, her backpack, with its unopened burden inside, sliding off her shoulder. Cold wind found her neck, and she shoved her chin further into her collar.

The lake was a blank mirror. No Bethesda angel would come to trouble this water, there was no divine cure, and there would be none, no matter how many leads she followed, people she accosted, pilots she hired. It was time to face it: Bean was gone. Fence kisses, Joan of Arc, hide-and-seek, all gone. Their whole long, brief time together, as though it had never been.

The backpack slumped against her feet, and she reached down, unlatched the clasp, and drew out a small brown paper-covered box addressed to herself at Annie's Northern Suites. Her strange, familiar handwriting and fumbling tape-job, her heart like ice.

Dona eis requiem. Words Rose had not thought of since church and childhood, suddenly in her mind. *Grant them peace.*

Trembling, she tore the paper off the package, broke open the cardboard case, drew out the three sleek knives Bean had once called her friends. Rose had kept them so long, they now seemed almost to be her own friends. They'd been a connection. A symbol of possible reunion, proof that Bean had existed, might still somewhere exist, be possible to know.

Holding the knives, Rose thought of a long-ago day, herself leaving for work, abstracted and busy, Bean, not much bigger than a real bean, watching her go. *Bye bye, Mama . . .*

She hefted the knives' cool weight in her hands: hello, bad old friends. Holding them lightly against each other, she noted for the last time their steel intelligence, their elegant length; observed her blurred reflection — her searching, tired eyes, her same worried face — in their clear blades.

Goodbye, old friends.

One by one she plunged the knives into the sand, each one delving as smoothly down as if this far shore had all along been its true home, to which it had finally been returned.

She sat back now and surveyed her work, the end of all her work: a signature of bone, blown by sand. And she thought of that other Thanksgiving weekend, the one when they'd watched the departure of the husband.

Was it because there'd been no pumpkin pie?

The wind was stronger now, pulling at her clothes, whipping her hair into her eyes. She stood slowly, hefted her emptied backpack, and walked away.

Abbey

What was it that she'd sensed, felt there in the weird, holy woods? She ran the way her T-shirt told her to, *like you stole*, not stopping, not looking back until she'd reached the cottage. Up its three wooden steps she fell, as her phone signalled an incoming email from Morrison, from whom she had not heard since the Bible was a three-page flyer, at least that was what it felt like. What the hell had happened to her since they'd left Kingston only twenty-four hours ago?

Despite the cold — she'd seen her breath out there just now — she was soaked with sweat and still felt weirdly sick. She surely must have picked up a bug, probably at school like she thought — after all, it was bug season. Saliva kept gathering in the back of her mouth, and she wanted water. And the thought of water made it worse.

What did Morrison want? Thank God, no sign of Parker and Iris yet. She thumbed in her password and swiped to email.

> ➤ *Hey gal, just had a gluten-free Thanksgiving dinner with my one kid, and it wasn't even bad. Ever heard of smoked tofurky? Me neither, till today. But anything tastes good if you drink enough with it. Thank God for the C-train. Anyway, I hope somebody out there fed you as good. So how's tricks? Haven't heard from you for a couple weeks. Must be coz you want to spare me the ugly truth of how you're gonna beat the crap out of me in Nov. Been following the new hill training schedule you sent last time you wrote, plus distance and weights, and some treadmill at night — great way to watch all of Yellowjackets, including out-takes! What about you?? I know, I know, you're planning to come first in your age category as usual. 'Way to go!*
> ➤ *Been thinkin, tho. Why don't we change the plans back and head out a few days early, do a bit of touring, stay*

in a nice place, eat some good food, maybe catch a
wine tour or two. It'd be like old times. Wouldn't mind
trying that Wild Valley one where you go all around in
a hummer (Google it up) and sample the best at every
stop. I know it's kind of last minute, so it's on me. Name
the day, and I can book for both of us. Lemme know!

She put down the phone. That damn old commitment-phobe, Morrison. Never satisfied with any plan until he'd reversed it twice. Never ready for anything, period, until it was too late. Though now the unready one was Abbey. How the hell was she going to run that marathon? She wasn't. Not if she stayed in the shape she was in right now. The race was only five weeks away, and she felt about as fit as Parker's kitchen. No amount of Red Bull would fix that at 32K. But they'd long-since registered and paid; she couldn't let Morrison down. Marathons were their thing. The thing they'd always done, despite all the stuff that didn't work, would never work, between them.

And a free week in wine country never hurt. She shook her head. Morrison had his bads, but he'd give you the singlet off his back, *and* his race number if he thought it would make you feel better.

Voices on the path drew her attention. Here came Iris and Parker, toting briquettes and marshmallows.

But wait. Wait just a minute. What, and when was she going to tell Parker about her long-standing little arrangement with Morrison, her ex, and so-called 'race partner?'

Parker was nothing if not laid back, but . . . And did she even want her long-standing 'little arrangement' with Morrison now? Now that there was Parker? Now that there was Iris?

Who at the moment, was complaining bitterly. "I'm cold! It's so cold! I hate it here!"

"We're almost there. See? There's the cottage. There's Ab."

"So what?" Iris made a fish mouth.

"That's not nice, Tad."

"I don't care. I want to go home."

"We're having marshmallows later. Don't you want to roast some marshmallows later?"

"Marshmallows are for *babies*."

Tears stung Abbey's eyes. Was she going to cry? And if so, why? Nothing was the matter except Parker and Iris bumping down the path, both of them hungry and cross. Which, far from a reason to cry, meant work for Abbey. Not just the delicate work of pleasing and teasing Parker, while subliminally shoring up Iris. Abbey'd be the one washing the salad greens and cooking the bloody burgers, and explaining that she couldn't go near their grease and carnal smell. Because she sure wasn't going to be eating burgers tonight, she could tell that right now. Even the word *burger* made her sick as a blood-poisoned cat.

Iris interrupted her litany of sorrow to look up and fling her hand outward. Was that a wave? A bug in her hair, an FU? In case, and in hopes of the first possibility Abbey waved, her eyes blurring. Maybe there really was something in the air out here. She was going to be so glad to get back to Kingston and her job, and her own place, her own friggin coffee in the morning, not that Folgers crap. Back to normal. Surely her stomach would settle once she was eating what she was used to again, and not all these damn hotdogs and Tater Tots that those two ate. And she'd be running on decent, predictable pavement, not creepy paths in haunted bushes. Bonus. The second they got back, she'd light out for the Running Room and grab some gear. She needed to get new shoes and break them in before the marathon; long ago she'd learned the hard way that you don't wear new shoes in a 42K race. That you never wear anything new in a 42K race, unless you want blisters in places you didn't know blisters were possible. Like underarms and nipples. New shorts were in order, too, and a decent-looking tunic. There was nothing like new running gear to make a person feel back to fucking normal.

And Abbey needed back to normal.

A breeze had come up and a mock orange bush scratched against the window, its expired blossoms frail as light. What had she sensed out there? Never mind, here was life, with all its ordinary rumpus and disorder.

She flung open the screen door to welcome a flesh-and-bad-tempered Iris and Parker. "Hey, you two, where've you been? It's time for dinner. And —" she looked at the kitchen clock on the wall above her "— we have to start soon; Dave'll be here in a couple hours."

She was so not herself. Did she really need to tell Parker anything at this point? Surely there was enough going on without rocking that boat. And life was always turning the order of things upside down; maybe she'd get lucky, and the whole damn thing would somehow solve itself.

Right now, as Morrison would say, she had other fish to fry.

Morrison

One advantage of Rose being up North: no damn shaving. Morrison closed his phone and rubbed his two-day-old stubble. A glance at his living-room window told him it was going to rain. Again.

He tried to imagine what Rose might be encountering up there, besides blackflies and bears. Not much, of that he was sure. Three and a half days till he was to pick her up at YYC, and he was nervous already; she'd take one look at him and know something was afoot. That gal, it didn't matter if she was off in the bushes somewhere or in the next room watching TV in her recliner, she had a way of smelling stuff if it concerned her. It wouldn't be long before she'd pick up on his damn expanded marathon plan. Why did he do the things he did?

If he could answer that one, he could quit running marathons.

The first drops of rain streaked the window, crossing the big panes in a thread of clear beads. What was the weather like where Rose was? He hoped she'd brought her long johns, and that her forensics at least served her current purpose. If anyone could find that weird kid of hers, Rose could. And for her sake, he hoped she did. Maybe if Rose finally tracked down Bean, there'd be more room in the world for Morrison.

Though now he'd gone and messed up again. Somebody he once knew said, "Who understands Morrison?" Morrison didn't understand Morrison. How could a person understand himself when he was walking around invisibly halved? When his self was both dead and not dead? When behind every bush, birthday, and Christmas tree lurked the undead, with its sad excrescences and sunk-penny eyes.

"Fetus Papyraceous." That had been one of her names, *Paper Baby*. A whole life, or what should have been a life, thinned and flattened to the size of a sheet of paper, a business envelope, a bad answer.

His own sister, drained to the spine by what? Him and his outrageous need to live.

But 'papyraceous,' he'd long-since discovered, was a euphemism, its dry tidiness suggesting art supplies and ancient scrolls, but instead referencing the unspeakable. He'd done his research, once Google'd become reliable; he'd had to, had had to know her in all her iterations, the fetal mouse cupped in surgical gloves, the wet marionette dangling from forceps, to be laid out in a stainless pan. One picture'd shown her as a crouching homunculus, an umbilical caricature of Rodin's thinker, all ponderous curvature and headless muscle. In another, she was a mucoid dancer, incipient feet jigging away from each other, bloodied head flung rakishly over a scrap of shoulder. Here she took the form of a beaten doll tied to a stump from which a set of bloated legs absurdly hung; elsewhere she might be an eyed placenta, a keychain skeleton, a flesh Martian with a thumb-shaped head of bone.

And all versions of her, whether flayed and dripping, or spread like taxidermy, he bore in himself — and all of them, in their eloquent abortion, had taught him one thing: She did not stay, the female part of him, would only shrink away.

If only. Because the thing was — how had he never seen this before? — she didn't shrink away. Not really. Here she still was in his fifth decade, and other than the sometimes good ones with his children, the only enduring relationship he'd had so far in his life was a grievous faithfulness to a bunch of teeth caught in one of his own organs. How pathetic was that?

It was getting late. For hours — hell, for his whole life! — he'd been parked in front of a fireplace where there was no fire. Dusk was spinning down like ashes, dissolving tables and chairs, veiling doors, filling up corners.

He knew he should get up and find a bite; sleep would tantalize and then flee him if he didn't. But he had a thing (he had so many things), and this one was about eating. There were times when he couldn't do it. Times when, if he merely looked at food, no matter how hungry he was, he'd be sealed back up in the room before time, the sly thief of his lost sister's space and oxygen and nutrition, his mere survival conferring upon him the status of murderer. Those were the times, like now, when eating wasn't worth it. When he'd rather shoot himself.

He could drink, though. And booze contained calories, too, last time he'd looked.

He yawned, wondering which bottle to open, yet not wanting to bestir his stiffened bones. What was the matter with his back? A heaviness and a painful catch made it hard to stand straight, an eloquent fling of pain kept hooking itself around one knee, a heated coat hanger, making him gasp. All those barrows of bricks he'd hauled to his garden, and the gardens of friends. All that running and racing. Maybe it was finally catching up to him. How was he going to run a marathon?

Abbey would leave him in her dust, that much was certain. Just like all of them. Remember when he'd told her about Danica? Back when they were together. Girl ran the fuck away. Couldn't deal with a ghost baby.

Who could deal with a ghost baby?

His gaze rose up the high wall above the stairs, to the sepia print of the marble lovers, with their sightless eyes and longing hands, their stone lips poised forever, a yearning half-inch from those of the other. *To Go Beyond.* Wasn't this what he'd always longed for? To go beyond with another person. Just one. Just once. Was that too much to ask? To *get* beyond all the weirdness and bullshit and disconnection that always happened with chicks, to that place of simply saying Yes.

What was it that eternally messed with Yes?

Morrison did. Morrison, whose yearning for oneness drove people away, whose bad-ass behaviors were driven by his craving for proximity.

He rubbed his aching knee, pushed himself up, then sank back into his chair, allowing himself just this once to be defeated. Too bad nobody'd ever come up with a remedy for the dead, a way to make them leave a person alone. If he knew the answer to that one.

The last daylight bloomed across the stone lovers, then faded. What would they tell him if they could talk?

He wished he could talk to Rose.

Rose

The pilot passed the Old Crow. "Here. girl. Good for what ails ya."

Rose thought, *You have no idea what ails me, much less what's good for me.* But she accepted the square bottle and swallowed down the burn. Warmth and ease, the fraudulent promise of temporary peace, flowed into her gut and out to her limbs, making them feel looser, younger, a little bit defiant. Defiant limbs. She liked that idea. The light breeze found her eyes, and she squinted, liking better the cold view of the lake. "I owe you."

"Comes with the service."

"Right." Rose made a face and took another swig, felt a fresh, more expansive wave of bone-pleasing heat. "Do you like being a pilot?"

"It's as good as anything else, I guess."

"What's good about it?"

"The sky."

Rose smiled. "Nice."

"And there's a freedom to it. I couldn't stand an institutional job, with all due respect." He tipped the bottle deferentially. "With this gig I can make my own hours, more or less, and there's nobody looking over my shoulder."

"Do you get tired of flying in and out of here all the time?"

"Never. It's always changing, up here. There's the different seasons. The animals. The weather. I like the wildness of it. But I do other stuff, not just this. I deadhead south once or twice a month. Vancouver mostly. Sometimes your neck of the woods." Another salute with the bottle.

"Cool." Rose scooched nearer the fire." You got any kids? You must have, you said you were done with that 'scene."

Byrd took back the bottle, drank, sighed. "Me?" He winced pleasurably. "Got a few."

"Well, lucky you."

"Guess that's one word for it." He drank again. "Not seein a lot of any of em these days."

"Oh. Why's that?"

"They're with different mothers, you know how it is, and living in different parts of the country. Kind of hard to keep track."

Rose gazed at the darkening horizon. "I get that."

Wind worried the low bushes near their guttering campfire, from which bits of bark and char sailed into their eyes. The sun would soon be gone. Above them, rags of sullen cloud hung like a purple blanket over the water that rolled, dark as a headache, toward the shore. Rose leaned closer to the fire.

"Cold?" Byrd kicked a hunk of driftwood into the flames and took another pull from the bottle.

Rose shrugged. "I'm good."

"Too bad."

Rose ignored that. Instead she concentrated on the alcohol's welcome assault on her veins and bones, her loosening tongue. "You're a pretty good fire maker."

Byrd sat back away from the heat, his lean face lit by the flames, and gave a comfortable groan of satisfaction. "Could be one or two other things I'm good at."

Rose grinned, she couldn't help it. "It would appear so."

"Hey, now." But Byrd grinned, too, and shoved his boots nearer the fire, held up the diminishing whiskey — "Little more? Nothin like a little more before turnin in, keep a person warm."

If there was a moment to stop, this was it. Rose imagined herself saying no thanks and making her way back up to the cabin. Even as she reached for the bottle she pictured her responsible professorial departure, the tossed-off excuse that it was going be a long day tomorrow traveling back to Calgary, etcetera, etcetera, and that she needed — this she'd say in her signature self-deprecating way — her beauty sleep.

Why, though? Why say it? Who cared? The blood was dried, the blades buried, she was out of touch with Morrison, who had his own weird agenda anyway, and the world as she had known, or hoped to know, it was done.

A fresh gust of wind snaked through, prickling Rose's neck and sending sparks up into the dark. Byrd leaned away from the fire, and toward her. "Why don't you head on up, and I'll make sure this is out. I'll catch up."

"You don't mind?"

"Nah. Just another part of the job."

"What about bears, or whatever?"

"All the bears've gone beddie bye."

"They better have."

"Don't worry."

"If you say so." Rose picked up her backpack. "See you in a minute." She looked toward him into the dark. "Right?"

"Yup. Gimme twenty minutes or so, to make sure."

"You got it."

"Hey, wait a minute, pretty eyes."

Byrd leaned away from the fire and toward Rose.

Abbey

Parker and Iris came crashing through the cottage door bearing shopping bags, a hamper, and a shared displeasure. How was she going to get the three of them through dinner? Her mouth was watering, and not from appetite, as she grated cheese and chopped tomatoes for lasagna, Iris's fave, and her own, too, under normal conditions, whatever those might be, anymore; what had normal been before? Abbey cycling to work in the morning, Abbey in a Danskin teaching privileged kids their pas de bourrée, Abbey alone in her skinny townhouse at the end of the day, the light fading quietly. Now look: Abbey sad as Lent in the summer home of people she didn't even know, and who for all she knew had no inkling their place had been invaded. With Parker, you never knew. He could've met them once at some drunken party and jokily accepted their 'you-should-spend-a-weekend-at-our-cottage,' only to find them mystified and polite when he later took them at their word.

It wouldn't be the first time. Earlier this very summer, Parker, who seemed to know, and be possessed of, invites from all people with pools, had magnanimously asked her to swim in a friends of friends' leisurely backyard oasis, only to have the friends of friends turn up, looking like they'd seen a ghost.

"Just because people say things like that, Parker, doesn't mean they mean them."

But Parker had laughed it off, enjoying the startled hosts' surprise, and turning the whole thing into an impromptu party. He appeared to be doing that now, getting into the cheese, sliding wine bottles out of brown paper bags, shaking out chips, wiggling his hips.

The sight of the wine made her stomach churn.

Despite the coolness of the evening, a film of sweat bloomed obscenely under hers eyes and breasts, which prickled and itched; her scalp itched; even the backs of her hands itched. She scratched, looked around, scrutinizing. Oh, God, did the place have bedbugs?

The thought caused a fresh wave of skin-crawling nausea to wash over her, and she steadied herself against the counter, where Parker was leaning to snitch pinches of waxy cheddar. "I love cheese when it's that temperature."

A flash of irritation lit her, causing her to sweat more. "Quit that, Parker."

Caught red-handed, Parker slipped the guilty hand and its accompanying arm around Abbey's waist, moving in close to nuzzle her ear. "Someone's in a bad mood today."

"Parker, I mean it, you're gettin me right drove today, with your foolishness."

"Aw, come on, Ab, just a little bit of cheese and kisses for a hungry marmot."

"More like an annoying idiot."

"Ah, but you know where I'm not an idiot."

"I know you're an idiot, that's enough."

"Ugh!" growled Iris, "you guys are disgusting. When does Dave get here?"

Parker pointed at the still-open door, through which could be seen Dave's red sports car. "Speak of the devil."

Dave

"Don't forget to wave," he said, as he pulled out of the cottage's rutted driveway, ransacking his brain. "Wave to your dad and Abbey." How was he going to keep Iris happy for the two hours of the trip back from the lake? She hadn't slept well the night before, Abbey'd said, and she was clearly not a happy camper. Dark skin circled her eyes, her hair was a snarl, and she was pressed up against the car door as though she meant to escape the second his head was turned. Fun times.

He gunned it up the dusty road, through deep trees and barbeque haze, past shelves of Precambrian rock and glints of smoky lake, the radio playing honky-tonk, Iris steadfastly glaring at her book.

Better try to make some kind of connection. "This darn car, I love it, but —" He shoved and struggled, trying to find a way to get all six-and-a-half ripped feet of himself comfortable in the cockpit. Never yet had he adequately managed it.

"I'm hungry."

He looked over at her. "I got gum. You want some gum?"

Iris had the look of a girl who very much wanted some gum. "No, thank you."

"It's Bacon Gumball. Ever heard of it?"

Iris stared out the window.

"Says here —" with his non-driving hand, Dave fished a foil tube out of the junk-filled cup holder "— that when you *chew* it, you get the crazy taste of smoked pork in your mouth, and you can make piggy bubbles." He savoured the small plug of tobacco he kept tucked inside his bottom lip. "A person should have at least one chance to make piggy bubbles in this life."

No smile from Iris.

"Aw, come on, man, don't you think?"

A slight away-movement of her thin shoulder.

Dude, he thought to himself, do better. "Or we could, like, listen to Quirks and Quarks."

"Huh?"

"You know what Quirks and Quarks is. We listen to it all the time at your mom's. On Saturdays, remember? It's on the CBC. It's that one where you can learn about glaciers and gluten and shit."

"Fine."

But Dave couldn't find Quirks and Quarks. "F — I mean, we must be out of range or something." Could that be? Was this the twenty-first century? He gave the radio a frustrated slap. "Jee — come on."

Iris turned from the window. "That's not nice."

"What's not nice?"

"Hitting radios."

Dave shook his shaved head, brows knitted. "I'm —"

"It's poor self-management to hit radios."

Dave heard Ali in Iris's prim comment, but chose to exercise proper self-management. "Can't argue with that."

They passed a stand of trembling birches with a whisper of winter in their leaves. Dave cranked the heat.

Iris studied her page. "Don't, then."

"Ouch."

A skunk waddled across the road in front of them on its tiny black-gloved feet, and Dave swerved. Both of them saw the animal disappear just as the car hit a rut.

Iris cried, "Did we hit it? Oh no, will it die? Will it make a stink?"

Dave tongued his tobacco plug. "We'd know if we'd hit it. Nah, this guy's just headin home from the bar. And anyway, if he does let rip, we'll be outta here by the time his perfume hits."

"I hate skunks."

"Skunks are citizens."

" I need to eat."

"I know a place that has pies."

"Pie isn't good for you. My mom says so. What kind of pies?"

"Cherry."

"I don't like cherry. My mom said it comes out of a can."

"No pie for you, then."

"There's more pies in this world than cherry."

"You sure about that?"

"I had peach pie last week! At my gramma's!"

"You never!"

"I did so. I had lemon, too. With *meringue* on it."

Trees streamed by, and more trees, their dreamy blur stitched with smoke and lake shimmer. Iris kept her eyes on her book, "I know a game."

"Is it a game you can play in the car?"

"Of course," Iris replied crossly. "It's would-you-rather."

Dave had never heard of it. "Hey, I love that game! You first."

But Iris had found Dave's tobacco. "Ew."

"You better leave that alone. It's not good for kids."

"Then it's not good for *grownups* either." She chewed her braid. "If you even are one."

"I thought we were going to play would-you-rather."

"We are."

Dave zoomed past a pothole. "Can you remind me how it goes?"

"You have to give the other person two horrible choices, and they have to pick whichever one they think is the least horrible one." She sniffed. "I can't believe you could forget *that*."

"Comes with old age." He shifted down to fourth. "Okay, fire away."

Iris took a moment to think. Then: "Would you rather . . . stay out all night in just your underwear, in November, or eat snot?"

"My own or somebody else's? That's kind of important."

"Aggh, you're disgusting!"

"And you're laughing."

"I am *not*." She struggled to manage her face. "Anyway, you're fat. Your arms are fat."

"And you're short. Besides, that's muscle, on my arms. Believe me."

"Well, you're old."

"And proud of it." Dave demonstrated with his best hideous, tobacco-plug- revealing, forty-nine-and-a-half-year-old grin.

"Plus you're, like, super annoying."

Dave chose to ignore.

"You really are."

"Somebody's gotta do it." Dave spit out the window. "Would you rather have ADHD and no medication, or serious bedbugs?"

"Bugs are cute. I would just be friends with them."

"Bedbugs're not cute, man, and they don't make friends."

"How do you know?"

"I've stayed in a few sleazy motels in my time."

"What's 'sleazy'?"

"They bite, you know, your cute friends. Sleazy means dirty and kind of . . ." He paused to think. They were passing a cottage. A mother, a father, two kids about Iris's age on a groomed lawn, playing Ring Toss. A scene from the innocent past. Was there such a thing as an innocent past? If there was, it'd been somebody else's, not his, with his workaholic parents and skulking siblings. He suddenly remembered another cottage, one from the not-so-innocent past, his father sunning on the lawn with his weekend girlfriend, while his mother lurked in the dark kitchen, downing G&Ts. "Sleazy motels are where bad guys go."

"So you're a bad guy." Iris snorted like she'd always suspected it.

"I'm your mom's partner. Guess that makes me a bad guy."

Iris sat silent, watching the autumn trees flash by.

"Would you rather . . ."

"What I'd rather is —" Iris folded her skinny arms across her chest.

Dave looked over. "Hey. Are you mad? Did I make you mad?"

Iris frowned. Her matted lashes shone in the late afternoon sun. Her hair was the bright red gold of the leaves blurring past outside the car.

"It's okay to be mad, you know." He looked over at her. "Wait . . . those aren't . . . are those tears?"

How the hell were you supposed to talk to a crying kid? Dave had only ever *been* a crying kid; he'd never had one.

Iris bunched up her shoulders and brought her elbows down hard onto her scabbed knees. A little puff of angry air escaped from her nostrils. "Would you rather have to live sometimes at your dad's crazy house and other times at your mom's baby factory, or have polio?"

"Where'd you even learn about polio? Mind if I smoke?"

"I read. And I smoke sometimes."

"You what?"

Iris yawned. "I smoke."

"Where the hell do *you* smoke?"

Iris's small body expressed resolve, her gray eyes on the far line of the water.

"Dude relax, I'm not going to rat you out." They drove on, Dave exhaling, Iris fuming. She kicked off her sneakers and stuck her bare feet on the glove compartment. Silver hairs gleamed on her brown legs, against which she leaned her battered copy of *The Secret Garden*.

Dave rolled down the window to let out the smoke from the cigarette he'd just lit. "You've always got your nose in that book."

"So?"

"So, what do you like about it?"

"I don't know."

"Do better."

"What if I don't feel like doing better?"

"We got a long drive ahead."

He offered the Bacon Gumball gum again, and this time Iris took a piece. "I like . . ." she said, half to herself as she savoured the sweet sourness . . . "that Mary Lennox — that's the kid in the story — lives in a *mansion*."

"Sounds kind of like our house!" He winked.

Iris grimaced. "I hate our house. Everything's always a mess, and it's *always* noisy. And there's nowhere for me to be alone, and I always have to help. My mom's always after me to do stuff."

"I know. I live there, too. But you gotta have patience with your mom. She's got a lot on her plate."

"So do I." Iris shrugged, her small silver-brown shoulder. "Well, Mary Lennox lives in an old mansion that has this other kid in it somewhere, in a wheelchair, and he never quits crying. The kid. And Mary can hear him sometimes in the night. At first she thinks it's just the wind, but it isn't."

"Sounds pretty creepy."

"Not really."

"Okay. But I still don't know why you like the book."

"Because Mary finds a special place. It's a garden, and it's inside a wall, but it's all grown over with weeds, and you can't hardly see any flowers at first."

"Can."

"What?"

"*Can* hardly."

"Who cares?"

"I care. And I'm telling you how to say it right because I care about *you*." Dave shot Iris a pretend-stern look. "So tell me more about Mary and her garden."

"Well, so nobody's taken care of it since the beautiful wife died. That's the boy's mother. And a robin lives in there. And there's a boy named Dicken who comes."

"What does Dicken do when he comes there?"

"He talks to the robin, and the robin comes and sits on his shoulder. And he and Mary get to be friends."

"I wouldn't mind being friends with a robin."

"And in the end, Dicken and Mary find the boy in the wheelchair, and the three of them fix up the garden, and it's theirs. It's their special place, right? And nobody but them and the robin can come there. And it's full of nice paths and leaves, and beautiful flowers that bloom just for them, and it's nobody's but theirs."

"Huh. I'd like to see that garden."

"Well, you can't." Iris was sulky again. "It's only in a book."

"But I bet a person could make a garden like that, if they had the right tools and a bit of help."

Iris pulled her Bacon Gumball gum out into a long gooey loop. "I don't know how to get any tools."

Dave flipped the end of his spent cigarillo out the window. "You know, my mom and dad separated, too."

"Were they mad at each other?" Iris asked. "My mom and dad sure were."

"Reason married people split up is cause they forget how to talk to each other." They were out of lake country now, and passing a field of poppies, acres of flame tossing in the late-day wind. "And the more they forget, the harder it is to start again, see, even if they want to." He rubbed his chin. "It's kind of like . . . gremlins get in."

"What do you mean, gremlins?"

"Well, like bedbugs. Anyway, it was a pretty long time ago, back when married people didn't do shit like that."

"What did you do?"

"I did what anybody'd do. I burned the school down."

A smile crept across Iris's face, and she struggled to master it.

"Now, I'm not proud of it, though." Dave fiddled with the tape deck. "You got that, right?"

Iris let her book slip between her seat and the door. "I feel like doing something like that sometimes," she said. "I feel like just . . . punching somebody. I feel like punching stupid Hugo."

"You feel like punching stupid me?"

Iris looked up.

"Go for it." Dave thrust out a muscled forearm. "Come on, I can take it."

"You're so dumb."

"First to agree. Come on. Hit me."

Iris considered. Then she hauled off, landing a timid punch.

Dave snorted. "That all you got?"

"Plus you're loud and — ugly, and you don't know *anything*." Now she was getting into it, the blows coming faster and harder. Dave could almost feel them. For driving safety, he pulled over under a shivering poplar, so that Iris, hair and snot flying, could shove and pound and despise him to her heart's content.

He waited until she started to slow down. "Girl, what's goin on?"

"I'm hitting you my *thoughts*." Under her tan, her face was flushed, eyes hard as heraldry. "And my thoughts aren't friendly." She caught him one on the chin.

"Ow. I can see that. Why?"

"Because you're just going to do what they all do."

"What? Who? What do who all do?"

"They leave. Always after a few months and I finally get used to them, all my mom's damn partners leave, same as my dad's! Abbey will too. And that's what you're going to do. You're just going to leave!"

"Iris." Dave turned in his seat and looked straight at her. "Iris, listen to me. Look at me."

She was sobbing, her eyes and lips swollen, hair matted across her scalded cheeks. But she looked.

"I'm not going to leave you." He pressed his lips together. "No matter what, I'm not — not ever — gonna do that. Ever. You hear me?"

Iris was picking at the scab on her knee, tears dripping into the soggy wound.

"I hope — Iris, I hope it's okay I said that."

Iris kept picking her scab. "Whatever."

He hadn't known he was going to say it, or that he'd had it in him to say. But now that it was out there, he knew that he was going to make it true. Whether things with him and Ali turned out good or not, he would be there for Iris in whatever ways she'd let him. For the long haul. Homework, hikes, the whole hullabaloo. He fished in the glove compartment. "Here's a tissue. Now let's go find ourselves some pie."

Byrd

The evening wind shirred the dark surface of Maxhamish Lake. Byrd stood and kicked sand over the last of the fire. "Gets cold quick up here once the sun sets. How about we head on up to camp?" His jeans, as he flung the sand, rode low on his scrawny ass.

Rose contemplated the ass with irritable wonder. All her life she'd disapproved of her body, deploring this curve, despising that contour, especially once age and gravity had caught up and got to work on her. How was it that men, even when past the meridian like this one, could still have these skinny adolescent asses?

"Sure." She stood, then stumbled through a head rush. When had she last eaten an actual meal? She couldn't remember.

"Woah." Byrd reached to steady her.

"Thanks. Sorry. I'm such a —"

The Old Crow asserted itself in her veins, slowing her thoughts, fumbling her words. Suddenly she felt shy.

Byrd was pointing, a grin spreading over his face. "Take a look."

"What? I don't — what is it?" The hand on her elbow was warm, reassuring. Was there assumption there? Should she withdraw from it? "I don't see anything." She drew her arm closer to her side.

But Byrd kept hold of the arm. "Man, use your eyes. Up there." He was pointing at a dark clump just like all the other clumps along the shore, one blurring into another as the day faded.

"I don't see anything . . . where?"

"Up in that — okay, look, see where those Saskatoons stick up behind that —"

"Oh! Oh my God, oh fuck . . ."

Byrd chuckled. "Not scared, are ya?"

"Christ, I thought you said there weren't any bears up here. Oh, God, oh my God, is it a grizzly?"

Bird grinned. "Guess I was wrong. Nothing to worry about, though. That's just a good old brown bear feedin up for winter. She's not interested in us."

Rose leaned hard into Byrd. "Jesus," she breathed, "Oh, Jeez . . ." Despite the cold, she was suddenly burning, sweat trickling between her breasts, pooling under her arms, finding her underwear. Of all the times for a hot flash. "Are you sure?"

"Steady, girl." Did he mean her or the bear?

The heavy animal raised itself up on its marshy hind legs, huffing and grunting, black rubber nostrils flaring.

"Oh, fuck, does she smell us? Is she smelling us?"

"Probably," Byrd whispered, "but did you see that fish jump a minute ago, there? That was a bass. Nice big guy. Place is full of em. That old girl don't care about us, she's heading on down to the water for a bite of supper."

As if on cue, the car-sized creature lumbered right past them toward the lake, feeble eyes peering, pie-sized feet smacking the trembling ground, sides swaying like a hay wain.

Byrd chuckled as if he'd dreamed up the bear himself, and set it going, just to please her.

"What's so damn funny?" Rose had recovered enough to feel the cold. And cold was always twice as uncomfortable after a hot flash.

"Just watch, now."

As if she had a choice.

The bear waded in, ignoring rocks and rolling logs, its ponderous head suspended from the mossy shoulder hump like a bucket from a rusty crane.

"She'll make her move here in a minute."

"Oh, fuck, *what* move?"

"Hold on."

Fish flipped and scattered in the shallow water at the bear's great feet, mouths agape, patterned backs like heat-sensitive missiles, turning the water to silver froth.

Byrd counted. "One thousand . . . two thousand . . ."

Rose wished he'd shut up. Now that it seemed sure the bear was busy with something besides eating her, she wanted to watch, to take in the strange beauty of its raw immensity. "You are as good as a chorus, my lord."

"Eh?"

"Noth — oh my God, look, she's got one, she's got a *fish*!" She squeaked the word, trying to keep quiet. "Oh, it's wiggling! It's so big! Why isn't she eating it? Why is she putting it on that log? Won't it get away?"

"Log's her pantry. She knows what she's doing. You watch, like I told you."

Twice more the bear plunged and pulled back, its leg-hold jaws flashing with catch, returning to the log to deposit its gasping prize.

"She'll tuck in in a minute now, and we should, too. Let's move while she's partyin down there."

Byrd grabbed Rose's hand and they scrambled up the bank in the fading day, Rose still watching the shape of the gorging bear over her shoulder. She felt envy, watching it. Envy of its life of hunger and satisfaction, of heat and slake, of sleep and feed. No past. No future, no conjecture or regret. Just this. Just fish.

"I wish —"

"If wishes were horses . . ."

"Are you saying I'm a beggar?" They were in the door. The cabin's only light was the dim remainder of this morning's fire.

"Nah, not a classy lady like you." Byrd turned to the fire. "Look at that. Still got a few embers." He grabbed a poker, tossed on a fresh log, shed his jacket as he dropped to the sad excuse for a couch that he'd slept on the night before. Rose was still standing just inside the door; she had that first-dance-of-high-school feeling, where you didn't know anybody yet, and you hung along the gym wall with the other losers, hoping, dreading, wishing you could just go home and watch TV, like you did on a normal Friday night. What was it they called you if you didn't have anyone to dance with?

Byrd regarded her. "Am I keepin you up?"

"Very funny."

Wallflowers. That was what they called those people. She moved closer to the fire.

Byrd smiled. "I don't bite, you know. You could always just come sit down; guaranteed to warm you up faster than standin there." He patted the couch beside him as a sudden rush of wind hurled a bush against the cabin window. "Not much to do out there till morning." A small oval of polished wood lay like an egg on the table in front of the couch, left there by some other party of hunters or fishers, and Byrd picked it up, working it between his thumb and forefinger like a worry stone.

Rose kicked off her boots; she couldn't exactly leave. "Will the plane be able to fly tomorrow?" she wondered, despising her cowardice. "I mean, with all this wind and everything."

Byrd canted his head in the direction of the beach, where the Cessna waited, tied off to a clump of small scrubs. "Never seen anything stop that little gal yet." He kicked the new log to turn it over, his cowboy boots businesslike. "Don't you worry. I'll have you back down to Annie's before you got your teeth brushed." He winked. "You did bring your toothbrush?"

Rose glanced at her watch. Nine-forty-five Calgary time. What was Morrison doing tonight? Probably still at his daughter's. Wasn't he going to her place for Thanksgiving dinner? It occurred to her that she'd never yet met his daughter. She must make a point of it, when she got back.

In the meantime, the cabin was getting warmer from the revived fire, and she let her coat drop to a kitchen chair by the door.

Byrd stood then, and took her by the hand to the couch, and she let him, blame her terminally bad judgment and the Old Crow; there certainly wasn't much else to do.

"There, that wasn't so hard, was it." He flung his braid out of the way, let his arm fall loosely across her shoulder, his jacket releasing its scents of sweat and suede.

In Rose, something stirred. A dark warmth that had nothing to do with the whiskey. She shook her head, No. But she didn't pull away. "I can't —"

Byrd picked up the wooden oval again, and began turning it, rolling and stroking it in his hands. As he tossed the oval from one hand to the other, his body smell came to her, grassy and peppery. "Can't what?"

Rose inhaled his smell, craved more. "This. I mean, I've got —"

"I know, I know." Byrd's lips found her forehead. "You've got responsibilities. You've got a house and a job and a handsome husband and . . ." He drew her face up to his, touched her temple, her cheek, the side of her mouth.

"I — well . . ."

He began kissing her now, his mouth hesitant, intelligent. The new log had finally caught, and was sending flares of dark light up the pine walls, transforming the rough cabin into a buttery cocoon surrounded by wind.

" . . . and a whole bunch of beautiful kids waiting for you to hurry home for turkey and stuffing . . ."

Rose thought, As if. She kissed back, though. She couldn't help herself. And she couldn't help that Byrd was unbuttoning her shirt, nuzzling her neck, fumbling with her belt and his own, pulling her down. In her mind she disengaged, backed off, made a stab on behalf of tomorrow's sober sanity. But her mind lagged well behind her body, which was obeying Byrd's hands. Her shirt was off now, her bra somewhere between the couch and the door, her legs languidly withdrawing from her trousers.

Byrd straddled her, studying, tasting, inhaling. "You're . . . God, you're so beautiful."

She looked up at him, embarrassed. "You know what? I honestly can't. I'm sorry. I feel terri —"

Byrd paused, playing dumb. "Can't what?"

"I . . . didn't come here —"

"To get laid by a stranger."

"Exactly. Thank you."

"What did you come here for? I mean — all the way up here." He was dampening the fire, fishing in his folded coat for a cigarette. "To nowhere?"

Rose pulled a rough blanket over her bare legs. She thought of the knives, buried out there in the wind, felt something move in her.

Byrd drew back to light up, stopped. "You're crying. I'm sorry. I'm really so sorry. Did I —"

"It's okay. You couldn't know. I came to bury —"

"You don't have to tell me. If it's too hard." He exhaled, the smoke ghosting out into the shadowed room. "What can I do? Is there anything I can do? I mean for you. Right now."

"Hold me. Please. Just that. Just let me fall asleep in your arms. Could you — could we — do that?"

He grinned. "That comes with the service, too."

Rose smiled through her tears "You're good. You are, you know." She was becoming dreamy from the cold and the long day and the bear scare, and the whiskey. "You're a good person."

"I'm a guy," he smiled. "Just a guy." Byrd fished for more blankets and found a down sleeping bag at the bottom of the bed. He unzipped it and pulled it up over them both, laid his arm across Rose's weary back. Rose turned away and at the same time pushed into him, exhausted, wifely.

Almost immediately she was asleep.

Outside, the storm kept on, bending trees and beach grass low, scattering driftwood, worrying the racing surface of the water. The wind in its tantrum grabbed at the sand, hurling it into the air and whipping it into arcane dunes, rocking the little sea plane at its moorings, sending animals to their dens. Inside the cabin, Byrd stroked her arm, and Rose tightened to him.

"Don't worry, darlin," he murmured, "all it is, is weather."

She slept then, out of the wind, with a man from nowhere curled warm around her.

Morrison

He was in bed, back in the house he grew up in. There was his same old dresser with the bits he'd carved out of it in grade ten and gotten in trouble for, and his desk, and the dormer window he used to sneak out onto the roof through.

But he was also somewhere else, some kind of Greek temple like the ones he'd seen years ago, in Corfu, back when he and Abbey ran their first pre-breakup race.

The house was dark and no one was there but him, lying in bed lonely, just like when he was a little boy after lights out, just like after breaking up with Abbey, just like always.

And like always, it all came back to the great questions. Where was she? Why couldn't he reach her? Why had she left him?

From his quilted bed he could see through the temple pillars the sober flares of stars, suspended like beacons in a clear cobalt sky, so close and yet so far away, always beckoning, always maddeningly elusive. How he yearned for them! Just as he had when he was a little boy, he held out a hand, in the fantasy that if he squinted just right, positioned his hand just so, held his breath long enough, he could catch one, he could hold a star in his hand.

But no star came.

Ranged around the room, which was somehow both a public space like an agora and his actual present-day catchall of a bedroom, classical Ionic columns rose to form a pediment. Unlike the Parthenon frieze, that frozen tableau of horses and warriors and whip-cracking charioteers, this surface bore the figures of the lovers from his yard-sale print. But instead of remaining forever poised and static as they did in the poster in his real-life living room, the figures now were alive and fluid, their muscular bodies breathing, sculpted lips softening out of the archaic smiles and into flesh.

A holy dread seized him as the adoring pair began to stir, turning their steadfast gaze away from each other's eyes, to look upon him, as he lay, so small and terrified below. The figures were silent. Static. And yet. Understanding flowed in a current from them to him. They were telling him something, their faces gentle, their draperies fluttering in the soundless wind. It was about her.

It was about Danica.

You named her for a star. Give her back to the stars. Be aware.

What did that mean? Morrison tried to speak, but no sound came. The stone figures turned back into stone. Above the pillars the stars burned on, solemn lamps hung in an unreachable sky.

Morrison woke up. It was fully dark now, and he was slumped in his grotty old recliner, and this time there was no doubt that he was hungry. He craved pickles. And cheese. And meat. He wanted cake. And he wanted good cold milk right out of the jug, to wash it all down.

On his way to the kitchen, he looked up at the picture of the stone lovers. Goodbye, he thought, goodbye. Who was he saying it to? He hardly knew. Maybe he was saying goodbye to Corfu.

How splendidly ruthless, how wickedly carefree he and Abbey'd been back then, hoofing it past temples and ruins, fantasizing about what they'd be eating and drinking later, full of the delicious shock of dumping each other, the anticipation of an alternate future.

And that future had come, the alternate one, that much they'd been able to pull off, but it hadn't turned out to be quite as grand as they'd each imagined, and it had nevertheless contained the other. Further races with each other. Outcrops and ambushes of the other, gaps where the other had been.

Why had they dumped each other? Too stupid to know any better. Too dumb to realize that you never really dump your past, that it's always waiting for you in a fresh disguise, around the next corner, after the next race marker.

And that maybe what you had wasn't actually so bad.

He found his way out to the fridge without turning on any lights; there was no need. Centered in the dark glass of his kitchen window was a bright curve of moon, whose light whitened the table, the chairs, the counter.

Below it hung a single star.

Stella

Standing in the hiss of grass on a wild crag above Nova Scotia's north shore, they survey what is there. Cape Split, perilous above its race of ocean, the riptides so far down they look like white stitches on ruffles of inky material; cormorants and gulls sailing on wind powerful enough that it nearly folds the few other hikers double and bends the long dry grass horizontal; wildflowers — daisies, vetch, false flax, blue cornflower — tossing all around, while swallows dive to nests hidden in mile-high cliffs; sky a blue wound.

They're dressed in leggings and a tunic, handmade leather boots the worse for wear. A silver medallion of a female warrior gleams on their collar. Tilting their head back into the lean of the wind, they swing their backpack to the ground and dig out their water can, consult a well-used map, fish for the remains of last night's hit. Almost out of weed. Soon they'll need to find some.

Though finding more weed is the least of their worries.

Nearly two years it's been since they went on the road, a month since they hitched out of Vancouver. Beds are becoming unfamiliar, and they can't remember the last time they had a good hot shower.

The weed performs its quick magic, mellowing their mind, freeing their thoughts. The past, with its brokenness and chaos come before them, but also their future, which is bearing down. *Ready or not, you shall be caught.* The thing is, now they want to be caught. They're ready for it. Now, after two hard years 'out there,' they know what Joan of Arc was trying to show them, with her strange get-ups and her burning vision, her willful isolation. In her own early way, the maid of Orleans had been an artist. An artist of armies and war, of heresy and spectre, but an artist nonetheless. She'd had no choice but to leave her mother's spinning wheel, her father's garden, to burn down the known world in order to make one she could live in.

And now she lives in Bean.

In Stella.

They pick up their backpack and turn toward land. It's time to take off the outward symbols of their calling, put on jeans and a T-shirt, and get found.

Abbey

Parker pulled up in front of Abbey's place to help her schlep in her stuff from the weekend.

Abbey said, "I feel bad about the way she left. At the end."

"The tadpole."

"Yeah, poor little duck. She wasn't happy when Dave turned up. And we didn't do marshmallows. I promised her we'd do that."

"We just ran out of time, Ab. Don't worry about it. Plus, she's always like that when she has to switch, remember? The tad'll be fine." He looked over at her. "You're the one I'm worried about. You gonna be okay? You need anything? Some 7-Up or anything? 7-Up's good for an upset stomach. I could go get you some 7 —"

"My period's late."

Parker paused in the doorway. "It's what?"

"It's late. L.A.T.E. Right?"

"How . . . late?"

"A week. Could be a bit more."

"Okay. But your periods *are* late sometimes, right? Sometimes you even skip one."

"They are. Sometimes. I do. Could be nothing. The flu was going around at the school last week. It's probably that. Anyway, I need to crash." She looked meaningfully up her stairs. "You should head home."

But Parker stepped back into the room and crossed to where Abbey stood. He took her hand in his, and raised it to his lips. "It wouldn't be the end of the world, would it? If there was a little tadpole in there?" His hand grazed her troubled belly.

Abbey took her hand back and ran it through her hair. "Well it wouldn't exactly be a picnic. My life's not set up for a baby. I'm old, for God's sakes. And we're not — you know what, Park, right now I'm tired. I just need —"

"You need to jump in the tub and cool off, that's all you need. By tonight you'll be right as rain."

Abbey managed a feeble smile. "Okay. See you later. Bye."

Parker gave her a peck on each cheek, a pinch on the bum.

"You'd look so cute with a tadpole tucked in your pouch."

"For fuck's sakes, Parker, there's more to being pregnant than being cute."

"Yeah," Parker grinned, "you'd be a mommy." He consulted his watch. "Or, I guess you'd say a 'mummy,' like the Queen of England. By the way, one of the guys and his wife from the market gardeners' association are throwing a party tonight. Down by the Time sculpture. Lots of cool people going to be there. Even some dancers, you'll like that, right?" He did a little ass-wiggling reggae move, then pushed a lock of Abbey's sweaty hair off her face, for better scrutiny.

Abbey waited. "What?"

"Nothing. Just lookin at you. You do look a little off. What happened to your tan? Your freckles look sorta . . . green." He shoved his hands into the pockets of his Bermudas. "Okay, call me after your nap. S'posed to be nice out tonight. Harvest moon, and not even cold. Be fun to bike down there later, check it out."

Abbey swallowed. "Okay, just let me get a rest first." She managed a grin. "Go."

"Kayseeyabye." Parker's breezy one-word leave-taking. He added his Elizabeth Regent wave, a hand raised and rotated like a stiff paddle. Then he jumped into his rattle-trap of a car — where did he get the energy to jump anywhere in this heat? — and roared off around the corner.

Abbey stared at her bags. They looked so stupid. So heavy. A fly buzzed idly in the entryway. She despised flies but didn't have the strength to deal with this one, a large and sleepy bluebottle. Saliva once again pooled at the back of her throat. Was she hungry? Thirsty? What did she need?

And why couldn't she tell?

It was two o'clock in the afternoon, an eerie time of day. Anything meant to happen was still far off, and anything that was going to start was by now long underway. Two o'clock was the daytime equivalent to the night's witching hour, especially on the weekend. At this time of day, anything could happen. She needed to get out of the house, with its vacant feel and stale air.

Instead of heading upstairs to bed, she shoved the bags to the foot of the stairs, shouldered her purse, and hoofed it, head down and sweating, to the neighbourhood pharmacy.

Hyper-fragrant air-conditioned cold smacked her as she pushed through the automatic door, making her gasp and turn up her collar. Glossily perfect women, to whom such things as rogue pregnancies would never happen, stared at her with flawless reproof from every Revlon banner. The store's bright aisles and cosmetic smells, always before so familiar and beguiling, were suddenly gateways to strangeness. Stomach churning, temples pounding, she found the 'Family Planning' aisle and selected a *Clear Blue Easy*. If *that* wasn't the euphemism of the century. What was it Mum used to say? "They won't buy the cow if they can get the milk free." Thanks, Mum.

The liquor store was right beside the drug place. Fronterra, her old fave, would be sitting on its usual shelf in there, waiting for her. Fuck, though. If she was pregnant, that was going to be the end of her old fave, and a few other faves, besides. She sighed. Only to her would this happen: pregnant at thirty-nine, single, and on contract. And no more wine to drown her sorrows in.

Though somebody once said it's okay to drink until you know for sure. And Abbey was going to a party, and she knew nothing for sure.

Blushing, she paid for the pregnancy test and then crossed to the liquor store. Maybe if she could go to a party and enjoy herself, things would be normal. Maybe if she did that, everything would go back to the way it was before.

Parker said, "They're super cool, I mean it." They were driving to the party, not biking, thanks to unforeseen rain. Also thanks to the rain, the evening's events had been removed to the home of the market guy and his wife. "She makes some kind of musical instruments — lutes? Is that a thing? — and keeps bees. Awesome, eh? And he's a chef. Food's always to die for at their parties." He paused to fondle a new peanut-butter critter that was perched on the dashboard. "They're super fun. You'll like em."

"Says you." All Abbey needed right now was super cool people. The nausea had fucked off, praise God, maybe that would be the end of it, but she was still weirdly tired from the weekend at the cabin. Could it be she had a bun in? Could it? The high hollow feeling was back, as though gravity were gone, and the world were about to be hit with the worst hailstorm. And mixed into all the other discomfort was something about Iris. Was Abbey annoyed with her? No. Was there something she'd meant to say or do before Dave came crashing in to pick the tadpole up? Not that she could remember. But the Iris-feeling did have to do with Dave picking the little gal up. There it was again, that pang, and suddenly she knew something. The pang was simply that the weekend was over, that Iris wasn't there anymore.

And that Abbey missed her.

Parker was off on the other side of the cool couple's courtyard, talking to somebody about finishing materials for decks, while Abbey hunched on a bench, studying the party and nibbling cool-people snacks. She wished she had the kind of taste and smarts and talent and balls that could result in an outdoor woodstove, a courtyard full of Edison lights, and a happy crowd of hipsters like these. She wished she could find some more Cheezies, and that she'd worn better shoes.

Most of all she wished she were home in bed, watching the CBC news.

Beside her on the floor, her bag hunkered like an unclaimed airport bomb, the pregnancy test poking through its soft side, an ominous elbow. She sipped her wine. Should she even be having wine? She looked over at Parker, who was egging on his neighbour, gesticulating with his beer. It wasn't fair. A man and a woman made a baby equally, and then all the real work and guilt and privation and boredom were handed to her. Here ya go, darlin, enjoy!

Screw that. Until and unless that test told her otherwise, Abbey was damn well going to enjoy herself.

More people were arriving. Was everybody at this party really going to be younger than herself and Parker? And when had that wee transition happened? Wasn't she supposed to be the youngest person at the party? She always used to be. She eyed a group of latecomers, so slim and tanned and belly-button-bejewelled, with their shiny hair and groovy wristlets, their downy babies in costly tribal-looking sleeves tied to their toned torsos, their superior ankle tattoos. Maybe she should get an ankle tattoo. Maybe she should put Edison lights in her weedy back yard, with its sad metal shed. Maybe she should plant more trees, make lutes, keep bees. She always filled up with furiously good intentions at parties, and the next day she predictably went back to being her same old self, which used to be cool, like these people. Somewhere along the line, it seemed, that had changed, too.

It turned out there weren't any dancers at the party, or if there were, they were choosing less aerobic forms of entertainment, such as standing around admiring themselves. Abbey was relieved. She didn't feel like dancing, or talking about dancing. She didn't feel like standing.

Corn was boiling in a cauldron, its queasy smell floating up into the autumn air, and hamburgers were grilling somewhere, as bottle caps flipped and wine clicked into glasses, and the patio gurgled with pleased laughter. Abbey kept catching herself yawning. Despite the high hollow feeling, she was hungry. And despite being back in town, she wasn't her old self. Every time she thought of Iris and her frustrating hair and the bedtime story of Alexander, her eyes welled.

Parker was fine, though, he was cool. He bounced across the courtyard and dropped to the bench beside her, his legs lean and brown from a summer outdoors. "Feeling any better?"

"Not much, actually."

"Nothing trivial, I hope."

"Jerk."

Parker took a pleased swig from his bottle, then brought his face close to her ear, his voice a confidential whisper. "I think you're going to have a little tadpole."

"I think I need to go to bed."

"Aw, so early?"

"So early. Look, I'll meet you at Jerry's for breakfast in the morning."

Rose

Who could endure flying? Even on perfectly normal flights, where everybody else was sleeping and watching movies and sipping gin and tonic (could she get one? Was it too close to landing? Could she get two?), Rose sat bolt upright in her seat, canvassed other passengers' faces for signs of alarm — what was the matter with them, couldn't they tell they were all going down? — and wished she'd remembered to bring an Ativan. Nothing would ever satisfy her that the plane was held up by anything save prayer and trickery. Only if the gods were busy elsewhere and Rose was beaming relentless concentration and prayer could a safe landing occur. Which by extension meant that a lapse in that concentration could send the silly ship and its two hundred and forty gullible passengers spiralling down.

To distract herself, she was writing — of all things — another poem. Not her forte, poetry, she was smart enough to know that, and she also knew she should be leaving the poetizing to those more competent but she wasn't on the ground yet, that was her excuse. What happens at thirty-thousand feet stays at thirty-thousand feet. Plus, she couldn't help herself.

Buried blades.

Animal hides.

A cold northern sunset.

Naked limbs in firelight.

A feeding bear.

Reeds leaning into winter.

Images from the wild lake kept rising inside her, and the only solution she trusted — the only one she'd ever trusted — was paper. She pushed the words and syllables clumsily back and forth, as though solving the puzzle of them might sooner bring her to the safety of earth.

Though earth couldn't save her from certain shocking new events of her own devising. Had she really just spent the weekend at mile three hundred of the Alaska Highway, and nearly screwed some dude with a braid, in an unfindable fishing cabin?

Her face went hot. Oh, God, she had done that. And what was worse: she couldn't stop thinking about said dude. And what had she accomplished up there, really, with her baffled heart and her backpack full of ghosts? A whacked bank account, that was about it. Though she'd known that much was likely. And she'd also known she'd had no choice. As long as there was a chance, the slightest hope of a chance — she'd had no choice.

Either way: satisfaction guaranteed.

Not.

The pilot announced that they were currently over Dawson Creek, and she paused her pen for a dutiful look down. Where was Byrd by now? Probably back in Fort Nelson, doing whatever bush pilots did when they got back to town. She tried to imagine him buying groceries, doing laundry, polishing up his boots, reinhabiting his place — an apartment? A house? She settled on something more makeshift, a rented room, a trailer at the edge of town, with space for his solitude and sky for his plane. He wasn't the kind who signed lease agreements, much less mortgaged and settled down.

The trees below looked distant, dark, impenetrable now, their secrets permanently sealed. Rose turned away, her mind bending toward the reality of Calgary. What awaited her there, besides a chilly house and Jeoffry's abandoned meow? Would Morrison take one look at her and know?

Did it matter?

The flight attendants were clanking down the aisle offering instant coffee, warm apple juice, stale pretzels. She had to pee, but couldn't bring herself to join the rumpled line-up outside the one roaring washroom at the back end of the cabin. Just such a lapse on her part could bring the plane down.

"Anything to eat, Ma'am? A cookie, bag of chips?"

Eat? At a time like this? "Not for me, thanks."

The movie of her last moments on the tarmac at Fort Nelson airport played in her mind as they lost altitude, the little red-and-white Cessna, its job done, standing primly still as though glad enough to be quit of her, Byrd in his aviators swinging down her luggage, that braid of his swaying in the bright wind, his face glanced with sun. Had all that been only this morning? Already it seemed years ago. She might not have believed it had happened if Byrd hadn't at the last moment slipped her the small oval of polished wood from the cabin's makeshift table. He'd looked up at the sky. "In case you need something to worry up there."

The way he'd used the word 'worry' in its first iteration, in the sense of 'grab and shake.' She'd loved him for that; how had he known it? But then, a casual wave. *So long*, the fringes along the sleeves of his suede jacket rippling in the breeze.

Across the aisle, an embarrassed mother jiggled and shushed a fussy baby, whose cheeks reflected her red jacket and matching cap. Rose wanted to warn the mother. *Don't scold her. Don't be embarrassed by her. Don't ever let go of her.* Instead she smiled, and offered the baby the polished wooden egg to take in her tiny hands. The mother was grateful. "No way I can read my paper with her this fussy." She handed Rose the paper. "Would you like it?"

"Sure, thanks." The paper was open to the real estate section. Sechelt, B.C. Property, water, clouds, trees. She imagined flying over all that wildness in a little Cessna.

She imagined touching down.

Abbey

Morrison's cell rang. It was two o'clock in the morning. Who the fuck would call him — was it Rose? Was something the matter with Rose? — at this time of night? Something must be the matter with Rose!

He fired himself across his bed in the direction of the bookshelf, and felt for his cell, knocking it and his glass of water to the floor.

"Yeah — ?" His voice sounded like wet crackers. "Hel —"

"Morrison, I'm so sorry —"

It was Abbey. She didn't sound right. "Hey fellow-marathoner, you know what time it is? You scared the shit out of me. What's up?"

"I can't — " She was crying so hard he could hardly understand her. "I think I —"

He sat up and turned on the light, as though that would help him hear better. "My God, kid, what's the matter?" His heart did a flutter.

Abbey cried harder.

"Jesus, girl, what's wrong? Are you all right? Are you drunk? Fuck, did somebody hurt you? If anybody hurt you, there won't be enough guys to pull me off the fucker."

"Yes," she wailed, though to what he wasn't sure, "No, no I'm fine, I'm —!"

Morrison was fully awake now, he even had his glasses on. "Abbey, give it up. What's going on?"

"I don't think — oh God, Morrison, I'm so sorry, I know we trained, at least you did, but I don't think I can do the marathon!"

"Okay, honey, but that can't be all that's the matter; I've never heard nobody cry that hard over a race before." This was classic Abbey, but he wasn't going to let himself get irritated. Helping women was what he lived for. Women, period, were what he lived for. "Look, there's one out in Sechelt, B.C, in November, and I'm not trained enough either. I was going to tell you that, but I guess now we're even. Why don't we scrap this one and try for the November one? I've got gobs of points, we could —"

"It's not that I'm not trained enough." Abbey gulped, blew her nose. It sounded like one of those old push mowers hitting a patch of wet grass. "It's that — I'm pregnant. I'm going — oh, my God, Morrison, I'm going to a have a baby!"

"How in the . . ."

The tears abated. "Fucksakes, Morrison, how do you think?"

"Jeez, I'm sorry. Ab."

"Sorry?"

"Well you're blubberin like a sonofabitch, you don't exactly sound like you're rejoicing."

A broken laugh. "It's exactly because I *am* happy, Morrison. I don't know what the fuck I'm gonna do, and I'm totally drove about the marathon, I really am, but I'm crying because —"

Morrison stared up into the shadowy air, as if it might contain an answer. "Have you thought about this? Girl, this ain't a race, where you just can go home after and shower the whole thing off; have you given this thing any serious thought?"

"Jesus Johnny, b'y, I just found out. Like, today."

"You ain't exactly a spring chicken. You're still on contract, you said so yourself. Do you even have benefits with that studio, you probably don't, right? Have you got a pension? Do you have any kind of leave arrangements? Have you told the — *him*? What are you going to do about him, eh? I presume it's that Parker dude. Is it him? Did he hurt you? Jesus, I'll —. And just tell me how you're going to teach dance when you're big as a barn door."

"I know! No, he didn't hurt me, it just happened! It was — do you think I haven't thought about all that, Morrison? Why are you being such an *article*, were you born on a raft?" Abbey blubbered again.

Good question. Why *was* he being such an article, as she called it? "Guess it's cause I am one." He smiled. "But right now there's more important fish to fry. For example —" he took a big breath

— "have you thought about the fact that this baby is going to need a godparent?"

Abbey laughed through the tears. "Oh, Morrison, you dear thing."

Mab

HomeSense was Mab's secret pleasure. Oh, she got happy in there! She couldn't resist its greedy jumble of kitchen and bathroom, its travel trinkets and food mills, its sketchy promise of a better life through brushed chrome and faux crystal. She wandered the untidily bright aisles, coveting stupid things like flavored coffees and bar stools, fondling table runners, gazing at gardening tools.

Though she wasn't here to browse and dream; Mab was on a mission. She consulted her list again. Curtains, dotted Swiss if possible; bedspread: matching? Would that be too cutsie? Lamp: anything available and tolerable; laundry hamper: size was the only criterion. Easy enough, all of it, to find here, but so neutral, so institutional; she wanted something more, something cozy and welcoming. She wanted something warm.

A shelf in "Sleep" sported edgy, self-deprecating teddy bears. Too young, she decided, even with the edge; could be interpreted as patronizing. What about a poster? In every conceivable theme and scheme they had them, but that could go sideways as well; who knew what pushed people's buttons nowadays, especially the young ones?

Comforters caught her eye in a cozy display, and she considered these, pushing back and forth the wheel on which they hung, until she found a star-sprinkled one the inky blue of the night sky. Some clever store arranger had thought of placing near it one of those kits of stick-on heavenly bodies, planets and comets, stars and moons, the kind that absorb light during the day and give off dreamy constellations at lights out. Mab was so pleased with the find that she rewarded herself with a bar of orange chocolate and a pound of raspberry-flavoured coffee.

Though when she got home, she changed her mind about rewarding herself. She didn't need the calories, and the orange chocolate and the coffee would be perfect additions to the comforter and the stars, She smiled, thinking how she would position the treats on the freshly polished and emptied dresser.

But then she sobered. What was she going to tell Rose?

How was she going to tell Rose?

Byrd

The coffee maker whistled. Byrd got up to yank out the cord — it pleased him deeply to hear its strident electric shriek sink to an insect whine — and pour himself one more. This was going to be his third. Maybe this pot would clear the cobwebs away. Three times lucky. And if it not, who cared? His social life wasn't exactly lively. Two days till his next gig, and caffeine was the only thing he could apply himself to. He looked with bemusement around his place. Damp piles of dirty laundry. Floors and windows grimy. Beer cans tossed in a cardboard box in the corner. Kitchen table covered in dishes and dusty to-do lists.

And all he could think of was a slender woman with guarded eyes and a backpack full of ghosts.

And of course, knives.

He shouldn't've, but he'd watched her. Out there on the beach, with her strange burden. It was a wonder she'd ever gotten through airport security. What, or who, had those blades been about? What had happened to her, to take her up there all alone on Thanksgiving weekend, with a bunch of knives, and no turkey to carve? He hadn't had the nerve to ask her. Though he could see by those eyes that she was carrying more than cutlery. Coffee in one hand, he started with the other to take his own utensils to the sink, run hot water, pour detergent. An orderly fragrance rose from the dishpan.

The knives wouldn't last long out there; she didn't know it, but he did. So while Rose was getting ready to leave, Byrd had pretended he was servicing the plane and instead walked down to the beach, found the log where she'd sat to bury them, and made them a proper grave.

Hard to believe that had been only yesterday.

He poured himself more coffee, turned off the tap, and set the pot down on top of the to-do list. The dishes could wait. He went outside and sat down on his steps to sip it, his eyes on the sky.

Iris

Wild geese were crossing the sky in a throbbing V. Lucky them, way up there, where it was empty and calm. Iris sat on the front step, whacking the heads off her mother's expired peonies, and eating a crab-apple jelly sandwich. An amber blob of jelly trembled on her left knee, magnifying her skin's small lines and creases. Sometimes that was all life seemed to be about, lines and creases. She wished she could live up in the clouds like the geese, and never-never come down.

Because where she lived, things were not so calm, thanks to a bunch of stupid grownups. As if things hadn't been bad enough before, now Dave was moving all his dumb stuff in. Plus, hello? He was bringing his new horn, that he was taking lessons on, and that sounded like Hugo's poop. Did anybody ask Iris what she thought of all this? Duh. Now she was stuck with Dave-*plus*-babies. She tore off a corner of her sandwich and stomped on it. Jelly blood spurted satisfyingly out from under her heel, and she imagined taking all the babies in the world and doing the same with them. Squish, there you go.

Except that now, far from squishing babies, they were getting a new one, and this one was heading straight for her dad's, thanks to stupid, knocked up Abbey. And guess what: when that baby came, Iris was going to move out to the treehouse, and she was never going to speak to the baby, or to her dad or to Abbey, no siree. She watched as a column of interested ants moved into formation to feast on the jelly, blithely unaware of how much danger they were in. Some of them were so dumb they climbed right up over Iris's giant shoe.

If only they knew.

The stupid grownups could tell her all day long that the new tadpole could be her 'very own baby brother or sister,' that she wouldn't have to share it with the others. Iris knew what that meant, and she wasn't buying it. She wasn't going to take care of Abbey's poopy-bum baby. Not ever. That baby could be sitting out in the middle of the road in a box, and she'd leave it right there.

Try to stop her.

The door creaked open. Dave stood in his sweats and bare feet, just like he was going to be standing there all the time now, until he went away. Because they always went away. Iris eyed him over her shoulder.

"Hey." Dave held a cup of coffee in one hand and a box in the other. A second bunch of geese flew over and then a third, talking goose talk to each other, as he lowered himself down beside her, his feet big and clean, and still showing faint tan marks from the summer sun.

Iris had never seen toes as humungous as Dave's. "Your feet are insane."

Dave took a sip of his coffee. "Why thank you. He looked up at the striving birds. Did you know that Canada geese can fly as fast as a car can drive?"

"No, and I bet it isn't even true."

"It is so. Google it up if you want to. With a tailwind, those girls and guys can do up to seventy miles an hour. That's enough to get you a ticket in a school zone. It's right there in Wikipedia."

Iris flicked away the crust of her sandwich, demonstrating boredom. "Wikipedia isn't a proper source of information. My teacher even said so."

"Don't believe everything you hear." They watched another bunch of geese grind by, the wind singing in their feathers. "Hey, I bet you didn't know that the collective noun for geese is 'skein.'"

Iris turned to look at him. "And I bet *you* didn't know that I came out here so I could be a-*lone*. For, like, once." The box Dave carried — she regarded it — appeared to contain gardening tools. She couldn't help herself. "What's that for?"

"Oh, this?" Dave asked, as though he hadn't realized it was there. "I picked it up the other day at Plant Nation."

"Plant Nation, what's that? That's a dumb name."

"I think it's kind of clever. 'Plant Nation.' You know, the nation of the plants. It's a nursery."

"Here we go again."

Dave laughed. "This one's not for starting babies, I know we've got enough of those. It's for starting plants. Did you know plants need a nursery too?"

"No, and I don't need any more teachers."

Dave let a small whistle escape around his tobacco plug. "Right, so, there's this neat little spot out behind your mom's shed. Kind of hidden and protected. Kind of babyproof."

"I know where that is. I go read out there. It's the only place that's quiet enough around this loony tunes."

"Oh, so you're the one who left the dishes and the teapot. Cool little spot, right?"

"Whatever."

"So when I saw these tools —" he rattled the box " — I thought maybe you and I could work that little patch up for next spring, maybe put a fence around it with a fancy-shmansy lock and key that only you would have, so it could be just yours, like in your book." He took a last slurp of his coffee, then tossed the rest of it into the flagging peonies. "I thought you might like to plant some irises in it."

"My mom wouldn't let me. She'd say" — Iris put on a smarmy English Country Garden sing-song voice — "'Oh, out there's just for the compost, nobody can . . .'"

"I already asked her, Tad. She said yes."

Iris shot him a look. "Don't call me that."

"I'm sorry. You're right. That was — That's your dad's —"

"My dad's the tad, not me, as in: a tad *messy*. Why can't he even clean his place up? What makes him collect toenails? Yuck! Half the time I don't have clean sheets on my bed, and he saves toenails!"

Dave looked at her hard. "We're going to make that garden. And you won't even recognize the place next spring. You'll come out here one morning, and it'll be amazing. We can even make paths."

"How do I know you'll even *be* here next spring." Iris spit the words out like bitter seeds.

"I'll be here."

"Yeah, right."

"We'll plant tulips and daffs. And irises. I promise."

"Promises are stupid. So are irises."

She gazed in the direction of the compost spot. "I forgot my name is a flower."

Rose

The magazine pocket in the seat in front of Rose held a crisp white barf bag and various other bits of information and diversion. Magazines. Menus. Maybe one of these would help take her mind off landing. She drew out the inflight magazine and flipped it open to an illustrated article — lakes, trees, more lakes — on Indigenous rites of passage. Vision quests among Sechelt's early tribes, the article claimed, included 'dream visions' or 'dream fasts.' Participants in the fasts were made ready for epiphanies by going without food and by sleeping alone in the wilderness. When they were prepared, they'd leave their community for an isolated place where, according to the author, they could be alone with their thoughts or dreams or night terrors or what have you. Depending on how effective the preparations were, sacred hallucinations would arrive, dispensed by the Creator and the ancestors, revealing knowledge about the participants' lives. Under conditions of privation, a dream visitor, or *pawaganak,* was thought to establish a relationship with the dreamer during the quest, and to serve as a guide for that person for the rest of his or her life.

Rose smiled wearily. Wouldn't that be nice. To have spent some hungry time in the bushes and emerge less fat, plus having a clue, for once, as to how one might carry on. Wouldn't it be great to be handed a vision of how to get through the remaining days, go to work, give a shit about what you ate for dinner, when the world no longer contained a centre.

If anybody could use a *pawaganak,* it was her.

She felt a sickening shift, and glanced out the window. The plane was tilting in its turn, moonlight spilling along its wing. She looked down. Calgary from the air at night was a glittering garden, a web of light. Rose obeyed the captain and put her table and chair in the upright position, then, to calm her nerves, tried to identify as many landmarks and neighbourhoods as possible.

The homing aircraft was following the north axis of the Deerfoot, itself named for an Indigenous visionary, a Siksika long distance runner known for his exceptional speed. Unlike their fleet namesake, the highway's lanes of hurtling traffic, viewed from the air, looked like bumbling lines of winter-stunned bugs far below, and yet so shockingly near. Rose watched the bug-cars with her usual mix of fascination and horror; thank God she wasn't driving down there. Though, was it any better to be teetering above that mayhem in a metal tube, in the air? At least in the air, she reasoned, someone else was the driver; she might get dead, but she wouldn't get arrested.

For Rose, whose stellar ineptitudes verged on the criminal, not getting arrested was a perk.

Now was coming the part she dreaded most: the hellbent descent, the apocalyptic roar of the braking mechanisms' reverse thrust, the leap of lights and land as the engines screamed, and the plane careened toward the outrageous fact of: runway. How was it — never in her life would Rose understand this — that thousands of people every day survived such arrogance and naiveté?

"Ma'am?" A young flight attendant who was probably about the age Bean would have been was moving down the aisle, collecting garbage. "Anything to toss?" She looked tired, which wasn't helped by the stagey heaviness of her makeup. Why did they have to get tarted up that way? The woman looked like a slightly frazzled version of one of those makeup ads on the oversize billboards you saw in the drugstore. Like if you got too close, you'd stick to her.

"No, but could I get a gin and tonic, please?" Just one. Just to get her down.

"Well, we're a little close to landing, Ma'am, but —"

"Actually, could you make it a double? Landing's not my comfort zone."

The attendant looked unhappily over her shoulder. "I'm not supposed — oh, sure."

Double G&T clenched in her hand, Rose gazed at the lighted stem of the Calgary Tower in the south; the cold twinkle of Canada

Olympic Park, and the orange blaze of sodium light that signified the new highway under construction westward to the foothills; the growing bedroom communities that kept the Deerfoot humming sprawled to the north. She recited to herself the ones she could remember. Ranchlands, Hidden Valley, Silver Springs, Rocky Ridge, all of them pastoral euphemisms for treeless hills cluttered with cheek-by-jowl rows of identical condos that, up close, she knew from having driven past them, looked more than anything like an epidemic of barnacles.

Somewhere to the southeast, her own small house lay nestled among old trees. It was a 'tear-down,' according to the real-estate agents and developers of the world — "It's the property that's valuable, not the house" — but compared to these herded suburban replicants, it was a monastic refuge, lamp-lit, hardwood floored, booklined, and guarded by her dapper valet, Jeoffry. A place to come home to. Now that she was so close, she was longing to be there, to unlock the door and smell the cottagey smell of the front porch, to drop her coat and put her bags down on a chair that was familiar. There. Even after these few days away it would feel unlived in; there'd be leaves to rake, the answering machine to listen to, the mail to go through.

But — now it hit her, and she trembled, her whole body shaking as the plane roared and hurtled — she wouldn't find Bean there. This time when she walked in the front door, she wouldn't even find the old habit of hope, that always before had lurked in hide-and-seek shadows and corners behind doors. An image of the buried knives winked on in her brain, their blades far down. Should she have left them? Had she been wrong to do that? By leaving them, did she make certain she'd never see Bean again? Morrison would call that superstition. Oh, Morrison. Thank God for dear old annoying Morrison. He was down there somewhere right now, God love him, waiting for her.

She polished off her G&T and craved another, but thought better. Instead, her mind went back to the knives, Bean's blades, sunk in that far, cold shore. No, it wasn't wrong to leave them. A bad habit of Rose's was hope. She had to quit. By burying the blades, she was telling herself to walk away, get over it. Stuff it. Relief might be possible now, if only a defeated relief. For two years, ghosts had greeted her every time she'd walked in that door. Maybe this time, for once, there'd be nothing there.

Maybe this time what she'd meet would be herself.

The plane's yaw became steeper, its pitching and shuddering more strenuous. Rose looked around at the other passengers, who continued chatting and checking their hair and eyeing their phones, just as if they were in their right minds. How in God's name did they do it? Now the crew were starting to take their seats. Rose folded her napkin and tossed her plastic cup into the trolley as the last attendant strove past, heading uphill toward the cockpit. The plane, having flown far enough south, was now banking north for its final descent, the wing — Rose was seated beside it — canted at a sickening angle, the busy highway tilting toward them. She closed her eyes and put her head down, she might as well relax; what did she have to lose anyway, if the thing went tits up?

But once again she was privy to the twin miracles of survival and arrival, the screaming roar and bounce of rubber on tarmac, a tsunami of forward energy suddenly hurled into reverse, cabin lights pinging and flashing, jolly little runway markers tripping past. Now she could see the trucks and trolleys that took care of the planes beetling back and forth, loading and unloading luggage, their drivers semaphoring light-stick directions, orange windsocks fluttering cheerfully. Mall music tinkled its inane reassurance through the stuffy cabin. Overhead bins were clunking open and slamming shut, flight attendants collecting newspapers and pillows, passengers unbuckling themselves and squeezing out into the aisle, as the plane taxied to its dock.

The world was back. The familiar was just outside the door.

Somewhere in the airport under his Tilley hat lurked Morrison, probably leaning near YYC's tacky wildlife-in-the-Rockies display of dusty stuffed bobcats and wax panners-for-gold, scrolling through his texts and emails, waiting for her. Would he want them to go home together? And if they did, would he sense that something had happened up there? She half wished he *would* sense it.

And that she'd booked a cab.

The intercom announced that phones could now be allowed out of airplane mode, so she touched in her password.

Two texts lit the screen, one from Mab, who never seemed to learn that you don't have to sign texts or emails, and one from Morrison.

> *Girl, where are ya? Waiting for you at Arrivals. Got some weird news. Wanna catch the Tuesday night special at Earls? Fifty per cent off on all bottles of wine. See you in five!*

Morrison had just learned how to use emojis, and he couldn't get enough of them. Cowboy hats, party decorations, sparklers, kisses, candies, and comets signalled his pleasure soon to be seeing her.

> *Hi Rose, been trying to reach you for the last couple days. Hoping your trip went well, and that we can chat soon. Shoot me a text when you get in, could you? Mab*

News from Morrison and an out-of-character 'I need you to text me' from Mab. And what news could Morrison have? A pulled muscle? A new recipe? A handy shortcut for making white sauce? Was Mab all right? All this before her feet hit the tarmac. Morrison would be chomping at the bit, but she didn't have to deal with Mab. Not yet. She sat back down to let an impatient businessman past, and felt something hard grind into her thigh. The wooden oval, from the cabin at Maxhamish Lake, dropped there by the baby across the aisle. She reached down and turned it for a second in her hand, running her thumb and fingers over its surfaces, so cool and smooth, so utterly inscrutable. What did Mab and Morrison need to tell her? What was so important each had had to send her a message ahead of time? The wooden oval dropped back into her pocket as she moved down the aisle and through the airport corridors to Arrivals, toward whatever awaited her, for her sins.

Two days away from home, and the world was stiff with news bulletins.

Abbey

Faded posters featuring plantar warts, fungal toenails, and STIs decorated the doctor's tiny consultation room. Waiting among them, she felt like a prisoner. Her offence: she was single, far from rich, preggers, and fast heading for forty.

The doctor, himself no beauty, scanned the results of the pregnancy test, and looked up over his metal-framed glasses. "Are you going to keep it?"

At first she thought he meant the Instant Pot she'd hastily bought before the appointment, and was already feeling buyer's remorse over. "Ex — sorry?"

"The pregnancy. Are you planning to keep it?"

Not the baby. The pregnancy. As if he actually *were* referring to the kitchen aid she harboured in the car. Just an object that could be returned if it was flawed, as long as you had the receipt.

She had the receipt, all right; already her bras were too tight.

The doctor was looking over test results. "Because right now the hormone levels aren't particularly stable."

Abbey swallowed. "I don't know . . . what's that mean?"

"Just what it sounds like."

Just what it sounded like to a doctor, maybe. Abbey blinked.

"Right now your progesterone and estradiol aren't in the right range. If they don't even out, you could experience a miscarriage. Wait a couple weeks. If that happens —"

"If what happens?"

This time the doctor removed his glasses. "Miscarriage, my dear. And of course we'll have to watch you closely for other irregularities . . ."

"Such as . . ." Her mind wandered to Parker, who at this point in the day was probably busy delivering his marvelous peppers, having just enjoyed a toke or two. She'd bragged she was fine to do this appointment alone. Now she regretted her folly.

"Older mothers run the risk of certain . . . chromosomal abnormalities, and as I said, the chances for miscarriage are higher, as is the risk of stillbirth. But give it a couple weeks or three, and if it hasn't self-aborted, come back and see me." He closed the file on which his very clean hands had been resting. Everything about him telegraphed *busy*. "Come and see me either way."

Older mothers. Here we go, she thought. 'Certain' risks. As in: Chromosomal abnormalities. Abbey supposed that meant Down's Syndrome. She'd seen Down's before. Back home on the Rock, with the neighbours next door. Little Binny, that she used to babysit for movie money, way back in high school. Dead these many years, of her heart. But such a character, with her scrappy red cheeks and patched corduroy overalls no bigger than your hand, and that fluff of ice blonde hair wafting like corn floss on the summer air. And you couldn't keep ahead of her; there wasn't a house in the neighbourhood that kid couldn't break into or out of, faster than a dog could lick a dish. She'd take your silver, your cheese out of the fridge, your cat, if she approved of it. By the time Abbey'd left for away, she'd helped herself to two or three cats. But popular! Abbey'd get her up on her shoulders and horse her all around the harbour, and take her to Kenickell's corner store for popsicles or licorice cigars, everyone smiling and waving at the pair of them. All that joy and fury, packaged into one 'chromosomal abnormality.' She stood up and shouldered her backpack. "Thank you. I'll let you know what happens."

She walked out into the small parking lot beside the clinic. There was a nip in the air that hadn't been there before. Late afternoon sun glanced off the crushed rock between the cars like regret. What had she been thinking of, putting herself in a situation like this? Her ankle turned on a piece of loose stone, and she grunted with pain. 'Thinking' was just what she hadn't been doing, all these months, with her foolish ideas about being too old for such a thing to happen. Her own mother'd had such a thing happen, and it was her!

A chucklehead she was, sure as you're born.

A sudden wind slammed a paper cup against the car. Abbey clutched her jacket around her neck, looked back at the clinic, that dreary home of green pre-fab siding and blind windows. To hell with that twit in there with his manicured hands and his steel wool eyebrows, she damn well *was* going to keep it, just watch her. But now a new shock bloomed in her mind. One way or another, keeping the baby — if the bloody hormones stabilized — meant keeping Parker.

In a heartbeat she'd keep Iris. Iris was why she'd stuck around this long to begin with, truth be told. But she'd never meant to carry on with Parker. Or had she? Who knew what a person really meant to do? Half the people on earth got here from people not knowing that.

The sun was gone from the parking lot, and Abbey shivered. Then she got in her car and headed straight for the most comforting place she knew: Buddy's Burger Bar. She was going to have a flame-broiled burger and serious onion rings, followed by a double chocolate milkshake, and to hell with that doctor.

So there.

Dave

'Plant Nation' was just the right size for a nursery, in his humble estimation. "I don't like too much choice" — he slurped his coffee in Iris's direction — "you know, like in some of those big-ass outfits like Sunharvest and places like that." Dave and Iris were pushing a two-tier shopping cart through aisles of potting plants and perennials. "You know what I mean?"

"Can I get an elf?" Iris pointed to a ceramic troll with a goofy hat and polka dotted overalls, cheeks like jolly boils. "I love elves."

Dave despised elves, with their runty bodies and faces of ecstatic criminals. "Get a couple if you want. You could get a girl elf and a boy elf. Or whatever floats your boat." He sucked back the last of his cold coffee, which still had the taste of being awake, of being on the move. "They could be friends." A person needed to be always on the move. He was craving more coffee — he was always craving more, of everything — and he'd spotted a McDonald's down the street from here. There was worse coffee than the Golden Arches variety. "Plus, they'll protect your garden, — elves have special powers, you know. Hey, you want to go to McDonald's after? I saw they got a two-for-one special on."

"Can I get a double-chocolate glaze?"

Dave knew Ali wouldn't approve. And he didn't want to rock that boat. So far, Ali was the one paying the dental bills. But he wanted to please Iris. "Yup." He winked. "Just between us."

"Let's go! As soon as we get an elf. I mean two elfs!"

"Elves. Two —"

"How about these two?"

A wind had come up, and Iris was cold. So they left the outdoor part of the nursery and were now working their way through the store's niftily expensive knickknacks and flowered gardening boots, its birdbaths, and expensively packaged seeds, its crocks and watering systems. A wall of barn board shelves boasted *Bulbs and Beyond*.

Dave scowled. "Why do they always have to do that 'beyond' thing? Beyond what?"

But Iris was busy playing with somebody's mutt. "Ooh, he's so cutey-cute, I wish I could have a dog! Why can't I have a dog instead of all those babies?"

"You got a problem with babies?"

"My mom sure does. She keeps on making them — example: Hugo the bubo. Plus, also? —" Iris made a cringe face. "Now *Abbey's* getting in the baby game."

"I did hear something along those lines." Dave scrutinized the bulb shelves. "Maybe it's something in the water."

"It is not."

"What is it, then?" Should he have asked that?

Iris gave a sly look. "You know what it is."

Dave plucked and tested crisp packages featuring pictures of bright blooms. Was he blushing? "Yeah. It's something in the water. We'll maybe get two or three kinds, I'm thinking. What colours do you like?"

"I don't like any colours."

"You do so. I know you like purple."

"I like pink better."

Dave smiled to himself as he pretended to read a seed package. "What if the new baby's a girl? You could dress her up all pink."

"And then babysit it. That's all I ever do. I hate babysitting."

"I get that. But this one'll be different. It won't live with you except when you're at your dad's or visiting us for a sleep-over. You can be its big special sister. You'll have fun showing it around and teaching it how to get on in the world."

"No I won't. Babies are all the same. Give em a year, and they're into your stuff."

"You know what, Iris, some people don't ever get to have any babies. I never have. I love you and Hugo and Pippa, but I didn't get to be your real dad. I wish I had. But now a new tadpole is wiggling into the world, and she — or he's — going to be part of your family. Well, of our family. I think that's pretty cool."

"Could I take it out in my playhouse at Dad's," Iris asked without a question mark.

"Why not? I mean, Abbey's going to be protective of it for a while, mothers are like that, and you gotta be patient, but Ab's pretty chill. She'll want you to be part of the kid's life. A big part, I bet. How about we get two or three packages of tulips and maybe a few more of the daffs. They're always a bit iffy — a bit daffy?"

Iris groaned. "You're so lame."

"Lame's my game. So, you need to plant lots of daffs, in case some of them don't come up." He looked into his coffee cup, as though he couldn't understand why it was empty. "And, way lots of irises, of course."

"Can we get pink irises?"

"I don't think they come in pink, but look at this" — Dave chose several glossy packages of bulbs. "You can get bearded ones! Did you know that there are irises with beards?"

"I want all bearded ones!"

"I'm all over that." He got out his plastic. "We could even plant one for the baby."

"We could show it to the baby after it's born."

"That would be swell."

"But," Iris darkened, "there's something you haven't thought of."

"Oh yeah? What?"

"It's fall, Dave, in case you hadn't noticed. They won't even be able to grow if we plant them now, and then the seeds'll be all wrecked. I learned about that in school."

"School doesn't know everything . . ." Dave scanned the planting information on the back of the package. He'd forgotten his glasses, and had to squint. "See, the deal with perennials is that you plant em in the fall, and they come up in the spring, it's not like with seeds. As long as you plant them before the ground's too frozen they'll do fine."

"What do they do under the ground all winter?"

"They party."

Iris pulled a spear from a dwarf cedar. "So funny I forgot to laugh."

"Hey, you break it, you bought it." Dave simulated a Popeye frown. "They do, though. Once they're down there under the ground they start developing root systems, so they can be ready to rock and roll once spring comes. In a way, it's magic."

"I didn't know anything could grow that's frozen."

"Sure they can. Even people can."

"That's dumb." She feathered her hand through the branches of the cedar. "How can people grow when they're frozen?"

"Sometimes people can be in a dark cold place for a while, too, right?"

"I don't like it in the dark."

"Most people don't. But sometimes grownups — and kids too — can find themselves somewhere they don't want to be. And that feels like a cold, dark place. Kind of like for the bulbs, under the ground. And when we're in a place like that, we don't know how long we're going to have to stay there, and that's pretty much the pits."

"Have you ever been somewhere like that?"

"Oh, yeah." They were approaching the counter with their purchases. So were lots of other people; they had to get in line.

"What did you do?"

"Not always much a person *can* do. You wait. I waited. 'Cause a lot of life is waiting."

"I hate waiting. Waiting sucks."

"Yup. But then when the waiting's over, and the light comes back, we appreciate the light more. And before you know it: irises!"

"And tulips."

"Right, and daffodils. It's like Easter. Ever heard of the resurrection?"

Iris raised an untrusting eyebrow. "That sounds like something my mom wouldn't let me do."

Dave mastered a laugh. "More than likely. You know, you're pretty smart."

"You're pretty not."

"And pretty hungry."

"Me too. Can we go to McDonald's now?"

"Would that make me smart?"

"It might be a start."

Rose

The captain's voice announced a problem. Too many planes trying to land in Calgary; they'd have to circle a while. Please keep seatbelts buckled, and seats in the upright position.

Rose had to pee, and she'd already read the inflight mag cover to cover. Where were all the *pawaganaks* when a person needed them? Somewhere in her carry-on was her copy of *To the Lighthouse*, so worn it was held together with an elastic band, the paper cover, with its art deco illustration of an abstract woman seated in front of a fireplace, jammed somewhere in the middle of the book for safe keeping. It fell open, as always, at the part where Lilly Brisco is thinking about the true reality of painting, about how you can plan and plan, 'airily,' away from the canvas, but that when it comes down to it, art is damn hard, and you just have to grind it. Many underlines where Lily reflects that the difference between an amateur and a real artist is that a real artist <u>finishes the picture</u>.

The words, always so satisfying before, were less so now. What picture had Rose ever finished? What, besides a few articles and two very amateur attempts at poetry, had she ever brought to fruition? The only thing that was done was Bean. There would never be grandchildren. She closed the book again. At least Lily Brisco's predicament, comforting if only in its familiarity, had distracted her long enough to get through the circling. The plane was now safely tethered to its gate. Rose stumped up the arrivals ramp, towing her carry-on with one hand and trying to tidy her hair with the other. What was Morrison's 'weird news'? Fear needled her. Morrison had cancer. No, Morrison wouldn't call that 'weird.' He'd call it 'stupid.' He was being transferred. Not likely. He was counting the days until retirement. *Spend your money and die.* That was his favourite saying, and he meant to make good on it, including a death race in Nevada when he was good and ready. Or he and Abbey were back together. Could he have managed that in a weekend? How far could a person go on points? And how would Rose feel about it if he and Abbey did get back together?

Considering. Firelight flashed briefly in her mind's eye, and she saw limbs, saw lips, heard the dark lake wind.

A woman was hurrying beside her, holding an infant in one arm and trying to manage a two-year-old girl plus carry-on with the other. Her sari had come partly untucked and was trailing, interfering with her feet. She smiled at Rose in mock frustration, and Rose looked at the little girl, then back at the mother, extending her hand. "May I?"

The woman smiled again, this time with relief. Rose bent and gathered the child up, parking her on her hip like laundry, the way she used to do with Bean, surprising how that came back, the wiry limbs clutching on, the knobby knees, the little girl smell of unwashed hair and sleep. Rose wanted to nuzzle in under the child's hair, have more. No, she told herself, no. Do not go there. Do the favour and get your butt out of here.

But 'here,' suddenly, was Morrison, under a fawn Stetson, being a cowboy for Rose's arrival in Calgary. "Hey, must be the new thing!"

Rose gave the child back to her mother and returned Morrison's bear hug, smelled his smell of fresh basil and soap. "What new thing?"

"Grandkids!"

"Nothing cryptic about you — what's this about grandkids?"

"You had one hangin off you a minute ago." He saw her bag come down the chute and lunged expertly to grab it. Then he winced. "Jesus. Ow. Damn knee. And now my hips've joined the party." He swung the bag onto a cart. "Good you put that pink ribbon on it. Makes it easier to tell from the others."

"Yes, Morrison," Rose grinned, "that's why I put it there."

"Where do you want to go for dinner?"

"I don't care." She reached to steady her case on the trolley. "That clearly wasn't my grandkid, but, anyway. And, did I say I wanted to go out for dinner?" But she was smiling. All things considered, it was a relief to see him.

"Well, I hope you do. Cause I made reservations at that new place up on MacLeod Trail."

"What new place? I thought we were going to Earls."

"And I thought tonight was Tuesday. They got a deal at Earls, on Tuesday. But it ain't Tuesday, it turns out. So instead we're going to Tabernetta. Way nicer. Italian. Gilchrist gave it a good review in the *Herald*."

Rose's phone buzzed, and there was another text from Mab. Mab, never wrote two texts in a row.

> ➢ *Haven't heard from you yet. Can you give me a call when you get a minute, please?*

Please. Mab never did 'please,' either. She slipped the phone into her pocket. "Okay, you can take me out to dinner. As long as I can have buckets of wine. You know me and flying."

"And you know how I feel about wine. Done." As they were moving past the Mac's Milk and through the doors to the parkade, a lean man in jeans and a suede jacket passed them, also on the way out. The fringe of his sleeve brushed Rose's arm as the doors swished shut behind him.

Parker

Where the hell was she? From the warm smell of the Boner's kitchen, Parker could tell the cinnamon buns were ready. Even the floury Tea Bisk blobs with minimal cinnamon weren't too bad, fresh out of the oven. Otherwise, it was better to stick with coffee. But Parker wasn't about to have blobs or coffee until Abbey showed. Maybe once they got talking he'd be able to swallow.

For the third time since arriving at the diner, he looked at the clock over the door. Abbey was still nowhere to be seen. The *Whig Standard* lay on a neighbouring table, and he pulled it over. Look at that: the damn thing was already stiff with Christmas, and it wasn't even Halloween yet.

By Christmas — the freight train of it suddenly bore down on him — the new tadpole would already be five months under construction, if the hormone levels steadied out, and with his luck they would. Jesus, what a dick he was. As it were. What an arrogant, dumbass dick! Knocking up somebody he hardly knew, and who had every right to give him the old heave-ho. At the same time, how could you not be happy about a new tadpole? He remembered when Iris was so small you could hold her in the palm of your hand. Those little sounds she'd made. Those fuzzy-wuzzy outfits with the stripes and snaps, that made her look like a junior criminal. The way she'd smelled! You could take her to parties back then and never see her all evening, thanks to everybody wanting to carry her around. For a while it'd been like he didn't even have a kid.

Though kids had a way of expanding. Before you knew it, the little beggars wanted to borrow your car. What was that thing they said about the little head thinking for the big head? That was the self-appointed definition of Parker.

"Hey." There she was finally, looking fresh and frightening.

"Man, you scared me! Where've you been?"

"In the can, darlin. Thanks to you, that's where I spend most of my time these days."

"You want a coffee?"

"Shoot me now."

"I guess that's a no. But you're nuts about coffee, you always have two or three!"

"I'm knocked up, remember? Right now that shit smells like earwax." She looked around the room at the muffins and buns and plates of eggs. "Everything in here smells like earwax." She swallowed. "And looks like it, too."

"So, Ab, what're we gonna do?"

"We don't even know if it's going to be anything yet."

"When will we know?"

"Next time I see that numbnuts of a doctor."

"Do you want it? You want it, right?"

"Do *you*?"

Parker slurped his coffee. "'Course I do!"

Abbey looked at her hands. "It's gonna be hard. But yeah, I do, too."

"That's the problem," Parker grinned. "It was hard."

Abbey looked at him as if she'd just received a notice of auditing from Revenue Canada. "You didn't seem to have a problem with that at the time."

"That's because I thought you were — that you couldn't get —"

"Coffee?" The proprietor was standing with a full pot at their table. Parker stuck out his cup for a refill. "Guess what, Jer,' Abbey might be having her own little tadpole." He looked from Jerry to Abbey. "Hey, Ab, wanna get married?"

"Actually" — Abbey, frowning held out her cup — "I've changed my mind. I do want a coffee." She looked up at Jerry. "Don't believe everything you hear."

Jerry grinned. " Eve and me got pregnant on our very first date."

"And now he's got seven tadpoles!" Parker put up his hand for a high five with Jerry. "Jer,' what do you call a bunch of tadpoles? A school?"

Jerry chuckled. "I call it Trouble!"

"More than one tadpole is a 'cloud,'" Abbey murmured, "a 'cloud' of tadpoles. And," she lowered her voice further, "'it's Eve and *I* got pregnant,' not Eve and *me*."

Parker grinned. And now, it's Abbey and me, myself, and I."

Abbey stared. "Parker, what the absolute . . ."

"Just trying to lighten things up."

"You picked a funny way to do it." She was fuming.

"I thought it was kind of romantic."

"Right. To announce to the whole effing place that I'm knocked up. It's not going to change anything, you know. The last thing I'm going to do is marry *you*."

"Nobody's forcing you to."

"Fuck you, Parker, who'd want to marry someone who keeps toenails in bottles" — she waved an impatient hand at the objects around the tops of the Boner's walls — "and thinks peanut-butter critters" — in air quotes — "are art, for the love of God? Never mind the fact that you can't even keep anything to yourself for five minutes!"

"Okay, I'm a loser." He tipped his head. "So what's the plan, non-loser?"

"Right now the plan is that I'm going the devil home." Abbey gathered her purse and her keys from the table. "The plan is that I'm going to take this — situation — one day at a time. If — IF — it's a viable pregnancy, as they call it, I'll raise it. I mean: her. Or him. We'll talk about the arrangements once we know. In the meantime, I have to scrap my marathon I haven't trained enough for. At least for now."

Parker for once could think of no smartass comeback.

Abbey shoved her chair toward the table as she turned to the door. "Fuck. Probably I'll have to can marathons forever."

Jerry's Diner wasn't very big. But suddenly it was very quiet. Parker regarded the room full of interested observers, as Abbey's furious departure set the branch of small bells above the door a-jangle. Then he stood grandly, hiked up his drooping cargo shorts, and addressed the room in general. "There goes my latest masterpiece."

He bowed.

The room broke into applause.

Rose

"So?" Morrison dipped a chunk of focaccia into a pool of flavoured olive oil, watching the oil and vinegar merge and separate and flow around the bread. His eyes narrowed with pleasure.

Rose was crunching hungrily on a curl of calamari — she hadn't realized how avid, after all that travel, she was for real food — and swirling her glass on its tall stem. "So what?"

"So what's *new*?" Morrison, who always drank faster, waved the server over for another. "We'll have a carafe of the same thing."

Though it was cold, they were seated on the patio behind the restaurant, heat lamps hissing companionably behind them. Sunset was nearly over, and the sky dropped its inky curtain through bare branches. Above them, strings of miniature electric stars pricked the thickening dark, spilling pools of warm light onto the hands and shoulders of the few other diners.

"Not much."

"I mean, didja *find out* anything up there?"

I found out I'm wicked and appalling, thought Rose with deep discomfort and a disconcerting undercurrent of pleasure. She felt a surge of adrenalin and the first itches of a hot flash — they always came when she was stressed — climbing her neck, needling the backs of her hands. Could Morrison tell? Probably not; he'd be teasing her about power surges if he did. Rose shook her head, sipped, nodded a lying 'yes' to the server's, "Everything good here?"

"It was a bit of a fool's errand."

(Emphasis on 'fool,' she thought).

"Aw, that's too bad. But you had to, though, Rose. You had to go."

The last of the trellised leaves whispered dryly in a gust of Halloweeny air. "I know."

"But I mean, what did you actually do? Up there. I mean, was it all awful or . . ."

"It was . . ." Rose temporized ". . . expensive." She took a sip of wine. "Considering that it yielded dick-all."

"Exes are always pensive," Morrison observed as he zipped his microfiber collar higher up his reedy neck. "Still though, imagine if you hadn't gone. You'd have always wondered."

"I would have, yes."

"So you talked to the locals and went to the police and . . ."

"Stuff like that, yeah. Though it wasn't all forensics. I did a couple touristy things, too. Went to their museum — they're pretty big on the taxidermy up there — and checked out a couple stores. I went to a church."

"Yikes," grunted Morrison. "What flavour?"

"Anglican." Rose smiled. "My weakness. One of them." She heard the muffled ping of her phone from somewhere deep inside her purse. "And I flew up to that lake, remember? The one on the postcard."

"That would've been cool. Wouldn't it?" He lifted his Grinchy eyebrows. "Good fishing up in those parts, if I remember. You do any fishing?"

Another gust swirled leaves around their feet. Rose felt its cold breath on her ankles, and pressed them tighter together. She hated winter. Heating bills. Frozen windshields, shovelling at five in the morning on eight o'clock teaching days. And it was coming. "No fishing. Though I did watch a bear fish for its dinner."

"Way cool!"

"It would've been cooler if there'd been so much as a clue. I mean — of her."

"Right." He looked up from his plate. "If there wasn't a clue, what all *did* you do up there? At that lake."

She looked down at her food. "Not a lot a person *can* do up there." Now wasn't the time. Right now, she just needed to eat and drink and find her feet. There'd be time enough to deal with the other. "Not really very much." She accepted a top-up of water from the server. "But I left those knives up there." She gazed past Morrison, to Maxhamish Lake. "You know the ones."

"I do."

It was quiet, the heat lamp bravely holding off the night.

"I had to do that much, at least, and I did it. To the tune of about five grand, altogether." She shrugged an *oh, well.* "It's just money." Now she could change the subject. "What did you get up to while I was gone?"

"Woah, not so fast! Did it help? I mean, to leave the knives? Where did you leave em?"

The server was suddenly there, two elegant plates balanced along one forearm, a giant pepper grinder brandished in his other hand. He lowered the plates, still hot from the warmer, with a deft flourish. Morrison surveyed his swordfish with canola and chia seed salmoriglio. "*Now,* we're suckin diesel." Rose's inhaled the fragrance of her smoked lamb shoulder, savouring its pretentious and lovely olive, anchovy, and fennel something or other. She breathed a grateful "We sure are."

"Okay, Miss Cryptic," said Morrison, deploying knife and fork, "I'm starving. I'll get more out of *you* later. By the way, what are you doing later?"

Rose ignored that. "Wait a minute. What's your news? Apparently *you're* the one with the news."

Morrison put down his knife and fork. "Okay, you're not gonna like this."

Rose waited, her own fork poised. "Okay . . ."

"Now, just hear me out. It won't be what you think."

"Do tell."

"Yeah, so, I found out Abbey hasn't been keeping up with the training."

"For your race."

"For Santa Barbara, yes."

Rose felt a small stirring of Schadenfreude, an emotion she disliked but allowed herself anyway. "Oh, how come?"

"Turns out she's preggers." He shook his head, as though he still couldn't fit such a thing into his picture of the world. "Jesus."

Rose chewed a mouthful radicchio. It was bitter. "Morrison, don't tell me . . ."

"Oh, Christ, it ain't me, if that's what you're thinkin."

"The guy out in Kingston, then."

"The same. The market gardener dude. Seems he fertilizes more than vegetables." Morrison tore off another chunk of focaccia. "Anyhow, life's sure gonna take a one eighty for that girl now."

Rose nodded. "A child does have a way of changing the world."

"Yep. And that's one change I'm happy to be spared at this point in my life." He snorted. "Can you imagine me changing diapers? Taking the little bugger out in the stroller? Worrying about lice and homework and vaccinations? Nosiree, that ain't my cuppa no more."

For once, Rose couldn't think of one thing to say. But she could feel a smile twitching the corners of her mouth as the Schadenfreude turned into a ripple of absurd relief. She wanted to laugh. Abbey pregnant? That was all? A desperate chuckle bubbled up somewhere inside her. Maybe their mutual follies would cancel each other out, and they could get back to normal. Whatever normal was for herself and Morrison.

Morrison leaned toward her. "But, what *do* you think?"

Rose looked straight back at him. "I think life happens."

Parker

The middle of the afternoon was a time of day that always made him feel unsettled. Parker unlocked the front door and let himself into his house. Stale, silent rooms. Tired light sifting like rain down the folds of the godawful drapes. Where had he even gotten those things? Some garbage yard sale? His Great Aunt Mildred, when she came back from being a missionary in India? He couldn't remember. He sniffed. Something was off in the kitchen; big surprise. He contemplated emptying the garbage, but instead gazed up the stairs.

"Tadpole? You up there?"

Then he remembered that Iris wasn't with him. He wished she was. He always wished she was. There were times, like now, when he almost couldn't stand how much he missed that little goofball. When he couldn't stand the ongoing toothache of not knowing exactly where she was. How can you not know where your own kid is? Or what she's doing. If she's even safe or not. Good luck with that. At this very moment his little girl could be — his mind's ever-available movie of kidnappings, drownings, car burnings, and superbugs unrolled on cue — but he couldn't let himself think about such things when Iris wasn't there. Instead, he kicked off his greasy Tutankhamun-era sandals and contemplated his feet, those hobbit's plates-of-meat he'd always been so pleased with.

What was so great about dirty big feet?

The stairs to the tadpole's room were silent, dim, hung in shadow. There was nothing else to do; he climbed them. Yard sale carpet. Stained walls. Dusty banister, still paint-flecked from some careless wall job or other. When was the last time he'd actually cleaned the place? He couldn't remember. The tadpole's door was ajar and he pushed it further. He needed to see her clothes, her bed, her books. He needed to smell her little girl smell of crayons and wool.

He sat down on the bed, still unmade from Iris's hurried departure with Dave at the end of the weekend. Something hard dug into him under the skewed sheet. A book. He'd seen her reading it, around the house and in the shack out back. He lifted it out, and studied the cover image. A Victorian school girl in a red coat, white skirt, brown old-fashioned boots, blonde hair flowing out from under a matching red cap. The child bent before a door that was almost hidden by a tangle of vines and leaves, a look of intense concentration on her small face, one hand on what appeared to be an ornate lock. Behind her on a branch, a fat robin, also keenly observing. Further back, a path along which Ent-like trees leaned. Around the picture grew a border of something pink — roses? — on a green ground, as though the verdancy of the scene had managed to creep out and into its very frame. An aura of intense mystery surrounded the child, as though she had stood there forever, frozen in time, waiting at that almost-hidden door. What was she waiting for? *Dad*, Parker could almost hear Iris saying, "If you ever read anything besides the leftover newspapers at the Boner you'd *know* what she's waiting for!"

And she'd be right. He was such a dork, with his 'art' and his Star Wars toys, his farts. What had he been doing with his life all this time? Aside from part-time hanging out with the tadpole: not a lot, he had to admit. What was he so scared of? Why was it he had to make everything funny? As though nothing were to be taken seriously. Not even life. Why was that? He hefted his daughter's well-used book in his hand, and it fell open along the worn spine. "One of the strange things about living in the world," it advised, "is that it is only now and then that one is quite sure one is going to live forever and ever and ever."

He snorted. In his case that delusion hadn't surfaced only 'now and then.' When had he ever thought anything about the world but that it would be happy to let him carry on, always, in his off-the-grid, quasi-bad-boy way, scorning the serious, sampling everything, committing to nothing? That kid on the cover wasn't the only one waiting. Parker was smart, he knew that. Why had he settled for building decks and growing peppers?

He stared down the hall at the odd shoes and bits of gear and piles of clothes waiting for someone to put them in cupboards and in the laundry. Why did he live in a dreamy mess that postured as a house, pretending he was an artist, and justifying his nutty creations with all that bull about subversion? 'Artist of subversion' — he rubbed his jaw at his foolishness — it was only a fancy way of saying: nonstarter. He studied the picture of the girl at the door. What was he waiting for? He'd already let Iris down bigtime, and he knew it. And now, thanks to the fact that he'd once again let the little head think for the big head, he was going to have even less time for her.

Did he want another tadpole? He was too old for another tadpole! But he'd been young enough to make one; now he'd better be ready to raise one.

And on top of it all there was the whole marriage business. He'd teased Abbey about getting hitched, and she'd gotten mad, as any sane woman would. But Jesus, what if she'd said yes? Parker'd always laughed at people who capitulated, who knuckled under, in big ways and small, to the Man. He'd called them 'bourgeois materialists,' with their tidy, tied-down lives. So dull. But what if those dull people were onto something? He stroked the book's cover, imagining it in Iris's small, purposeful hands. At least those dull people got to live where their kids were.

And: biggest question of all, what about Abbey? Did he want her? Or rather: was he man enough to want her? He sensed the room's presence, so hushed, so absent. Was this the first time he'd been quiet enough, alone enough to feel it, to feel all of what was there, and wasn't?

Abbey's wonky little house was just around the corner. What was she doing over there? Probably not a whole lot; she wasn't feeling very good, thanks to him and his gonads. What was her expression for a surprise pregnancy? *Up the duff.* The way she'd roll that off her tongue in happier times. The cheek of her! And the funniness and the smartness, the flaming, impossible beauty. The thought of all that still made the wicked pecker stir. Yes, God damn it, he did want her.

A greasy jumble of gray towels and cluttered hair products beckoned him from the bathroom, the walls and the fixtures still bearing the wear of long-gone roommates. How did Iris stand it? How did she stand *him*? He'd seen her little attempts at grown-up femininity — a hint of her mother's lipstick here, a guarded look there. She was getting to the age where she'd soon be able to see him for what he was. What kind of example did he want to set for his only — Jesus, *so* far his only — daughter? He turned and creaked back down the stairs. The living room — look at it! — was a cross between a yard sale and a mortuary. Unless you counted his Star Wars figures, nobody'd used it very much except for parties, for years. Nothing matched. The mantle had become a catch-all for stuff that wouldn't fit anywhere else. Thirsting plants languished like cornered orphans. And the crowning feature: the toenails, that looked more murdered than subversive, crammed like dead-guy parts in mayo jars.

When had he managed to eat so much mayo? Desolately, he scratched his ass. It was time for a new art form. It was time to explore the unfamiliar and truly subversive genre of: clean.

He picked up one of the jars of toenails, then lifted down another. Blurry and discoloured, they hadn't been added to in years. He didn't want them anymore. Didn't want to see them anymore. He started grabbing. Here. And here. And here. Get them. Put them on that table there. No. Haul them straight to the kitchen and out the back door. Get rid of the table too, the ugly old thing. And those fucking funeral-home drapes! He began yanking the heavy fabric, shoving the panels upwards to unhook them, sneezing from the sudden shower of ancient dust and dead critters.

He started stacking chairs.

The phone rang. For some obscure past sin of commission or omission, Revenue Canada was intending to break his knees, and those of his family. That's what happened when you answered the phone in the middle of the day. So he ignored the phone, went out to the kitchen, grabbed the greasy tea towel, then came back and cleared everything off the mantle, and wiped it clean. That done, he went at the clutter of books and magazines and old coffee cups and bits of curled-up toast on the table. He felt shocked, thunderstruck. Why hadn't he done this long before?

Now he saw — for once he really saw — the hallway, with its frayed mats and smelly boots, its heavy old hulks of winter coats. Through the bleary front window the verandah sprawled, a Steptoe's Junkyard of caned rocking chairs from the houses of long-lost ancestors, yellowing telephone books, tossed there and never brought in, garden implements rusting and forgotten.

But first the mess in here. Where was the vacuum cleaner? Somewhere, sometime, he'd stashed his mother's ancient Black and Decker.

And he better have filters somewhere.

So help him God, this place and everything in it was gonna get scoured .

Morrison

The server finished refilling the glasses and stepped away. Morrison raised his glass to let the light from the Edison bulbs above them gleam through. He squinted at Rose through the bright wine. "So, girl, I told you my news. What's yours? I know there's something. Did you really find nothing out about Bean? Did you at least get a lead? Yikes, I almost said 'laid.' You can tell my mind's in the gutter. Anyway, from the looks of you, something happened up there."

Before Rose could pee her pants with horror at Morrison's unwitting indictment, her phone lighted up. Mab again. Saved by the bell. "God. I'm sorry, Morrison, she keeps texting. I'm going to have to look at this."

R u back yet? Call me a.s.a.p.

That didn't sound like the twinkly, self-deprecating Mab Rose was used to. She didn't even write out the words properly, opting instead for those white-trash abbreviations both Mab and Rose had always said they'd never, ever stoop to. Something was wrong. Also, Morrison was keenly studying her, waiting for her so-called news. All the times she'd been bad tempered about Abbey, someone Morrison had known and loved for years, and now, here she was packing a one night stand with some guy in the bushes, while everybody else was decently passing the holiday pie.

To hide her confusion, she fished for her watch, which she'd taken off to change the time, and then forgotten to put back on. "How late is it out there?"

Morrison looked out to the street. "Same as it is in here, I figure."

"Out East, nimrod. Toronto."

Morrison consulted his phone. "It's nine o'clock here; so, it'd be eleven there. Just about. She's up, obviously; why don't you phone her."

"What, here?"

"What's wrong with here?"

"Don't be pissy."

Morrison laughed. "*Who's* being pissy?"

"Call Mab," Rose, with an eye-roll, commanded Siri; she still got a kick out of being able to do that. As the call went through she watched Morrison across the table, nodding when the server offered water.

"Rose?" Mab's familiar — but this time decidedly tense-sounding — query. "Finally!"

"Sorry, I was on a plane until half an hour ago. What's up?"

"Where are you right now?"

"What?" She looked at Morrison. "At a restaurant, having dinner with Morrison. He picked me up when I got in."

"I assume you're sitting down, then."

"Mab, for *God's* sake, what — ?"

"Rose." Mab sighed. "Rose."

"Jesus, Mab, are you all right? You're not sick, are you, is there something the matter? Are you in some kind of trouble? Mab, are you in financial trouble? Is something the matter at work?"

"No, no, nothing like that, everything's — all that's fine."

"Well what's going on, then?" Annoyance began to replace her alarm. "What's with all these 'urgent' calls? You're scaring me."

Mab breathed and took a pull on something. It sounded like a cigarette.

The server paused again. "Everything still good here? Little more wine? More pepper? "

Rose heard Mab exhale. The breath sounded shaky.

"Rose . . . it's about . . . it's Bean."

Rose put her phone down and went white. "What?"

Morrison leaned toward her in alarm. *What?*

She shook her head, made a hard little gesture of NO. The hot flash had passed as quickly as it had struck, and left her soaked, and shivering. Her voice was gravel. "Mab, get on with it."

"Rose, I can explain." Mab paused, as though waiting for Rose to do the explaining.

"Oh my God, Mab, she's — is she —"

"No, no. It's not, it's nothing like that."

Rose waited, not breathing.

"Rose, She's — they're — okay."

Not kidnapped or battered. Not waterboarded or murdered. Not so much as bored. "They?"

"I'll explain."

"Okay."

Okay. The outrageous banality of the word, with its implied habits and routines, its ascending of steps and choosing of tops, its routine boarding of trains.

The ordinary cruelty of it.

Rose's mouth was dry, her hand shaking as she passed Morrison her cell. "I can't." She watched Morrison take a quick sip of water, say Hello, ask Mab to talk to him. Watched him nodding, saw his eyes widen then narrow again.

Morrison looked up at her over his glasses, mouthed, "She's there."

"What? What the — what do you mean, *there*?"

Morrison paused the conversation, covered the phone. "With Mab. In Toronto." He winced. "She says Bean said not to tell you, or she'd have let you know sooner." He reached a hand across the table, pressed it down over Rose's. She looked back at him, gripping his hand hard.

"How long? Oh, here. Gimme that." Rose grabbed the phone. "It's me. You better talk."

"Well, Rose, I've been *trying* — anyway, they got here last — Rose, they've been here a week. Stella. They go by Stella now. Just a week."

Stella. She looked up. The first stars winked in the deepening sky, smug as graveyard cherubs. Nothing surprised her any more, or ever would again. "Okay." That goddamn lie.

"They actually got here at the end of September, but they didn't turn up at my place until —"

"What are you talking about?" Tears trembled in her eyes, and a commotion was building in her throat. She looked around to be sure of the washroom.

"I know, Rose. I know this must be —"

"Let's get one thing straight: *you* know nothing." But she had to ask. "Where was she? Before. Where has she been? All this time." She wanted to hurl the phone across the courtyard, crack the wall with it, see its ridiculous electronic guts spilled like jellybeans over the nice, civilized flagstones.

"They didn't say. Didn't want to talk about any of that. Not yet. Just said they'd been hiking around the last while, staying with friends, working a bit when they needed money, mostly in B.C. Mostly in Northern B.C., apparently."

So, she'd been there after all. Possibly even at Maxhamish Lake. Certainly in Fort Nelson. Rose might have run into her on the street if she'd been there a month earlier, or asked the right person, turned a lucky corner. She could have been this young person in a plaid jacket and backpack, writing in a journal in a café window; that hip young Starbucks server, whipping up lattes and making winsome heart designs on cappuccinos; one of the shiny guides at the ostentatious museum, redolent with deft youthfulness and superior knowledge. The nerve of them — she shook her head — of all of them. Them! What was this 'them'? They depended on you for everything for the first half of their life and the minute they were strong enough to stand on their own, they dumped you like dung.

All those fence kisses. All the bedtimes and morning times, all the long, slow hurry of school time. All that agonizing searching time, waiting time, aching time.

Them.

She shook herself. Wake up. "So, where is she — is she there with you now?" And what *was* she now? Did she still go about in Byzantine regalia and hedgehog hair? Had she gone prim and preppie? Did she trick herself out all in black, wear an earring in her bellybutton, sport a burlap sack?

For all Rose knew, she'd turned up in a news anchor's do, and professional chic.

"Yes, Rose, they're here."

"With you." She looked up at Morrison again, shaking her head in amazement. "Can you — can you at least put her on." Next question: Could Rose survive such a thing as talking to Bean, after believing, all this time, that she was dead, buried, gone? Could she really just pick up a phone and shoot the breeze with her, at a restaurant, where people were chowing down as if this were just any old day?

She could try.

"Rose, I can't." Mab's voice dropped. "I can't put them on."

"What do you mean, you can't put my daughter on?"

Morrison shot Rose a look. People at other tables were starting to pause in their conversations and show a special interest their food, in the way that meant that you could tell they were listening.

Rose lowered her voice to a hiss. "What do you mean you can't put her on, Mab, what is this? You tell me."

"Oh, God. I don't know how to tell you this."

"Tell me *what*?" She looked around the restaurant, at all those comfortable, self-satisfied people, whose own children, presumably, were delivering their papers or babysitting, or doing their chemistry homework, and who'd be where they were supposed to be when their parents came home.

"Mab this is not easy for me!"

"It's not exactly a picnic for me, either. Rose, it's just that they're not ready yet." A long pause. "To talk. Another pause. "But I think they're getting there." Mab exhaled again. "There's just . . . a lot to — work out."

Rose sat back in her chair. She wanted to laugh. She almost did laugh. Of course Bean didn't want to talk to her. Why would Bean, or Stella, or whoever she was these days, want to talk to her own mother? Bean had run away from her, hadn't she? Not only that. She'd wanted to do it so badly she'd crawled out a basement window as if escaping from some cruel orphanage, and disappeared.

And what did Rose get for a by-your-leave?

A tidy little post card from beyond the grave.

Clearly, she was not a person a resurrected Bean would wish to consort with, dead or alive.

Though surely, by fence kiss and hide-and-seek and winter afternoon, she would want, after all this time, to see her mother in person. She would need her. Wouldn't she? After all she'd been through? "I'll be there tomorrow."

"Rose . . ."

"It's no problem. I haven't even unpacked yet, I'll just go home and sleep for a couple hours and tell work there's a family emergency, and get on the red-eye if I can get a seat. There's always seats."

"Rose."

"Now what?"

"Bean, Stella, needs . . . um, they're going to be —"

"Morrison can take care of Jeoffry." She looked enquiringly up at Morrison, who nodded, of course. "Don't worry about picking me up or anything, I'll just get there when I get there, I can take a cab."

"They don't — I don't know how to say this."

Rose waited, breathing hard.

Mab sighed. "Rose, they need — she — Bean just needs some time."

"She doesn't want to see me." Rose felt her face go numb. "That's what you're saying, isn't it."

Mab sighed again, more heavily this time. "They will. Want to. I'm sure they will. Soon. We just can't rush it, though, Rose." She lowered her voice. "We don't know what she's — what their life's been like."

It must have been quite the adventure, to turn her into a 'them.' What did that even mean, 'them'? That suddenly she was plural? "Right. Of course. How could I be so selfish?" Bean had been anonymously hitchhiking and playing her guitar through the world for the past two years, while all her mother did was sit around in her empty house, wondering if her daughter was a sex slave, or down some abyss in the Andes. Shame on her for wanting to see her, now that she'd finally surfaced. "So what, is *they* going to be living with you now?" She hated the tone of her voice, knew she was being a harridan. Worse than. But she couldn't help herself. Some lid that she hadn't even known was screwed tight on an active volcano, was about to blow. "Is that it?"

"I'm sorry, Rose. I know how hard . . ."

"You know dick." She signalled the server, why she didn't know. "*You've* never been a mother." Then she realized what she'd said. "Oh my God, Mab, Jesus, I'm sorry, oh, fuck!"

"You know what, Rose?" Mab's voice was trembling. "I didn't ask for this. I've got my own life, such as it is, and my own ghosts, too. And God knows I wasn't expecting a kamikaze houseguest out of the blue, with no job and no place to go. But what was I going to do when she turned up on my doorstep? Say no? I knew how — Honestly, fuck you."

"Mab!"

"You know what, Rose? I love you, but right now I'm done with this conversation."

"Mab, I'm — you know I'd never —"

"Yeah, I know you'd never. But you did. Anyway, you know where they are, at least you know that much now, and you can rest assured I'll give them a home as long as they need one. They've got your number. Maybe once they get themselves sorted out, they'll be ready to talk. I'm sure they will be." Mab's voice trembled. "For now, it's been a long day and it's really late here, and I'm going to bed. Goodnight, Rose."

Rose clicked off her phone, looked back at Morrison.

The server cruised by. "Can I clear that for you?"

Rose heard in her mind the reply a colleague once used to deliver at such restaurant moments: *Not unless you want to pull back a bloody stump.* She wanted someone to pull back a bloody stump. It might as well be him. She glared.

The server blanched, backed away.

Morrison held his credit card between two signalling fingers. "We're good. We get the bill, please?"

Rose crouched in her chair, a trapped wolverine. She didn't even offer, like she usually did, to split the bill with Morrison. Bean was in the world. The world contained Bean. She should be rejoicing. Instead, she felt something darkening inside her, ink soaking into paper towel. "How can you say that?"

Morrison paused. "Say what?"

Rose narrowed her eyes. "That we're good?" Something feral coiled in her throat, something unfamiliar and dangerous. And the feral thing had an appetite. "You know what just happened."

"Yes, and I was just dealing with the bill, or trying to, so you wouldn't have to."

"Just the way you deal with everything."

"Kid, you're under a lot of stress. Anybody'd be freaked right now. But look, I mean. Rose. Are you going to say something you're gonna regret here?"

"It's about time I said what I felt like."

"Okay." Morrison waited.

The feral thing stirred again, more cruelly this time. "So . . . now that Abbey's pregnant . . ." Her lips curled unkindly around the hateful word and she despised herself as she said it, "what's going to happen about your marathon?"

"Not sure yet." Morrison managed to grin. "Wanna come?"

"Oh, so now that Abbey's out of commission, I'm good enough to take."

"Rose . . ." Again, he signalled the server, probably to come save him.

"At least I can get laid when I feel like it. At least *my* body works."

"What's that supposed to mean?"

"At least I don't have some kind of weird marathon arrangement . . ." She made a sound of distaste.

"Rose, I adore you, you know that, but I'm starting to lose my sense of humour."

Rose couldn't help it. Something inside her, both cold and hot, had been lit. The strongest need she had right now was to lash out, cause hurt, bring down judgment. "Fuck you, and I mean it!" The twisted words spilled out like blisters. *Fuck you,* all right. And she didn't mean just Morrison. She meant everything and everyone. She meant Mab and Morrison, and Bean, and most of all herself. Only a loser's prodigal daughter would finally turn up, and then disdain to see her. Rose's nose began to run, the first sign of impending tears.

"All set here?" The server presented the debit machine as though offering his arm to an alligator.

"I'll take that." Rose grabbed the machine, pulled out her own plastic, ignoring Morrison's, and paid the bill, adding an absurdly large tip. At this moment, she didn't care that Morrison looked spectral, that she'd hurt him, that the entire courtyard was silent, except for the soft mockery of the heat lamps' hiss. She shot a brief look at the innocent but interested pasta-havers and wine-sippers, then threw up her hands. "What are *you* looking at?"

Her chair clattered against the uneven floor as she half ran, half fell out of the courtyard.

"Rose," Morrison gamely hurried behind her, "girl, you forgot your purse!"

Also — her luck — her luggage was smugly stashed in Morrison's car. So much for a dramatic departure. How was she going to get home? Outside the restaurant, it was cold as Edmonton, the night a black galaxy. A wind had come up, one of those mean little pre-Christmas bitches that tell you there's only one way forward, and it's going to be icy. She sat down hard on the stone step and looked up at the stars through a blur of tears. So many times she had thought of this moment. The moment of finding *out*. So many scenarios. So many ways it could have gone down. Bean arriving at her front door, older and wiser; a wary but not-unwilling Bean, asking to meet her somewhere; Bean dead, and Rose getting some official goddamn letter, which would at least afford closure.

But Bean here and not here? Bean returned, and refusing to see her? She had to laugh at her own stupidity, not to have thought of that one. Her hope-springs-eternal naiveté. There was no understanding life.

"You wouldn't have gotten too far without this." Morrison stood on the step behind her, dangling her purse.

Rose said nothing. There were no words. There was cold, though, seeping up through the concrete step and along her bare neck. Somewhere far down, an ominous soberness was starting its chastening work.

Morrison sat down beside her. "Hey, it ain't every day your kid comes back from the dead and tells you to keep on fuckin off. And it's not . . ."

"Don't try to tell me it's not my fault."

"You were — you are — a great mom." He flung a pebble across the parking lot. "Whatever. A great mother."

"How do you know, you never even saw me be a mom. I could've been a monster. I must have been one."

"I've seen your house. I've seen the places where she isn't anymore. The cushions she used to lean against when you had your bedtime talks. Her room, that you've kept the same. The door you never open. The gaps on the wall where the pictures were."

Rose wiped her nose on her sleeve. "I must've done something. I must've done some terrible thing, some awful goddamn, terrible thing." She was freely crying now, her mascara bleeding tartily down onto her cheeks. "What did I do? Morrison, what did I do?"

"I got a better question. If you can quit blubberin long enough."

She looked at him warily, through wet lashes.

"Abbey's up the stump."

"We covered that."

"And if there's anything I hate, it's runnin a race alone. I was only half joking when I suggested you come along."

A great tiredness began to settle in her bones. She stifled a yawn. "You're still going?"

"I registered for it, may as well get a fuckin T-shirt out of it."

This time she didn't stifle the yawn. She pictured her white bed in the dim light, her down comforter, a purring Jeoffry backed up against her, using her for a heating pad. Sleep beckoned like a kind of homesickness. "You'll kill yourself, you dummie."

"Like I always say . . ."

"Spend your money and die."

"Words to live by." The grim grin. "So anyway, I've decided to run closer to home, and do the half. Just to say I did it.'."

"Makes sense, I guess. When?"

"Taking a long weekend. First of November."

"Where?"

"Sechelt, B.C. Be nice out there at that time. Not too hot, tourists gone. Why don't you come keep me company? Just company, no pressure." A sleazily raised eyebrow. "Unless you want some pressure."

"Morrison, you are . . ."

"Come on, girl, it'll be fun. I'll run my race and then we can hang out, do all the goofy little shops you like, take in an event or two. Get your mind off the whole damn thing." He paused. "Hey . . . hey! You know what? It's only a half. Anybody and their *dog* can do a half." A light, half-mischief, half-rapture, dawned in his runner's eyes. "Why don't you do it with me!"

Rose couldn't help smiling a little bit. "I don't like where you're going with this."

"Just hear me out. You don't have to be some super-athlete, all you have to do is finish. And take it from me, there's nothing for the suffering soul like 21K."

Rose considered. Twenty-one K. Water, clouds, trees, anonymity. A chance to punish her body. Away. Considering the shape she was in, maybe it'd be her very own death race and she'd be done with the whole nonsense experiment by the finish line. She looked up at him. "Fuck, why not."

Morrison chuckled. "I'm gonna hold you to that."

Parker

Almost time for the tadpole to show. Parker glanced out the door. Barely November, and already it looked like snow. White light brimmed in the emptied rooms. He'd explained to Iris on the phone about the house-cleaning project, but he was nervous anyway; Tadpole didn't like change, not even good change. From the scoured kitchen, the kettle sang, and he set his roller in the tray, to go make himself a cup of tea. Chamomile, ginger, peppermint, peach. Which would be the best tea for painting a nursery? More importantly, how was he ever going to be good enough to live with Abbey? She was so smart, so strong, so damn beautiful. He couldn't believe he'd actually gotten her pregnant, much less managed to persuade her to move in with him.

And what kind of tadpole would the new one be? And — oh, fuck — what if it was a boy? His gut tightened. With Iris, he'd been lucky. The kid had been born reading. And she'd never had colic or teething problems or temper tantrums. No weird shit at school, no eating disorders or bad report cards, no mean friends or bullying. All you had to do was talk to her the way you would to anybody else and let her stay up late occasionally, and she was good to go.

But a boy. Parker had no clue what to do with a boy.

Pomegranate. He tore open the foil packet and inhaled the red of it, poured the boiling water in, sipped.

Its clarity entered him.

As he looked out the window, he spotted Dave's car moving down the street and slowing to a stop in front of his house. He wished he had that guy's pipes, but he wasn't willing to live in a weight room. Like, who could stand that? He raised his teacup in a wave as Iris toppled out and came bumping her backpack up the walk. "We got it, Dad, we got it right in the back!"

Parker grabbed Iris and tried to lift her to his hip. "Damn, you're getting big." He looked where she was pointing, to Dave's car. "You got what? I know one thing you got: ice cream on your face.

Let me guess . . . chocolate." He winked at Dave, who was labouring to eject himself from the driver's seat. "Dude, you need smaller pecs or a bigger car."

Dave ignored the tease. "It's butterscotch."

"We brought the bassinet," Iris called. "My mom cleaned it. Dave's going to get it out right now."

Parker did a double take. Even though the tests were solid and the pregnancy was now good to go, he was still in shock that it was happening, even more shocked than he'd been when Abbey'd actually said, Yes.

Life, he thought. There was no accounting for the turns it could take. One minute you're a boho bread-maker with bare feet, scorning the establishment and selling necklaces made out of teeth; the next you're just an ordinary guy past forty, hurrying up to get respectable, and not too much to do it with. But he was sure going to try. What more could a person do, than try? He thought of his unfinished teaching degree, forsaken in a fit of 'originality.' All he needed was his practicum and one last course in pedagogy.

He swung Iris out into the late-autumn day. "A nice clean bassinet. We're in business!"

Rose

A cat-faced clock, one of the few remaining artifacts of Bean's childhood, meowed eight p.m. from Rose's office wall. Fast-food containers teetered on the corner of her desk, her mouth tasted sour, and the stack of essays on Hamlet's antic disposition, waiting since before the Thanksgiving weekend, sat half marked under the circle of lamplight. The students were rightly complaining; she had to finish the marking before she left tonight. The Sechelt half marathon was coming up, and the work needed to be handed back before she left town.

From the window behind her desk, she could see yellow leaves in the streetlight, twirling down to the concrete paths where, far below, the occasional student crossed. She'd go brush her teeth before tackling the rest of the stale pile. Anything to stave off the brain cramp of combing through another eighteen papers with little to recommend them beyond Wikipedia.

Rose loved Hamlet. Loved his bravery and passion, his reverence and humour, his hot heart, his infuriating, so-human hesitation. How could the students not see that they were just like him? Instead they bridled because 'waah, it's Shakespeare!,' and complained that he had no relevance for their lives. She snorted. Wait 'til they got themselves hexed and vexed, and betrayed and martyred. Wait till they lost their wits, their eyes, and their narrow little minds.

I loved you ever.

Wait till they lost their daughters.

The cleaning staff had arrived, unlocking doors and banging containers, shaking out garbage bags. Rose took the moment to grab her toothbrush and her phone, head to the washroom. Maybe she'd treat herself to one of those too-sweet vending machine coffees. That way she'd have an excuse to go brush her teeth again before too long. Anything to pause the marking.

Her phone lit up as she pushed her chair back. A non-Calgary area code. She didn't recognize the rest of the number on the display. But she was reasonably lonely, and terminally bored. Right now she'd suffer a telemarketer's inane questions about the lady of the house and possible chimney-cleanings, to have a human interaction.

"Yes?" Her don't-fuck-with-me voice.

"Rose? Is this . . . Rose Canning?"

The voice was faintly familiar. Where had she heard it before? She summoned her automatic response to such queries. "What can I do for you?"

There was a pause on the other end of the line, a faint intake of startled breath. "I don't know if you remember me . . ."

"Who's speaking?" She wanted that coffee. Irritation, the reliable harbinger of a hot flash, began to prick her neck.

"It's Byrd. From . . ."

The pilot. Distant images of a cold sky and a dark lake, hungry bodies and whiskey-fueled embraces, flickered in remembered firelight. "Oh." She sat back down. "Hello."

"I hope I'm not disturbing you."

Of course he was disturbing her. He was disturbing her plenty. "It's fine. Nice to hear from you," she lied. "How are things up north?"

"Far as I know, they're fine."

What was that supposed to mean? "Okay. I mean, that's good. I guess."

"I'm actually not in the north right now."

Rose couldn't get a grab on any shape of sentence. Her thoughts were a slow jumble. "Oh?"

"Yeah, I deadheaded in to YYC this morning. Been walking around a bit, admiring the view. Wondered if you might feel like meeting up for a bite of dinner somewhere. I'm in town until tomorrow noon."

Now the voice came back. So did the tanned skin, the lean limbs. The swinging braid as he hefted down her luggage that last morning, his aviators glinting in the sun. The hands. Hunger, wayward and absurd, stirred in her. Christ Almighty, he was here.

"I'm um . . . I'm . . . I'm kind of marking to a deadline tonight."

"Oh, hey, no problem, it's not like I gave you a load of notice." He laughed, a pleasant sound, and she remembered it. "I'll find something to do."

Now Rose laughed, surprising herself. "This is Calgary. After sunset it's pretty minimal out there. Trust me."

"I brought a book."

"You'll need it."

"Guess that's a no."

Today was Thursday. Tomorrow morning she was heading out to the airport herself, to fly to Sechelt with Morrison.

But what was her commitment to Morrison? She wished she knew. And when would she ever see Byrd, that strange citizen of the sky, again? "The marking can wait a little longer." Famous last words. "I'm about to leave town myself for a couple days, so it'll have to be short, but there's a sports bar around the corner from my house. It's called Wicked Wings." She named the cross streets. "I can meet you there for a quick drink in forty minutes."

"See you at Wicked Wings."

Emphasis, Rose thought, on 'wicked.' What the hell-on-wheels was she doing?

Parker

Parker put Iris down and hitched up his pants to go help Dave get the bassinet out of the car. Now he remembered the beribboned basket, an adorable whim of Ali's, though he hadn't seen it since the tadpole'd been bouncing in it. The first tadpole, that is. The one who right now was about to run upstairs to the little back room, to clear a space for all things infant. After Iris, the bassinet had been resurrected for Pippa, and then for Odessa and Hugo. Though it had been cleaned, the bunting was grey looking, and the headboard had seen better days. Paint in places was chipped off, showing the metal underneath. He'd need to give the dear old ugly a bit of a going over out in the shop.

"Got your end?" Dave lifted and shoved the front end out over the hatchback, and Parker hauled from the trunk. Their eyes met somewhere in the middle, and Dave paused. "I don't know how you're feelin about this, buddy," he said. "If I were you I'd be scared. Anybody with a brain would be, and I know you got one. He winked then paused again, trying to find words. "But I'd also be the fucking happiest dude on this planet." He looked uncharacteristically shy. "I hope you can be."

Parker ran a hand up his brown belly. "Appreciate it, man." He yawned. He was tired from moving furniture and painting walls. "Tell you what."

Dave waited.

"Any time you want, you can borrow the little rug rat. And I mean that."

"Deal. And I mean it, too."

They shook.

Iris

It was clean. Like, super-duper clean. Her dad's house was actually cleaner than her mom's! Iris gazed around. The kitchen gleamed. The old chairs in the living room were stacked for disposal, and the new ones were bright and inviting. No more junk cluttered the wooden table, which shone. The toenail jars were gone. The dumb-bum drapes had been replaced by cool dangly panels that could be slipped back and forth with a magic wand that hung down. She liked it so much!

But what about upstairs? She tiptoed up the newly scrubbed steps to her room, and found it tidy, her clothes folded away, the shoes and puzzles and books all tidied into shelves and hampers.

All except one. On her desk lay *The Secret Garden*. She sat down on the bed and held the old book, and it fell open in her hands. "If you look the right way," it suggested primly, "you can see that the whole world is a garden."

Yeah, right, Iris thought, a *baby* garden. She went downstairs and found a Popsicle in Parker's gleaming fridge. It was orange, her favourite, and she wandered out onto the doorstep, licking it. In front of the car, Dave and Parker were still debating the best way to get the bassinet up the narrow stairs, which had a crook in it before the top floor landing. Somebody had to take charge. "You guys, hurry it up," she commanded crossly, "we need to get to work in the new tadpole's room!"

Morrison

"Cape Blomidon Reel" rang through the house as Morrison tossed singlets, shoes, and an emergency flask of Appleton Estates into his carry-on. He had a weakness for old-time fiddle music. A long time ago, his father'd been a fiddler. A prairie fiddler, of all things. He'd actually written fiddle music, despite being landlocked and musically illiterate, and some of his tunes had been used on a long-extinct TV program called *Don Messer's Jubilee*. As a kid, Morrison had never missed that goofy old show. He'd loved it when his mom made popcorn and gave him a big buttery bowl of it on the couch, so he could watch Marge Osborne and Charlie Chamberlain and the Buchta Dancers, their bodies solid as the furniture of the nineteen forties, faces frozen in expressions of quaint jollity. He could still remember the one time he'd seen his old man on the show, playing the fiddle his own father had made for him in the shop behind his house. Morrison, thrilled to be up past his bedtime and scandalized to see his father grinning at him out of the mysterious flashing box, had waved at the black-and-white RCA, then dived into the couch, popcorn flying, the cat's startled hiss, his whole five-year-old body shouting, *Yes!*

Tonight he felt that same crazy affirmation, packing and drinking wine, and listening to those rickey-tickey old tunes, preserved now in their accessible hundreds, on YouTube.

Tonight, for whatever reason — was it the music? The trip with Rose coming up? The imminent race? The he felt full of *Yes*. He wanted to say Yes to Rose, whatever that might mean, Yes to the run, Yes to Danica, there or gone, Yes to the goddamned untrained-for marathon.

Now as he tossed gear into his bag and eyeballed the race package pick-up schedule and popped a few last cherry tomatoes into his mouth, he was listening to "What Can You Do With a Drunken Sailor," a fast and melancholy jig he remembered his old man singing and fiddling, and he began to belt the bawdy tune himself.

"Shave his belly with a rusty razor," he yodelled as he tossed, and sorted, and made himself a little more drunk, "earl-eye in the mor-ning!"

Earl-eye in the morning he'd be cabbing it to the airport to meet Rose. Strange that she hadn't answered his last message confirming their meet-up time, and advising her to travel light. He hated the new twenty-five dollar add-on they were charging just to take your fucking luggage to your destination, and planned to thwart them. He was hoping that for such a short trip, they might both dodge the stupid fee.

He pulled out his phone to check one more time. Nothing. May as well fire off a quick one before he hit the hay.

> ➢ *Girl, you've sure been mighty quiet today. Cat got your tongue? Been getting ready all evening, and gonna crash now. Will be out to the airport by 7 a.m. sharp. Don't forget to pack lots of energy gel; you'll need it after 10K. Did you pick up the one I said? 'Espresso Love?' Stupid name, but it beats the bejesus out of Strawberry. Sleep tight and rest those purdy feet, they'll thank you.*

Should a person use emojis? Did real adults enjoy, or ignore such foolishness? He plugged in a craven ☺, yawning as he powered down his phone and poured a tall glass of water to go with the morning's Aspirins. The picture of the stone lovers gazed down on him as he climbed the stairs, and he raised his glass to them in a kind of pre-runner's high bliss. There was nothing — nothing in this world — like the night before a race.

Rose

Why did she do the things she did? One of life's great mysteries, that one. Rose was getting ready to leave the office, throwing essays into a satchel in case she got a moment on the plane, or in a Sechelt café. She knew how likely that was, but she'd always been a sucker for superstitious gestures. She glanced up at the clock. How had it gotten this late? The phone call had thrown her off, and she had nothing ready for the trip tomorrow morning. But instead of going home to finish packing, what was she doing? Sneaking out to meet Byrd the pilot, who was unbelievably at this very moment waiting for her not a mile from her house. Her heart beat faster at the thought. Then came the inevitable question: Why was she inviting such a complication into her life, when it was plenty complicated enough already?

The answer that came back more and more often, to such questions, was: why not? Why worry about making sure you've packed the dental floss, when your daughter's lost? Why care if you're packed up, caught up, loved or literate, when your motherhood's in question? Because if anything in this world was in question, it was Rose's motherhood. So many questions. Why had she scorned the Lululemon mothers with their designer coffee cups, back in the days of the schoolyard? Why hadn't she hung out with them for at least a minute here or there, listened to their lacquered gossip, praised their Pinterest tips? She'd thought she was being responsible all those years, marking during dinner, shovelling in the dark, hurrying to work. She'd imagined that late nights prepping and early mornings rehearsing was being a good parent.

Had that — all that striving nonsense — been, instead, one of the signs?

She crammed the last of the papers into her bag, and pulled her office door shut. She should have paid attention to all that Joan of Arc stuff, instead of 'enabling' it, as they said nowadays. Because Joan of Arc, it turned out, had been no mere affectation; she had been the beginning of a death, the harbinger of a long and devious disaster.

No — Rose was walking now to the underground parkade — that whole escapade with the funny clothes and the pious notions had signalled a worse thing than a death. With death, there's an end. You can pay your respects and grieve your grief, and after a while you can move on, if you're lucky, start again. But — *a man may smile and smile, and be a villain* — Joan of Arc was a mindfuck. Gradually, right under Rose's nose, the virginal warrior with God for a father and shorn hair, and impenetrable armour had colonized, and then lured, her daughter.

And now her daughter was a 'them' who didn't want to see her.

Rose located and unlocked her car, which was now nearly alone in the parkade. Not over a beetling cliff, it turned out, had Joan of Arc lured Bean into the sea; not to her untimely demise, which Rose could eventually, in some maimed form, have survived, a picture of her expired child held in her mind for all time. Instead she'd changed her into an indifferent stranger, a person who now had the nerve, after two years, to turn up in life again, and to return, not to her mother, but to a person she hadn't even known all that well, on the other side of the country.

Or had she? Maybe Bean *had* known Mab well. The startling idea bloomed in her mind with a quiet new chill. Maybe they'd been having a dandy old time all along, the two of them. Maybe they'd been secretly snickering at her in phone calls and letters, shaking their heads about Bean's pathetic excuse for a mother, all along.

What the fuck did Rose really know about anything?

On the passenger seat — Rose waved her pass and the parkade barrier lifted, letting her out into the wet night — lay the letter that arrived just yesterday, trust old school Mab to use snail mail for emphasis. She noted the letter's neat folds, and huffed out an explosion of angry air at its almost pious reasonableness:

Dear Rose,

I don't know if you'll want to hear from me at this point or not, but it seemed only right to fill you in a bit from this end.

'From this end.' Rose had huffed with tearful disgust. As though there were two ends to Bean's return. As though she were in any way included in the grand resurrection.

Stella's doing really well. Better than when they first arrived. They've put on a bit of weight and started looking for jobs. They've even got a couple leads! I suggested they look into some upgrading courses, but what they really seem to be interested in is the two-year visual arts program at Sheridan. They want to be an artist, Rose! Doesn't that just explain so much? I can't wait to see them put all that imagination into something creative, but I've suggested they maybe take journalism along with it, as a bit of a fallback.

How splendid of you, Rose thought, how absolutely, marvelously parental! Art, though? She snorted. Journalism? Couldn't you at least suggest something that would make her — them — some money? Maybe they should consider 'dental technician.' Perhaps you could recommend pastry chef. She always liked to be ready for battle; how about chainmail maker? Maybe a blacksmith course; maybe you should point her in that direction. Maybe you should just mind your own business, Mab!

Will they continue living with me? That remains to be seen, but I've told them they're welcome for as long as they want. When they get working they can pay me a bit of room and board, and we'll take it from there.

I know you must be hurting —

Fuck you, Rose thought, flinging the letter across the car, only to snatch it up again.

— but, at least you'll know where they are. You'll know they're okay. And I'll be encouraging them as soon as it seems right, to consider a visit to Calgary. I don't know if I should even say this, and I hope you'll forgive me if I've made a misstep here, but having them here — you know, just while they're getting their sea legs — I think it's good for me. You remember back when I lost the baby. Well, that — the ache of that, of never having a real end to it or any recognition of it — has always eaten at me on some level. Somehow having

Stella around is helping. It's a chance, Rose. A chance for me to give something to a child. And the fact that it's your child makes it even more important. I couldn't help but say Yes . . .

And so forth. The traffic was heavy for this time of night, and rain had begun to streak down, pasting wet leaves across the windshield; she fumbled for the slow wiper setting. Mab was right. Rose knew she was right, and she knew she was going to have to get the hell over herself. But it was going to be a while before she replied to that letter. She'd talk to Morrison about it during the race, if she could keep up with him for five minutes. He was always good to bounce things off.

But she'd never keep up with him!

Nor he with her, it seemed. A pang of guilt stabbed Rose as she thought this, but Morrison was a chameleon, and the two of them had no real commitment beyond their friendship and their few fumbling encounters and their love, which, though real enough, had not changed the world.

And life — she realized this now — life was going one way. And hers was well past the halfway mark.

So that was why. All of that was why she did the things she did. And it was why she was about to do *this* thing, whatever it would be.

She pulled into the parking lot. There it was. Wicked Wings, its good-time lights wavering gaudily across the puddled pavement. The car had got there as though by its own navigation. Maybe — in her nervousness she almost smiled — the car could be blamed for her arrival. She turned off the engine and listened to the small ticking sounds of its cooling. He would be in there by now, she knew he would, seated alone at the bar, braid shining, suede jacket pocked with rain.

She could take off. Even now she could turn around and scram the hell home, text him something lame and professorial about overdue work and immanent travel. She could do what she always did, and what Bean had done.

But Rose had told him she'd be there, and whatever else she was, she was nothing if not dutiful; she was going in.

Abbey

The house was so small, her little house. How had she never noticed? A hobbit house. Abbey sat on the floor in her tiny spare bedroom, contemplating its quiet emptiness. All afternoon Parker and a couple of his delivery pals had been there, carting her life off to join his wacky establishment. At least, thanks to his new cleaning obsession, his place was less wacky than before. And all this newfound polishing and organizing and tossing, it seemed, was for her, and for the new 'tadpole.' Whose sex she now knew, and whose name was growing in her.

She leaned tiredly back, gazing up through the plastic bubble of skylight, with its remote net of stars. What was the word she'd learned in high school Latin class, for 'star?' Danica. She'd once had an officious aunt named Danica. Was that why she'd not liked the name? It suddenly seemed a beautiful name. A fine name.

A wave of nausea moved in her, reminding her of the new life she harboured. She would name her baby Danny. For Morrison, who'd lost his Danica, and for this last look, from her skylight, at the night sky.

Cold was creeping down the bared walls, and she hugged her sweater around her, remembering how happy she'd been to find this goofy little place, a townhouse about as wide as a French fry and about true as one, around the corner, it had turned out, from Parker's. Her mother — "You can do the same for my coffin!" had cosigned the loan.

Right, Mum. Or 'Mom,' as they said out here. Ever the comic, Mum. Probably she'd meant it; she had no money. Who on the Rock had money? Not ever Abbey's family, and she was boldly carrying on the tradition.

She couldn't believe she'd actually gotten the loan. How brave she'd been, or how stupid, renting that dumpster and starting over, painting the walls herself, ordering in brand new unaffordable carpet. A pink carpet! Dusty rose, no less! And placing her antique table and chest just so, and seeding the towel-sized scrap of lawn, and planting nasturtiums. Even now — in her mind she saw them in their dark beds — they continued to bloom, their receding crimson flare a reproach for her departure.

What are you doing? They seemed to ask. How could you go? Abbey didn't know. What did anyone ever know? You just had to make a stab, strike out in faith, like some desert father in the wilderness.

You had to say Yes. At some point, didn't you have to?

So when Parker'd asked her to "move in. Why not? What've we got to lose?" she'd thought hard, and then decided. After all, she was only renting her place out, not selling it. She could always come home if it didn't work out.

Boots sounded in the front hall. "Hey, Ab, you up there?" Man sweat floated on the air. They were back for the big stuff. She stood, dizzy, leaning her newly unfamiliar body against the wall. Parker sprinted up the echoing stairs. "You ready?"

Abbey heard: Are you ready to grow up? But she didn't get mad. After all, wasn't that what Parker was doing? He was growing up, and he was doing it, beautifully, for her sake, and for the sake of their baby. The least she could do was respond in kind. She took a big breath, and she smiled. "Ready enough, I guess."

Rose

No getting out of it now. Rose turned off the car and pulled her
purse from the passenger's seat. As usual, the handles caught on
the stick shift. As usual, she took it personally. More speedily than
usual, though, she got over the affront, and did a last superstitious
fix of her face in the rearview. Rain cooled her skin as she crossed
the parking lot to Wicked Wings.

He was there. She could see him from the door. Just as she'd
imagined, he was nursing a beer, braid snaked across his shoulder,
the suede jacket marked by rain. From the stale entryway she
imagined she could smell the rain on his jacket: her back yard on a
spring night. Leaves. Chives. Earth.

She still could escape.

A movie — Byrd was eating pretzels and watching the
wall-mounted TV with apparent interest — was showing on the
monitors above the bar. The genre seemed to be horror. Was that
an omen? Byrd's back remained turned. Maybe she'd just stand
here and watch the movie for a while, and then go home, like a sane
person with promises to keep. She could text him from the safety
of her kitchen, Jeoffry looking patiently on, tell him something had
come up. After all, things do come up. A flat tire, a chimney fire.
How about a half marathon?

Too late. Byrd turned, grinned. "Hey." He indicated the empty
stool beside him, and Rose slid onto it. A pristine glass of wine was
there. "You seemed like a Chardonnay lady."

Lady. Despite her alarm, Rose smiled at the vaguely courtly term.

Byrd slid the wine in her direction. "I figured dry."

"Good guess." She lifted the glass. "Thank you." Word person
that she was, she didn't know what to say, how to behave. How
do you behave when you've signed up for something outrageous?
When you've purposely thrown what could be a mortal spanner
into your life? Who the hell was this guy, anyway? Where was he
going to go after their impromptu date at Wicked Wings? And how

come these questions hadn't occurred to her when she said she'd meet up with him? She hoped to God there was someplace pilots went in their deadhead destinations, at night. She sipped the wine. It was good. It was a relief. "How was your trip?" Immediately she blushed, remembering that for a pilot, deadheading to another city was hardly a trip. On the screen, the crazy nurse was berating the battered writer, calling him a 'dirty bird.'

The pilot laughed. "Hey, that's me."

Rose chuckled, too, at the odd coincidence, and drank, realizing she'd had no dinner. The wine hit her stomach with reassuring heat.

A second bowl of complimentary pretzels arrived at the table. Byrd offered them, and Rose scooped a handful. "Thanks."

Byrd tipped a menu her way. It was called 'So Many Wings.' You could have Buffalo wings and maple wings and jerk wings, and jalapeño wings, even, if you were the adventurous type, apricot-glazed wings. Her companion looked a little apologetic, as though he suspected that chicken wings weren't professor food. "Would you like something real to eat?" He scanned the menu with touching earnestness. "I mean, is there something you'd rather have? A salad?"

"I'm good." Good was the last thing Rose was. The reality of tomorrow's trip and the race ahead, was finally beginning to sink in. In a matter of hours she would be on a plane with Morrison.

Though the bar was three-quarters empty, eighties music rocked it from one end, the creepy movie from the other. Byrd leaned toward her, his gaze steady. "I've thought about you." He placed his hand near hers on the wet-ringed table. "A lot." The server came by and asked if everything was okay. Byrd asked for a repeat of what was on the table.

"I've thought about you, too." Was that true? She realized it was. Sitting here, seeing his smooth skin and his arms, his shoulders, remembering how he'd looked, swinging down her bag from the Cessna that day, remembering how he'd smelled, she realized it was definitely true. "Though . . ."

"Hey, no pressure, I know you got a life. I was just passing through, as they say, and I thought it might be cool to see if you were around, that's all."

She had to know. "How — how long are you here for?"

"I told you." He winked. "Heading out in the morning."

She shouldn't ask. But that was what you did, when people were passing through. "Do you have, like, a place to stay?"

"Figured I'd crash in the Westin out near the airport. It's what I usually do." His gaze remained steady. "I'll just grab a cab from here, later."

The second round had arrived, and Rose helped herself. She knew she was playing with fire. She could tell because she had let her own hand rest dangerously near Byrd's. His hand moved to cover hers. Rose drew hers away. Byrd used the rejected hand to gather more pretzels. "That was — gosh, I'm sorry."

Rose blushed. "You showed me hospitality, up at that lake. In the cabin there."

"Nah, that was just —"

"I know." She smiled. "Part of the service."

The server had arrived again. "Can I get anybody anything else?"

Rose shook her head. She didn't feel like sitting on a barstool. "Just the bill." She smiled, embarrassed by her bluntness. "Thanks."

Byrd raised an enquiring eyebrow.

Rose got out her card. "There's no point in you getting a motel. I've got a spare room. You may as well stay at my place. Save a bit of money. But I've got to be up and gone by six. Got a plane to catch."

Something was working in her. Some combination of the same old Bean-despair and a dark new Rose-defiance. She knew she was doing something stunningly risky.

She didn't care.

Byrd said, "I'd like that. If it's okay. But I'm paying the bill here."

"Fine," Rose said, "I mean, thank you. Thanks." Had she had too much to safely drive?

Probably. No fool like an old fool, Mab always used to say. Fucking Mab. She felt a fresh surge of anger, remembering the letter. Bean living at Mab's place, going to school from there, looking for jobs from there. Being a *them*, from there. But she couldn't think about that stuff now. Her house was just around the corner; cops were less likely to be out in bad weather. She could probably get away with it. "My car's just —"

"I know where."

Should she be gratified or appalled by this precocious knowledge? It hardly mattered. In any case, it was too late. Already they were crossing the parking lot.

She unlocked the car.

Byrd got in, buckled up, stared straight ahead, remarked, as if commenting on a sonata or some tropical sunset, "So beautiful."

Rose started the car and shifted into first. "What is?"

"You."

"Oh, spare me." She tried to shift into second, and did that nervous damn grinding thing with the gearshift, that always infuriated and terrorized her. "Did I mention? I forget. Did I say I have to leave really early in the morning?"

"You mentioned that, too, yes." He rolled down his window, and his thin face gained a kind of repose as the night flowed in. "That happen often?"

"What? Does what happen?" She could feel a free-floating irritation. Why was she being mean? She'd invited him. Did she have to be such a bag?

"Grinding it. In second."

With her free hand, Rose tipped out a stick of Wrigley's, and offered the package to Byrd. "Gum?"

"Thanks." Byrd lifted out a fragrant layer. "Because if you make a habit of it, there's no turning back. Right?"

Screw you, Rose thought, *I know how to drive my own car.* "Oh yeah? Why's that." She was wheeling out of the lot now, signalling her turn.

"Cause gears are kind of like interlocking teeth." He hooked his fingers through each other, demonstrating. Rose caught a glimpse of the fine smooth skin, the long fingers. "And they have to be sharp, right? Gears. So they can fit into each other. It's like a marriage. Kind of." He smiled.

Oh, brother, Rose thought. "Okay." The rain was coming down harder, and Rose set the wipers on high. Despite the weather, she'd seen a cop car glide around the corner ahead of her. Likely it was finding itself a nice out-of-the-way spot on a side street, from which to nail her.

"Yeah, cause once those teeth are all rounded off, you can't fix em. And changing the transmission fluid won't do anything anymore. The synchronizers won't grab the shaft hard enough, and you'll have to replace the gear set."

"Sounds like cause for counselling."

"Well, it's cause for cash, all right." He raised the window, to keep out the rain. "Can be up to two thousand dollars, depending how bad it is."

"You're Mister Good News, aren't you." They'd safely reached her house, which stood dark and forsaken on the eve of the Sechelt weekend. Rose, terminal homebody that she was, felt an immediate pang, not to be entering it alone on the night before leaving it. She unlocked the front door. "Well — here we are." Something streaked past them in the dark. It was Jeoffry, making a scandalized beeline for shelter, as the door opened and showed him a stranger. "That's just my cat. He was a rescue, so he's got a few issues. But what can I say? He's a servant of the living God. Don't mind him."

"I don't." Byrd slipped off his damp jacket and handed it to Rose. "Got an old fleabag myself that comes 'round when I'm there." He peered into the dark. "Can I meet him? Is it a him?"

"You can if you don't mind crawling under my bed. That's where he always goes when he's scared. It's a 'him,' yes. But I can't answer for whatever else is under there." Rose pointed the way to her room, imagining single socks and drifting dust balls and long-lost underwear; she never quite managed to clean under there. On her bed, reassuring proof of her claim to be leaving, lay her half-packed overnight case. Thank God she'd got a start on it before heading to work this morning. But, what was she supposed to do now? She tossed Byrd's coat across the couch in her office. "Can I offer you anything? A cup of coffee, another glass of wine?"

Byrd

Byrd lay on his side on the bedroom floor, knees drawn up, quietly conversing with Jeoffry, as though they were old pals. A low purr rumbled from under the bed. Rose smiled, "God, you're a regular cat whisperer. Usually he won't purr for anyone but me."

Byrd looked around for his wine. "I'm actually not too bad with animals. Lord, though," he swallowed a sneeze, "you got a few dust bunnies under there." He added with a smile, "I have other calming talents, too."

Rose snorted. "One of which would seem to be bullshitting."

Byrd gave his regards to Jeoffry, and slid out from under the bed to accept his wine, which Rose had set behind him on the bookshelf. "Beautiful." He leaned against the bed, kicking off his shoes and patting the spot beside him. "Come."

Part of Rose thought him presumptuous. Another part stirred, and, in keeping with the new 'defiant' Rose, she moved beside him.

"You are, you know," Byrd said.

Rose tossed him a tolerating look. "I are what?"

"Beautiful."

"Oh," Rose laughed, "I thought for a minute you meant —"

"I know what you thought. But it was you I meant. I meant that you, Rose, are beautiful." His eyes, in the shadowy room, were large and grave, gazing upon her with an animal dignity. They made her want to touch his face, the way you might stroke the face of a standing horse.

Instead, she turned down the lamp. "What I am is a hundred."

"What you are is stupid."

"Maybe. Probably." Either way, she didn't care. He was undressing her now, unapologetically, and she wasn't stopping him. When he dumped her jeans in a heap, she reached for him.

He paused. "You okay?"

"I'm . . ." What was she? A braided cowboy she hadn't known two months ago was undressing her on her bedroom floor, on the night before a marathon with Morrison. "Okay."

"Sure?"

Rose nodded, moved against him. "You're almost a stranger. We are. Strangers."

Byrd shrugged. " Or, you could say we're human."

"Touché."

"Tell me." He bent over her, brushed the corner of her mouth with his. "Tell me what you want."

"I just . . . want. I want." Dreamily, she thought of the expression's first meaning: I *lack*.

He touched her face. "I want you."

Rose laid her own hand over his.

"I know." He paused.

"What do you know?"

"I know why you went up to the lake, that weekend, I wasn't just cooling my jets while you were up there."

Rose smiled. "You were spying on me?"

"A person can see things without spying. If they're paying attention. You were there to say goodbye."

"You're pretty smart — for a guy who just dropped in out of the blue."

Byrd unbuttoned her shirt, found and unhooked her bra, kissed her neck, her collarbones, her hands. "Isn't that what birds do?"

She smiled. "You."

And he moved upon her and entered her, the force of his entry half pain, half pleasure, making her gasp as though this were the first time, ever. Gently, gently, Byrd began to move deeper into her. Rose licked her fingers and reached between her legs, stroking herself while he moved inside her, his breath harsh, arms trembling, legs tense, his long back filmed with sweat. Waves were building deep inside her, gathering and rising, then racing away, soon to stream back again, pushed higher each time by the force of his thrust, of her own knowledgeable touch. Her breath was becoming shallower, sweat flushing her skin, her heart opening wide, the very walls and cells of her peeling outward in a kind of jubilant greed.

Rose came first, and her coming brought on the man's passion, and their hunger shuddered through them until they cried out in unison.

Tears trickled down, wetting her cheek, snaking across her neck. "I'm sorry, I'm so —"

"It's okay." Byrd kissed her cheek, her neck, licking her shoulders, drinking up the tears. "You're okay. You'll be okay, you'll see." He reached into the blankets, and found her hand.

They lay together in the dark then, their bodies recovering, sleep moving in. What was going to happen to her now? What about tomorrow and the run? What about Morrison? As she struggled to think about these things, she began to drift, images and puzzles detaching from the day, turning into dreams. Beside her, Byrd was breathing in long sweeps, already well asleep. Rose studied him drowsily, the smooth skin, the long limbs, the shining otherness of him. Who was he? How on earth had this wild flier found his way into her life? And what was she going to do about that now? Sleep slowed her breathing, tugged at her eyelids.

Never mind, she'd be like Scarlet O'Hara. Yes. She'd worry about that tomorrow.

You've reached Bean. Well, actually, Joan. I'm a revolution. The voice was the one recorded on Bean's childhood cellphone greeting, left behind, as everything had been, when she'd run away. Rose, sinking into dreams, smiled at the familiar words and pauses, hearing the peculiar turns of phrase formed in the same architecture of bone from which she produced her own. Not whatever register Bean may have grown into, whose adult inflections Mab, not Rose, could now hear and answer, day by recovering day.

The voice was silver. An eight-year-old's dazzling chime, preserved by technology, held forever in her dreaming memory.

Please leave a message.

Dave

Yellow leaves whirled behind the speeding car as Dave, zooming back to Peterborough, cranked the speakers. The Volkswagen rocked with the zap and smack of "Blues for Alice," but in his mind, he called the joyfully hectic tune "Blues for Iris." He didn't like to think how much he already missed the kid. Would she be okay at Parker's? Would he feed her? He better feed her. But there was barely any furniture there anymore. What had that hairy-toed hobbit done with it all? Had he needed to sell it for breakfast? At least, finally, the place was clean. But Iris's bed — Dave had carried her suitcase and backpack up to her room — had been a musty mess, the sheets in a twist and clearly not washed. He was longing to buy her new sheets. Would it be wrong for him to buy Parker's kid new sheets?

Probably it was wrong. What wasn't wrong, nowadays? But here he was, at the exit for Portage Mall. What was it Prince Charles or somebody'd said? Never miss a chance to take a pee or the exit to a mall. Something like that. He groaned at his own dumb joke.

Sheets or not, he needed a coffee, and he could use a gas-up. There'd be a station and a Tims there, and a Bed, Bath, and Beware, or whatever. First he'd check out Winners.

Sheets were on sale at Winners, two sets for the price of one: he'd take that as a sign. Quiet pleasure lit his face: why not get her two fuckin sets so she could wash one, wasn't she getting old enough to do her own laundry? And put the other one on the bed, like real people. Yup — he hunched his shoulders race-car-driver style as the car took the ramp — he was even going to teach her how to do those goddamn hospital corners, so it looked like a professional job. They'd have it on YouTube. He'd Google it up.

He spit a mouthful of tobacco juice into the can he kept between the front seats. While he was at it, he'd get them a decent laundry hamper. God knows, they'd need one, with the new tadpole. Would he still be able to be a part of Iris's life once there was a new tadpole?

New tadpole or not, he promised himself standing there amidst the bewildering stacks and columns of sheets, he was going to be part of the life of Iris.

And his own life? What about that? It wasn't perfect. He knew that. One thing he shared with his pal Parker was that he'd got started late, stupid late, on the real stuff, the important stuff. But at least, like Parker, he'd *made* a start, and now, thanks to that little gal with the big words and the small patience, he knew what mattered. And he was going to live it, like Charlie Parker said, so it came out his horn. It didn't matter how you lived it, he figured, as long as you managed to make life happen somehow, somewhere.

Rose

There are fifty-five thousand steps in a marathon. Rose read that somewhere. Thank God she was only running half of them. Also, that she'd managed to do a few weeks of last-minute jogging. Even with the training, she had strong suspicions that even a half was going to humble her.

It was race day, and a light rain was falling in the early gray. The forecast — it had been the big topic at the pasta dinner the night before — was uncertain. Rose and Morrison, surrounded by thousands of angular and well-prepared Lycra-types in their fancy gear, jogged on the spot, trying to generate some heat under the garbage-bag raincoats they'd improvised back at the hotel. Later, if the weather report was right and the sun showed, they'd discard the bags somewhere along the course to be collected by race monitors, and get down to business. Rose cinched her running belt tighter and felt along it with her hand, checking to make sure she had her energy gel and her emergency Red Bull, and that her cell, without which she went nowhere, was safe in its waterproof container.

"Take a hit now." Morrison pointed at her belt of gels and water.

"Already? Should I?" She wanted to make sure she had enough to get her through. It was so damn cold. She ran her breath back and forth along her reddened knuckles, zipped her collar higher. "We haven't even —"

"Yeah, but you don't want to wait until you feel like you need it, cause by then it'll be too late. Gotta give yourself a good boost at the start and then just keep taking little sips all along the course. That way you don't get too wasted. Keeps your energy from dipping too low."

"You're the expert." With her teeth, Rose tore the top off a foil package of 'Espresso Love' and sucked back a mouthful of the sweet goo. "Yum. Where has this stuff been all my life?"

"Ain't any good for ya, except for racing. 20K's when you need it, not sittin on your arse, watching Netflix."

"Ha ha, fuck you, darlin,'" Rose laughed, "this is my first race and my last. Just for you." But she was starting to feel the excitement, the skin on the back of her neck prickling with more than cold.

"Never know, girl. Racing has a way of growing on a person."

"On *your* person, maybe!" Rose took another small suck of the energy gel, and clutched her garbage bag raincoat tighter. Of all the things a person might be doing early on a Saturday morning, standing in the rain in a garbage bag at six a.m. wasn't one Rose had ever aspired to.

Though life, she'd noticed, had a way of dressing you in garbage bags and standing you in places you never meant to stand. Maybe all these hard-ass sprinters were onto something. Good times and wicked discipline. Trained-for pain versus random pain. She would revisit that, the concept of that, after a bath and a glass of wine.

Despite the cruel hour, crowds of fans and supporters were lined up on both sides of the street, cheering, rubbing their hands together to keep warm, waving clappers and flags. The breath of hundreds of runners hung in the cold air as mascots twirled and bowled in front of the Start line. People trying to get in a last good-luck pee stood shivering in front of the besieged Porta-Potties, whose anxious stink flowed back along the ranks of runners, making even the just-relieved ones wonder if they should get in line for one last one, too. Far above in the swirling skies, police helicopters spluttered, waiting to fly the first few K with the let-loose marathoners. Rose gazed up at the ranks of choppers and felt a tightening in her throat. She was part of something. When had she ever been a part of anything? Ever since Bean had vanished, she'd been alone in her house, with only Jeoffry and the ghosts, a ghost among ghosts. But today she was part of this. Of this incredible surge of energy and good will, and hope, and unkillable love: here and there in the crowd stood people whose shirts featured photos of loved ones they had lost, presumably, to illness or accident or other forms of mayhem. The shirts bore captions with the names of the lost ones.

I'm running for Bob.

I'm running for Ama.
I'm running for Jean.

Now that she'd started to see them, they were everywhere, these lost and run-for ones, some of whom, judging by the photos on the T-shirts, were even children, or had been. Where had they gone? What catastrophe or cruel complacency had deleted them? Who was to blame? And why — a thought she'd never had before this moment, huddled, of all places, among hundreds of shivering strangers on a rainy race course — did she assume there was anyone to blame?

What if — she looked up into the churning sky — what if no one was? What if losing someone you loved was just something that happened? Relief, the possibility of relief, moved through her. What if Bean's disappearance had been as random as the rain, and as unavoidable?

What if it wasn't a sign of anything at all?

The countdown had begun. *Ten. Nine. Eight* . . . a swell of nervous energy rippled through the excited crowd. The elite runners, the ones who were in it to score and take home parcels of cash, were ushered to the front of the line, relegating mere amateurs like herself to steerage, where they belonged. Rose and Morrison took their place in these more humble ranks as the numbers counted down. *Seven, six, five* . . . Rose finished her Espresso Love. Morrison grinned. "Don't spend it all in one place, girl."

Rose smiled back. "The things you put me up to."

The gun went off with a bright crack, launching the immeasurably slow process of a marathon's beginning. All those feet, all those elbows, all the numbered bibs jockeying for position. At least the rain, true to the weather report, was temporarily letting up, leaving behind a dull shine on the wet pavement. Rose looked over at Morrison. "Should I take off my raincoat?"

"Yeah, let er go."

"But isn't that littering?"

"They'll sweep the course later, don't worry; you already paid for it with your entry fee. Though if you're worried about more rain, just pull it through your belt, it doesn't weigh anything." He looked around him, and showed Rose that the clumps of shivering runners were beginning to thin out as the faster ones took off, and the rest took up their own, less illustrious pace. "Okay, girl, giddy up."

Rose settled into a warm-up trot beside Morrison, careful to conserve her energy. The hundreds of runners were spreading out now and finding their long-distance strides, some chatting and laughing, others like herself, contemplative.

Morrison nudged her. "Penny for your thoughts."

"Oh, nothing too deep." She adjusted her running cap. "Just looking forward those bacon and tomato sandwiches they said would be on the course. And the chocolate chip cookies. And the smarties. For once, I'm going to stuff my face!"

"That's fine, as long as it don't knot up on ya. Just try to pace yourself a bit."

"Yes, Dad."

Already the town was behind them, streets and bus stops replaced by the deep silence of trees, though already, Rose could tell she wasn't going to be able to keep up with Morrison. "I have to — I need to — phew."

"What's up? Need a quick water break?"

"I'm going to have to —" she puffed "— you go ahead, I'm going have to dial this back to a —" Now she did need a drink, and she stopped to pull her bottle out of the pouch in her water belt — "Morrison, I think I need to slow down." She gulped, letting some water escape out the sides of her mouth and down her neck. "Ah."

"Nah, you can do it, remember, all we're doing is the half."

"I didn't train like you did, remember?"

"Got a confession." He tossed back a gulp of Gatorade. "I hardly trained myself. But, hey, if that works better for you, I'll catch you at the finish and we can go find some eats."

He eyeballed the weak sun, whose rays were starting to strengthen. "Christ, she's gettin hot already." He took the cap off his bottle and tossed water over his hat. "Stay hydrated, girl, and don't let these guys —" he looked around at the scampering marathoners

" — tempt you to run too fast, that'll come back to bite you in the butt."

And he was off, his white tunic flowing over his lean back, grasshopper legs pumping like pistons, race bib jockeying with the other bobbing numbers. As he rounded the corner, he turned and yelled, "This one's for the morning star!" He waved his dripping Tilley at the skies. "For all of them!" Rose gave a half-baffled thumbs up, and watched Morrison dissolve into the haze.

The next time she checked her watch, noon was on the horizon. She'd made it to the shoreline leg of the race, and was running on packed sand that was strewn with downed twigs from last night's rain. Her right knee was aching, and she wished she had a Tylenol. Hunger — it had been a while since an aid station — was starting to declare itself, with an attendant dip in energy. She felt for her gels. Only one left. She'd hold out a while longer. Where was Morrison by now? she wondered.

She looked up from her mesmerized gaze at her tired feet. Wet leaves were still solemnly dropping to the surface of the water; sea birds wheeled in the bright air. Apart from a few dogged runners before and behind her, she was alone. Blisters were starting to bite both second toes. By night — she'd seen Morrison's feet after some of his long runs — the nails would blacken and bulge over bubbles of water. Later, she'd lose the nails. Thirst was threatening to shut down her throat. If she was desperate, she supposed she could moisten her mouth with ocean; there sure was plenty of it around. But how was she going to get to the end of this ordeal? (Which the race was starting to become; she felt for the reassuring curve of her can of Red Bull.) How to get to the finish line? Morrison would say: one foot in front of the other.

Though now there was no Morrison around, to encourage or provoke her.

True to the CBC's prediction, heavy clouds were building again, over the water. Between their piled folds shimmered dazzling bands of watery light, reminding her that somewhere her sunglasses had slipped off her hat and gone missing, grabbed by a wave and washed away, the universe's revenge for her secret bad habit of pocketing other people's left-behind accessories. Despite the intermittent rain, her shoulders and arms were starting to feel pinched, and she knew that meant sunburn.

Thank God for her hat brim. From under its unflattering shelter she could see shoreline properties across an inlet, cottages tucked between trees, docks extending, an occasional person standing, legs like white ribbons reflecting down into green. A realtor's sign fronted one of the properties, calling attention to a small blue-and-white cabin tucked behind yellowing birches and poplars. At a slanting dock, a peeling rowboat rocked. To judge by the shape it was in, the place hadn't been used for a day or two. What did the rooms inside look like? Her gaze lingered on the place as she laboured past, her lower back aching, feet rubbing, mind imagining pine walls and plaid couches, a pot-bellied stove, a computer on a card table in front of the big window, a sign on the wood-panelled wall: *Do write as you please.* A scribbler's eyrie.

A runner had silently come up behind her, and had slowed to Rose's near-walking pace, in order to take a drink from her water bottle.

"You doin okay?"

She could hardly get the words out. "Do you know . . . next aid station?"

"Only 5K left," the woman puffed, "there probably won't be any more this point."

Was it the mention of 5K or the desolation of no more aid stations? Rose felt tears welling up, just like when she was a little kid, homesick at a sleepover. "Whoops, God, I'm sorry —"

The other woman reached a hand over to Rose's pumping arm. "Happens to most people at this point. You get emotional." She extended her water bottle. "Try this."

Rose took a drink, felt an instant and shocking surge of relief and energy. "What *is* this?"

"Iced tea. Old running secret. Never leave home on race day without it." The woman grinned. "Dig deep, girlfriend, you got this."

And she was gone, grinding heavily across the sand and around the bend, her water belt bouncing at her back. Had she been real? Who knew, at this point, what was real, and what wasn't? Real or not, the woman was running, she was keeping her commitment to herself, and if she could keep going, Rose could at least try. She returned to a wounded trot, concentrating on the thought of the vacant cottage to take her mind off her feet, her knees, her screaming back.

The cottage window had been blank, a pane of dark water. What was behind it? Why — a shocking thought — couldn't Rose be? She imagined sitting at the rickety table in front of that window, the charged post-storm leaves touching down on her own view of the stilled water. What was holding her in Calgary anymore? Bean wasn't coming home. Jeoffry'd be pissed, but he was portable, and the new kitten would be happy as long as he had a warm place to sleep, and kibble in his dish. She could find a job of some sort, she didn't need much. She pictured herself behind the counter of some café, pouring tourists' coffee, Academy-free. A shiver, though not from cold, dazzled through her. She could at least find out what they were asking, if she survived this nutty ordeal. Now, there was a goal. Maybe someday Bean — No. No, and no. She couldn't let herself think a thought like that, not anymore. If recent events had proven anything, it was that such thoughts were not profitable. The great drama was over, and it had ended not with a bang, as the saying went, but with a whimper, as usual: hers.

At least now she knew where Bean was. Bean was in the world. Maybe the world as it was, was going to have to be enough.

A sign showing the remaining distance inched by as rain, fat cold drops of it, started to fall, and real thunder to roll. A fork of lightening skittered over the water, a bright skeleton taunting its merry Halloween. Wouldn't that just be her luck: to be fried within sight of the finish line. She had to laugh, lifting her face to the ragged sky, which now was beginning to hurl the first grapeshot of hail, mean and small, but hard enough to smart. She looked around. Nothing human was near. The hunger and cold had become their own kind of pain. Where, by now, was Morrison?

This was what happened when a person didn't train.

She dropped to a walk, no point running anymore; the blisters bit and stung, her gels were gone, her heels raw to the bone, the race itself — she looked for other runners, saw none — pretty much in the can, and she was on her own in a frigging typhoon. There was nothing to be done but to grind it the rest of the way in. She'd be lucky if she could accomplish that much. Would they find her the next morning, balled up beside some drift stump, stiff and frozen, a few leaves stuck to her sandy cheeks? There were worse ways to go, she figured, than a quick heart attack on a silver shore, the story over. A stump lay on its side in front of her, and she considered simply sitting down on it, hail and all. Right now that stump looked beautiful.

Aw, come on, you're better than that. Mab's voice.

Rose started, looked around. "Wha . . . ?"

Nothing was there but trees and water. She began to lower herself to the log, just for a minute, just until she caught her breath.

None of that, now, up you go.

"You know what, Mab? Fuck you." That's what she wanted to say, had wanted to say since getting that impossible call from Toronto. *Just fuck you.*

Fine. But you get your arse off that log.

"Why? You tell me why."

Well, for starters, because you paid the fee.

She'd paid the fee, alright. She'd conceived and carried and given birth to a daughter, and done her best to raise her, and what had it gotten her? *Stella's decided to stay here for a while.*

Samuel Barber's Adagio — she'd brought the CD to the hospital — had played all during the gruelling hours of the birth, twenty years ago, its notes like the wind at the end of an age, as darkly triumphant as the pain she rode to bring her child to be. Blood — there had never been so much — had gushed that night until you could hear the medical team's feet squishing through it, and the room had smelled like iron until at last Rose was delivered. But of what? In the emergency of the delivery, no one had thought to tell her what she'd produced until, weakly, she'd asked the room in general.

"It's a little girl," someone had called as though to say the pizza had arrived. As the doctor worked on her nether parts, his needle-and-thread whaling like a sailmaker's, she'd heard the first sounds of her newborn.

Of her daughter.

The tears had come then, merciful as rain.

Okay, fine. Have your little cry. But then you get your butt up off that stump, and you run.

Rose wiped her face with the soaking sleeve of her tunic. "Why? Why should I? What's the point? What's the point of anything? I'm never going to see her again."

You don't know that.

"Oh, and what do *you* know?"

I know it isn't over till it's over.

The hail had stopped. Tears were mixing with snot as she stumbled up, and started back along the deserted beach, which began now to roar with the cheers of the bystanders. She couldn't listen, couldn't stand the distraction, even of encouragement. The only thing she could let herself hear was: *You got this.*

With all she had left in her, she chugged the last of the Red Bull, and began to limp the few hundred remaining feet to the Finish. What was she running for? Now it came to her. She was running for the same thing those T-shirt wearers at the Start were running for: unkillable goddamn love. And she was going to keep on running this whore of a race, but she wasn't going to run away anymore. From now on, no matter what life demanded or answered, Rose would be running toward.

She was practically puking, and colder than winter in Poughkeepsie, but finally: she was in. And she was miserable. Returning runners and their sopping gear were everywhere, and she staggered among them, looking out for Morrison, who must be done already, but in the chaos of the finish line, she couldn't see so much as his hat. Instead, she stumbled to a massage tent where volunteers were handing out foil blankets against hypothermia, and grabbed one to huddle under, feeling for her phone, which was buzzing, and once again, it was Mab.

"Rose? Rose, what've you been *doing* all day? I've been trying for hours to get hold of you!"

"Sorry," Rose huffed, "just running a marathon, nothing special." With her T-shirt, she mopped at her face. "But anyway," she gasped, "Thanks for the help out there, I couldn't have —"

"Help? What help? Where?" Mab exhaled. "What are you talking about, Rose?"

"Whoops, just a brain-fart. But Mab, I'm really glad you called. I've been wanting to say — Jesus, girl, I just want to say I'm sorry. I honestly am. All you did was offer my kid a home when she needed one, which was beyond amazing of you, and I was the one who —"

"Yes, sure, thanks, never mind all that, Rose."

"What, why, what for, I mean, why not?"

"There's someone here who wants to talk to you."

"Mab? What do you mean? What —"

There was the shuffle of the phone being handed over, and then, "Mom?" A voice she almost recognized.

"Oh my God, Bean, is this, oh God —" Down came the tears again, but this time someone handed her a towelette.

"It's me, Mom, and I know you just ran a marathon and everything, but I —"

Right there in the hypothermia tent, Rose rolled off her chair and fell on her knees.

Iris and Dave

Silver spring sun made the world drowsy, but Iris was busy. She was busy lots now, watching out for the new baby, who sat big as life under a rhubarb leaf in her car seat, waving her fat arms and grabby baby paws, while Dave showed Iris how to repot greenhouse plants.

"You just turn them upside down real gentle, see, like this," he demonstrated, "and then give the pot a little squeeze. See? And you gotta make sure your other hand's under the plant, so when it comes out, it doesn't fall headfirst on the ground." He demonstrated. "Kaboom."

Now the darn baby was making hungry noises, she was always hungry. "Look at her," giggled Iris, "she's trying to eat the actual dirt!"

"Oh my God, Dave, stop her!"

"Hey, Mom," Iris called, "I can repot things."

"Hey, honey, that's so cool!" But she was looking at Dave.

"Ali, my love," Dave said, squinting up at her, "In this world everyone must eat her pound of dirt." He set down the plant in his hand. "Or his."

"Well, not Abbey's baby when we're taking care of her, I hope." But she was smiling. "Here." She lifted baby Danny up out of the car seat, and put her on her hip. "You come with me, my little dirt-eater, and we'll get you something that's good for you."

"Wait, Mom," begged Iris, "I won't let her anymore, I promise. Can we keep her out here if we don't let her anymore?"

Ali considered. "I thought you were babied out."

"I only get to see her part time, though, Mom, and there aren't any other kids at my Dad's and Abbey's. She needs me to show her how stuff works."

"Well, it doesn't work to let her eat sand," Ali reminded her. "No more sand, okay?"

Iris fished in her pocket for a digestive. "Here now, you stop eating dirt, and have this proper cracker, baby."

Dave paused in his digging and leaned on his shovel. "You know what? You're a good old kid." He tilted his face to the sun. "Someday if you want to be, you're going to be a great mom."

Mercy

"Where do you want these, Mom?" Stella hefted a basket of fresh laundry just in from the makeshift clothesline. "Over there's fine," Rose smiled, indicating the couch, "I'll fold it when I get done here; or you can, I know you're going need some of your things for tomorrow." It was the end of their second week at the Sechelt hideaway, and Stella was getting ready to head back to Calgary, where there might be a summer job, and where the house—Rose had decided she couldn't bring herself to sell after all — needed a bit of tending to.

"Somebody's gotta deal with the chives," Stella joked. "Plus, I need to buy a few clothes."

Rose said, "Won't you need the car for that?"

"Nah," thought Stella out loud, "All I need's a couple pairs of jeans and some shirts, something a little less medieval than my usual." A little laugh bubbled out of her. "Can't very well show up to an interview at Mark's Work Warehouse in a surcoat and girdle."

"Who knows, maybe they'd go for it," observed Rose as she scanned the uncertain sky. "Maybe there's a load of closet knights out there, who'd just love to get their gauntlets on a tasset or two. Did I ever tell you I dated one once?"

"A tasset?"

"No, silly. A closet knight. After your father left."

"You did not."

"Seriously. He was a member (he told me this quite proudly) of the 'Society for Creative Anachronism.'"

"You're kidding me."

"I kid you not. So, this one night we were relaxing, or so I thought, after a very nice meal, he was a good cook, I'll give him that, and suddenly he reaches under the couch, and pulls out a seriously authentic 'hauberk,' or whatever he called it. And *then* he tells me that if he seems extra well-built above the waist, it's from wearing fifty pounds of chainmail on a regular basis—"

"Lord, Mom, now I *know* I should never have left home." Stella took the emptied Kleenex box from Rose and tossed it into the waste basket. "You're going to have to unpack that for me in the car."

Rose regarded her tall daughter. The sprigs of shorn hair were now an auburn braid; the tunic and snood had been replaced by some old sweats Rose had around the place, and an ordinary hoodie that said, "In my defense" on one side of the zipper, and "I was left unsupervised," on the other. The intelligent face, formerly impassive as funeral statuary, had somehow become a merry bloom.

Two months, already, they'd owned Scribbler's Eyrie, and for two solid weeks day and night, they'd been talking nonstop, from the morning pots (and pots) of coffee to the start-up of the stars.

And last night the talking had finally had to come down to a terrified, vertiginous, anguished: "Why?"

Stella pointed.

Rose looked. All there was, was her battered copy of *To The Lighthouse*, which she'd just finished reading for the millionth time. "What?"

"Well, you always used to talk to me about that book."

"I was such a bore."

"Only when you made me eat cauliflower. And you weren't responsible, either. For—"

Rose turned to the window. "Yeah, I bet." Here came the damn tears again.

"You were stressed, and you were tired, and sure, you weren't always easy to live with, but that's not why I left."

"Oh, fuck."

"Mom." Stella folded her arms across her chest. "Stop."

"Well, then, maybe *you* could *start*. Tell me." Rose took a deep, shuddering breath. "Maybe you could just tell. Me." Her voice did that trembly croaky thing her own mother's used to do, that she hated. "Why."

"It's just that I was like her." Stella pointed again at the book. "Or I was going to become like her.'

"Virginia Woolf? I hardly —"

"No." Stella made a tolerating face. "Like Lily."

"Lily Brisco? Oh, come on. Lily is just this scrawny little plain, self-effacing creature who lives somewhere off the Tottenham Court road —"

"You need to read your book again. And you need to listen."

"I'm listening." She was also snotting and snuffling, and irritatedly shoving the day's deluge off her face. Now that it had started, it seemed that the flood might never be going to stop. "Oh, I'm listening, all right."

"Well, maybe Lily's all those things you said, I haven't read the book for a while either, but she's also a lot more, Mom." Stella picked up Rose's tired old, beautiful book. "A lot more."

"Still listening."

"See, Lily can talk as good as any man about art with the so-called 'real' artist in the book, the stupid, full-of-himself dude who everybody *thinks* is the real thing, when in reality, it's Lily—and she also can show softness, remember, and actual caring for Mrs. Ramsay, who has to run the house and help the poor, and take care of the useless men, with their big fat brains. So in a way—"

"Guess you *did* read the book."

"When I worked in that bookstore, we had it in there, and I bought myself a copy because—well because you always were reading it, I guess, and it made me feel somehow close to you. And I liked how, because Lily had her painting, she could be both intellectual (what Woolf called the 'male' principle) and nurturing. She could be both both — or neither. Thanks to her being an artist, Lily Brisco could be any old thing she wanted." Stella smiled softly. "Even a star."

Rose drew a fresh tissue. "Okay, fair enough."

"Remember how you used to talk all the time about how Lily laid down her brush in extreme fatigue and drew a line in the centre, to show that she had had her vision?"

Rose snorted. "So it *was* my fault, then."

"Well, maybe in a way it was. It was your book that showed me it's possible. To have that."

"Have what, Bean. Stella. Whoever."

366

"A calling, Mom. A passion. From as young as I could even know things, I didn't want to live like all the other kids. And like all the other people, when I grew up, just working boring jobs and making money and eating and buying things, and finally croaking. That's why I liked that old newt in the Grade 2 classroom, because, maybe all he got to eat was flies, but he was never going to have to do all that shallow shit. I wanted to do something that mattered. To have something real. A *vision*. And Joan of Arc, via Lily Brisco, via *you*, gave me a way to find the way to mine." Stella handed her mother the Kleenex. "Here. These work better than your shirtsleeve."

"Jerk." Rose took a tissue. Then she snatched the box. "But why — just curious — why did you end up going back to your birth name? I mean, all those years you were this and that, and then something else. . ."

Stella gazed out toward the water. "You named me for the stars. And the stars are neither 'one nor t'other.' Didn't your friend Virginia say that somewhere? They just are. And I thought if I was going to have a vision, my birthname was as good a place as any, to start one." But suddenly Stella was laughing.

"Excuse me," Rose demanded, "what's so funny about your birthname?"

"Look!" Stella was pointing out the window.

Rose shifted Scottie, who was no longer a kitten, to her other knee so she could see Jeoffry from the cottage window. She had to laugh too, snot and all, seeing his striped butt wiggling with strategy as he monitored the spot where he watched for voles. Crouched in the reeds at the edge of the dock, he lurked where the smells of water and mud and rotting wood made a crafty disguise for his own predatory scent. By evening he'd have a string of the poor stiffened creatures lined up on the step for Rose to peruse, and she would dutifully do so, giving him an approving scratch behind the ears, in that place he couldn't reach himself. Though she felt some conflict about this collusion, having always had a soft spot for small things, she was also well aware that the more of them that ended up on the step, the less damage there'd be to the cottage's old wiring, which she couldn't yet afford to replace.

That was a job for next spring.

"He's a terror, that one," Rose smiled.

"And I'd better turn into one, too," Stella remembered. "Not long till plane time. You're driving me to the airport, right?"

"Mom's taxi," Rose grinned. "Best job I ever had."

Meanwhile, there was time to do a bit more on the little story she was writing for the community newspaper. This one was about some person who had got onto spiritual living, about which Rose knew dick and cared less, unless you counted wine, but she'd been hired to write the piece, she needed the cash, and one thing she did believe in was fiction's true lies. Even in a piece on spiritual living, she figured she could work in a few of those.

"Mom, do you think I could borrow your backpack, the smaller one, just for the trip? I seem to have more stuff than I did on the way out."

"Always happens," Rose smiled. "You know where it is, right?"

"Yup." Stella paused. "And Mom?"

Rose clutched herself. Here it came. The fatal blow, the great, goddamn final revelation, the blade she'd been dreading all those seven hundred and thirty or so days.

Stella sat back down, and took their mother's hand. They actually did that. "We're lucky, Mom."

Rose started to breathe again. "We . . . are?"

"Yeah, we are." They smiled. "Because we found our way back, all this time later. To each other."

"Seven hundred and thirty days later. Or so. Not that anyone's counting."

"But Mom, here's the thing." Stella's face wore a little lump-in-the-throat expression.

"What," Rose whispered then, faint as a sheep in a fog. "What's 'the thing'?"

"It's just that — well, there's still time."

"Okay." Rose held hard onto Stella's found hand, every cell in her body suffering such an onslaught of mercy it was hard to tell it from dismay. She swallowed, recalling a long-ago little girl down in the basement, watching bravely as her mother got ready to leave her behind for yet another day. "And I'm not even going to cry."

Though time was doing what it always does, conspiring to cause lateness. She had to get Stella to the airport, there was no food in the fridge, and she was expecting company. This was supposed to be Morrison's weekend, but his part-time girlfriend needed help painting her living room and it had turned out that Byrd, right now was girlfriend-free, deadheading to Ganges Harbour, and hoping to see her. "You go, girl!" Morrison had hollered via email, "I'm out there at the end of the month again, and I'll be bringing all the stuff for my famous super-spicy paella, so you better watch out!"

 Life and a lover, Virginia Woolf was ever fond of saying. Rose chuckled again at Jeoffry's antics. How, out of this whole impossible, beautiful mess — life — had she ended up with not one, but two lovers?

 Shit happened, she guessed. Sometimes lovely shit.

 There was nothing to do but say yes.

Acknowledgments

Major signs of YES to all the friends at the University of Calgary Press — including Alison Cobra, Helen Hajnoczky, and Melina Cusano — for your constant patience and positivity.

More such signs to my editor, Naomi K. Lewis, for your steady sensitivity, ready cheerfulness, and consistent brilliance. You never overwhelmed me, always isolated exactly the right things for me to take another look at, and answered my questions quickly and with kindness.

To my best pals and first readers Ali Bryan and Paulo da Costa, so many pains au chocolate from Cobb's are owed. The times we've spent in bookstores, pubs, masks, and in each other's living rooms have shaped and graced my literary life, and my life in general. There isn't a meeting when I don't pause, look at you, and wonder how I could be so lucky as to have you in my life.

To John and Saskia McKee, my long, long, long-loyal running pals, thank you for all the miles on the hard old path — your presence and support over the years have meant more than you know.

Thank you forever to Jerry for your constant support of—and generous belief in—my writing, for bringing me microwaved coffee, for eating leftovers yet again, for more or less staying out of my office, and for loving me. I don't know how you do it.

My gratitude finally to Esme, for the extraordinary and transcendent person you are, for the time we had as Mum and kid together, and for your presence in my life now.

Thank you, Esme, for coming back.

Photo Credit: Gerald Mills

JUDITH POND has published fiction and poetry in a wide variety of literary journals. She is the author of four poetry collections, including *A Shape of Breath*. *The Signs of No* is her debut novel.

 BRAVE & BRILLIANT SERIES

SERIES EDITOR:
Aritha van Herk, Professor, English, University of Calgary
ISSN 2371-7238 (PRINT) ISSN 2371-7246 (ONLINE)

Brave & Brilliant encompasses fiction, poetry, and everything in between and beyond. Bold and lively, each with its own strong and unique voice, Brave & Brilliant books entertain and engage readers with fresh and energetic approaches to storytelling and verse.

No. 1 · *The Book of Sensations* | Sheri-D Wilson
No. 2 · *Throwing the Diamond Hitch* | Emily Ursuliak
No. 3 · *Fail Safe* | Nikki Sheppy
No. 4 · *Quarry* | Tanis Franco
No. 5 · *Visible Cities* | Kathleen Wall and Veronica Geminder
No. 6 · *The Comedian* | Clem Martini
No. 7 · *The High Line Scavenger Hunt* | Lucas Crawford
No. 8 · *Exhibit* | Paul Zits
No. 9 · *Pugg's Portmanteau* | D. M. Bryan
No. 10 · *Dendrite Balconies* | Sean Braune
No. 11 · *The Red Chesterfield* | Wayne Arthurson
No. 12 · *Air Salt* | Ian Kinney
No. 13 · *Legislating Love* | Play by Natalie Meisner, with Director's Notes by Jason Mehmel, and Essays by Kevin Allen and Tereasa Maillie
No. 14 · *The Manhattan Project* | Ken Hunt
No. 15 · *Long Division* | Gil McElroy
No. 16 · *Disappearing in Reverse* | Allie MᶜFarland
No. 17 · *Phillis* | Alison Clarke
No. 18 · *DR SAD* | David Bateman
No. 19 · *Unlocking* | Amy LeBlanc
No. 20 · *Spectral Living* | Andrea King
No. 21 · *Happy Sands* | Barb Howard
No. 22 · *In Singing, He Composed a Song* | Jeremy Stewart
No. 23 · *I Wish I Could be Peter Falk* | Paul Zits
No. 24 · *A Kid Called Chatter* | Chris Kelly
No. 25 · *the book of smaller* | rob mclennan
No. 26 · *An Orchid Astronomy* | Tasnuva Hayden
No. 27 · *Not the Apocalypse I Was Hoping For* | Leslie Greentree
No. 28 · *Refugia* | Patrick Horner
No. 29 · *Five Stalks of Grain* | Adrian Lysenko, Illustrated by Ivanka Theodosia Galadza
No. 30 · *body works* | dennis cooley
No. 31 · *East Grand Lake* | Tim Ryan
No. 32 · *Muster Points* | Lucas Crawford
No. 33 · *Flicker* | Lori Hahnel
No. 34 · *Flight Risk* | A Play by Meg Braem, with Essays by William John Pratt and by David B. Hogan and Philip D. St. John, and Director's Notes by Samantha MacDonald
No. 35 · *The Signs of No* | Judith Pond